THE KA OF GIFFORD HILLARY

*

The Ka of Gifford Hillary is a Black Magic story by Dennis Wheatley, who writes: 'I, personally, have never assisted at, or participated in, any ceremony connected with Magic—Black or White. Should any of my readers incline to a serious study of the subject and thus come into contact with a man or woman of Power, I feel that it is only right to urge them, most strongly, to refrain from being drawn into any practice of the Secret Art in any way. My own observations have led me to an absolute conviction that to do so would bring them into dangers of a very real and concrete nature.'

BY DENNIS WHEATLEY

NOVELS

The Launching of Roger Brook
The Shadow of Tyburn Tree
The Rising Storm
The Man Who Killed the King
The Dark Secret of Josephine
The Rape of Venice
The Sultan's Daughter
The Wanton Princess
Evil in a Mask

The Scarlet Impostor
Faked Passports
The Black Baroness
V for Vengeance
Come Into My Parlour
Traitors' Gate
They Used Dark Forces

The Prisoner in the Mask
The Second Seal
Vendetta in Spain
Three Inquisitive People
The Forbidden Territory
The Devil Rides Out
The Golden Spaniard
Strange Conflict
Codeword—Golden Fleece
Dangerous Inheritance
Gateway to Hell

The Quest of Julian Day
The Sword of Fate
Bill for the Use of a Body

Black August
Contraband
The Island Where Time Stands
Still
The White Witch of the South
Seas

To the Devil—a Daughter
The Satanist

The Eunuch of Stamboul
The Secret War
The Fabulous Valley
Sixty Days to Live
Such Power is Dangerous
Uncharted Seas
The Man Who Missed the War
The Haunting of Toby Jugg
Star of Ill-Omen
They Found Atlantis
The Ka of Gifford Hillary
Curtain of Fear
Mayhem in Greece
Unholy Crusade

SHORT STORIES

Mediterranean Nights   Gunmen, Gallants and Ghosts

HISTORICAL

A Private Life of Charles II (*Illustrated by Frank C. Papé*)
Red Eagle (*The Story of the Russian Revolution*)

AUTOBIOGRAPHICAL

Stranger than Fiction (*War Papers for the Joint Planning Staff*)
Saturdays with Bricks

IN PREPARATION

The Ravishing of Lady Mary Ware (*another Roger Brook story*)
The Devil and all his Works (*Illustrated in colour*)

Dennis Wheatley

The Ka of Gifford Hillary

ARROW BOOKS

ARROW BOOKS LTD
3 Fitzroy Square, London W1

AN IMPRINT OF THE HUTCHINSON GROUP

London Melbourne Sydney Auckland
Wellington Johannesburg Cape Town
and agencies throughout the world

✳

First published by
Hutchinson & Co (*Publishers*) Ltd 1956
Arrow edition 1961
Reprinted 1965
This new edition 1969
Second impression December 1969
Third impression July 1970
Fourth impression June 1971
Fifth impression June 1973

*Made and printed in Great Britain
by The Anchor Press Ltd,
Tiptree, Essex*

ISBN 0 09 908220 9

Contents

Author's Note

It is fairly widely known that I was specially commissioned in order that I might become an additional member of the Joint Planning Staff, and that I worked in the famous fortress basement of the War Cabinet Offices for three years.

It is therefore important that I should make it absolutely clear that no statement on military matters contained in this book is in any way inspired. During the eleven years since I put off my uniform as a Wing Commander I have had no contact, other than social, with any member of the Joint Planning Staff; and the views of my fiction characters upon future strategy and the reorganisation of the Fighting Services owe nothing to any member of it past or present.

D.W.

1

Statement Begun Saturday 1st October

I am in prison awaiting trial for the murder of my wife's lover. When I was arrested I had excellent reasons for refraining from telling the truth about the crime. Now they are no longer valid, and by revealing the whole awful story there is just a chance that I may save someone who is very dear to me from ruin and a long term of imprisonment. I have little hope that I shall be believed. My version of what occurred is so utterly fantastic that it is certain to be taken as an attempt by me to show that I am mad. But the doctors have already agreed that I am sane; so for myself I see no escape from the gallows. Nevertheless, I swear by Almighty God that all I am about to dictate into a recording machine is the truth, the whole truth and nothing but the truth.

My name is Gifford Hillary. In 1949 I became Sir Gifford by inheriting a Baronetcy that had been given to my father for his services in the First World War; but my oldest friends call me Giff. I am forty-two years of age, but people say that I look a good bit younger; perhaps because I am a big muscular chap, broad shouldered, six feet one in my socks, and have always kept myself reasonably fit.

My job is boat building. The Hillarys have been shipwrights for many generations. Some of them helped to build the ships-of-the-line in the Beaulieu River that fought under Nelson at Trafalgar; and my own company of Hillary-Compton and Co. has been established well over a hundred years. Our offices and yards are at Southampton and, apart from the early years of the war, I have worked there ever since I came down from Cambridge. On my father's death I came into the biggest block of shares held by any individual in the Company, and succeeded him as its Chairman of Directors.

As my mother had predeceased my father, I also inherited

the family mansion, Longshot Hall, Lepe. It is not a very big or pretentious place, but a comfortable late Georgian house with some thirty acres of grounds and really beautiful views across the Solent to the Isle of Wight. In 1950, when I married again, I had it done up and took my second wife, Ankaret, to live there.

My first wife, Edith, divorced me in 1943. I had married her against my father's wishes when I was only twenty-one. By her I have a daughter, Christobel, now aged twenty, and a son, Harold, aged eighteen. Our separation during the early war years put an end to the few interests, other than the children, that had kept Edith and me together; so on my return from India, we agreed to part.

Seeing her again, and the children, a fortnight or so ago in most exceptional circumstances shook me badly. I had always thought of myself as rather a good chap; but many things I learnt during the fateful week before I was arrested have made me wonder if the pace and pressure of modern life, together with my determination to get my own way in anything on which I was really set, have not often caused me to act with almost brutal lack of regard for the well-being of others. Anyhow, it became clear that my family didn't think me half such a fine fellow as I thought myself; and if I did get off I'd try to—but that is out of the question. Broadmoor for life with criminal lunatics as my companions is the best I can possibly hope for, and all the odds are on my suffering an ignominious death at the end of the hangman's rope.

A little way back I mentioned that I was away from my firm during the early years of the war. Since we are boat-builders, and particularly as for many years a considerable part of our business has consisted of building small fighting ships for the Admiralty, I could easily have got an exemption. But in 1939 I was only twenty-six and a very fit young man; so I should have found it quite intolerable to remain in an office while most other people of my age were in one of the fighting services.

In view of the family's long association with the water, the natural thing would have been for me to go into the Navy; but one of my best friends was a test-pilot at Vickers' works nearby on the Hamble. Owing to him I had become fascinated with flying, and was myself already in the process of learning to fly. In consequence, I joined the R.A.F.

By the time I got my wings the worst of the Battle of Britain was over, so my squadron was among the first to be sent out as a reinforcement to the Middle East. Then, when the Japs came into the war, it was transferred to India. Shortly afterwards I was shot down and although the physical injuries I sustained were not particularly serious it resulted in my developing a number of infuriating nervous reactions, such as involuntary twitchings of the hands and face. For some months all attempts to rid me of this humiliating disability failed, until an Indian doctor suggested that I should try some of the rudimentary Yoga exercises. I did so, and by working hard at them was soon completely cured.

However, a Medical Board decided that I was not fit to undertake further flying duties, and it seemed to me that I could be of more use to my country back at the boatyards at Southampton than as an administrative officer in the R.A.F. I wrote my father to that effect and he applied to the Air Ministry for my release. It was duly granted and I returned home towards the end of 1943.

I have made this mention of my war-time activities only because they have a definite bearing on my present situation. Strange as it may seem, it was my decision some seventeen years ago to join the R.A.F., rather than to go into the Navy, which has landed me in this cell; for had I not done so I think it most unlikely that Sir Charles would have ever approached me to act as his stalking-horse—or that I should have consented to do so.

And the method by which I cured my disability in India is now the most damning piece of evidence which the prosecution will bring against me when I am taken to Winchester to stand my trial for murder.

I think that is enough about my background; so I will now put on record the extraordinary series of events which has caught me like a wretched fly in a spider's web from which there is no escape.

2

Events Over the Week-end
3rd/4th September

It was three weeks ago last Wednesday that I had my interview with the Minister of Defence, and it was not until
after it that I understood his reason for wishing to keep our
meeting secret.

The appointment was made with the usual unobtrusive
skill that one associates with high-ups in our Government.
Martin Emsworth had rung up on the previous Friday night
to say that he was staying with friends near Lymington; so
might he look me up sometime during the week-end? He was
an old friend, or perhaps I should say an acquaintance of very
long standing, for, although we had been up together at
Cambridge and were members of the same Club, we had never
been really intimate. All I actually knew about him was that
he was still a bachelor and had done very well in the Civil
Service. I had an idea that he held a fairly important post
in the Treasury; although I wasn't even certain about that.
But, naturally, I said I'd be delighted and we fixed up for him
to come over for a drink before lunch on Sunday.

Sunday proved to be a lovely day, of the belated summer
type that we sometimes do get in England in September.
Normally over every week-end at that time of year the house
would have been full of people, but four weeks earlier my
wife had had a bad fall from her horse. Its worst effect had
been to twist a muscle in her thigh, and the nerves there had
given her the most awful jip; so, greatly as she loved company,
she felt that until the bouts of pain, which sometimes caught
her unawares, had ceased, she really could not cope with
visitors. In consequence we had no one staying and I spent
most of the morning on my own, swimming and pottering
about our half mile of private beach; then I settled down in
the beach-house to wait for Martin.

I should, perhaps, explain that Longshot Hall stands on a slight rise several hundred yards from the shore, and that what we call the beach-house is really a charming Georgian pavilion consisting of three rooms and a wide veranda. When we have bathing parties we use the two side rooms for changing, and the larger, central, one is furnished as a lounge; in it we keep all the usual facilities for picnic teas and drinks. Soon after twelve o'clock my man, Silvers, brought Martin out there to me.

He duly admired our view, which was at its best on such a day with dozens of little yachts out of Cowes tacking up and down the Solent, and for a time we talked of mutual acquaintances; then, after a brief silence had fallen, he disclosed that his visit was not really a casual one by saying:

'Look, Gifford; the Minister of Defence is anxious to have a chat with you on a highly confidential matter, and he's asked me to arrange it.'

'Really!' I replied with some surprise. 'What on earth does Sir Charles want with me? I've met him only two or three times at public functions, so I hardly know him.'

'That's neither here nor there,' Martin shrugged, 'and I'm afraid it is outside my terms of reference to tell you what he wants to see you about. But he would like it to be this week, and for reasons which you will appreciate in due course the meeting must be a strictly private one. Naturally, like all these chaps, his book is full to overflowing but he is keeping Wednesday evening open, and said he would be particularly grateful if you could arrange to be in London that night.'

I had nothing particular on, so said that I could; and Martin beamed at me:

'That's fine. Then I think the best plan would be for you to meet in my flat at Whitehall Court. I'd like to give you dinner somewhere first; but we don't want to put ideas into people's heads and it might do just that if you were seen dining tête-à-tête with anyone in my sort of job; so you must forgive me if I don't. Just come along to my flat at, say, nine o'clock on Wednesday evening; and I shouldn't make any arrangements for later as it may prove quite a long session. I need hardly add that Sir Charles counts on you not to mention this meeting either before or after it has taken place.'

Considerably mystified, I agreed, and a few minutes later

Ankaret suddenly appeared round the corner of the beach-house. She was still using an ebony stick, but her leg had given her much less pain recently, and evidently she had decided that to walk down from the house to join us would not put too much strain upon it.

Martin had never met her, and as she came up the steps on to the veranda I saw him catch his breath. I was not surprised and only mildly amused, because I had seen dozens of men react in the same way on first coming face to face with Ankaret.

She was certainly something very special in young women; although I doubt if Hollywood would have found a use for her, as she was poles apart from the curvaceous blondes that box-office receipts prove to have the maximum appeal to the primitive emotions of the masses. Ankaret's beauty was of another age; her lure a more intimate one and very difficult to define. It did not lie only in her tall willowy figure, the Titian hair with rich gold lights in it that she always wore framing her pale face and curling down on to her shoulders, her firm well-modelled features, or even in her big grey eyes. It was something in the way they were set, wide apart between her high cheek-bones and tapering eyebrows, and in their expression.

At first glance they looked as clear, wondering and innocent as those of a young girl about to go to her first Communion; but a second later, when her classically-curved mouth broke into a smile, one caught something very different in their depths. They seemed to be full of secrets, and to see right through you with faintly cynical amusement at what they saw going on in the deepest recesses of your mind. Eve's eyes must have had that quality after she had eaten the fruit of the forbidden Tree of Knowledge; and that appraising look that Ankaret gave to every new male she met was almost as if she had said out loud: 'I know you would like to sleep with me, and I'd let you if I thought it would give me a thrill; but very few men have a strong enough personality to do that.' They were the eyes of a Fallen Angel—as old and as wicked as sin, but oh how beautiful.

According to *Debrett*, she was British to the backbone; but privately I have always held the theory that one of her ancestors in the long line of Ladies Le Strange, that goes

16

back to the days of the Conqueror, must have had an affair with an Italian—perhaps a music-master, or someone of that sort—and fathered the result of her liaison on her Lord, and that Ankaret was a throw-back. If painted with the technique of an old master, her picture could easily have been passed off as a portrait of a Medici, Colonna, Sforza, or lady of some other noble Italian house of the *cinque cento*; and her swift subtle mind added to the plausibility of such a theory.

Ankaret was much younger than myself—twenty-six against my forty-two—and we had been married for five years. During that time many men had openly envied me my luck in having her for my wife, quite a number had endeavoured to take her from me and a few had succeeded. But only for brief periods and, as far as I knew, all her lapses had occurred while she was on holiday abroad without me. There had been occasions when I was tempted to wring her slender neck, or would have given her away with, or without, a packet of tea, and been—temporarily at least—heartily glad to be rid of her. Yet it had never come to that.

The first time I found her out I was frantic with rage, jealousy and grief. But she did not express the least contrition and even laughed about it. She told me then that I was a long way from having been the first with her and certainly would not be the last. Unless I could reconcile myself to that I had better take steps to divorce her; but she hoped that I wouldn't because she loved me and didn't give a button for the other fellow—he had meant no more to her than trying out a new car.

I was still desperately in love with her; so, of course, I forgave her, and tried to regard as nervous braggadocio what she had said about being unfaithful to me again in the future. But a few months later, when I joined her in the south of France for a short spell before bringing her home after she had spent six weeks there, I found good reason to suppose that she had been. When I charged her with it she adopted the same attitude as before, and, moreover, flatly refused to give up going abroad for holidays for much longer than I could take time off to accompany her; so I could no longer shirk the issue.

Had I been younger I don't think I could possibly have brought myself to go on with her under those conditions;

but age teaches one to control anger, the repetition of an offence dulls resentment of it, and the longer one lives the more tolerant one becomes of the faults of others. On a third occasion when I remonstrated with her she said that she was driven to her lapses by an insatiable curiosity to know whether other men who interested her could fulfil their apparent promise as lovers; but I incline to the belief that some maladjustment of her glands made her by nature almost a nymphomaniac, and that only her sense of values restrained her from becoming a real tramp.

However that may be, she handled her illicit affairs with great discretion, and never gave me the least cause to reproach her during the greater part of each year while we were living together. That she never ceased to love me, after her own fashion, I am convinced, as time and again she could have left me for some much richer or more distinguished man, but never even hinted at any desire to do so. Her physical attractions apart, she had many very lovable qualities, and I have never met a woman who was capable of giving more in the way of intelligent and charming companionship.

After each of our brief separations she invariably returned to me brimming over with happiness to be back, as if I were the only person in the world with whom she had ever wanted to be. So I can honestly say that, however much pain she caused me during the early years of our marriage, she brought me far more joy than sorrow in the long run; and I do not believe there is the least reason to suppose that our marriage would ever have broken up, had it not been for a terrible misunderstanding that bore its evil fruit the week-end following that on which Martin Emsworth came over to Longshot.

Mentioning his name brings home to me that I have made far too long a digression about Ankaret; but I shall have plenty more to say about her later. After another drink and some mildly amusing chit-chat Martin left us, and I have not seen him since; but I duly kept the secret appointment he had made for me.

3

The Evening of Wednesday 7th September

Being by nature a methodical and punctual chap, it was nine o'clock precisely when I pressed the front door bell of Martin Emsworth's flat on the Wednesday evening. A few blocks away Big Ben was still pounding out the hour as Sir Charles himself let me in.

Actually we are much of a height, but close up he seemed even taller than myself; probably because he holds his spare figure very upright. Undoubtedly that, and his invariably well-groomed appearance, are both legacies from the years he spent in the Army, although one is apt to forget that he reached the rank of Major before he went into politics. In spite of his prematurely-white hair he looks much younger than his age and remarkably fit for a man who can't get much time to be out in the open air. His wide mouth broke into a friendly grin and he said:

'Good of you to come, Hillary. Sorry about all this mystery, but you'll see the point of it before you're much older. Martin has got rid of his man for the evening and discreetly taken himself off to his Club, leaving me to play host to you. Come along inside.'

In the centre of the big sitting-room there stood a large table. On it were Sir Charles's brief-case and a number of papers upon which he had evidently been working before I arrived. Along one side of the table a comfortable sofa faced the grate, in which a bright fire was burning. Motioning me to sit down, he walked over to a drink cabinet and asked me what I'd have. I chose brandy, so he poured two good rations into small balloon glasses, handed me one, gave me a cigar, and settled himself at the other end of the sofa. For a few minutes we talked about Martin, and a few other acquaintances we had in common, then he opened up as follows:

'I don't know if you saw the last White Paper on armaments, but during the past two years I'm sure you must have read any number of articles in the press dealing with the same subject. I mean, of course, the fundamental change in methods of warfare which must be considered as a result of the introduction of nuclear weapons. It is that which I want to talk to you about.

'One result has been extremely severe cuts in the Army Estimates, and the scrapping or conversion to new purposes of numerous formations. But such measures are really only begging the question; and the controversy is still raging. Some people maintain that we should bank entirely on the incredibly terrible devastation which could be wrought by H-bombs, and scrap practically everything else. Others hold the view that, whether thermo-nuclear weapons are used or not, we would still run an unacceptable risk of defeat unless we maintained our present strength in the types of weapon with which the last world war was waged. For simplification, when we are discussing armaments we now speak of these two schools of thought as the protagonists of either the New Look or the Old Look.

'Our difficulty is, of course, that we cannot possibly afford to have it both ways. The colossal cost of producing nuclear weapons is known to everyone and since 1913 the cost per annum of maintaining our fighting services with their conventional weapons has increased from seventy-four millions to over one thousand three hundred millions. In relation to the increased cost of living that means that our bill for men and arms has more than quadrupled; so it is already a grievous burden on the people, and to create a New Look alongside the Old Look would break the nation's financial back.

'That, of course, is just what our enemies would like to see. Whether they will ever challenge the N.A.T.O. nations in an all-out hot war I have no more idea than the next man; but it is quite certain that any measure which tends to undermine our economy, and so cause depression, discontent and dissatisfaction with the Government, suits their book. By the devious means of which they are past masters they will bring influence to bear on all sorts of well-meaning people and bodies to press us to continue with a "middle of the road" policy, knowing that it must inevitably result in increased taxation without either the New Look or the Old being developed to its maximum efficiency. But we—and in this instance I am speaking of the Prime Minister and the Cabinet —are determined not to fall into that trap. And the time has come when we must take a definite decision one way or the other.

'Whichever way we do decide there is going to be the most frightful outcry from the side our verdict goes against. Either the scientists and New Lookers, or the warriors of the Old School, are certain to raise Cain. They'll write to every newspaper and shout from every roof top that we are betraying the nation. The Government may well have to face a vote of confidence in the House with the unhappy knowledge that many of its staunchest supporters will be against it; although, of course, as an offset to that one can be certain that a proportion of the Opposition will be in favour of whichever decision is adopted. The issue is a non-party one, but it is bound to split the nation; and it is in the belief that, if you will, you could be of great assistance in carrying the ship of Government over these dangerous rocks on a spate of public opinion that I asked you to come here tonight.'

I made no comment. There was nothing new to me about the problem. Like most other peole who habitually scan a few of the more serious papers, I had read dozens of so-called 'informed' articles on it by every type of expert both scientific and military. In what way Sir Charles thought that I could materially influence public opinion I had not the faintest idea; so there seemed nothing useful that I could say. After sipping his brandy he went on:

'I need hardly add that I shall not ask you to do anything which would be contrary to your own convictions; neither have I any intention of endeavouring to influence your judgement. I propose only to lay a variety of opinions before you. Should you form the same conclusion from them as I have, I shall then tell you what I have in mind. If not, that will be the end of the matter, and I shall only request that you will not divulge any information which you may have acquired during the course of this evening.'

'That's fair enough,' I agreed. 'Naturally I haven't a notion what you have in mind; but if we do see eye to eye in this I'll willingly give you such help as I can.'

He nodded, and smiled at me like a wise white owl through his thick-lensed glasses, with the heavy tortoise-shell rims. Then he asked: 'Do you know anything about the workings of my Ministry?'

'Not much,' I replied, 'except that the majority of its staff are hand-picked bright boys on about Colonel's level from all three Services, with a few Foreign Office types, scientists and economic experts thrown in. I only know that much because a nephew of mine has recently been posted to it.'

'Really! What's his name?'

'Johnny Norton. He put up a pretty good show in the war and in Malaya and has since passed out near the top from the Air Staff College; but he's only a very junior Wing Commander so he thinks it quite a feather in his cap to have been selected for the Joint Planning Staff.'

'And he's right, of course, because we do skim the cream. I haven't met him yet; but in due course he is sure to have to sit in for his G. One at one of the bigger conferences, and I shall then. Has he told you of the system by which we get the answers to our riddles?'

'Gracious me, no. Johnny is much too security minded even to drop a hint about the nature of his work.'

[*Before proceeding further with this account I feel it only right to state that the details of my secret conference with Sir Charles have no bearing on my personal tragedy. It was the action which I took as a result of it which later had such disastrous consequences, and I am recording the details only because they explain that action. In consequence any reader of this document who is uninterested in future strategy and our measures for countering the threat of Soviet aggression will lose nothing by omitting the next few thousand words and resuming this account on page 40*)

Sir Charles' friendly grin came again and his pale blue eyes smiled through the pebble lenses as he proceeded to enlighten me. 'The Joint Planning Staff, which forms the backbone of my Ministry, is the only equivalent that Britain has ever had to the German General Staff, but it is infinitely smaller. It had its modest beginnings in Palestine in 1937 with a single team of a Lieutenant Commander, a Major and a Squadron Leader. Even during the war it was never expanded beyond six teams of three each with the addition of a few civilian specialists. It is divided into two sections, the STRATS, or Strategic Planners, who deal with more immediate problems, and the FOPS, or Future Planners, who tackle questions of long-term policy. Every single problem concerning any theatre of war, or possible theatre of war, or redistribution of forces, or creation of new bases, or undertakings to the N.A.T.O. countries, or terms of reference for special inquiries, or directives to force commanders, or important innovations in any of the Services, is submitted to one or other of these two sections. In addition they are expected to think for themselves, and on any matter which they may decide requires attention draw that of their superiors to it by writing papers which begin: "In anticipation of the wishes of the Chiefs of Staff." '

'Then they must have their plates full,' I said with a smile.

'Yes. The hours they work would make every shop-steward in the country faint; they get no overtime for it either. It seems that there are just as many urgent problems to be dealt with in the cold war as in a hot one; so it's not at all unusual for the STRATS to be still at it at two o'clock in the morning preparing final briefs for the Chiefs-of-Staff's daily meeting eight hours later. Most of them work on Sundays too, although there is no meeting of the Chiefs. It gives them a chance to catch up.

'But to go on with what I was saying. Each problem is first argued out by a team of G. Two's. They state the object of the paper, set out the arguments for or against this and that, and give their conclusions. It then goes to a team of G. One's who reargue it, redraft it and pass it on to the Directors of Plans of the three Services. The Directors of Plans argue the pros and cons in their turn, amend it as they think fit and submit it to the Chiefs of Staff. The Chiefs, who in the meantime have been separately briefed by their own personal staffs in their respective Ministries, then discuss it. If they are not satisfied that the recommendation is the best answer to the problem they refer it back with their comments to the J.P. for further consideration. If they are satisfied they pass it, and copies are sent for action to whatever departments may be concerned. That is the drill with regard to all bread-and-butter Service matters. But all questions of major importance, or ones in which the Foreign Office, or other Ministries, may be concerned, are placed before me; and on issues of the highest import, such as this business of the New Look, I, of course, have to consult the Cabinet.

'I'm telling you all this because I want to impress upon you that the papers they produce are not just cock-shies at a subject setting forth the views of a few clever but possibly prejudiced people. Initiated by promising young officers who are full of enthusiasm, and who sometimes have most revolutionary ideas, they go up stage by stage till they receive the well-balanced scrutiny of the men who have had greater experience of such problems than any others in their profession. So in their final form these papers embody the consolidated opinion reached by a majority among a selection of men all of whose brains are well above par and some, probably, as fine as any in the country.'

Reaching a long arm over the back of the sofa, Sir Charles picked up some sheets of foolscap clipped together at the top, handed them to me and said: 'This is a paper got out some months ago on the New Look. I want you to read it and tell me what you think of it.'

The first page of the paper had a printed heading with TOP SECRET in inch-high letters above a red line; the rest of it was stencilled. Great skill and experience had evidently been used in drafting it, as it did not contain a single redundant word and the whole subject had been reduced to the barest essentials. It was only three pages in length and consisted of a number of neat paragraphs each with a separate sub-heading.

In effect, it stated that while we could not afford to fall behind our potential enemies in the development of thermonuclear weapons, it was essential that we should retain a sufficiency of orthodox formations to enable us to meet aggression in cases where it was unlikely that either side would resort to nuclear warfare—such as that which had taken place in Korea.

It referred to our undertaking to keep four divisions on the Continent, to our commitments elsewhere, and to the vital necessity for adequate convoy protection to keep Britain's sea communications open in the event of a major war.

In conclusion it stressed the danger we should run if we

were caught changing horses while crossing the stream; and expressed the opinion that no further major reduction of forces would as yet be acceptable to any of the three Services.

When I had finished it I glanced across at Sir Charles and said: 'This doesn't seem to get you very far, does it?'

Again the boyish grin, that contrasted so strongly with his thatch of white hair, flashed out. 'It doesn't get us anywhere. Mind you, normally there is a great deal of give and take between the three Services, but that could hardly be expected where the New Look is concerned. The airmen feel that in any major war they, practically alone, will be called on to hold the baby. The soldiers fear a still greater reduction in their numbers unless they can make a case for taking over a big share of the airmen's responsibilities, and the sailors know that they are fighting for their very existence. It is not surprising that their views are entirely irreconcilable.

'Realising that, as a next move, I asked the three Chiefs of Staff to have the officers of their own Services in my Ministry in consultation with the Planners in theirs, to prepare separate papers on the subject: The results were very interesting.'

Standing up, Sir Charles gave me three more papers, all considerably longer than the first, and said: 'Now while you read these I'm sure you won't mind if I do a little work.' Then he moved round to the other side of the table while I got down to reading.

The Admiralty paper was the shortest. It opened by taking the bull by the horns and stating somewhat bellicosely that Britain owed her rise to greatness and her security through the centuries to sea-power; so any suggestion that the Royal Navy should be reduced to an inferior status was unthinkable.

There followed paragraphs to the effect that: The employment of atomic weapons could not alter the fact that the country would become incapable of continuing to wage any form of war at all if, for more than a few weeks, its sea communications were severed. That the Russians were building great numbers of ocean-going submarines; so it was more important than ever before that we should increase to the maximum possible extent our building of submarine-killing craft of the latest design. That whereas airfields and rocket-launching sites presented fixed targets for nuclear missiles, aircraft carriers possessed the advantage of mobility; therefore, should all land establishments be wiped out, the Fleet carriers might still survive as a means of retaliation, and guided missiles from them prove a last trump card which could give us victory. That the Royal Navy had ever adapted itself to changing conditions and had taken to the air simultaneously with the Army, developing in the Fleet Air Arm a weapon of proved value which could be operated with maximum efficiency only under the direction of naval officers; and that logically Coastal Command should form a section of that Arm instead of being the responsibility of the R.A.F.

It was a good vigorous paper full of blood and guts, but despite the buccaneering project of seizing Coastal Command, one could not escape the impression that the Admiralty were on the defensive, and, clearly, by their demands for more ships and craft of all sorts and sizes, their Lordships definitely favoured the Old Look policy.

The War Office paper was much more subtle, as it started off with the frank admission that in a thermo-nuclear war some of its present formations would prove of little or no value, although it qualified the statement further on by remarking that should certain of these be eliminated the difficulties of suppressing outbreaks such as had occurred in Malaya and Kenya would be enormously increased.

Having nailed the old flag to the mast, that by whatever means an enemy is rendered incapable of further effort large bodies of troops are still required to occupy the conquered territory, it went on to examine what the results might be should we succeed in inducing our allies to agree to our withdrawing our land forces from the Continent—that being the only practical means by which we could reduce our number of standing divisions. Such a withdrawal, and the precedent it would set, might so weaken the N.A.T.O. forces in Europe as to encourage our enemies to invade our allies' territories while refraining from using nuclear weapons. In such an event, would we be the first to press the button? Our Government might well prove unwilling to plunge the world into chaos until all possible means of securing a ceasefire had been exhausted. Yet the price of such hesitation would prove ruinous. The forces the Russians could deploy were so overwhelming that within a few days Free Europe would collapse under their impact. In one stroke we should then have lost the war potential of allies whose populations total over two hundred million, every advance base on the Continent, billions of pounds worth of war-like stores, and have the Russians on our door-step at Calais.

The Soldiers pointed out that they had already shown their willingness to accept radical changes by the Territorial Army's handing over of Anti-Aircraft Command to the R.A.F. Regiment. Moreover they were even now examining the possibility both of reducing personnel and attaining greater flexibility by reorganising the Armoured Formations, eliminating a high proportion of old-type Artillery Units as atomic cannon became available, reducing the size of Divisions, and relieving Battalions of their heavier types of weapon.

The foregoing led to a statement that only by increased mobility could the Armies of the Allies hope to hold the greatly superior Land Forces of their potential enemies, and that the real key to the rapid movement of fighting units lay in an unstinted allocation of aircraft, particularly helicopters. Several other types of aircraft were then enumerated and it was insisted that, to obtain maximum efficiency, the pilots of these should obviously be integrated in the Army units concerned, as had been the glider pilots of the Airborne Divisions in the last war.

This proposed foray into the territory of the airmen was promptly followed by another. Attention was drawn to the fact that all the major German victories during the early days of the last World War were in large part due to the Luftwaffe's having been subject to the orders of the Generals, which had enabled them to utilise it with maximum effect. As far as our own Army was concerned the creation in the latter stages of the war of Tactical Air Forces, to operate in close co-operation with our ground forces, had been a most valuable innovation. But it was not the proper answer. For any Army in the Field to operate to the best advantage it was requisite that its Tactical Air Force should be just as much an integral part of it as its Artillery, Engineers or Supply train; as there could then never be any difference of opinion between Air and Land Commanders as to its employment or—its diversion to assist in Air operations elsewhere at, perhaps, a critical time for the Land Force to which it was nominally attached.

It had recently been accepted that in a thermo-nuclear war Land Forces must not expect air cover. That, of course, was on the assumption that such a war would be over very quickly. But, as stated previously, in order to hold the enemy at all great mobility would be required. This could be achieved only by air transport, and that, in turn, would render a combat Air Force essential for its protection. It should also be remembered that the close cooperation of aircraft with land forces was still required for local wars, and the suppression of organised terrorist activities in our dependencies. Under both heads it was therefore recommended that an Army Air Corps should be formed forthwith, and all suitable types of aircraft henceforth diverted to it.

Passing then to long-term policy, it was accepted that when nuclear weapons had reached their full development in a major war, practically all old-type armaments would become redundant. Tanks, artillery, warships would all be out-moded, fighter aircraft would be replaced by land to air missiles, and eventually bomber aircraft would be suppressed by long-range rockets.

But, for the present, in view of the possibility that a war begun with nuclear weapons might have to be finished with orthodox ones, the advisability of making any serious reduction in conventional forces in the immediate future might well be questioned.

This clever, vigorous paper was so well reasoned that I found it most impressive; and I felt that the Soldiers were on a very strong wicket in their contention that the responsibility for maintaining, or restoring, order in our overseas dependencies fell much more largely on them than on either of the other Services; therefore to the Army the New Look could not be acceptable in its entirety as long as there was liable to be trouble in such places as Kenya, British Honduras, Cyprus, etc.

The Air Ministry paper was obviously written by men who felt that they had nothing to defend, and had complete confidence in their own Arm. It was actually headed with a paraphrase of Churchill's message to Roosevelt in 1940: 'Give us the tools and we will tackle the job.'

It opened by quoting a statement by the Supreme Commander of the Allied Powers in Europe, to the effect that the disparity in conventional forces between ourselves and the Soviets was so greatly in favour of the latter that we could redress the balance, and hope to win a full-scale war against them, only by the use of thermo-nuclear weapons. Therefore our policy was now founded on this necessity and to plan for any other form of major conflict would be suicidal.

It then outlined the type of conflict which must be envisaged, the kernel of the matter being that so destructive were the new explosives that it was impossible to conceive of a long war. With the present potential of the United States and ourselves it was estimated that we could kill fifty million Russians in the first five days; and although the present stock-pile gave the Allies a superiority over them in a ratio of five to one, it must also be accepted that the damage they would do us was incalculable.

It followed that our first defence priority must be to ensure that we were able to win the nuclear campaign in the shortest possible time, and by a bombardment of the utmost intensity force our enemies to sue for peace before we ourselves were totally destroyed.

The briefness of the convulsion envisaged determined beforehand which arms could be usefully employed in it and which would prove redundant. In so short a time only units already in being, or such as could be mobilised within forty-eight hours, would be able to play a part, and then only if they possessed the qualification of being in a position to engage the enemy.

For all practical purposes the latter requirement ruled out the Navy, as its contribution during the first week could, at best, be only trifling. And that first week was all that mattered. During it, with due allowance for the destruction of stocks by enemy action, no serious shortage of food could arise in Britain; nor in that time could our reserves of raw materials be increased by imports to a degree that would have the least influence on the outcome of the battle. We should have to fight on what we already had in the national larder and petrol pump; for before even a first convoy, immediately despatched, could cross the Atlantic the war would be over.

Thus the Navy's historic task of keeping the sea-lanes open for our shipping no longer arose, and its offensive value in a thermo-nuclear war could be rated at less than that of a

29

single Bomber Squadron; so the fact should be faced that its maintenance on its present great scale was against all common sense, and an entirely unjustifiable expenditure of both man-power and money.

Having disposed of the Navy, the paper tackled the Army. It pointed out that alone among the great nations Britain had developed her Air Force as a separate Service, and proceeded to contend that had it not been for this independence we should have lost the last world war. The German Generals had used the Luftwaffe as flying artillery, and only owing to the great initial losses it had suffered in support of land operations had its numbers been sufficiently reduced for the much smaller R.A.F. later to meet and defeat it in the Battle of Britain. Even so, it had been a desperately near thing, and had our Generals had control of the Air Arm they might well have been tempted to use and dissipate it with disastrous results.

The principal functions of an Air Force were first to seek out and destroy the enemy air force, then so to disrupt the enemy's economy as to render him incapable of continuing hostilities.

It was accepted that the Allies must maintain Land Forces on the Continent; otherwise the way would be open for enemy spearheads to advance unopposed and, even in a few days, overrun Western Europe, doing great damage to cities and industrial plant before they accepted orders from their Government to surrender. The Air Force would, therefore, have to support these Land Forces in order to redress the disparity of numbers, and assist in blocking such breakthroughs as might occur.

However, it should be borne in mind that, while the Land Forces at present on the Continent were a necessary commitment, it would be pointless to maintain Reserve Divisions in Britain with a view to their reinforcement, or to mobilise others on the outbreak of hostilities, as it would prove impossible to transport any but a limited number of light units to the scene of action in time for them to participate in the battle.

It was also accepted that the Army must maintain a sufficiency of conventional forces to deal with eventualities arising outside Europe, and that for such operations Air support would be required. But this commitment, together with that of supporting our Land Forces in Europe, must now be regarded as a second priority to that of preparing swiftly to win a thermo-nuclear war by the use of Air Power; and no project of diverting aircraft or pilots for any other purpose could be entertained.

In the future, aircraft production should, with a minimum of necessary exceptions, be devoted to turning out aircraft to win the air war. Only so could the R.A.F. hope to counter the might of the Soviet Air Force; and unless this was agreed neither the Home Country nor our Land Forces on the Continent could hope to survive.

The paper then passed to the defence of the Kingdom. It said that we must expect nuclear explosives to be directed against our cities both by means of bombers and guided missiles. It was hoped that the latest scientific developments would enable us to explode a large proportion of these in the air, well before they reached their targets. For this purpose both fighter aircraft and missile to missile weapons fired from the ground would be employed. These two methods of defence were now in the process of being co-ordinated and would be controlled by Fighter Command.

Coastal Command had, like the Navy, become redundant, as in the brief space of a one-week war it could serve no useful purpose.

Finally, the Airmen went right to the core of the matter. Having courteously deplored the necessity brought about by a new age virtually to disestablish the Royal Navy and reduce the Army, the suggestion was put forward that the time had come to combine all three Services in a Royal Defence Force.

It was pointed out that Technicians, Gunners. Signallers, Supply, Medical and other specialist Services could all be integrated without difficulty; that two-thirds of the personnel of the Navy were now employed in its twenty Fleet Air Arm Stations and in Aircraft Carriers, so were in fact already Airmen; and that it should be possible to find administrative posts for the majority of officers still on the purely nautical side.

Finally, it was stated that a nuclear war would be determined neither on the sea nor on the land, but in the air. Therefore the training of personnel to fight in such a war, and the direction of operations should it come about, must be mainly the province of officers who had qualified for high command by a life-time of service in the R.A.F.

So that was that. By offering to sink their own identity in a Royal Defence Force, the Airmen had at least proposed a means by which the 'face' of the Navy could be saved, and which should prove much more acceptable to the Army than having to surrender its missile-launching sites to Fighter Command.

I should add that I have mentioned only the salient points in these papers, and having only the ordinary man's very limited acquaintance with their subjects may even have unwittingly somewhat distorted an opinion here and there. They dealt with many other subjects, including the potentialities of numerous secret weapons of which I had never heard, and their length may be judged by the fact that they took me over an hour and a quarter to read.

After re-reading a few paragraphs to verify statements made in them, I put down the papers and looked round at Sir Charles. Catching my glance, he said:

'Finished, eh? Well; what d'you think of them?'

'All three, each in its own way, are brilliant,' I replied. 'And you must know that I am not competent to give an opinion; but, since you ask me for it, I think that, by and large, the Air people have put up the most logical arguments. Their paper is the only one which really faces up to the possibility of a nuclear war. Of course the Army has a cast-iron case for insisting that orthodox formations should be retained for dealing with Communist-inspired risings such as that of the Mau Mau, but I notice they side-step the question of armour, and if the New Look were adopted I take it tanks are one of the items that would have to go on the scrap heap. As for the Sailors, what can the poor chaps do but heat up the round shot to defend their wooden-walls.'

Sir Charles nodded. 'It's good to hear you express such a balanced view, Hillary; but I thought I could count on you for that, because although all the traditional interests of your family lie with the Sailors, you served as an Airman in the war. My belief that I should find you impartial was one of the reasons why I picked on you to play a hand in this extremely tricky business. That is, of course, if you agree to do so. But first there is one more paper that I want you to read.

'You will appreciate that, having considered the three papers you have just read, I felt that the alternatives involved were much too weighty for any single individual to take a decision upon. Naturally, anything I decided would have to go to the Cabinet, but every member of it is up to his eyes with problems of his own; so short of the P.M. coming down heavily against me, it was more or less a foregone conclusion that, in the main, whatever recommendations I made would be accepted. I don't think anyone could accuse me of having shirked my responsibilities often, but on this occasion I was not prepared to shoulder them until I had had a further opinion. To procure it I decided to resort to a secret Court of Enquiry. For its chairman I secured one of our younger Judges, who is perhaps one of the most brilliant men who has ever practised at the English Bar. Then as members I co-opted a Civil Servant, whose abilities have brought him very near the top of his profession, and a Trade Union Leader, who is a patriot through and through and has more good, sound, common sense than any man I know.'

'It certainly sounds as though you got a first-class team together.'

'Yes. I doubt if it could have been bettered. To these three chaps I submitted the papers you have read; then I arranged that every type of information they required should be furnished to them, and that any Service or scientific personnel they wished to question should be made available to give evidence before them.

'You may have noted that the papers date from the late spring. During the four months since they were got out the members of the Court have very generously given up a great deal of their leisure time to reading scores of others, giving much more detailed particulars of the organisation and the functioning of the three Services. They have also listened to the sworn testimony, given in camera, of well over two hundred serving officers, scientists, and armament experts. I received the findings of the Court ten days ago. Here they are.'

I took the document Sir Charles handed to me, and settled down to read it. No doubt the Judge had played a major part in directing the enquiry, and drafting the admirably lucid phrases in which the Court's conclusions were set out; but both the ingrained regard for caution of the Civil Servant and the blunt good sense of the Trade Union Leader came through.

The paper was not very long but very much to the point. It opened with the statement that in a conflict with the Soviet Union two sorts of war might be envisaged: orthodox and nuclear. In either type it was to be expected that, as far as Europe was concerned, and apart from isolated pockets of resistance, a decision would be reached very swiftly.

In an orthodox war, two factors weighed against us. Firstly, the forces of the Soviet Union and its satellites, on land and in the air, were much superior to those of the N.A.T.O. powers in Europe. Secondly, the forces of the Soviet Bloc would be directed by a single will, whereas those of the N.A.T.O. powers would almost inevitably suffer from the divided councils of numerous Governments; who, as had been demonstrated in the last war by that of France, whatever their undertakings to their allies, could not be restrained from entering into a separate peace. Therefore, a strong N.A.T.O. Army might delay, but could not prevent, the Russians arriving at Calais.

In consequence the dictum of the Allies' Supreme Commander—that our only hope of emerging victorious from a full-scale war with the Soviets lay in our using thermo-nuclear weapons—could not be contested. Indeed, it compelled us to the further conclusion that, in the event of Soviet aggression, we must use nuclear weapons even if our enemies refrained from using them, and at once; otherwise such initial advantage might be gained as to cause us to lose the war almost overnight.

There was good reason to believe that in these new weapons we were ahead and, with the co-operation of the United States, could keep ahead of the Soviet Union. If we concentrated on them, there was a very real hope that rather than risk the total destruction of their economy the Soviets would never dare to launch a full-scale war against us; and that, should their Government prove irresponsible enough to do so, there would still be a good chance of our emerging as victors from the ruins. But, in order to build up a potential of sufficient magnitude to achieve either of the ends stated above, the development of nuclear weapons, and preparations for their employment with maximum efficiency, must now be accepted by all three Services as an overriding priority.

Any endeavour to create a New Look of the strength required to act as a really powerful deterrent to aggression, while seeking to maintain an Old Look at all comparable to present standards, would be to play the enemy's game. Taxation would be forced up to such heights that our economy would be disrupted. It was, however, estimated that a satisfactory New Look could be achieved if some two-thirds of the sum now expended on orthodox Naval and Military armaments could be diverted and added to that already allocated to the production of nuclear missiles, and the means of despatching them to their targets.

To achieve this re-allocation of expenditure it would be necessary to scrap the entire Naval building programme; to reduce production of heavy armoured vehicles to a point sufficient only to cover our present commitments in Germany; to abolish much other equipment in current use with the Army; to disestablish all Reserve formations in the United Kingdom which could never expect to reach the battlefield before a decision had been achieved, and to do away with both our Coast Artillery and Coastal Command.

It was appreciated that this question of going over to the New Look was giving as much concern to our Allies as to ourselves; and it was to be regretted that the United States, as the major arms producing nation among the N.A.T.O. powers, still seemed reluctant to give a lead in the matter. But that did not relieve us of our responsibility; and, as the strongest power in Western Europe, we were now being looked to for guidance by our own Continental Allies.

It was now a considerable time since the Supreme Commander's dictum had been accepted in principle by the military advisers to the Allied Governments. For many months the staffs of S.H.A.P.E., and those of the Commanders in Chief who would come under it in the event of war, had been redrafting their plans on the assumption that thermo-nuclear weapons would be used by us as an immediate reply to Soviet aggression. But it was futile to rely on plans unless they had as their basis a definite assurance that the full resources to implement them would be forthcoming.

At present the rate of build-up of these resources was far from satisfactory, because the Government had not accepted the full implications of the Supreme Commander's dictum. It had failed to face the question squarely; and, although it had allocated a considerable sum to the development of thermo-nuclear weapons, it had shirked the unpleasant task of scrapping or reducing many costly forms of armament which would prove of no value in nuclear war. Yet only by such economies could the development of the new weapons, and the means of despatching them to their targets, be accelerated to a degree which would enable us to smash our enemies so utterly and so swiftly that we might ourselves expect to survive with damage which, although heavy, would be by no means irreparable.

That this must be our aim was beyond question. Therefore the Supreme Commander's dictum must now be accepted not only in principle but in practice; and the two senior Services must be called on to submit to drastic cuts in their establishments in order that the Air defence of the United Kingdom and the bombardment by Air of the Soviet Union might be rendered more effective, until such time as full development of guided missiles made both Fighter and Bomber aircraft also redundant.

It was appreciated that one of the major difficulties of bringing this about swiftly and effectively lay in the present practice whereby each Chief of Staff submitted an estimate of the expenditure to be allocated annually on his own Service, and fought tooth and nail for its acceptance. Since the New Look demanded such revolutionary changes it was strongly recommended that this method of procedure should be discontinued. Instead, the whole sum voted for national defence should be placed at the disposal of the Minister of Defence, and, after he had consulted with his advisers regarding priorities, it should be his responsibility to determine the types of weapon to be produced and the allocation of funds to each Service appropriate to its commitments resulting from these decisions.

The paper then expressed the opinion of the Court that the amalgamation of the three Services into one Royal Defence Force would call for much skilful negotiation, but, given goodwill in all concerned, should be practicable; and was infinitely to be preferred to the only alternative, which called for the virtual dissolution of the Royal Navy, as such a measure would inevitably arouse great and natural protest, and possibly obstruction, throughout the whole kingdom.

It was suggested that the opposition could be overcome with a minimum of friction if the matter was taken out of the hands of the Services, and that a Royal Commission should at once be set up to examine the problem, then decide on a programme by which integration could be achieved with as little hardship as possible to all concerned.

The acceptance in practice as well as principle of a New Look policy meant that in any case the Navy must suffer severely. But an amalgamation of the Services would go a long way to softening the blow, as it should be possible to find employment in the new R.D.F. for all naval personnel other than the more senior officers, and the diversion of the pilots of the Fleet Air Arm to land-based aircraft would, after a comparatively short period of training, prove an invaluable reinforcement to our Air Power for the waging of a thermo-nuclear war.

The Army would not be called on to accept change to anything like such a degree. In addition to our commitment in Germany it was evident that a field-force must be maintained; so that a suitable contribution could be made to any U.N.O. Army formed to counter local Communist-inspired aggression of the Korean type, or for despatch to dependencies such as Cyprus in which organised terrorist activities broke out. This meant that a high percentage of its present units would have to retain, more or less, the Old Look; but it must be accepted that there would be a reduction in the types of weapon and organisation with which this field force would be equipped. Even so, the retention of such a force would entail the expenditure of at least four hundred million annually, as the economy in heavy weapons and elimination of certain Reserve formations would be more than offset by the necessity of continuing to maintain the majority of the Old Look training establishments.

With regard to Man-power, it was evident that all Arms required personnel with an ever greater degree of technical efficiency, and this could be achieved only by long-term service engagements. The aim should be for quality rather than quantity, and in this the benefits of National Service were dubious. It was therefore recommended that a reduction of intake should be offset by a really worthwhile increase in pay for all ranks as an inducement to increased enlistment of regulars who would make the Service a career.

By the laying up of the majority of our war vessels, and the reduction of the Army's heavy weapons, Reserve units, etc., it was estimated that we should save some three hundred and fifty million annually. This would enable us to pay for a greatly increased programme of nuclear weapon and aircraft production without placing a further burden on the taxpayer. But our object should be to reduce taxation if possible.

Should the full implications of the New Look policy be accepted and put into practice by the British Government, it could be regarded as certain that our Continental Allies would shortly follow suit by laying up the bulk of their Navies and making similar economies in their Land Forces. This would enable them to make very considerable savings in their Defence budgets; but, unlike ourselves, they could not transfer their savings to the increased production of weapons for a thermo-nuclear war, because the processes of manufacturing such weapons had not been divulged to them.

That our Continental Allies should be placed in a position to relieve taxation while we could not do so would be manifestly unfair to the British people. It was therefore suggested that our Government should enter into discussion with the Governments of our Allies on the following lines, and, as an extension of the proposal, that the Minister of Defence should take over from the Service Chiefs the allocation of all funds voted for Defence purposes.

Instead of the present system, by which each country votes a sum annually for the maintenance of its Navy, Army and Air Force, the whole allocation for its Defence should be placed at the disposal of a new committee to be set up at N.A.T.O. The committee would consist of the Defence Ministers of all the countries concerned, and they would decide in conference how the total defence budget of the Continental Allies should be expended.

Thus, should Britain continue to be the only producer of thermo-nuclear weapons in Europe, she would no longer be automatically saddled with the whole of their cost. Such an arrangement would moreover lead to increased efficiency in the forces of the N.A.T.O. powers, as from it would emerge a far greater degree of uniformity in arms and equipment than existed at present. Lastly, if all our Continental Allies reduced their Sea and Land Forces on the same scale as was proposed for ourselves, all the countries concerned should be able to grant some relief from taxation to their peoples, yet still contribute to a central N.A.T.O. fund sums which would enable a much greater allocation to be made for the production of nuclear weapons than Britain alone could afford. Indeed, with the combined military budgets of the European Allies at its disposal, it would not be unreasonable to expect the N.A.T.O. committee to devote one hundred million per annum to this purpose.

This, then, was the optimum solution to be aimed at. Could it be achieved, the N.A.T.O. nations would possess such overwhelming superiority in the Air and in destructive power that the likelihood of the Soviets challenging it must be remote; while, should they do so, the Allies might confidently expect to destroy all the principal cities of Russia within thirty-six hours and bring the war to a victorious conclusion so swiftly that they would have sustained only comparatively minor damage themselves.

As I put the paper down, Sir Charles asked: 'Well, what d'you think of it?'

I sighed. 'It's pretty tough on the Navy.'

'I know. If the New Look goes through, I'll never again be able to look any of my sailor friends in the face. But we must be realistic. To allow ourselves to be influenced by sentiment would be to betray the nation. The point is, do you agree with the main conclusions in that paper or not?'

'I do. How can one help doing so? The whole thing is so damnably logical.'

He stood up, came round to collect my glass, poured another ration of brandy into it, handed it back and said with a smile: 'You're going to need that, Hillary. The admission you have just made entitles me to make to you the request I have in mind. Of course, you've complete liberty to refuse it; but I hope you won't.'

Sitting down in the corner of the sofa opposite to me, he stretched out his long legs and went on: 'As I've already said, when this thing goes before the House, as it must if we are to combine the three Services, there is going to be the very devil of an uproar. Even the cockneys, whose only experience of the sea is a trip to Brighton, are going to wave their wooden legs in defence of the Navy. "All the nice girls love a sailor" too, so even the women will be against us. As for the Admirals past and present, just think of the opposition they will stir up. That's the trouble. There is a very real danger that the Bill will be thrown out; and you know what that would mean?'

'If the Government were defeated on such a major issue, it would have no alternative but to resign and go to the country.'

'Yes, and that would be bad enough; but far worse would follow. If we went out on that issue we'd have to fight the Election on it; and as the People are far more sentimental than the House it is a hundred to one that we would remain out. That would result in the status quo being maintained and the New Look being shelved indefinitely. If that happens, within another five years we'll be completely at the mercy of the Russians.'

I nodded. 'Yes; from those papers I've read I'm convinced now that drastic measures provide the only solution. I'm still completely in the dark, though, about how I might be able to help.'

'I'm coming to that. After much thought I've come to the conclusion that the only way we can hope to get this thing over is by preparing public opinion beforehand. Do you remember the high explosive shell business in 1915?'

'No, I was only a babe in arms then.'

'But surely you must have heard of it. After the first great land battles the Germans dug themselves in. Ninety per cent of the shells supplied to our Field Artillery were shrapnel. They had proved very effective against troops in open warfare, but were no earthly use against trenches and concrete pill-boxes. In consequence, the C. in C. of the B.E.F., General French, asked for less shrapnel and a big increase in high explosive shell. Lord Kitchener was Secretary of State for War. He was, of course, a great administrator; but the public thought of him as much more than that. His prestige with them was enormous, and being a very self-opinionated, dictatorial type of man, he took full advantage of it. On military matters he rarely bothered to consult his colleagues in the Cabinet, but just told them afterwards as much as he judged it good for them to know.

'Receiving no satisfaction in the matter of the shell business from the War Office, French took steps to acquaint some of the principal Ministers with the situation. They tackled Kitchener, but he adopted the attitude that what had been good enough for him to use against the Boers in South Africa was good enough for Sir John French to use against the Germans, and flatly refused to do anything about it. As Kitchener was the idol of the public, to have forced his resignation might have brought the Government down; so they sought the aid of Lord Northcliffe.

'He was the most powerful Press Baron of the day and he used the freedom of the press to attack the War Office. Soon, people who had never even heard of shrapnel before were saying in every pub in Britain how futile it was to burst shells filled with shrapnel bullets twelve feet above deep trenches, and indignantly demanded that high explosive should be sent to blow them in. The public assumed that Kitchener was far too busy directing the strategy of the war to be responsible for types of ammunition: so it was the poor old War Office that got the raw end of the deal. But there was such a storm about it that he had to give way, and the B.E.F. got the shells it needed.'

I nodded. 'Yes, I do remember now once hearing some story on those lines. But I'm no Press Baron, and I can't imagine it would cut much ice if I wrote to *The Times* as a private individual, urging the adoption of the New Look.'

'No; but it would if you wrote as Chairman of your Company, and you had some very concrete reason for doing so.'

'Such as?' I asked, now agog with curiosity.

Sir Charles stubbed out the butt of his cigar, and turned his pale-blue eyes, that looked so enormous through the pebble lenses, full upon me. 'It would be on the subject of E-boats,' he said slowly. 'The Admiralty has just passed an order for six more of them; and you know how much they cost—a million apiece.'

'No, no!' I protested. 'I feel sure you've been misinformed about that, Sir. I only know the cost of the hulls; but I really can't believe that arming them brings the total up to anything like a million.'

'It does, Hillary. I've been into every detail. I know the share you shipbuilders get is only a fraction of that sum, and the biggest item is not the armaments either. It is all the scientific gadgets with which every ship of war now has to be packed. There are scores of them, and most of them cost a small fortune. I assure you that by the time a new E-boat has now completed her trials she has cost the country a million pounds sterling.'

'Good Lord alive! That's as much as a Dreadnought, which had twelve-inch guns and took a thousand men to sea, used to cost in 1914.'

'I know; and another Dreadnought meant something in those days. But in a nuclear war these six new E-boats will be no more use to us than six fishing smacks.'

'Then you want me to write to *The Times* calling public attention to what you have just told me?'

'There is more to it than that. Your Company's tender has been accepted for building two of these boats. The acceptance is probably already in the post to that retired Admiral who is your Sales Manager—what's his name? Yes, Sir Tuke Waldron. When he informs you of this nice order he has secured, I want you to refuse it.'

'What!' I exclaimed, sitting up with a jerk.

Sir Charles smiled at me. 'I know that what I am asking is a bit hard on you and your shareholders; but I'm sure your Company is much too solid a concern to be at all seriously affected by the loss of this order. Quite frankly, I am appealing to you on patriotic grounds. You did not know about this contract before I told you of it, so you can honestly say that it was obtained without your knowledge. I want you to reject it, then write to *The Times*, saying what you have done, state the convictions you have formed this evening about the urgent necessity of our adopting the New Look, and say that in view of them you could not square it with your conscience to be a party to such a scandalous waste of the public's money.'

I said nothing for the moment, and he went on:

'That will send the balloon up. The following day it will be front page news in every paper in this country, in the

United States, and on the Continent as well. Your obvious integrity will be evident from the sacrifice you are making. Logic is on our side. We'll have spiked the Admiralty's guns and have the nation behind us. You have it in your power, Hillary, to enable the Government to go to the House on this thing without risking defeat—more, by enabling us to act in time, you may save us from annihilation by the Soviets in a few years from now. Will you do it?'

'Has the Prime Minister approved this idea for catching the Old Lookers napping?' I asked.

Sir Charles made a little gesture with one of his long slim hands. 'I don't think we need go into that. We all know that, even if it meant the fall of his Government, he would still face the House and ask it to do what he felt to be the right thing for the nation. It's my job, and that of my colleagues, to lighten, as far as we can, the burden he has to carry; and the heaviest one in a democracy is that of persuading the mainly ignorant masses to accept a programme that sound evidence has shown to be the best for them.

'Of course, I am fully aware that my proposal to you is highly unorthodox, and if it got out that I had made it I should have to resign; but you wouldn't think much of me if I did so for no apparent reason and left the baby for some other poor devil to hold, would you? Or if I shirked facing up to the issue?

'Frankly, Hillary, I believe that if we continue with the Old Look, or even try to have it both ways, Britain will be as much a thing of the past within ten years as Greece or Rome; the only difference being that any of our grandchildren who may survive will not even be allowed to know about the great achievements of their race. That is why I don't feel the least scruple about asking you to do this thing.'

I realised then that by my last question I had implied that he was doing something vaguely dishonest. He had taken it very well; but, actually, that was the very last thing I had had in mind. No one could have been more of an anti-thesis to the modern politician whose eyes are always flickering round to catch sight of a band-wagon on to which he can climb with the hope of doing a bit better for himself. Sir Charles was a most modest and retiring man. Rather than seek office he had been pushed into it by those who appreciated his many gifts. He was a younger son of one of our great families, who, like the Cecils, the Stanleys, the Churchills and the Seymours, had served the country with little thought of self for many generations.

Smiling, I said: 'That you feel the way you do, Sir, is quite good enough for me. But there is just one point that I have to consider. I am the largest individual shareholder in my Company, but I don't hold a controlling interest. Our next Board Meeting is on Friday. It is then that Admiral Waldron will produce this order he has secured for two E-boats. When he has done so it will be up to me to turn it down. Naturally, my co-directors will think I've suddenly gone crazy; so, to win most of them over to support me in this altruistic sacrifice of the Company's financial interests, I shall have to produce some very strong arguments. I realise, of course, that I must keep you out of it; but I'd like you to give me an idea how far I may go in using this material that you've shown me tonight?'

After a moment, he replied: 'I see your point, and it's a very sound one. You must not disclose that you have seen these papers, as to do so would as good as give the game away; but providing you warn your co-directors that, for security reasons, what you are saying should go no further, I see no reason that you should not use the arguments in them. They won't know where you've got them from, but they are so convincing that they should do the trick.'

Later I was bitterly to rue the fact that he had given me such a free hand, or at least had not warned me to avoid quoting figures and the mention of certain special passages; but I suppose he took it for granted that I should keep those to myself.

We had another drink together and talked on in a most friendly fashion for a further half hour. Then he let me out, and as I walked up Whitehall I felt the thrill that must come to every man chosen for any form of special mission. Little did I guess then what would have happened to me by that time on Friday night.

4

Friday 9th September

I have found already that dictating this account helps to take my mind off the harrowing and unnerving vision of myself standing in the dock at Winchester and the Judge putting on the black cap to sentence me. So, while continuing to adhere to the strict truth in everything, instead of confining myself to bare facts as I had originally intended, I shall give free rein to the tendency to be discursive—where the matter warrants it—as indeed, it seems that I have been already to some extent; and so by this occupation may stave off the morbid contemplation of my only too well-founded fears. To resume my narrative.

During the war poor old Southampton took a terrific pasting and our offices were among the many buildings destroyed in the blitz. For several years we suffered considerable inconvenience in a higgledy-piggledy collection of pre-fabs, but at last we got a rebuilding permit and were able to erect a fine modern glass and concrete block. The new Board-room is on its top floor overlooking our yards and with a vista of Southampton Water.

At two-thirty on the Friday the Directors of Hillary-Compton assembled there, and before going any further I had better give some account of them.

Our Managing Director is James Compton. His father started in the firm at the age of ten, in the bad old days of child labour, and by hard work, initiative and ability progressed right to the top. As a reward for his long and valuable services my grandfather made him a junior partner a few years before the concern was turned into a Company. James has not only benefited by a proper education but inherited the old man's drive and knowledge of our craft; so my father took him on the Board in his early thirties. He is now just over sixty, and the mainstay of the firm. He knows far more about the practical side of the industry than I do, handles our labour problems with firmness and tact, and has his whole heart in the business. In matters on which his opinion differs from mine he fights me tooth and nail; but on the majority of questions we see eye to eye, and no man could have a more loyal and honest partner.

Angus McFarlane is our Chief Engineer. He is a tall thin bachelor, who says very little and, I believe, spends most of his leisure poring over his stamp albums. But he is a first-class technician, and I have never known him advise us wrongly about types of engines for our speed boats and motor launches. When he had been with us for some years we decided to give him a seat on the Board as being more convenient than having to summon him so frequently to it.

Charles Toiller is the Secretary of the Company and has been with it since my grandfather's time. He is a Chartered Accountant and has all the Company's financial affairs at his finger tips. In addition the little man carries all our principal transactions for many years past in the egg-shaped dome of his bald head. He is getting on now, as he was nearly sixty when my father died; and it was then that James Compton and I decided to promote him to a Directorship.

Admiral Sir Tuke Waldron, K.B.E., D.S.O., etc., has, since his retirement from the Navy, been our Sales Manager; but his connection with the Company goes much further back than that. His father was related to mine by marriage, and when our business was floated as a Company he took a large block of shares in it. By inheriting them, the Admiral became, after myself, the largest shareholder. As we are boat-builders to the Admiralty, he was naturally precluded from holding a Directorship during his service career, but it had for long been understood that on retirement he should join the Board.

He was retired as Vice-Admiral, so is still only in his middle sixties. To look at, he is the choleric type of sea-dog, with a red face, bushy white eyebrows and an apparently unlimited capacity for despatching pink gins; but he is far from being a stupid man, and has a most likeable personality. I do not, of course, suggest that Admiralty contracts can be obtained by taking people out to lunch, but in securing any business the personal touch does count where tenders are equal; and he has many friends in the right places. He had not been long on the Board before he began to produce results; so in due course we made him our Chief Salesman, and in the five years he has been with us we have never had reason to regret it.

The Right Honourable Annibal William Fitz-Herbert Le Strange, 14th Earl of Wiltshire, Viscount Rochford and Baron Blackmere, known to his friends as Bill, is my father-in-law. The only serious row I have ever had with James Compton was due to my insistence that Lord Wiltshire should join our Board. At the time I was so ashamed of foisting a 'guinea-pig' on to my colleagues that I tried to sell them the story that as he had always been a keen sailing man it was intended that he should join the principal yacht clubs round the coast, and so would be able to bring us a lot of business; but the truth is that landing him a Directorship was part of the price I had to pay for Ankaret.

The Le Stranges are one of those very old families which have seen lots of ups and downs. At present they are in a 'down' from which I think it unlikely that they will recover. One of them had come over with the Conqueror, and they had done very well for themselves in Norman times. Under the Plantagenets a line of Barons Blackmere had been possessed of great estates, and held numerous castles for the Crown. But they backed the wrong horse in the Wars of the Roses and for a hundred years or so wilted into little more than country gentry. Under Henry VIII they had popped up again, as they were close connections of Sir Thomas Boleyn.

Sir Thomas's principal claim to fame was that Bluff King Hal, having seduced both his daughters, became so crazy about the younger of them that he divorced his wife and made her Queen. Papa's reward for his complaisance was to be created first Viscount Rochford then Earl of Wiltshire, upon which the lady's brother took by courtesy the lesser title. The cousins Le Strange were brought to court and secured some valuable pickings. But their luck did not last, as the lively young Queen was accused of jumping into bed with several gay sparks, among them Rochford. So both sister and brother had their heads chopped off on Tower Hill, and the rest of the family fell into disgrace.

Yet in the long run the Le Stranges got a big boost as a result of the King's amour and the incest of which Anne

47

Boleyn was accused. By the first they had become kinsmen of Anne's daughter, afterwards Queen Elizabeth, and by the second the Earl of Wiltshire was left heirless; so that on his death the peerage fell into abeyance. Half a century later another handsome Le Strange persuaded the Virgin Queen to revive both titles in his favour, and, in addition, wheedled some very profitable monopolies out of her.

For the next fifty years the family were in clover; but when the Great Rebellion broke out they naturally sided with the King, so they lost everything and had to go into exile. Charles II restored most of their lands to them, but on his death they once again backed the wrong horse by siding with Monmouth against James II; and two generations later they made another blunder by joining Bonny Prince Charlie in '45; so from 1685, for about a hundred years, they were very much under the weather.

Then there had come a sudden revival, obviously due to the Earl of the day having married the daughter of a Sheffield Alderman. This heiress brought into the family not only a considerable fortune but also business acumen. Her son cashed in on the industrial revolution and by the time Queen Victoria came to the throne the Le Stranges were once more immensely rich. But by the middle of the century, probably without realising it themselves this time, they had begun to go downhill again.

To all the extravagances to which the more empty-headed of the Victorian nobilty were prone they took like ducks to water. Scores of servants, a plurality of houses, ceaseless entertaining, grouse moors, yachts, villas in the South of France, cards, horses, and secret establishments for pretty ladies, reduced them in three generations from great land-owners to titled people of only modest fortune.

Courage they had never lacked; so two of them fell in the 1914 war. The double death duties administered the final blow to the already crippled estate. The family seat, the town house and the last acres all had to go. In 1918, at the age of eighteen, Bill came into the title. Of course, he had been educated at Eton and was already an ensign in the Life Guards; so his friends were mainly young men with extravagant tastes who did not have to worry much about money. In the circumstances one can hardly blame him for having dissipated, during the gay early twenties, the few thousands that had been saved from the wreck.

In 1923, as a means of averting bankruptcy, he had married an American heiress; but he was much too transparent a character to disguise for long that his heart was not in the match. He must have been extremely good-looking. I'm told that when it was discovered at Eton that his first name was Annibal, his school fellows had nicknamed him 'handsome Annie'. Anyhow, women had fallen for him like ninepins and he had had scores of affairs; yet the fact remained that the only person he had ever really loved was a second cousin of his, the lovely Lady Angela Chippenham, and she was just as much in love with him.

The young American wife soon tumbled to the situation, and she was not prepared to keep her coronet at that price. One cannot blame her, but I think she might have been a little less malicious about it. Not only did she throw her Earl out on to the pavement from their flat in Grosvenor Square, but nothing could persuade her to refrain from citing Lady Angela.

Actually I don't think Lady Angela minded, because it meant that she would get Bill for keeps. Proud as they make 'em, she refused to deny the charge and said some pretty cutting things about plain little girls who thought they could buy love with dollars. As soon as the divorce came through Bill made an honest woman of her; but her family were by no means wealthy, so he had to leave the Guards and try his hand at commerce.

As a peerage was still something of an asset for shop-window dressing in the business world of those days, he managed to keep himself afloat; but only just, because he was too lazy to make the best of his opportunities, abhorred routine, and got so bored with his jobs that he chucked most of them up after a few months.

Meanwhile, his wife had presented him with a son and daughter. Fortunately in 1928 Lady Wiltshire was left by an aunt the income for life on quite a tidy sum. It was anyhow sufficient for her to meet the expenses of a medium-sized house in one of the streets off Belgrave Square and to educate the children; but in 1946 she died from injuries received in a car smash, and her income reverted to another member of her family.

The four years that followed proved far from easy ones for Bill. His boy, who enjoys his second title, Rochford, and is known as Roc, was then nineteen, and Ankaret was two years younger. From 1928 onward Bill had been quite content to let his wife foot the household bills, while he devoted such money as he could pick up to shooting, fishing, a little mild racing and such other pastimes as he had been brought up to enjoy. At her death he suddenly found himself up against it.

Roc was far from being a young man of promise. He had all his father's bad points and few of his good ones. In fact he has turned out to be about as decadent a specimen of the British aristocracy as one could find if one raked the shadier West End night-clubs for a month.

To do his National Service he was, of course, put into his father's old regiment, the Life Guards; but he failed to get a stripe, much less graduate for a N.S. Commission. When he came out Bill got him a succession of jobs in the City; but he could not hold down any of them and, as his father could afford to give him only a very small allowance, he took to downright dishonesty.

For a time he got along by sponging on his friends and borrowing all he could from them without the least prospect of being able to pay them back. Having exhausted all such sources, he then got engaged to a rich widow twice his age and pawned her jewels without her knowledge, counting rightly on the fact that she might throw him over but would not face the humiliation of bringing an action. Next, he got in with a set of rogues and lent himself to a little bogus company promoting. He escaped from the results of that only because he had the luck of the devil; and twice, since I married Ankaret, I have had to come to the rescue financially to save him from being sent to prison. Recently he seems to have become a bit more canny and is now picking up a living at some sort of job in the film industry; but one never knows from one day to another when we shall suddenly be told that he had started issuing dud cheques again.

After Lady Wiltshire's death the house had to be given up, and Bill had Ankaret left on his hands. But his problem about what to do with her was solved by the 'family' rallying round. One of her aunts undertook to present her, and, while none of her relatives could afford to give her a permanent home, they agreed to have her to stay in turn for long visits until Bill could make some suitable arrangement for her to live with him.

Even if he could have earned enough money, I don't think he would have attempted to do that; because having unloaded Ankaret suited him very well. He settled down in a small bachelor flat and salved his conscience by occasionally buying her a few clothes or sending her a cheque for pocket money. In consequence, after her coming-out season the poor child had practically to live in her boxes, mostly at country houses but occasionally in London.

Being young and healthy she took it quite philosophically; but from one point of view it was most regrettable. She has a real flair for art and four years of this unsettled existence deprived her of all chance to study it properly. Had she spent them at the Schools I am sure that by now she would have made a name for herself; as it is she can draw really beautifully, but her paintings lack something which only a mastery of technique can give. That apart, such a life is far from being a good background for a girl of her age and temperament, as no one was really responsible for her, and, providing she behaved tactfully, the different relations with whom she stayed all allowed her to do more or less as she liked.

Being Ankaret, she soon started to make the most of her chances; and, as she told me sometime after we were married, there had been quite a number of occasions on which, between visits, she had spent week-ends with young men at discreet country pubs without her relatives ever getting to know of it.

I imagine that most girls in such a precarious situation would have done their damnedest to hook the first likeable man who came their way and was in a position to give them a comfortable home of their own. No doubt, too, in view of the devastating effect that Ankaret had on men her relations had never anticipated that her rounds of visits to them would continue for as long as they did; but until she was over twenty-one, and met me, she never became even temporarily engaged.

I suppose that fairly frequent changes of scene and company, coupled with her self-taught painting and her clandestine love affairs, kept her reasonably contented. Anyhow, expensive clothes, jewels and rich furs were no temptation to her, because she had everything a woman needs without them; and she never bothered her beautiful head about the future. I well remember that if on parting I ever said to her 'God bless you, darling' her invariable reply was, 'Thanks; He will.'

What she saw in me that she had not found in other men I have no idea; but she did not take very long about making up her mind after I'd asked her to marry me. She asked only one night to think it over; then next morning in the garden of Ewefold Priory, where we were both staying, she said:

'I'm not a woman's woman, so sooner or later it is quite possible that you may hear catty remarks to the effect that I have a past. I shall neither admit nor deny them; so you must believe them or not as you like. But one thing I don't think anyone will accuse me of is being a gold-digger. All the same, I feel that I have certain obligations to my family.'

She told me then, perfectly frankly, about her father and brother, and went on: 'I'm afraid that any attempt to turn Roc into a respectable citizen would prove quite hopeless; so all I ask for him is that should he land himself in further messes you will do what you can, within reason, to save him from being sent to prison. Daddy, on the other hand, is a very different matter. It isn't altogether his fault that he has been reduced for some years past to living on a shoe-string; and as he gets older his situation is bound to get worse instead of better. He has never even hinted that I could help him by marrying a man with money; but I have always felt that if I did have a rich husband I ought to ask him to make the old boy an allowance of a few hundred a year. He has become used now to living quite modestly but I would like him to have enough not to have to worry where his next quarter's rent, or the subscriptions to his Clubs, are coming from.'

The night before she had admitted that she loved me, and now she added that she felt differently about me from any other man she had met; so it must be that she was really in love for the first time, and she did want to marry me. But if, after what she had said about her family, I would prefer to forget that I had asked her, she would perfectly understand.

In view of the very special feeling that I had aroused in her, it seems most unlikely that she was making any mental reservations about being unfaithful to me later on; so the way she put matters to me could hardly have been fairer and I willingly agreed to do something for Bill.

Had we been living in pre-war days I could, with my present income, quite well have afforded to give him five hundred a year without embarrassment. But the coming of the Welfare State has made a difference to men in my position that few people of moderate incomes realise. In the 1930's, ten thousand a year meant everything for which one could reasonably wish. Now, Income and Super Tax bring it down at one fell swoop to the three thousand five hundred mark; and as a pound today buys less than six and eightpence did then, the actual purchasing power remaining is less than twelve hundred.

Even that must sound pretty good to most people; but there is not much to spare if one has a largish house to keep up and an ex-wife and two children to provide for. In addition I was about to marry again; and to a girl who had not a penny of her own.

Nearly all my capital is tied up in my own Company, and I certainly did not feel like selling out a large block of my shares to form a Trust fund for Bill. The obvious way out was to put him on the Board, which would net him five hundred a year in Director's fees. Perhaps that was slightly dishonest, because I knew he couldn't really pull his weight; but that is what I did, and how he came to be there.

I feel that I have devoted a lot of space to my father-in-law, although he played little part in the events that follow. But it has enabled me to give an account of Ankaret's background, and that is important.

Now for the last, and most junior, of our Directors: my nephew, Wing Commander Johnny Norton. He is the only child of my half-sister, Betty, and she was the only child of my father's first marriage. As she was fourteen years older than myself and ran away from home when she was twenty, I have only the vaguest memories of her.

I gather she was rather a hoydenish young woman with neither beauty nor charm, and that her one passion was motor racing. Apparently this led to her spending a great deal of time with my father's chauffeur, who was also an enthusiast, and in his off duty hours was jigging up an old car that he had bought with a view to doing a little amateur racing himself. They became secretly engaged and when they broke it to my father that they intended to get married there was hell to pay.

Not unreasonably, perhaps, as Betty was such a plain girl, he assumed that Norton was after her for what he could get out of it; so he sacked him on the spot. Betty declared that she meant to marry him anyhow; and her papa said that if she did her husband could keep her, for he certainly would not, and that if she even saw Norton again he would cut off her allowance. She made a pretence of giving in, but one morning about a month later her room was found to be empty, and a few days after that she wrote from an address in London to say that she had become Mrs. Norton.

It was natural enough that my father should have been averse to his only daughter marrying a working man, but I am sure that in threatening to cut her off he believed that he was protecting her from an adventurer; for he was by no means hard-hearted by nature. He told me himself, years later, that, if at the end of a year she was still happy with Norton, he had meant to forgive and forget, buy them a house and take Norton into the business at a decent salary. But he felt that their having to make do for twelve months on a chauffeur's wages first would prove a real test for both of them; although as far as they knew he was through with Betty for good.

Unhappily, Fate forestalled my father's good intentions. Ten months after her marriage Betty died in giving birth to Johnny. When my father was informed by Norton of her death, he was terribly upset by the thought that she had died in some poor lodging, and might not have died at all had they had the money for her to have the baby in a nursing home attended by a Harley Street gynaecologist. He wrote to Norton bitterly upbraiding him for not letting him know that Betty was about to become a mother, but offering to take full responsibility for the baby; and Norton wrote back with equal bitterness, asserting that his wife's death had been due to her father's snobbery and meanness. He added that as her father had done nothing for her while she was alive he need not expect to have any share in her son now she was dead, and that he was quite capable of bringing the boy up without any assistance from his Hillary relatives.

Later, my father made an attempt to patch matters up with Norton so that he might at least arrange for his grandson to receive a good education. It was learned then that Norton had come into a little money, so had returned to his native town of Huddersfield and opened a garage in one of its suburbs. Johnny had been there since an infant in the care of Norton's mother; and I have since learned that the garage business prospered to a degree that enabled his father to send him to a Grammar School and give him a very respectable middle-class upbringing. But Norton remained adamant in his refusal to accept any assistance from my father, or even to let him see the boy.

As far as I was concerned the whole affair was one of hearsay and dim memories; so I had virtually forgotten that I even had a nephew when, by pure chance, I was introduced to Johnny some three years ago. I met him while having drinks before dinner at the Royal Air Force Club with another regular R.A.F. officer with whom I had become friends during the war. He is what used to be considered a naval type; fair-haired, intensely blue-eyed and with a square chin having a slight cleft in its centre. He is nearly as tall as I am, but slimmer and, again like the naval type, has that quiet good-humoured manner of the man of action who makes little fuss but sees things through.

Our names, of course, rang bells in one another's minds, and as both our fathers were by then dead we saw no reason whatever to prolong the family schism. Moreover we took to one another at once, so I asked him down for the weekend. My sister having been so much older than myself he would really have fitted better into the role of a younger brother than a nephew, and during that first week-end we came to like each other a lot.

Before he left on the Sunday night he said that sometime he would like to see over the family business; so I asked him down again and took him round the yards. James Compton knows the family history as well as I do, and being twenty years older remembered much more about poor Betty's affair than I did myself; so naturally he was most interested to meet Johnny, and he went round with us.

Both James and I were greatly impressed by the intelligent questions Johnny asked, and the shrewd comments he made on this and that; and this tour of the yards he had made with us set me thinking. James had no sons and my own boy is set on becoming a chartered accountant; so there is no one to take the place of either of us should one of us drop out. When the routine flying days of R.A.F. officers are over quite a high proportion of them have to be axed, and Johnny was already aSquadron-Leader; so in a few years' time he might be only too glad of the chance to go into business. Moreover, ours was his own family concern, and but for circumstances over which he had had no control he would have been given the chance to go into it as a youngster. Had he done so he would by then have been far better off than he was, as he had not even been mentioned in my father's will, and the proceeds from selling his own father's garage brought him only a little over a hundred a year; so he was practically dependent on his pay.

The more I thought about it the more I felt that, having been left nearly the whole of my father's fortune, it was up to me to do something for Johnny. When I spoke to James about it he agreed at once that Johnny would be an asset to the business, and had at least an ethical right to some share in it. We agreed, too, that even if he was not prepared to leave the R.A.F. right away, we might, with future possibilities in mind, run him in by making him a Director.

When I put it to Johnny, he said that he wanted to go on in the R.A.F., but that as he had recently returned from two years in Malaya, and previously to that done a tour of duty at Gibraltar, all the odds were on his being stationed at home for the next few years; so he should be able to attend most of our monthly Board meetings. He was keen as mustard about the idea; and most charmingly grateful when I told him that he need not sell out any of his capital to buy qualifying shares, as I meant to make over to him five hundred of mine.

During the past three years he has more than fulfilled his promise, and now has an excellent grasp of all the Company's affairs. Whenever he attends a meeting he always spends the night at Longshot Hall, and we are no longer like uncle and nephew, but the closest friends.

These, then, were the six men whom I had to do my best to persuade to join me in refusing a valuable order for what

I was convinced were patriotic reasons, but might well appear to some of them to be very far-fetched ones.

As I took my seat at the head of the table I felt inwardly excited and a little nervous. It was not that I lacked confidence in myself; but I knew that I was in for a battle, and the thought that what I was about to do might even lead to an open quarrel with men I liked and respected was a far from pleasant one.

On glancing down the agenda, I saw that 'Sales report by Admiral Sir Tuke Waldron' was item number five. That meant that I would have to control my patience for at least an hour; for, much as I should have liked to plunge into the matter of the E-boats right away, and get it over, I had to wait until he told us about the new contract. To have done otherwise would have given away the fact that I had previous knowledge of it, and it was of the utmost importance to avoid giving them grounds for suspecting that I had been put up to the line I meant to take by anyone associated with the Government.

The clock ticked round with maddening slowness to three-forty, while I strove to concentrate on the normal affairs of the Company; but, at last, I was able to call on the Admiral for his report. Even then a further ten minutes elapsed while he told us about the past month's activities by his sales staff. Evidently he was saving his own coup for a *bonne bouche*, and, at length, with pardonable satisfaction, he produced it.

A murmur of congratulation ran round the table, then I said: 'To have landed us this order is a fine feat, Admiral; and you certainly deserve the thanks of the Board. But recently I have been giving a lot of thought to this question of E-boats, and I have come to the conclusion that we ought not to accept contracts to build any more of them.'

It would have been more truthful to say that for the greater part of the past forty hours I had been wondering how the Board would take my bombshell, and rehearsing in my mind what I should say in an endeavour to bring as many as possible of its members round to my view.

They reacted much as I expected. Toiller, McFarlane, Lord Wiltshire and Johnny all stared at me in swift surprise. The Admiral exclaimed: 'Lord alive, man; why ever not?' And the good solid James, who was seated on my right, said:

'I haven't a clue what's in your mind, Giff; but perhaps you'll enlighten us?'

Looking at old Toiller, I asked: 'As Secretary of the Company, would you say that its financial situation is a satisfactory one?'

'Why, yes, Sir Gifford,' he replied after a second. 'You must know yourself how well we've been doing since the Conservative Government brought prosperity back to the country, and that during these past few years we have been able to put large sums to reserve. Our affairs are in better shape now than they have been for a very long time.'

'Thank you,' I said, and turned to James. 'Will you tell the Board how we stand about work to keep our people going for the next twelve months or so?'

He shrugged. 'We've plenty of that; and the demand for small boats is still on the up and up. My problem is to get enough skilled labour.'

'What's all this to do with it?' the Admiral exclaimed impatiently.

He was on my left, and glancing at him I replied: 'It is just that I wished to have recorded in the minutes what we all already know. Namely that the financial position of the Company will not be seriously impaired, or a number of our people thrown out of employment, should the Board decide to decline this Admiralty contract.'

'But why should we?' he asked in a puzzled voice. 'What the devil are you driving at?'

I gave him the works then. My heart was beating a little faster but I said quite calmly: 'No doubt you have seen a lot of the articles that have appeared in the papers in recent months, stating that in any major war our only hope of victory lies in the use of thermo-nuclear weapons and that in order to develop them to the maximum extent we must sacrifice everything which in a nuclear war would prove obsolescent. Personally I accept that view. But it means that, among other things, the whole of the Naval building programme should be scrapped.'

Naturally, that put the fat in the fire. His rubicund face went two shades redder, and he burst out: 'What; scrap the Royal Navy! Good God, man, to advocate such an idea comes damn near to treason! Those scribblers you've been reading ought to be locked up. I'm amazed that anyone of your intelligence could take them seriously. They are talking through their hats, and don't know the first thing about such matters. Neither do you.'

I had been expecting something of the sort, so I proceeded to say the piece I had mentally prepared for the occasion. It was, of course, a brief résumé of the arguments in the papers I had read, to the effect that we could not hope to defeat the Soviet colossus with orthodox weapons, and that the country's finance would break under the strain if we continued the present policy of trying to run with the hare and hunt with the hounds.

Only the good manners that were natural to Sir Tuke enabled him to hear me out without interruption. The moment I had finished he burst forth into a swift series of denials, assertions and general counterblast.

'It was nonsense to say that we could not face up to the Russians if they used only orthodox weapons,; and that was the type of war it would be. Fear of reprisals, and of much heavier stuff than they had themselves being launched from the United States, would deter them from starting a nuclear war. And anyway, if they did, it would not be all over in a few weeks, as some of these morons who wrote in the papers predicted. Whatever happened, we should fight on, just as we had always done. But the country must be fed, and our convoys could not survive without naval escort. In either type of war the Navy would play a leading role. The Soviet Fleet was not the second largest in the world. Only by increasing our numbers of aircraft carriers, submarines and E-boats could we hope to prevent it from blockading us. The Fleet Air Arm, based on the carriers, would be both the eyes of our intelligence and the modern equivalent of big guns. The carriers and many other types of vessel would also prove far less vulnerable than land sites for launching guided missiles. The whole matter had been gone into with the greatest thoroughness and eighteen months ago a White Paper had been published on it. The Army, of course, had had to accept considerable weapon cuts, but the Navy had been fully vindicated, and an increased building programme authorised. These more recent attempts to upset those decisions were little short of criminal, because they were playing into the hands of the enemy. The Prime Minister and his advisers were not a pack of fools. During the past year or so there had been no major new development to cause them to alter their last publicly-expressed opinions; and on matters of Service policy it was up to all decent people, whatever their politics, loyally to support the nation's leaders.'

In my turn I heard him out. Then I made the blunder which was later to have such serious repercussions. Having said my piece, I should have stood my ground. I should simply have replied that I counted myself just as patriotic as himself, but could not agree with him; and that it was upon those very grounds of patriotism that my conscience would not allow me to accept the contract. As I had never had any hope of winning him over, and could look for backing only to some of the other members of the Board, I ought, as a next move, after letting him blow off steam, to have asked them for their opinions.

No doubt I was influenced by the vigour with which he had spoken, and a fear that the confidence he showed in his case would deprive me of the support I had hoped for from the others. Anyhow, I fell into the error of endeavouring to counter his arguments; and I was now speaking without the book.

By that I mean that whereas my first speech had been carefully thought out, this was extempore and discursive. It so happens that I am a very fluent speaker, and at times that can prove a mixed blessing. Pleasant as it is to have the most telling expressions trip off one's tongue without having to search the mind for them, it tends to make one talk far too much and, occasionally, get carried away by one's own eloquence to the point of saying things without giving due weight to their import.

Sir Charles had given me more or less *carte blanche* to use the ammunition with which he had provided me; so, having prefaced my remarks by saying that I must request the Board to consider anything which was said during this discussion as highly confidential, and not repeat it to anyone outside, I launched forth into facts and figures about the Soviet forces and our own. Short of actually describing secret weapons which were still in the development stage, I gave them everything I'd got.

I had been talking without interruption for a good ten minutes, while they all sat round obviously fascinated, when the Admiral pulled me up.

'Excuse me for breaking in, Gifford,' he said sharply, 'but where did you get all this?'

Collecting myself quickly, I replied: 'I didn't get it from anywhere. Everything I have said could easily be deduced by anyone with a little common sense from facts that have been published in the press.'

His blue eyes bored into mine with an icy stare, and his voice had the snap in it that must have made midshipmen jump the length of the quarter-deck, as he retorted: 'I do not agree! And if the press was your only source why should you have warned us not to mention to anyone else these things you have just been saying?'

That was a nasty one; but I countered it smartly. 'Because I believe my guesses to be so near the real mark that public discussion of them might put ideas into the heads of our enemies.'

'They cannot all be guesses,' he snapped back. 'I insist on knowing who it is that has supplied you with this information.'

I shrugged. 'You are right, of course, that I didn't get all of it from the newspapers. I have quite a number of friends who are now fairly high up in the Services. You know as well as I do that while such men are invariably security-minded about their own spheres of activity, they are often open to discussing more general problems with a responsible person like myself. They know what they say will go no further, and in my case it certainly would not have done, had it not been for our present divergence of views. That is the real reason why I asked the Board not to repeat any part of the discussion. As for giving you the names of my friends, I shouldn't dream of it. What is more, it would get you no further if I did, as I can't even remember now which of them told me this fact or that. I must ask you to accept it that my conclusions are based upon considerable reading spread over several months, backed by a certain amount of reliable information picked up here and there, but arrived at independently by myself.'

This lie spiked his guns for the time being and enabled me to secure the reactions of the others. On the sound principle

61

of Courts Martial—that the junior member should be asked to give his opinion first—I looked across at Johnny and said:

'Well, Johnny; what is your view about this?'

He had, all the time, been eyeing with me growing surprise and a highly speculative look. Now he massaged his square cleft chin with his hand for a moment, then replied: 'If it comes to a vote, I'm with you, Sir. But in view of my present job on the Joint Planning Staff, I'm sure you will excuse me from giving my reasons, or entering into any discussion on the subject.'

The Admiral grunted, and I said: 'Mr. McFarlane, what about you?'

With true Scottish caution the Engineer performed a skilful hedging operation. 'There's much to be said on both sides, Sir Gifford. However sound the Company's financial situation may be it would be a sad pity to throw away such a valuable order. Against that, if the country's interests are really at stake I'm sure none of us would be influenced by the thought of profits. But I'd be glad to hear what Mr. Compton has to say before committing myself; for maybe it would help to clarify my mind.'

I called next on Bill Wiltshire. His Lordship had arrived at the meeting in a far from good humour, as he was spending the week-end with friends near Winchester and to attend had necessitated his having to make do with a sandwich lunch after abandoning a day's shooting half way through. Had he been summoned to a business meeting while in London, he would have turned up impeccably dressed in conventional City attire; but he was still wearing aged tweeds and had mud on his boots. Thrusting his hands deep into the pockets of his jacket, and tipping back his chair, he stared at me with an uncertain look in his slightly protuberant blue eyes, and muttered:

'You're putting us in a devilish awkward situation, Giff. Of course, I can see how strongly you feel about this, and you're not the sort of chap who is given to getting bees in his bonnet; but, well, I mean—we couldn't scrap the Navy, could we? That would be going a bit too far.'

'Either that, or in another five years' time we may see the whole country scrapped for us by the Soviets,' I remarked sharply. 'And, personally, I prefer the lesser evil.'

Lowering his head, he placed both his palms against his temples, so that his fingers temporarily hid a good part of his slightly wavy, sandy hair, and remained like that for a moment. Whether he still had a hangover from the previous night, or was endeavouring to cudgel the few brains he had, remained uncertain. Looking up, he said with a sigh:

'I should have thought, myself, that Admiral Waldron knew best. Still, if you put it like that. Anyway, it was you who got me on to this Board, Giff; so it's not for me to let you down. I'll vote the way you want me to.'

Inspired by loyalty though it was, he could hardly have made a more embarrassing admission that he was a 'guinea-pig'. So with a hasty word of thanks, I quickly looked down the table at Charles Toiller and asked his opinion.

Knowing that the old boy guarded the Company's resources like a dragon, I had thought it likely that he would prove most averse to agreeing that we should forgo the handsome profit to be made out of two E-boats, for what might seem to him an exaggerated fear about the future. But I was right off the mark.

Holding up his left hand, from which two fingers were missing, he said: 'That's what I got out of the 1914 war, gentlemen, and I was one of the lucky ones. Half the young men of my generation died in the mud of Flanders. Last time, as some of you will remember, I was an Air Raid Warden. No one who hasn't done it knows what it's like to drag mangled bodies and screaming children out from underneath beams and rubble, often with fires raging nearby, night after night, week after week, month after month. And if there's another war it will be a hundred times worse. So, short of surrendering without a fight, it is up to all of us to do everything in our power to prevent it happening.

'Most of my life has been spent in totting up figures; but there's little point in doing that unless you can make them show you a picture when you've assembled the results. Those Sir Gifford has given us of the Russian forces as compared to those we could send against them make a very clear picture to me. In an old-fashioned war we wouldn't stand a hope; and in either kind of war it looks as though it will be the end of Britain.

'For years past, Sir Winston and Sir Anthony Eden have

been telling us that our only chance of survival is by making ourselves so strong that the Russians will not dare to start anything, and I believe they are right. Well, if we can't muster anything near the number of troops and ships and planes that they can, we've got to try to get the lead of them some other way, haven't we?

'Again and again this country has been near defeat by evil men, but God has held His hand out, and given us time to save ourselves. In the sort of war we are thinking of it looks as if we should need more than that to save us, so I believe that this time He is giving us our chance in advance. It is only by the development of these new weapons that we can hope to become stronger than our enemies, and He has given us the means of doing that. Even if the refusal of this order meant running the Company into financial difficulties, I would still vote for its rejection; because I believe that everything else shoud be sacrificed for this one hope of protecting ourselves from being conquered and made slaves.'

I think we were all moved by the old man's reference to the way in which God has so often saved Britain from the logical consequences of her unreadiness and blunders, and the faith he showed in His continuing to do so. I know I was; and having thanked him I turned to James Compton.

Addressing me directly, he said: 'I was going to go against you, Gifford, but I must admit to having been a bit shaken by what Charles Toiller has just said. Still, we've got to consider the full implications of the decision you and he are urging us to take. If we refuse this order and our reasons for doing so get out, it will be the end for us as far as the Admiralty is concerned. They will never give us another.'

'Huh!' grunted the Admiral. 'It's good to hear someone talking a little sense at last.'

Ignoring the interrutpion, James went on. 'So it is not just a question of our financial situation at the moment, and our work programme for the next twelve months. We have to think of next year, and, much further than that, to how we might find ourselves placed in five or ten years' time.

'By then, the Socialists might have got back into power. We all know what that would mean because they've told us themselves—increased Welfare State benefits at the expense of the middle classes. They call it a policy of further levelling incomes; but call it what you like, to take the jam off the bread of those with the brains or the guts to earn it means a return to austerity for all. Now, we can hardly keep pace with the demand for small boats; but within a year of the Socialists getting back we'd have to turn off half our workpeople. God forbid that they should, but they might; so can we afford to throw overboard the one big customer that neither booms nor slumps affect, and whose orders for naval craft could be counted on to keep us going?'

'That is all very well, James,' I replied. 'But in ten years' time . . .'

'I know, I know.' He held up his hand. 'If the present Government fails to take the steps you advocate we may by then have all long since been blown into the middle of next week. I'll admit that to be a very real and terrible danger. But I don't quite see why we should have to be the people who stick their necks out in order to give it a lead.'

I shrugged. 'Someone must; and there are not many firms in the kingdom as well placed as ourselves to do so.'

He nodded. 'That's true; and on the broad issue I am inclined to agree with you. But I feel this is much too big a thing for us to decide here and now. We've no call to send a formal acceptance or rejection of the order right away. How about taking the week-end to think it over, and meeting again same time on Monday?'

'I'm afraid I couldn't manage that,' said Johnny, 'but I have already given my opinion, and nothing anyone could say would alter it.'

The others nodded, except for the Admiral, who snapped: 'I'll be here, of course; but I warn you, Gifford, that should the Board accept this monstrous proposal of yours on a show of hands, I shall ask for an Extraordinary General Meeting to be called so that the matter can be put to the shareholders.'

His threat caused me no concern. If James came over to me, our holdings, together with the qualifying shares held by Johnny, Toiller, and Bill Wiltshire, would be more than sufficient to render the calling of a General Meeting pointless. But if James sided with the Admiral and a meeting had to be held, the result of the voting was of little consequence. My address to the shareholders would send the balloon up. The Press would get hold of it and make it front page news in no time; so by that means I should equally well achieve all that Sir Charles had asked of me.

With our minds still on the big issue we felt little inclination to spend long over the last three items on the agenda, and as soon as they were despatched the meeting broke up.

Since the early summer Johnny had been taking a lively interest in Sue Waldron, the Admiral's daughter; so although he was staying with me, he had a date to dine with them that evening over at Beaulieu.

He had come down from London in his car and it was parked at the far end of the yard; but, as we left the building together, instead of making for it at once, he walked a little way in the opposite direction with me. As soon as we were out of earshot of the others, he said in a low voice:

'Of course, you're absolutely dead right about this business. But who on earth let you in on all that Top Secret stuff you were spouting?'

'Was it Top Secret?' I pretended surprise. 'Well, that's news to me. I've only picked up bits here and there these past few months from various people I know; the rest was simply putting two and two together. Are you going to be late tonight?'

'Not very. Sue and I are not going dancing; so I expect I'll be back around midnight. Still, best leave the key under the mat as usual. If you have gone to bed before I get back I'll see you in the morning. I was due for forty-eight hours, so I haven't to start back to London at crack of dawn tomorrow.'

He certainly saw me in the morning, but in most unexpected circumstances. Poor Johnny. If only he had set out for London first thing, as he had after attending most of our other Board meetings we had held since he had been posted to a job there, he would not now be in a cell charged with complicity in murder.

*   *   *   *

Johnny turned away and I walked on towards the firm's private pier. Lepe lies just outside Southampton Water, a mile or so along the coast to the west, whereas the city is situated near the top of the estuary but on its eastern side. To go round by road entails a twelve-mile run and it is less than half that distance by water; so, unless the weather is exceptionally bad, I always go back and forth in my motor launch.

Young Belton, who also acts as my chauffeur, usually pilots the launch, as that leaves me free on our trips to and fro to think of what I am going to do, or have been doing, during the day. He is a rather uppish young man, but good with the engines, and one can't expect everything these days. As I came down the steps he said:

'We've got another passenger this afternoon, Sir. The Prof's in the cabin.'

It was typical of Belton that he should refer so casually to Professor Evans as 'the Prof', although I will admit that Evans has neither the age nor the personality to inspire much respect. He is in his early thirties, a short, dark, hairy little man who buys his clothes off the peg, and without them would be hardly distinguishable from those Celtic ancestors of his who fought the Romans to a standstill in the wild Welsh mountains.

Like many of his race he had a mystic streak and, coupled with genuine brilliance in higher mathematics, it seemed to get him the answers to all sorts of problems; some, but only some, of which had a commercial value. That, of course, was the trouble; he was erratic, pig-headed and only with difficulty could be persuaded to work for his employers' advantage rather than on the things that suddenly caught his own interest. Had he been more amenable he might have done very much better for himself with some great industrial corporation; but then we could not have afforded to employ him, as the problems connected with boat building are not numerous enough to warrant the retention of a highly paid scientist.

I had come across him eighteen months before in connection with some experiments concerning the resistance of various metals to corrosion by sea-water. He had then been out of a job and, on learning by his own admission the reason, I had offered to take him on at a nominal salary but with quarters and board found. The result, as far as the Company was concerned, had proved moderately satisfactory; as he had produced a paint to which barnacles appeared to be allergic, a solution which lengthened the life of ropes, and several other products which, although expensive, we had found worth using ourselves, and had also marketed in limited quantities at a profit.

However, I must confess that I had been led to suggest the arrangement in the first place by a private interest. I have already mentioned that out of an income of ten thousand a year seven thousand now goes in taxation; and after having been married to Ankaret for five years I was finding it increasingly difficult to make ends meet.

It is not that she was unreasonably extravagant; but I naturally made her a fairly generous allowance and paid for her winter holidays abroad, and I still had to weigh out for my first wife and the children; so running a fair-sized house and doing quite a bit of entertaining there had begun to make me scratch my head when I had to pay the bills. I could, of course, have sold a few hundred of my shares every year without seriously depleting my income, but I am old-fashioned enough to be averse to spending capital, and for some time I had been wondering if I could not put a part of Longshot Hall to a use which would enable me to reduce the cost of its upkeep.

The secrecy with which, in these days, all scientific experiments are conducted fully justified my installing Owen Evans in my home instead of at the Company's yards; and by making over about a third of the house to his use I was able to save that proportion of rates, heating, light, etc., without having to partition it off or in any way surrender my rights over it. Had he proved a flop I should have felt it incumbent on me to reimburse the Company; but that was a gamble I had taken, and it had come off.

Stepping down into the cabin of the launch, I nodded a greeting and sat down opposite him. A wharf-hand threw the painter down on the forward deck. Belton gave a twist to the wheel and we were nosing our way out into the channel; but it was not until he had the engine going full throttle that Evans leaned towards me and said in a voice that only I could hear:

'I have got it.'

My mind was still dwelling on the meeting I had just left, and, anyway, for quite a long time I had not given a thought to his activities; so I replied both absently and ungrammatically, 'Got what?'

The dark eyes beneath his bushy black brows were bright

with excitement, as he answered impatiently: 'The ray, of course.'

That made me sit up. During the early summer he had been working on a fog-solvent; his theory being, as I understood it, that if certain rays could be projected into fog they would so agitate the mist particles as to cause them to change their structure and disappear. To maintain such a ray for considerable periods over a big area, such as an airfield, would, he had believed, prove too costly; but he thought that it might be developed in a small apparatus with a range of perhaps twenty yards which, if flashed only at intervals, could be brought within the means of the owners of large motor launches and the more expensive makes of car. I had naturally encouraged him to go ahead, as I saw great possibilities in the idea if it could be made a commercial proposition. The public would be certain to demand that buses should be fitted with it, and City Corporations might adopt it for use in beacons at main street crossings.

But, one evening late in June, Evans had told me that, for the time being, he had abandoned work on the fog ray, because the principles involved had given him a line on a much more fascinating problem, and he now hoped to produce a death ray.

I was far from pleased; for whereas I had seen the prospects of a lot of money for my Company out of his first idea, I saw little prospect of making anything out of his second. There is already, I believe, a ray which will form a barrier over an open window and kill any insect that flies into it, and although Evans asserted that his would be powerful enough to kill cattle at a limited range I could think of no practical use for it; except perhaps as a humane killer. It was, of course, just possible that the Ministry of Defence might take it up, but it would obviously be much too dangerous to leave about as a sort of 'dumb sentry' and the limitation of its range would render it of little use as an offensive weapon. In consequence, I had tried hard to get him back on to fog dispersal; but he had become sullen, dug his toes in, and flatly refused to be diverted from following up his latest inspiration.

Realising that he must now be referring to his death ray, I was considerably taken aback. After all, it is one of the things that scientists have been endeavouring to discover for several generations, so a great feather in his cap. Moreover, sub-consciously I had formed the impression that he was only wasting his time and would never achieve practical results; so I exclaimed:

'D'you really mean you've found a way to kill . . .'

He silenced me with an angry gesture, swivelled his eyes warningly towards Belton, who was at the wheel only some six feet from us, then nodded vigorously.

'Have I got it, man? No real cause had I to come into Southampton this afternoon; but took the chance to do a bit of shopping, so as to come back with you. All evening I doubt but you'll be with Lady Ankaret, and I've no wish to speak of this in front of her. I thought, though, maybe you'd like to see a demonstration; so this would be as good a way as any to get you alone and ask. Then what about this evening, after dinner, eh?'

'Fine,' I agreed at once. 'It is a great feat to have pulled this off; and I shall be immensely interested. What sort of—er—dish do you propose to cook?'

'Rabbit,' he replied tersely.

I nodded. 'I'll come through to your lab at about half-past nine, then.'

We fell silent, and soon afterwards the launch was turning west past Calshot Castle. Another five minutes and Belton shut off her engine to glide silently in alongside the jetty that juts out from the private beach below Longshot Hall.

The greater part of the house consists of a solid two-storey block. On the ground floor the principal reception rooms look out over the Solent, and upstairs, in addition to what the Americans term 'the master suite', there are two double guest rooms and an extra bathroom. The kitchens and the servants' quarters are at the back. That is ample accommodation for most people in these days, but there would not have been in the era of large families; so my forebears had built on a wing containing a number of smaller, less lofty rooms, and it was this which I had, more or less, turned over to Owen Evans.

I say 'more or less' because I had reserved the right to put up single guests in two of the bedrooms on the ground floor if I wished, and to use another as a store-room; but Evans had three rooms for his private use and the greater part of the upper floor had been gutted, then roofed over with glass, to make him a laboratory.

Even had he had more in common with Ankaret and me, to have had him with us all the time would have become very irksome; so it had been agreed that he should have his meals sent through to him on a tray from the kitchen and, fearing that he might find such a life lonely, I had also offered to foot the food bill if from time to time he cared to have a friend to stay. But he seemed to be one of those solitary types to whom work is also wife and friends, for he had never made use of his guest room.

On entering the hall we gave one another a vague smile and parted. I got rid of my outdoor things and went into the drawing-room. Ankaret was there curled up on the sofa reading a book. She was wearing a 'shocking pink' silk house-coat, and looking very seductive. But she always does; and even after having been married to her for five years there were still times when I felt my pulses quicken at the sight of her.

As I bent over her from behind she tilted back her head, threw an arm round my neck, and pulled my head down. I gave her a long kiss on the mouth, then asked what sort of a day she had had.

'Oh, all right,' she shrugged. 'But I get bored to tears all by myself here.'

'Now that your leg is no longer painful, you should have asked someone down for the week-end,' I told her. 'I did suggest it.'

'I know you did, Giff, and I ought to have. I'm afraid having done damn all for five weeks has made me terribly lazy.'

'You can't have it both ways,' I said with a smile.

'No; I suppose not. I really must make an effort and snap out of it now I can get about again. We'll ask the Wyndhams or the Beddinghams for next week-end. But what about to-night? Let's ring up Hugh and Margery, or General John, and ask ourselves over for drinks after dinner.'

I shook my head. 'Sorry, darling, but the Prof has just completed a new toy, and I've promised to look into the lab to see him work it. The little man is no end excited about his success, so I'm afraid he'd be terribly upset if I let him down. But tomorrow and Sunday I'm all yours, so make any arrangements you like.'

Ankaret was never sulky or unreasonable, and she shrugged philosophically. 'Oh, never mind, then, I'll fix something for tomorrow. How did your meeting go? From what you said this morning I gathered that it was rather a special one.'

'It was. It didn't go too badly. I'll tell you about it over dinner; but I must leave you now to get down to my Friday chores.'

My Friday chores were the wages, and the payment of bills for the running of the place which lay outside the regular list of Ankaret's household accounts. The awful spade-work of figuring out tax deductions and proportions of contribution to insurance stamps was done for me by my secretary at the office; so I really had only to see to it that the staff got the wage packets she made up for me by passing them on.

Silvers was my butler-valet, and his wife was our cook. Ankaret had known them since childhood and, hearing that their late mistress had died, had got them to come to us soon after we were married. I had blessed her for it, as it is far from easy to get servants even to consider taking a place at Lepe. The trouble is that this little corner of Hampshire is right off the beaten track. There is not a High Street or a cinema within ten miles of us. But the Silvers were elderly and did not seem to mind that. They adored Ankaret and were dependable old-fashioned servants whom it was a pleasure to have about the house.

Besides them we had only one girl living in, a well-grown eighteen-year-old named Mildred Mallows. She was a local who had not yet found her wings; or perhaps was temporarily enmeshed by the glamour of maiding Ankaret, which was for her the jam on the bread and butter of ordinary housemaid's work. But, of course, we also had two daily women in to help both her and in the kitchen. There was, too, the outdoor staff: old Eagers, who had once been head gardener of six, but now had to make do with a buxom land-girl and a boy; but the garden produce that was sold paid nearly half their wages. And Belton, of course, was carried by the firm. All the same it was quite enough to have to pay out every week.

Silvers was in his pantry, and having given him the wage packets for the indoor staff I took the others out to Eagers. In return the old boy handed over to me the week's takings, which were falling off now that most of the fruit was over; but he told me that he hoped to do quite well with his grapes and chrysanthemums later in the year.

After ten minutes' chat with him about the garden I returned to the house and went into my library. It hardly justifies the name, as it is quite a small room at the corner of the house and only one of its walls is lined with books; two of the others have windows in them and the fourth a doorway that leads into Ankaret's drawing-room.

On Saturdays I don't usually go to the office, but I often bring work home, and if there are people staying in the house I can shut myself up in the library secure from interruption. I have a big old-fashioned roll-topped desk there, which is not a very elegant piece of furniture but highly practical; as I can just slam the top down and lock it at any time without having to tidy up the papers on which I have been working. Opening it up, I put the garden money in the petty-cash box, emptied my brief-case of the papers I had brought back with me, and set to work on the bills.

There were not many requiring immediate payment; so writing the cheques and envelopes, and a letter of condolence to a friend who had lost his wife a few days previously, took me only about twenty minutes. When I had done I locked the desk, then went over to the drinks cupboard in the corner, mixed a Dry Martini, and took it through to Ankaret.

While we had our cocktails I told her about the meeting that afternoon. Of course, she knew nothing of my interview with Sir Charles, and I did not even hint to her that anything more than my own convictions had led me to take the line I had. In fact, when she said that she thought having forgone a handsome profit on ethical grounds did me great credit, I felt distinctly embarrassed; but I swiftly slid away from that aspect of the matter by making her laugh with a description of Admiral Waldron's indignation.

In due course I went up to have my bath and put on a smoking jacket; then, at eight o'clock, we went in to dinner. It was during the meal that I mentioned that Johnny would

73

not be leaving first thing in the morning but going up late on Saturday night; and Ankaret asked:

'How is his affair with Sue Waldron going?'

'I don't really know,' I replied. 'But he seems as keen as mustard about her; and as he is a determined type of chap I should not be surprised to hear at any time that they've become engaged.'

'It would be a good match for him; Sue is quite an heiress, isn't she?'

I nodded. 'That may prove a snag, though. You can bet that the Admiral has been hoping she'll marry someone with a place, or anyhow a chap who can afford to keep her in better style than could a Wing Commander with little but his pay. The old boy may dig his toes in; and I don't think she's got any money of her own.'

'Oh, she'll marry him if she wants to, and make her father give her an allowance into the bargain.'

Somewhat surprised by Ankaret's declaration, I glanced across at her. When we are alone we always sit at the sides of the table, so that we can see one another between the two candelabra. Against the dark background of the room, her pale face with its aureole of gently curling Titian hair, the richness of which was brought out by the candlelight, looked more than ever like a painting by an old master, come to life.

As she caught my glance, her beautifully curved mouth broke into a slow smile, then she asked: 'What are you looking so surprised about?'

'What you just said. Sue is an attractive little piece; well educated, nice manners, no fool and with plenty to say for herself. But she's only just twenty, and I've never seen any indication in her that she has a particularly strong character.'

Ankaret's grey eyes showed her amusement. 'What poor judges of women you men are, Giff. You never look beyond the obvious. Just because Sue is small, inclined to be plump, and has a merry eye in her rather highly-coloured little face, you write her off, beyond granting her the intelligence normal to any girl with her upbringing, as a "smack bott for Uncle".'

'Not this Uncle,' I grinned. 'I prefer them blonde and blue eyed.'

She had been moulding a bread pellet, and she flicked it at me. 'I know what you prefer, darling; or I wouldn't be here. I mean I would have left you long ago if you hadn't taken the trouble to get to understand me; and that can't have been easy. But I'm the only woman you ever have understood. You didn't know a thing about your first wife, and you haven't a clue about Sue.'

'Tell me about her, then.'

'I like her. That is, as much as I am capable of liking her sort of person. She is unimaginative, honest, reliable, and would go a long way out of her way to help her friends; but woe betide anyone who gets up against her. Next time you see her forget the pretty pink cheeks and take a look at her side face. You'll see a replica of the Admiral's battleship chin. Then look at her hands. They are firm and square with short square-tipped fingers. If that is not enough, I've once seen those merry eyes of hers go as hard as agates. Given the natural cunning of the female in addition to all that, I bet you she'll make rings round her father.'

I made a grimace. 'If you're right about all this, and Johnny gets her, I hardly know whether to be glad or sorry for him now.'

'Oh, you needn't worry on that score. If she loves him enough to marry him she'll be on his side; and Johnny has quite enough personality to hold his own with her. Given a little money, and with her behind him, he can hardly fail to become an Air Marshal.'

'Well, here's good health to them,' I said, raising my glass of hock, and Ankaret joined me in the toast.

When we had finished dinner we took the Benedictine bottle into the drawing-room, so as not to delay Silvers clearing away and finishing with his work for the night. Until nearly half-past nine we talked of those trivial common interests that are the staple conversation of married couples and give them an occasional laugh; then I said it was time for me to go along to Owen Evans.

Ankaret knew that his experiments were more or less secret; so she never asked me about them. And, as she had not the faintest interest in science, I don't think she would have anyway. She said that she had just started a very witty travel book called *Blue Moon over Portugal* that had come in with the latest batch of library books, so she would go early to bed and read; but she hoped that I wouldn't be too long.

75

She preceded me upstairs, a tall graceful figure with the voluminous skirts of her 'shocking-pink' house-coat swishing about her heels. I locked the front door and those of the rooms that gave on to the hall, put out the downstairs lights, and followed. Up on the broad landing she had turned left. I turned right and went through the connecting door to the Prof's domain.

Beyond the door was a sort of antechamber, which he used as an office. It held a small desk, with a telephone, and was fitted up with shelves to hold his reference books and files. A further door led into the laboratory, which from there ran to the end of the wing. By removing the roof and substituting one of glass I had ensured a maximum of light during the daytime, without spoiling the appearance of either the front or back of the house, and the windows on both sides had been covered over inside with asbestos sheeting. The glass of the roof was frosted, to prevent glare, so at night nothing short of strong moonlight came through; but the long room was made bright as day by neon strip lighting.

A broad bench, on which stood a variety of scientific instruments, ran all down one side of it, and at the far end, in the middle of the floor, there was a four-foot square table. On it was a conglomeration of lenses, brackets, screws and levers, which, as Evans was tinkering with the contraption, was evidently his new toy.

Having given me a curt nod, he continued working on it for some minutes; then he brushed his hands together, as though to cleanse them of invisible dirt, frowned at me from under his thick black eyebrows, and said in the superior voice that a school-master might have used to a newly joined pupil who had only just managed to scrape through his entrance exam:

'Naturally, Sir Gifford, it would be too much to expect you to understand a detailed description of the processes that I'm proposing to demonstrate to you this evening; but you might get the broad principle of the thing—that is if I use simple language.'

'It will have to be very simple,' I smiled, 'but I'll do my best to follow you.'

He launched out then into a maze of technicalities, in which I endeavoured to show intelligent interest but was soon completely lost. His lecture lasted for a good twenty minutes, but all I had really gathered at the end of it was that he had been playing around with radio-active forms of various elements, and that these isotopes, as they were called, could be used to bring about important changes in the physical properties of both inanimate materials, such as plastics, and living bodies. As far as the latter were concerned, he claimed that at short range his machine, if directed on an animal, would have the effect of stopping its heart.

When he had said his say he, literally, produced the rabbit. It was a nice fat Belgian hare, in a fair-sized cage, happily chewing away at some leaves of lettuce. Lifting the cage from the floor, he set it on a broad shelf which ran along the end wall of the laboratory and was about on a level with the table.

Beckoning me forward, he asked me to stand up against the table, so that by looking straight over his apparatus I had the best possible view of the rabbit. Standing on the left of the table he made some final adjustments to the machine. While he was doing so I heard the old clock over the stables strike ten. Then he made a sign to me to look at the rabbit, and pressed a button.

Instantly I felt a fierce pain pierce my heart. Next moment my whole body was contorted with agony. It was so excruciating that it paralysed all thought and movement so that I could not even let out a shout. But the torture ceased almost as swiftly as it had begun. My nerves refused to register further and my mind became a blank.

After what cannot have been more than a few seconds, my brain began to function again; but I no longer felt even a suggestion of pain, or the breathlessness that should normally have been its aftermath. In fact I felt no physical sensations at all.

I was still standing up against the table with Evans's apparatus just in front of me. Staring straight over the top of it I saw the rabbit in its cage still happily nibbling away at the lettuce leaves. Then, without any particular reason for doing so, I glanced down towards my feet. My mind positively reeled at what I saw.

Where my feet should have been a body sprawled upon the floor. And it was mine. I had not a shadow of doubt about that. The face was half hidden by an outflung arm, but it had my neatly-brushed brown hair, the burgundy-coloured velvet smoking jacket I had been wearing, and the evening trousers with the double braid stripe, which should correctly have been worn only with tails, but were a pair that, as one wears tails so rarely these days, I was knocking out.

It flashed upon me then that I must be dead. Evidently, through some frightful oversight, Evans had got his apparatus reversed, so that its ray had been focused on myself instead of on the rabbit. Looking up at him I expected to see his face distraught with consternation, and that in a moment he would fling himself down on his knees beside my body in a wild effort to revive it.

But that wasn't how things were at all. He had not moved from beside the table, and he was looking down upon what had been me. On his lean face there was no trace of panic or distress, but a faint smile of elation. I knew then that I really was dead, and that he had deliberately murdered me.

*　　*　　*　　*

My feelings were extraordinarily mixed. Shock, horror, amazement and dismay jostled one another in my whirling mind. It was still striving to grasp the idea that it had suddenly become disembodied; yet no other explanation fitted the facts. Although I no longer had feeling in any part of myself the conscious 'me' was still standing beside the table, while sprawled on the floor lay my corpse.

Evans's reactions to my collapse showed beyond doubt that he had planned to make me the victim of his infernal machine. Why, I had not the faintest idea. The most likely explanation seemed to be that, all unsuspecting, I had been employing a madman; but in these frantic moments my distraught brain was far more concerned with the implications of being dead.

Like most people, I had never been afraid of death; only of the pain which is generally inseparable from it, or, worse, the failure of some vital faculty by which a man may be reduced to an unlovely caricature of his former self and must suffer a long drawn out dependence on others before his end. I had often expressed the hope that I might escape such agonies or ignominy by a sudden death. Now, apparently, my wish had been granted; yet I was very far from being happy about that.

As a healthy man only just entering on middle age I had expected to live for a long time to come. There was still a lot of things I wanted to do and places I wanted to see. I had, of course, made a will, but there were many matters that I would have tidied up had I only had a little warning. Absurdly enough, two quite trivial things flitted across my mind—a begging letter from an old friend fallen on evil times that I had left unanswered, and my intention to increase the pension of Annie Hawkins, the long-since retired nurse of my childhood.

Then it was suddenly borne in upon me that I would never now read Grey's *Elegy*, or see that masterpiece of Moorish architecture, the Alhambra at Granada, or witness from Stonehenge the sunrise on a midsummer's morning—all things that I had vaguely meant to do at some time or other. I had left it too late. Yes, 'too late', the saddest words, as someone once remarked, in the English language.

These thoughts all raced through my mind in a fraction of the time it takes to set them down, and I was still staring at Owen Evans. As I watched him with mingled bewilderment and anger the smug little smile of self-congratulation faded from his face, and he began to tremble.

After all, it is one thing to contemplate killing a man—even if obsessed with the desire to secure the final proof of the effectiveness of a new scientific weapon—and quite another actually to do it. Apparently, the realisation that he had allowed his disordered imagination to lead him into committing a terrible crime had suddenly come home to him. His face went as white as a sheet and, although he was quite well shaved, the incipient stubble on his chin showed blue in sharp contrast with it.

For a moment I thought he was going to be sick; but he got hold of himself, stooped down, grasped my body by the shoulder, and shook it. As he let go, the rolling head became still again and the arm flopped back, without a quiver, into immobility. Drawing a sharp breath he turned and walked towards the door of the laboratory.

It was then, for the first time since the ray had exerted its deadly effect on me, that I attempted any form of movement.

Naturally I supposed that, as a disembodied spirit, I should be able to flit from place to place without effort and, having no weight, I—or rather the mind of which I now solely consisted—could remain poised high up in the air or sink to any more convenient level as I desired. But it did not prove quite like that.

Although I could not feel the floor the force of gravity apparently still operated sufficiently to keep me in a normal relationship to it unless I exerted my will to impel myself forward. Then I rose slightly and drifted in the direction I wished to go, but only for a few yards, after which I became static again till I once more made a conscious effort to advance. The movement can best be likened to that of a toy balloon which having been thrown with some force bounces in slow graceful arcs across the floor. It was a most pleasant sensation and I recalled having on rare occasions experienced it in dreams.

I was, obviously, invisible to myself and also to Evans; for had my spirit been clothed with the tenuous outline of a ghost it is quite certain that he would have seen it and fled in terror.

He had already reached the door and was about to close it as I came up behind him. For a moment I feared that he would shut me in, but the next second I became aware that no material object was a barrier to me. My last quick forward impulse carried me through both the half-shut door and his forearm as he pulled it to.

While he locked it behind him I waited in his little office, wondering what he was about to do. My guess was that he would go down the back stairs to Silvers and tell the old boy that I had died as a result of a terrible accident; then they would telephone the police. As Evans had no apparent motive for murdering me there seemed quite a good chance that if he kept his head under cross-examination he would get away with an accident story, anyhow as far as a capital charge was concerned; but he would have to stand his trial for manslaughter and, as such an accident could have taken place only owing to crass carelessness on his part, the probability was that he would be sent to prison for a couple of years.

The cold-blooded little rat deserved far worse than that

and, while I am not normally vindictive, had I had the power to do so I would have seen to it that he paid the full price for his unscrupulous experiment. As it was I could be neither seen nor heard; so far as I could judge for the time being there were no means by which I could any longer influence the future of anyone.

However, it soon transpired that my speculations were right off the mark. Instead of making for the servants' quarters, or down the main staircase to telephone the police, he walked straight across the landing to the door of the bedroom that I shared with Ankaret. Without even knocking, he flung it open and marched in.

As I followed, I saw that Ankaret was sitting up reading in her side of our big double bed. Sometimes she wore a little fluffy bed-jacket, but the night being warm she had on only a semi-transparent night-dress of pale blue chiffon. Its delicate colour was well chosen to throw up her Titian hair, big grey eyes and milk and roses skin. It was not to be wondered at that as Evans halted a few feet from the bed he gave a sudden gasp at the picture that she made.

I jumped to the conclusion that the little brute, lacking as he was in the finer feelings, intended to blurt out a story about my accidental death, instead of giving Mrs. Silvers a chance to break it to Ankaret gently. But again I was quite wrong. Next second he flung himself upon her, bearing her backwards and kissing her violently on the mouth.

Ankaret's slender limbs concealed a surprising strength, and she was as supple as an eel. In a moment she had wriggled free and was thrusting him off. Her voice was tense with anger, but deliberately kept low, as she exclaimed:

'Have you gone mad, Owen? Where's Giff? If the two of you have finished in the laboratory he may come in at any minute. Should he find you here he'll half kill you.'

Her words and tone shocked me profoundly. They had a conspiratorial air about them which conveyed as clearly as anything could that she was having an affair with Evans. She was angry with him not for having invaded her room and forced his kisses on her, but because she believed that he had taken an unwarrantable risk in coming there at a time when I might easily appear on the scene and catch them in *flagrante delicto*.

It flashed upon me then that Evans's motive for killing me had little, if anything, to do with his desire to prove the capabilities of the scientific device he had invented. He had evidently been inspired to the crime by madness of quite a different kind—an insane jealousy of me as Ankaret's husband.

That he should have fallen for her I could well understand; but what she could see in him passed my comprehension. It seemed utterly unnatural that so lovely a creature as Ankaret should willingly submit to, let alone welcome, the caresses of this little dark, morose, uncultured runt of a man. Yet in such matters women are incomprehensible, and I could only assume it to be a case of beauty fascinated by the beast.

Urgently, angrily, but still keeping her voice low, she repeated her command that he should leave her; then she endeavoured to scare him into doing so by swift graphic phrases depicting the explosion which was certain to take place if I came in and found them together.

After she had thrown Evans off he made no further attempt to grapple with her, but neither did he make any move to leave the room. Instead, pouting slightly, he perched himself at her feet, near the end of the bed, and, as soon as he could get a word in, said in his lilting Welsh voice:

'That will do, now. No need to be fearing any more that Giff will surprise us. The job is done, look you. Worked like a charm, it did: could not have gone better.'

'What on earth are you talking about?' she asked in a puzzled voice.

'Why, of the plan we made to be rid of him.'

Ankaret jerked erect in the bed as though she had received an electric shock. Her mouth fell open, her big eyes widened to their fullest extent, her voice came in a hoarse whisper:

'You . . . you don't mean . . . you can't mean that you've killed Giff?'

He nodded; then they exchanged a few swift sentences which gave me the key to what had been going on. It was not so much what they said, and Ankaret made no admission of the game she had been playing; but knowing her so well enabled me to fill in the blanks and reconstruct the psychological processes of the two of them which had led up to my murder.

Having been confined to the house for several weeks, owing to her injured leg, Ankaret had become so bored that she had encouraged Evans in his violent passion for her; but evidently she had not been attracted to him physically so had played a rôle which had enabled her to continue to amuse herself with him without giving way to his attempts to seduce her.

As he could have known nothing of her past amours, it had been easy for her to pretend to be a virtuous and faithful wife who was unappreciated and misunderstood; so might, in certain circumstances, be willing to leave her husband for a man she loved.

What those circumstances were did not emerge. She might have told him that I would never consent to divorce her and that she could not face the furtive life of living with him 'in sin'. Or perhaps she had spoken sorrowfully of his inability to support an extravagant and idle wife. Anyway, she had evidently raised some such obstacle as a counter to his pressing her to run away with him; and it must have been this, coupled with his obsession to possess her whatever the cost, that had put into his head the idea of resorting to desperate measures.

To murder me provided a solution to whatever obstacle Ankaret might have raised. Not only would it free her without the difficulties and delays of a divorce, but he could be reasonably certain that she would inherit a large enough share of my considerable fortune to keep them both in comfort.

It seems that he must have first mooted his idea to Ankaret as a sort of day-dream. Possibly on some such line as 'What a stroke of luck it would be for us if Giff met with a fatal accident. He might, you know, if some time he came into my laboratory and monkeyed about with some of the things I've got there. As a matter of fact, I was thinking only this morning that if I were in there with him I'd only have to give him a push in the right direction to send him marching up the Golden Stairs. I suppose that sounds pretty frightful, but I love you so terribly that there are few things I'd stick at to make you my own.'

That Ankaret had not taken him seriously was beyond question but, horrible as murder may be in actual fact, there

83

are few women who could help their most primitive emotions being stirred by the thought of a man loving them so desperately that he would even toy with the idea of killing another in order to get them for himself.

Probably the conversation had developed by her saying that murder was not as easy as all that; all sorts of things might go wrong, a single slip was enough to give the police reason to believe that there had been foul play, and that once that happened they nearly always got their man.

That would have led to a discussion, on his part in concealed but deadly earnest, on hers simply as an intriguing sort of game. Together they had worked out how the job could be done and made watertight against suspicion even, as transpired shortly afterwards, to my apparently not having met my death in the laboratory but in quite different circumstances.

While they planned the crime Ankaret, I am convinced, was thinking of it as an entirely hypothetical case, and had not for one moment visualised myself as the victim. The horror and distress she now displayed were ample evidence of that. But she had played with fire once too often. The passion-crazed little Welshman had assumed that she was willing to become his accomplice and, without warning her that he was about to do so, staged the 'accident' that had so abruptly terminated my life.

While I was swiftly piecing this background of the crime together, the couple on the bed were hurling useless recriminations at one another.

Amazed and appalled at Evans's deed, Ankaret gave free vent to her horror at it, and swore that she had not had the faintest idea that he really intended to carry out the rôle he had cast for himself in the nonsense they had talked together one afternoon a fortnight or so ago.

He, with equal intensity, declared that she was lying, and now attempting to back out of giving him the help she had promised in disposing of my body.

At that she cried: 'I'll see you damned before I do anything of the kind! In fact I mean to ring up the police.'

As she stretched out a hand for the bed-side telephone, he grabbed her wrist, and snapped: 'Is it mad you are, woman? Indeed now, and you do that, we'll both be in the dock; and like as not to hang, see?'

'You may,' she retorted. 'I will not, for I am innocent, and no one can prove me otherwise.'

'Don't be too sure of that,' he warned her. 'You're in this thing with me up to your lovely neck, see. Too late to job backwards now. Spare you I would, if I could. But your help I've got to have. Big man he was too! I cannot shift him alone. Do you come down now to give me a hand. Get him into the wheelbarrow we will. Then we'll tip him into the Solent as we planned.'

'I won't. I won't.' Her voice rose to an hysterical note.

'Do you listen, lovey,' he strove to calm her by adopting a gentler tone. 'We daren't leave him in the lab, see; you know that. Didn't we agree that if we said he'd had it through monkeying with some of my gear then the police would insist on my explaining just how? Clever lot of devils they are these days. For sure they'd call in one of their tame scientists to check up. And there is only one way, look you, he could have caused his own death in the lab: my Death Ray Machine.'

'Death Ray?' she repeated hoarsely.

He nodded. 'A new invention of mine. I used it on him. And no one knows of it so far. So no one can even suspect the real cause of his death. But did I have to show it to the police and there's murder will be in their minds in a jiffy. That's why we've got to get him out of the lab, see; make it look as if he drowned himself—just like we said.'

Ankaret violently shook her head. 'I tell you I'll have no hand in this. It's all too horrible—too frightful even to think about.'

'Ah, and you will.' He was sweating now, evidently from fear that her refusal to help him would lead to his having to pay the full penalty for his crime. Pulling a crumpled silk handkerchief from his pocket, he wiped his face with it, and went on more quickly.

'Suspicious the police are! Ask questions without end they do. But stick to what we said we'd do, we can put ourselves in the clear about having fallen for one another. Deny it, see, and there's rope enough to hang us both. I doubt but the Silvers have ideas about us, even if young Mildred Mallows kept her mouth shut. Anyhow, her walking in on us, and me sitting here on your bed last Wednesday evening when Giff was in town. For sure the police will have that out of her. And there's the motive they'll be seeking should they find Giff's body in the lab and I have to show them the Death Ray. 'Twill be all up with both of us then. Swear certain sure you are completely innocent; they'll still charge you with complicity. Look you, help me is what you've got to do.'

'I suppose you're right, that I'm bound to be dragged into it,' she admitted with an angry frown. 'But at worst Mildred's testimony could be taken only as evidence that you were my lover, and a woman can have a lover without inciting him to murder her husband.'

He gave a heavy sigh and stared at her gloomily. 'And maybe you'd get away with it if you had nought to answer but servants' talk. 'Twould not be quite like that though. I hate to force you to it, but it seems I must, for my own life now hangs on the help that only you can give me.'

'Force me to it?' she repeated. 'What do you mean by that? You have no hold over me.'

'Have I not? Think again. You'll see I have.' His voice rose a little and he spoke with sudden passion. 'I had no quarrel with Giff. Treated me decently enough he did. I killed him only to free you from him. Or, if you will, to get you for myself. Anyway, by doing what I've done, I've won the right to you. Do you take me for a fool that I would now let you jeopardise that? Am I to hang because you've suddenly turned squeamish, and are trying to go back on your part of our understanding? No, lovey, no! You're mine now and I mean to keep you. I'll not go to my death and leave you behind to be bedded by some other chap. Either you'll get up now and do your bit to put us both in the clear, or should I be charged with Giff's death I'll let on that it was you who urged me to kill him. Yes, indeed, and after the judge has heard young Mildred's evidence he'll be telling the jury that you're a second Lady Macbeth.'

Ankaret had gone white to the lips. For over a minute she remained silent, and I could sense the frantic working of her very able brain as it weighed up the chances in the horrible dilemma with which she was faced. At last she said:

'All right, then. Go and make certain that the servants are asleep, while I get some clothes on.'

86

A grin of relief spread over his dark face, and he exclaimed: 'Land of my fathers, now! 'Twouldn't have been natural, mind, if you hadn't been a bit upset, but you'll soon get over that. If all's quiet in the courtyard side of the house, I'll get the wheelbarrow round to the back door of the hall.'

As he spoke he stood up. Ankaret had never been particularly modest. In fact she took such delight in her beautiful figure that she often walked about her bedroom with nothing on, so that she could admire it in the mirrors. Now, with her thoughts obviously elsewhere, she flung back the bed-clothes and thrust her long legs over the side of the bed. The sight of the lovely body that he had committed murder to possess acted on Evans like a spark to kindling. Stooping suddenly he stretched out his arms again and threw himself upon her.

This time she did not fight him off, but, up to a point, let him have his way with her. It was not until he had given her two long fierce kisses that she clutched at his hands, jerked aside her head, and said with a calmness which told me that he had entirely failed to rouse her:

'No Owen, no. This is no time for love-making. You must be patient just a little longer.'

'It's early yet. The night's all ours,' he muttered thickly.

'No, it's not,' she countered. 'If we leave . . . leave what we've got to do for too long Johnny may come in and catch us red-handed.'

Rolling off her, he sat up, his mouth twitching and his eyes wild with fright. 'Giff's nephew! Staying here the night is he?'

Ankaret sat up beside him and nodded. 'Yes. He is dining with the Waldrons and when he does that he and Sue usually join some party or other to dance afterwards. The odds are he won't be back till three or four o'clock in the morning, but we can't afford to take any chances.'

'*Sospan bach!*' He smiled again. 'Scared I was—for a moment; but we'll be through with our job well before midnight.'

Putting an arm round her shoulders, he drew her to him and added: 'Just one more kiss before we get to work, and tell me you forgive me driving you to do your bit. Indeed

87

I'd not harm a hair of your lovely head, but I had to rouse you up somehow.'

She gave him the kiss and murmured: 'Of course I forgive you. I behaved like a fool; but you didn't give me even a hint that you meant to do it tonight, and the shock was so great it caused me to say all sorts of things I didn't mean.'

I felt certain that both of them were lying. Rather than lose her now Evans would have seen her go to the scaffold with him, and Ankaret knew it. That accounted for her change of attitude. She was playing along with him because she realised that to do so was the lesser danger; but I would not have given much for his chances of reaping the full rewards of his crime.

So intrigued had I been by the revelations that had emerged during the battle of personalities, of which I had been the unseen witness, that for some time I had hardly given a thought to my own strange state. And even now, as Evans left the room, I thrust from me the tendency to start speculating on my future, because I was so anxious not to miss the smallest development of this gruesome drama in which my own dead body was the central figure.

Evans had hardly shut the door behind him when Ankaret suddenly went limp. Uttering a low moan, she let herself fall back on the bed and lay there with closed eyes. After a few moments two large tears welled up from under her eyelids and ran down her cheeks.

There was no escaping the fact that my death lay at her door. Had she not amused herself by leading Evans on he would never even have thought of using his Death Ray upon me. It was beyond dispute her vanity, egoism and complete lack of principle that had cost me my life. Yet, even so, I felt no trace of resentment against her. On the contrary, she was still to me the gay, generous, lovely darling; a born pagan but in no way evil. And I longed to comfort her.

Moving over to the bed I brought my lips down on to hers. I couldn't feel them and she made no response, but in silent words I said to her:

'Take courage, darling. You must go through with this, then send that little knave packing as soon afterwards as you possibly can.'

88

At that she murmured: 'Oh Giff, dear Giff. What have i done to you?'

Whether that was a spontaneous utterance of remorse, or in reply to my thought wave, I had no means of telling. Hoping that it was the latter, I said: 'Don't worry about me. It hurt only for a moment and I'm perfectly all right. Pull yourself together now, and do what you've got to do. But when the police come, for God's sake keep your story simple and don't budge from it by a word.'

She gave no further indication that my efforts to console and counsel her might be getting through to her mind; so I was reluctantly forced to the conclusion that she was unconscious of my presence, and abandoned the attempt.

For some five minutes she lay there motionless, then she rolled over, put her feet to the floor, and walked unsteadily into the bathroom. I remained where I was but the sounds of splashing water told me that she was bathing her face. When she emerged her mouth was firmly set, and the clean-cut Le Strange jaw, that she had inherited from those ancestors of hers who had held many a fortress, stuck out with evident resolution. Slipping off her nightie she quickly got into her underclothes, pulled on over them a pair of slacks and a dark coat. Then, instinctively, I suppose, she sat down at her dressing-table to make up her face. She was still at it when Evans came back into the room.

'All's clear,' he told her. 'Not a light or a sound from the Silvers's room or young Mildred's. Had I not known they were all early-to-bedders I'd have waited a while before coming along to you; but I felt that the sooner we could get things over with the better.'

As she stood up, he added: 'Best put on a pair of gloves, lovey, so as not to leave any finger-prints, see. We can't take too many precautions.'

He already had rubber gloves on, and when she had done as he bid her they left the room together. I followed them across the landing to the lab, and on entering it I saw that he had had the forethought to tie his blue silk handkerchief over the face of my corpse, so that the sight of it should not upset her.

As she looked down on the body her lips parted slightly,

showing that her teeth were tightly clenched; but that was the only sign she gave of the emotions which I could guess would be harrowing her mind. The next quarter of an hour must have been an appalling ordeal to her, but her courage proved equal to it.

'Need his jacket to put the suicide letter in,' Evans muttered, 'best take it off now and leave it here.'

She made no move to help him as he turned the body over and wriggled the limp arms out of the sleeves, but when he had got it off she said: 'He keeps his desk locked so I shall need his keys to get into it. You'll find them in his right-hand trousers pocket.'

Evans fished them out and gave them to her. Then he took the body by the shoulders and she picked up its feet. The dead weight of a big male corpse must be pretty considerable. They could only stagger awkwardly along with it, and had to let go for a breather twice before they got it down to the hall door. I suppose, at a pinch, Evans could have managed to drag it downstairs on his own, but that would have taken far longer and been a most exhausting business. However, it was not for that alone that he had counted Ankaret's help essential if he was to get away with his crime. The really vital aid that he had to have from her was in providing evidence that I had committed suicide, as she alone was capable of producing that.

Their mention of a letter to put in the pocket of my jacket, of the key to my desk, and of the fact that if they stuck to what they had originally planned it would put them in the clear about having fallen for one another had enabled me to guess the means by which they intended to create a false impression of how and why I met my death.

Ankaret, as I think I have already mentioned, possessed artistic gifts of a very high order. Her ignorance of technique debarred her from making a name for herself as a painter, but she could probably draw as well as anyone in the kingdom. Quite apart from original drawings of her own invention her eye was so good that she could draw from life or copy any other work with extraordinary swiftness and accuracy. It was this latter ability which enabled her, if she wished, to forge other people's handwriting with very little trouble.

I knew nothing of this until, while on our honeymoon, I asked her one day how much she thought she could do on as a dress allowance. With a laugh she had replied: 'Make it what you like, darling. If I get short I can always forge your name to a cheque and I'll bet you any money that your bank will cash it.' Then, without a second's hesitation, she had written my name on the back of a magazine she was reading and handed it to me.

Of course she was only joking, and had never forged my name to anything, but before marriage she had made use of this unusual gift as an adjunct to one of her hobbies. History was one of her chief interests and, in addition to two or three hundred volumes of memoirs, etc., that she had collected, she owned a big scrap-book. From time to time she had bought and pasted in it small etchings, colour prints and cartoons of famous people or incidents. Then, when staying for a while in London, she had spent a few mornings at the British Museum. There she would get one of the staff to hunt out for her some original letter or manuscript written by each of the people who appeared in the pictures she had recently bought. Selecting from them interesting passages, she would copy these out on separate sheets of paper, add the appropriate signature, and later paste them under the picture with which they were associated. Of course, from the paper on which they were written, an expert could have told at a glance that they must all be forgeries, but the ink gave them an apparent reality which no photographed facsimile could have done.

I had not seen this historical scrap-book of hers for years, but either she must have dug it out and shown it to Evans or, while they were planning—as she thought—my hypothetical murder, she had mentioned to him her capabilities as a forger. It was that which must have given one of them the idea of the suicide letter. To write one in my hand would be easy for her, and if written on my private paper it would be even more readily accepted as genuine; that was why she had wanted the key of my desk.

What she intended to put into the note I could not be certain, but I would have taken a good-sized bet that she meant to say on my behalf that I had found out that she was having an affair with Evans and was so cut to the heart that

I meant to throw myself into the Solent. In my case neither ill-health nor financial difficulties would be regarded as a plausible motive for suicide, but no one was capable of assessing the depths of despair to which I might have been reduced on discovering that Ankaret was being unfaithful to me. Moreover, by conveying information of their guilty passion to the police in this way, and when questioned admitting it, they would forestall and render harmless any otherwise dangerous tittle-tattle that the police might pick up from the servants.

If I was right in my surmise they had certainly thought out a most ingenious way of covering up the truth and, anxious as I was that my dear, wicked Ankaret should not have to pay for her folly with her life, I could not help feeling that it would be intensely interesting to see if the police accepted the false evidence at its face value or spotted some little detail that the murderer had overlooked and, with dogged persistence, gradually unravelled the whole plot.

As yet, however, while I speculated on the ultimate stages of their plan, they were still occupied in getting my body through the door and arranging it in the wheelbarrow that Evans had brought round there. To do so satisfactorily was by no means an easy job as it may sound; for the load was weightier than the barrow was built to take and so awkward in shape that each time Evans started to wheel the barrow forward it tended to tip over.

With a mutter of lilting curses and sweating under the strain he ran it down the path a few feet at a time, while Ankaret tried to keep it steady by walking alongside and hanging on to the shoulder of the corpse's shirt. After progressing about twenty yards trial and error made the tricky business somewhat easier for them, and by a further five minutes of laborious effort they succeeded in getting the barrow down to the pier.

On reaching the end of the pier, Evans tipped the body out so that it fell face downward, then stood beside it panting for a few moments. There was no moon but the sky was not overcast, so the stars gave ample light to see by. Ankaret had turned her back upon the corpse and was staring up at them. What her thoughts were at that moment, God alone knows; but I pitied her. As an accompaniment to Evans's heavy breathing I could hear the constant slap-slap of the water as it lapped against the wooden piles. When he had got back his breath he retrieved his silk handkerchief from the corpse's face, touched her on the arm and said:

'Come, lovey, now to get done with it.'

Evidently she had been screwing herself up against this gruesome moment, for she turned without hesitation, stooped down, and again took the corpse by the ankles. He took it by the wrists. Having lifted it they swung it between them, while he counted, 'One! Two! Three!' Then with a final heave they let go. Still face downward it hit the water with a loud splash; a moment later only a few flecks of foam, dimly seen in the starlight, showed where it had disappeared beneath the surface.

Without a word Evans took the handles of the barrow and began to wheel it back towards the house. Ankaret followed, her face, as far as I could judge in the dim light, set and very pale, but quite expressionless. While he took the barrow back to its shed she went into the house and upstairs, but instead of going to her room and collapsing, as I expected, she went into the laboratory.

The lights were still on and, apart from my velvet smoking jacket, which was lying across a high tubular stool, there was not a thing to show that just under an hour before a murder had been committed there. The rabbit, all unconscious of the evil deed that had been enacted in its presence, was still busily nibbling at its generous supply of lettuce, and the Death Ray machine looked no more malefic than would have some new scientific labour-saving device.

Ankaret halted within a foot or two of the spot where I had fallen when struck down by the ray. There she remained, staring straight in front of her and making no sound. Her hands hung limply at her side: and her face was as blank as that of a white marble statue. I was beginning to fear that this terrible business had unhinged her mind, when Evans came in and said to her:

'What are you doing up here, lovey? I thought to find you downstairs. Indeed but you must not delay in writing that letter. Maybe you're right about Norton and his girl being out dancing most of the night; but say he came home early and caught us still up, how would we explain Giff's disappearance?'

To my relief Ankaret replied in a low but normal voice: 'Johnny won't be home for hours, and I came up here to see your Death Ray. Is it that thing on the table?'

He nodded. 'Ah, that's it. Explain it to you sometime; but not now. Get you downstairs, lovey, and do that letter; so that I can stick it in the pocket of his jacket and take that out to leave on the end of the pier. We'll be in the clear then, and nought to fear from anyone. 'Twould be wisest for us to wait a few months, but we can be married in the New Year.'

With the infuriating disregard for playing safe that women sometimes show at times of crisis, she said with a shrug, 'We have plenty of time. I want to see how you operate your Death Ray machine. Show me how it works on the rabbit.'

'By damn!' he exclaimed impatiently. 'I couldn't now, even if I would. It needs recharging; and, look you, to prepare it for action is a long business and expensive.'

Her request that he should demonstrate the Death Ray to her on a rabbit, while one would have expected her mind to be still occupied to the exclusion of all else by tumultuous thoughts about his crime, had struck me as strange. But a moment later I jumped to the conclusion that, for some reason or other, she was playing for time; as, with equal irrelevance to their present situation, she remarked:

'In that case it can't be much good as a commercial proposition.'

'No, indeed?' His tone had changed from impatience to excited enthusiasm. ' 'Tis scarce past its experimental stage as yet; but there's a fortune in it. 'Twill need money, of course, to develop it into a long-range weapon with quick repeating action. But now Giff's dead we'll have plenty of that, and for every shilling we put into it the Government will later pay us back a pound. Bringing it to perfection will be just the thing to keep my mind busy till we can get married and I can go to bed openly with you at nights.'

Suddenly she swung upon him and cried: 'I'll not put a penny into it! And you can disabuse your mind once and for all of the idea that I'm going to marry you. Get out of here! Get out!'

He stared at her in amazement and his jaw dropped in dismay. But he recovered himself quickly and said in a soothing tone: 'You're over-wrought, lovey; and I don't wonder. You'll feel different in the morning, be your sweet self again. In your bed you should be, with a good sleeping draught. But you must write that letter first. Come now, let us go downstairs and get it over with.'

'I won't,' she snapped. 'I'll see you damned first!'

'Then you'll be damned as well as me, if you do not.' The angry note had crept back into his voice, although he was obviously endeavouring to control it. 'See now, how otherwise can Giff's disappearance be explained, and his death, when his body is washed up? He'd not a worry in the world. He'd no reason to commit suicide, and we've got to provide one. Do we fail, and the police will start ferreting around. They'll get your Mildred's story of finding me in your room. Him being so heavy the wheelbarrow must have left a track. When they begin looking, they'll find it. Ah, and once those human bloodhounds are on the trail there's no knowing what they'll unearth that may tell against us. Remember, he was dead before we put him in the Solent. Well and good, all will be if the letter is found in his coat. There the reason will be for his drowning himself, and drowned everyone will believe him should his body be fished out of the water. And do we not put suicide into their minds there'll be post-mortem! 'Twill emerge that indeed he did not die by drowning whatever but by shock. They'll search the place with fine tooth-combs, and there'll be no pulling of wool over the eyes of the experts they send to examine this lab. 'Twill be found that there's a machine here capable of giving the heart of a man a shock strong enough to kill him. Then what with Mildred, and the barrow track, and maybe other things we've not thought of, 'twill be plain to them that he was murdered here. Ah, and that guilty love being the motive it was yourself that helped me get him down to the shore. Have some sense, woman. Do you not write that letter, curtains it will be for both of us.'

Again Ankaret's resolution gave way. After moistening her lips with her tongue she said harshly: 'Very well, I'll do it. But I never said that I would marry you, and you may as well know now that I never had the least intention of doing so. I suppose I must put up with your presence until this awful business has been straightened out, but I won't for one

95

moment longer than I have to. As soon as the household has settled down you are to pack and go. That is an order. And if you make any trouble about going I'll send for the police to eject you.'

She showed no trace of hysteria, and the sudden expression of consternation that came over Evans's face made clear his realisation that she had both fooled and finished with him. For a moment his mouth worked furiously, then he burst out:

'Eject me, is it? Cast me off after getting me to kill your man for you so that you could have your freedom. And I like a fool worshipping the ground you walked on. Who would have thought that behind that angel face of yours lies the mind of a double-crossing bitch. Ah yes, indeed, but it's a big mistake you've made to think to play Owen Evans for a sucker. I've paid your price and I mean to have you. Yes, indeed! Saint or devil you're going to be my woman for as long as I want you. Not yet for a while, maybe; but you'll not spoil for a few months' keeping. 'Tis true enough that I can't stop you from having me turned out. Indeed, I'll go without the least fuss, whatever. But I'll be waiting for you, and you'll either come to me or go to the gallows. I'll take ship for South America. I'll let you know where you're to join me. I'll have changed my name and the police will never get me. But they'll get the lovely Lady Ankaret unless I've bedded her by Christmas Day. Fail you to come at my bidding, and a sworn statement goes to Scotland Yard telling how you tempted me into committing murder for you.'

Ankaret heard him out, then, as swiftly as a gangster could have pulled a gun, she snatched up a steel rod from the nearby bench and struck at him with it.

The stroke caught him full across the face, breaking the bone of his nose. As he staggered back blinded by pain, she struck at him again and gasped out:

'You swine! You filth! You miserable fool! How dare you think that I would ever live with you.'

With a wail of agony he thrust up his hands to protect himself. Her second blow descended on the back of one of them. Uttering another screech he jerked it away, but attempted to run in and at her.

Side-stepping swiftly she lashed out at his head. The steel

rod sliced down on his ear, half tearing it from his head, then thudded on to his shoulder.

As she beat at him she was speaking all the time, her voice vibrant with hate and fury. 'Take that, you beast! Had you been the last man on earth I'd never have let you have me! I am no angel! I've had a score of men, but never one like you! Women like me do not allow themselves to be defiled by the sweepings of the gutter.'

Her fourth stroke landed on his head. His knees gave and with a moan he fell upon them. But she did not mean to show him any mercy, and told him so as she continued to strike down with all her strength at his untidy mop of thick black hair and feebly flailing hands.

'Take that for Giff! And that, and that! Tonight you killed the only man I've ever loved. A man whose boots you were not fit to lick. But two can play at murder. I'd have tried to kill you with your filthy Death Ray had it been working. This rod is better though, for you don't deserve a sudden, painless death. Get down to hell where you belong, and stay there.'

*   *   *   *

I have never been given to physical violence, but I must confess that the sight of Ankaret attacking my murderer aroused intense excitement in me and, in the early stages of the conflict, had I been able to do so I would certainly have given her my aid; for even after her first blow had deprived him of the full use of his wits, had he succeeded in clutching the steel rod he could easily have wrenched it from her, then, maddened with rage, frustration and pain, as he was, quite possibly have beaten her to death with it.

After the fourth stroke she had him at her mercy, and what followed was horrifying to behold; for she must in all have struck him not less than twenty times before he ceased squirming and lay, his head, face and hands a broken bloody mess, sprawled out on the floor. But her own admission while beating at him showed that before he returned to the laboratory she had already made up her mind to revenge my death;

so she could hardly have been expected to let up when well on the way to accomplishing her purpose.

Apart from the final agony that Evans must have suffered, I did not feel in the least sorry for him. He was a mean-spirited little man and capable of the greatest baseness, as had emerged in his threat to denounce Ankaret to the police should she refuse to go out and live with him in South America. Moreover, to satisfy his own lust he had killed a man who, far from doing him any injury, had given him employment when he needed it and had always treated him decently.

On the other hand any impartial person given full knowledge of the whole affair would, I feel sure, have considered that he had had a raw deal. Having been brought up in a poor home and spent his adult years in intensive study as the only way of making a career for himself, he had had neither the time nor means to travel or to mingle with what are still termed the upper classes. And the cinema is no real substitute for that, as it is only a temporary transportation to make-believe in which neither settings nor characters are real. In consequence, even the modest luxury of Longshot Hall, and the quiet but gracious life we lived there when entertaining guests over week-ends, must have seemed to him like entering another world.

It follows that in his eyes Ankaret must have appeared even more glamorous than she did to sophisticated men like myself, and utterly unobtainable. No doubt he had fallen for her in quite a humble way, and would never have dreamed of letting her know it, had she not so wickedly decided to amuse herself with him. Even if she had not actually said that she would marry him after they had got me out of the way—and the plan for that had been thought of by her only as in the nature of a plot for a thriller play—she must have given him grounds for believing that she would be willing; so there was no escaping the fact that she was fundamentally responsible for my death, as well as his.

All the same, while I felt intense umbrage against him for cutting short my life, I felt none against her. Perhaps that was partly because she had, in a sense, acted as my champion and proclaimed her love for me with such vehemence while striking him down; but much more it could be attributed to the old saying that to understand all is to forgive all, and knowing and loving her as I did I could not wish her any ill for what she had done.

On the contrary, I was now intensely worried on her account. It appeared not only that she had forfeited her chance of clearing herself of having had a hand in my murder, but that there could be no escape for her from being convicted of that of Evans's.

She could, of course, tell some version of the true story twisted as far as possible in favour of herself; then say that when she learned from Evans that he had killed me, maddened by grief and shock she had attacked him while temporarily out of her mind. Unfortunately that did not tie up with her having helped him to get my body down to the pier, and if her having done so came out few people would believe that after participating in such a cold-blooded act she had suddenly become the victim of a brainstorm. There was also the certainty that, unreasonable as it might be in this particular case, any jury would regard the fact of her having beaten Evans to death as a much more heinous crime than if she had simply shot him. To sum up, I feared that there could be little hope of a recommendation to mercy for her and that, unless she could get away with a plea of insanity, she might, just as Evans had threatened to make her, have to face the horror of being pilloried as another Lady Macbeth. It can, therefore, well be imagined with what distress I watched her at that awful moment.

Panting from the exertions, she threw the steel rod down on the floor and walked quickly out of the lab, across the landing, to her own room. There I expected her to be hit by the reaction to her terrible deed, and fall prostrate upon the bed. But she was made of sterner stuff than even I had thought. Pulling off the gloves she had been wearing for the past half hour, she again went into the bathroom and bathed her face.

When she had done she went downstairs to the drawing-room and from a drawer in her writing table got out a packet of letters, then she went through to my little library. Opening the bow-fronted cupboard where I kept glasses and our drinks, she poured herself a stiff tot of liqueur brandy and drank it off. Next she lit a cigarette; but after inhaling a few long pulls from it she took the butt into the drawing-room and stubbed it out in an ashtray there. She then returned to my room, produced my keys from a pocket in her slacks and unlocked my roll-top desk.

I guessed then that she still meant to forge a letter purporting to have been written by me; but for the moment I could not see how it was going to help her, or that by it she could possibly account for Evans's death as well as mine. As she took up my desk pen and drew a blank of sheet foolscap towards her, I watched over her shoulder with the greatest interest.

After several false starts she drafted a letter in her own hand which apparently satisfied her. It was a fair length but, I suppose, as short as she could make it if she was to put over all the essential points which would explain the two violent deaths without involving herself in either. It was addressed to herself, and ran:

Ankaret, my love,

At first I could not take seriously your confession that you have been flirting with Owen Evans. I thought you possessed better taste. But I was compelled to believe you this evening when you were driven to admit it by the necessity of asking me to get rid of him, because he assaulted and attempted to rape you when I was in London last Wednesday night.

When I charged him with it in the lab he had the impudence to deny that it was assault. He boasted that you were a willing party, and maintained that you had told me of your affair with him only because you feared that the servants might fore-stall you in doing so, and that if I learned from them that he was your lover I might kick you out of the house.

I suppose I was a fool to believe him. But the thought of him and you together drove me into a frenzy. I snatched up a steel rod and the next thing I knew was that I had killed him.

There is not a hope if I stay and face my trial. At the very best it would mean a ruined life dragged out at Broadmoor. So I've decided to end it. I have kept some dope from the days when I was in India that is supposed to rev up the heart. If I swallow the lot and chuck myself into the Solent that should ensure me a pretty swift finish.

If you keep your mouth shut, the reason that I killed Evans may not come out. So you had better destroy this. But I wanted you to know that now I'm in my right mind again, I'm sure that he lied to me about you.

And that I still love you.

Giff

Her brain had been several jumps ahead of mine, and I thought her skilful elaboration of the original plan truly masterly; particularly the new line about my having taken an overdose of some heart dope before diving off the pier. Actually I had never had any such stuff, either in India or elsewhere; but no one would be able to prove it, and this brilliant bit of improvisation would account for the lungs not being full of water if my body was recovered from the Solent. I began to have hopes that, after all, she would get away with it.

I could see now that the packet of letters she had brought in were from myself. Opening it up she began to glance through them, evidently with the object of refreshing her mind on the details of my calligraphy. Now and then she paused to read a passage, and after some minutes one of special tenderness so upset her that her face twisted grotesquely. I feared for a moment that she was about to break down and find herself unable to go through with the job, but she got quickly to her feet, poured herself another brandy and tossed it off. The neat spirit made her gasp and shudder, but it did its work, and with new resolution she sat down to the desk again.

Taking some sheets of the paper that I use for my private correspondence, she began to copy her draft letter in my own hand. At her fourth attempt she completed one that had it been produced in court would have been sworn to without hesitation by anyone familiar with my writing. Having written her own name and 'Personal' on an envelope she slipped the letter into it and stuck down the flap.

It was at that moment I heard a slight noise from the direction of the drawing-room. She had heard it too and, quickly pocketing the letter, turned to stare apprehensively in that direction. The door, which she had left ajar, was pushed open and Johnny walked in.

Instantly, it struck me that here was one of those unforeseen occurrences that are said so often to wreck the most skilfully-laid plans and bring murderers to the scaffold. Ankaret believed that Johnny had gone out dancing, so would not come in before three or four o'clock in the morning. As he had told me his plans, I knew that he would be in much earlier; but when she mentioned to Evans that Johnny was staying in the house I had still supposed that they would have a clear field until well after midnight. Yet here he was, although it was not yet half-past eleven. If I had had any breath to hold I would certainly have held it as I waited to see how his untimely arrival would affect Ankaret's chances of clearing herself.

I have already mentioned that I retained my big roll-top desk, in spite of its being rather ugly, because I could always pull the roller down and so save myself the bother of keeping it tidy. As usual it was littered with papers, some of which Ankaret had pushed aside to make a space to write on. As the door opened, in order to hide her draft letter and the three first forgery try-outs, she swiftly shuffled some of my papers over them. Then, evidently feeling that to be insufficient protection for the evidence of her guilt, she pulled the roller down and locked it.

Catching sight of her gesture as he entered, Johnny said politely, 'I hope I haven't disturbed you. I came in for a nightcap.'

'No; not a bit.' Her voice held a slight quaver, but I don't think he noticed it, as he was looking somewhat distrait; and she added quickly, 'Do help yourself. I only came down to hunt out an address that Giff said I would find here; and I've just come across it.'

With a word of thanks he walked over to the drink cabinet, fixed himself a large whisky and soda, and plumped down into the arm-chair near it, as she remarked:

'You don't usually get home from your evenings with Sue Waldron as early as this.'

'No,' he replied non-committally; and, stretching out his long legs, he stared with a worried frown at his feet.

Having recovered from her fright she gave him a puzzled

102

look and asked: 'What's the matter? Have you quarrelled with Sue?'

'No,' he repeated, and I formed the impression that although he was in some sort of trouble he had no intention of telling her what it was. Until the previous autumn he and Ankaret had been on excellent terms, but from the beginning of last winter, while her attitude to him had not changed, I had thought on several occasions that he had become a trifle stand-offish with her. His present uncommunicativeness confirmed the change that I had noticed and I wondered what could have caused it. In due course I was to learn.

After knocking back a good half of his drink, he asked: 'Where's Giff?'

'Up in the lab with the Prof,' she replied promptly. 'They are trying out some new gadget. It's something to do with photography, I think. Anyhow he said that it might be a long session, and that if anyone rang up they were not to be disturbed, as if the door was opened the light would get in and ruin everything.'

Again I metaphorically took off my hat to her for producing such a fast one, while Johnny said: 'I see,' in a disappointed tone. Then, finishing his drink, he asked: 'May I have another?'

She nodded. 'Of course; finish the bottle if you like. But Johnny, dear, what is wrong? You seem to be fright-fully upset about something. Won't you tell me what it is; then perhaps we'll find some way in which I can help you.'

That was typical of Ankaret and the sort of thing that, despite her faults, made her so lovable. No woman could conceivably have had more on her mind than she had at the moment, yet she would not allow it to prevent her trying to comfort a friend who was in trouble.

Johnny helped himself again, gave her rather a shame-faced look, and said: 'Well, I haven't exactly quarrelled with Sue but I've had one hell of a row with her father.'

'What about?' Ankaret enquired.

He passed a hand worriedly over his fair, rather rebellious, hair. 'It arose out of the Board Meeting that we held this afternoon. Giff sprang a pretty startling piece of policy on us, and in support of it he produced a mass of facts and figures

103

connected with Defence. After dinner, over the port, the Admiral tackled me about it, and as good as accused me of having put Giff up to this idea then briefed him for the meeting.'

'And you hadn't?'

Johnny's blue eyes opened wide. 'Good Lord, no! This stuff is dynamite—Top Secret and known only to a few dozen people outside the high-ups. But the devil of it is that I might have, because as a member of the Joint Planning Staff I am one of those few dozen. It's our job to do the spade-work for the Chiefs of Staff, so we have to be in on all their secrets.'

'Where did Giff get it, then?'

'I haven't a notion. There must have been a colossal leak somewhere; and to let half the things he said out of the bag would mean cashiering if it could be brought home to whoever did brief him. It is owing to the field being such a narrow one that makes the Admiral suspect me; and the old boy was hopping mad about it.'

Ankaret nodded. 'One can hardly be surprised about that, seeing that if Giff's proposal was adopted it might lead to the dissolution of the Navy.'

'You know what took place at the Board Meeting, then?' Johnny said, raising his eyebrows.

'Yes. Giff told me about it before dinner.'

'Then you'll appreciate what a jam I'm in with the Admiral. He knows that, whether I briefed Giff or not, as an airman I am one hundred per cent behind what he plans to do. To the old boy that is little better than High Treason. After saying that he had half a mind to put the Security people on to enquiring into my reliability, he ordered me out of the house and forbade me ever to enter it again.'

'Poor you. What rotten luck,' said Ankaret sympathetically. 'Does Sue know about this yet?'

'Yes. Before leaving I collected her and we went out and sat in my car. We spent well over an hour together while I tried to explain matters. She accepted my word for it that I knew nothing of Giff's intentions, but the Navy means nearly as much to her as it does to her old man; so she took mighty badly my admission that I would help to get it scrapped if I could. She just wouldn't listen to reason, and before we parted she told me that she would prefer not to see me again until I was willing to leave Navy matters to men like her father, who understood them.'

'Don't worry too much,' Ankaret endeavoured to console him. 'That she believes you is what really matters. The woman isn't born yet who would sacrifice her lover for a question of strategy. I'm sure she'll come round before long. Anyhow, you can talk it over with . . .'

I felt sure that now submerged in his problem her mind had temporarily blacked out about the events of the past two hours, and that she had been about to say 'talk it over with Giff in the morning'. As it was she suddenly went deathly white and substituted '. . . we can talk it over again tomorrow.'

Fortunately he was once more staring unhappily at his feet, so he did not see the blood drain from her face; but when she added quickly: 'Now, what about getting to bed,' he looked up again, and replied:

'If you don't mind, I'd rather accept your offer of a third noggin of Scotch, and sit here for a while. I want to try to think out if there is not some way by which, without letting my side down, I could patch matters up with old Waldron.'

Ankaret glanced at the locked desk. It was evident to me that she was most reluctant to leave the room without retrieving the evidence of her forgery; but I could also see that she was just about all in. Forcing a smile, she said: 'Good night' to Johnny and walked through the drawing-room to the hall.

There she took the forged letter from her pocket and looked about her uncertainly. Perhaps she had momentarily forgotten the original plan to put it in the pocket of my smoking jacket and leave that, as though I had thrown it off before jumping into the water, on the end of the pier. Or perhaps she decided that with Johnny about it was too great a risk for her to leave the house again. Anyhow, after a moment's hesitation she walked to the front door and put the letter in the letter-box.

Slowly and wearily she went upstairs. On the landing she paused for a moment to stare at the closed door leading to the laboratory; but she did not go in to collect my jacket, and had she done so I hardly know where she could have left it to better advantage, short of taking it down to the pier. After all, I would not have been likely to have thrown it off in the house before going out to commit suicide, but I just might have done so before attacking Evans.

At last the terrible strain that Ankaret had been through was taking its toll of her. The effort required to appear normal during her ten minutes' talk with Johnny, had exhausted her last reserves of will-power and control. Within a few moments her face had become drawn and haggard. Her steps were faltering as she reached her room and closed the door behind her. Still fully dressed she flung herself face down on the bed. For a while she remained silent and motionless. Then she stretched up a hand and switched out the light; but the blessed forgetfulness of sleep was as yet a long way from being granted to her. In an agony of distress she moaned:

'Oh Giff, darling Giff; what shall I do without you?' And after that anguished cry she began to choke with such awful rending sobs as one could expect to hear only from a woman whose heart is broken.

My own heart, or rather its spiritual counterpart, was so wrung that, since I was debarred from comforting her, I could not bear to remain in the room any longer. Withdrawing from it I passed downstairs and through the garden door out into the night.

At last I was alone. Now that the actions of others, fraught with such potent possibilities, and anxious speculations about the way their minds were working, no longer fully occupied my attention, I had become free to consider my own situation.

There could be no escaping the fact that I was dead, and although a witness to all that had passed, a silent and unseen one. There was no way in which I could help Ankaret during the ordeal which she must still go through when the deaths of myself and Evans were discovered. I could only pray for her. I now had no more power to influence the lives of the living than the stones of the terrace a few feet above which I floated; yet for some reason that I had no means of guessing, apart from the fact that I no longer had a body, I felt no more dead than I had two hours before.

The moon was now up and by it I could see the silent prospect of the Solent as clearly as if I had still been living. Like most people, I had always assumed that to die was to solve the great mystery, yet to me death had so far revealed nothing. All the same, I found it impossible to believe that I should continue in my present state for long; and as I heard the grandfather clock in the hall strike midnight, I wondered a little grimly what strange experience the new day would hold for me.

5

Saturday 10th September

In the Age of Faith, when religion played a major part in
everybody's life, and a belief in the powers of saints and
devils was accepted as naturally as the fact of life itself,
ninety-nine people out of every hundred had fixed convictions
about death. They accepted without question the teaching
that at the moment of dissolution their souls were either
carried triumphantly away by waiting angels or dragged off
to eternal torment by remorseless fiends. In consequence those
who led godly lives could meet their end with complacency
and sinners generally had the opportunity of making a death-
bed repentance which enabled them to rely with some
confidence on forgiveness and mercy.

But, apart from the few who still faithfully follow the
Christian precepts, the Age of Reason has deprived us of this
happy certainty of our fate in the hereafter. Even so, the idea
has become pretty generally accepted that while we need no
longer fear hell-fire, and that punishment for our short-
comings will probably be no more drastic than having to suffer
a certain period of distressing remorse, our personalities will
continue after death and we shall be received on the other
side by loved ones who have preceded us.

I was, of course, brought up in the Christian faith, but from
the time of leaving school had never been a regular church-
goer and, like most men of this bustling, highly competitive
modern age, had given little thought to religion. In consequence, had I been told the previous morning that I was
to die that night I should certainly not have expected to be
wafted away either by angels or devils; but I should have
expected somebody or some power to do something about me.
Could I have reconciled myself to being so suddenly snatched
from those I loved on earth, I think I might even have looked
forward to death as a great adventure, and I should certainly

have counted on meeting again friends who had gone before me.

Yet here I was, a ghost—even if an invisible one—a wraith, a spirit, utterly alone, with no means of communicating with either the living or the dead, and no indication whatever that I might shortly be taken care of.

It was a most unhappy situation and there came into my mind a frightening thought. What if the God in whom I had been taught to believe at my mother's knee watched over only those who proved faithful to Him? As I had abandoned Him perhaps He had abandoned me, and I was condemned to wander the earth alone until some far distant day when there was a final judgement. Such a possibility was utterly appalling.

Bordering on panic, I took refuge in the Christian teaching that the Mercy of God was infinite. Although I could lay no claim to having led a saintly life mine had certainly not been an evil one. My neglect of religion was not a sin of commission but omission; so surely He would not inflict such a drastic punishment upon me.

Yet of that hope I was promptly robbed by the beliefs I had formed since becoming adult. It had seemed to me highly questionable that the Christian teaching was a reliable guide to the hereafter. What of the millions who placed their faith in Mahomet and Krishna? And to me, the impersonal philosophies of the Buddhists and Confucians appeared much more plausible. Admittedly I had never thought about the matter really seriously, but I had more or less subconsciously come to the conclusion that God in the image of Man did not exist at all, and that the affairs of mankind were directed by some remote power, who left it to each individual to create his own place in some future existence.

Again I was chilled by the possibility that I had been right; for, if so, I could not hope to be pardoned and rescued by a merciful God who was aware of all things, even to the fall of a sparrow; but must somehow work out my own salvation, despite the fact that I had not the faintest idea how to set about it.

One comforting thought came to me; there must be countless thousands of people in the same boat as myself. In Europe and America and in every part of the world in which

109

white communities of some size were established people must be dying every minute; and a high proportion of them, although brought up as Christians, must have died with the same lack of positive faith in the Church's teachings as I had. Therefore it could be only a matter of hours before I should meet some kindred spirit in a like state of puzzlement who, for lack of a better phrase, had also recently 'passed over'.

That theory seemed sound and reassuring until I suddenly remembered that I had actually been present at Evans's death. Although I had never discussed these matters with him, at odd times during general conversations he had let drop enough for me to be quite certain that he was an agnostic. That being the case, our spirits should have had enough in common to meet with more or less similar treatment in the 'great beyond'.

Therefore it was only reasonable to suppose that as his left his body he would have been aware of my presence, and that I should have realised that he too, although now invisible, was still in the lab and also watching with the keenest interest what Ankaret would do next. The different backgrounds which had given us so little in common while alive, and even any antipathy we felt for one another owing to each of us, in a sense, having been the cause of the other's death, should surely have been submerged in mutual concern for our futures, and an instinctive urge to get together and compare notes about our sensations.

But nothing of that kind had occurred. When Ankaret had finished with Evans I had regarded him only as a repulsive and bloody mess. Not a whisper, or even a thought, had impinged on my consciousness to suggest his spritual survival and arrival on this same 'plane' as myself. And that having been so in the case of a person with whom I was at least well acquainted, there did not seem any great hope that I would shortly run into some elderly person who had just died in a neighbouring village, or one of the several people who during the past twenty-four hours must have given up the ghost in so large a city as Southampton.

While I was gloomily pondering this—no doubt because certain terms used by spiritualists, such as 'passed over' and the 'great beyond', had recently drifted through my mind—

another idea occurred to me. From the little I had read of such matters, most occultists were of the opinion that on leaving the body a spirit rarely sped direct to its new field of activity. Some even failed for a time to comprehend fully that they were dead, while the majority were still so deeply concerned with the people or projects and possessions that they had left behind that, for varying periods, they remained earthbound. The period, according to this belief, depended on the strength of the emotional ties, and it was only when these had weakened to a point at which the craving of the spirit for fresh interests submerged the old ones that it could move onward to a higher sphere.

Unquestionably from the moment of my own death until midnight I had been entirely absorbed by happenings connected with my past life; so there seemed fair grounds for supposing that the reason why I had so far made no contact with the spirit world was because I was still earthbound. At least such a premise had logic to recommend it, and with a slightly more optimistic outlook I began to contemplate its implications.

For Ankaret and Johnny I could do nothing; so, should I have the ability to leave their vicinity, there was really no point in remaining longer in it. On the other hand, my love for her and affection for him still filled me with deep concern for their future. Before 'going on' I was most anxious to know if she would escape being implicated in the crimes committed at Longshot Hall that night, and if he would succeed in persuading Admiral Waldron of his innocence concerning the leakage of those Top Secret matters to which I had been made privy by Sir Charles.

Personally, I have never believed in the old adage that 'one cannot have one's cake and eat it'. Like most successful men, by the tactful handling of affairs I have, on most occasions during my life, succeeded in deriving benefit and enjoyment from the things I won without having to surrender them later. Now my personality having in no way altered on account of the loss of my body, I saw no reason why I should not attempt—literally in this case—to have the best of both worlds.

Tomorrow, unless prevented by some cosmic law that was still outside my comprehension, I would return to Longshot Hall and again become a silent witness of all that took place

111

there. But the night was still young; and during it I would do my utmost to leave earth and penetrate the higher plane of existence on which I now felt that a future of some kind must be awaiting me.

Since I was no longer subject to the physical limitations imposed by a body, my first thought was to make my way towards the stars. Willing myself to rise, I managed to force my consciousness up to the level of the roof of the house; but there the effort to ascend further proved such an intolerable strain that I had to give up and on abandoning the attempt I slowly sank back to my previous level, some six feet above the terrace.

Considerably disappointed in the result of my first experiment, I next decided to see how fast I could move, and facing in the direction of the beach I set off towards it. The sensation of progressing in long swift bounds was an extremely pleasant one, but I soon found that I was not going much faster than a fast run; and when I pulled up on the shore I was conscious of a definite sense of fatigue. It was not breathlessness, for I had no lungs, but I knew instinctively that I could not have kept up that pace for very much longer, and several minutes elapsed before I felt up to trying anything else.

While I remained stationary, just above the tide-mark, to recover, it occurred to me that it would be interesting to find out what would happen if I advanced towards Cowes. I thought it probable that I should be able to move over water as easily as I could over dry land. It also seemed possible that I might be able to rove about under the surface as though I were wearing a diver's helmet, and the prospect of exploring the sea-bottom at my leisure intrigued me greatly. In any case it was quite certain that I could not drown, so I once more projected myself forward.

Within two minutes of leaving the shore I found that neither of my ideas had been correct. As I crossed the shallows, bound by bound, I sank lower until the essential 'me' had dropped to within a little less than a foot above the water; but at that level it remained until I forced it under, and then, when the effort to keep it there was exhausted, it bobbed up again.

On metaphorically 'plunging in' I was not conscious of

any change of temperature, or pressure from the water, but my movement was slowed down to the sort of pace I would have maintained had I been swimming, although I was not consciously using my invisible arms and legs, and my range of vision was now limited to that of a bather with his head just above water.

For a time I drifted about, then I again became aware of a sense of fatigue; so I returned to the shore and went up to the beach house. As long as it was warm enough to bathe we always left several lounge chairs out on its veranda and, instinctively, I performed the equivalent of first sitting, then lying down, in one of them.

There seemed no other experiments I could try, so my thoughts turned again to Ankaret and the shattering events of the past few hours. Gradually my mind became hazy, and before I realised what was happening my consciousness had faded out.

*   *   *   *

When I became conscious again it was morning. The sun was well up, lighting the familiar scene and sparkling on the wavelets. I heard a slight noise nearby and saw Johnny throw off his bathing robe on to one of the other chairs. It must have been his arrival that had roused me.

He was a fine figure of a man, tall and well set up, his body marred only by a long scar across the ribs where a Malayan bandit had sniped him. His resemblance to my father was much closer than my own, but his fair, slightly wavy, hair had come from the other side of his family. It was not surprising that his looks and physique, coupled with a rather reserved manner, made him very attractive to women; though as far as I knew he had never had any really serious affairs until he met Sue Waldron.

The thought that I had unwillingly been the cause of their quarrel distressed me very much. Had I only been permitted to have lived for another day I could have gone to the Admiral and given him my personal assurance that Johnny had no more to do with the proposal I put before the Board that afternoon than he had. And that was the real crux of the matter. Old Waldron was too honest a man to endeavour to prevent Johnny acting in accordance with his convictions. His resentment was due to his belief that Johnny had made an unscrupulous use of secret information in an attempt to put a fast one over on the Navy. Sue's attitude sprang entirely from sentiment, and I felt sure that it needed only an assurance from her father that Johnny was doing his duty as he saw it to bring her round. But now there was nothing I could do about it. I could only hope that Sue's feelings for him would get the better of her very natural championship of the Service which she had been brought up to regard as the pride and shield of Britain.

Johnny waded into the water and when up to his waist flung himself into a crawl with such powerful strokes that he was soon nearly a quarter of a mile away from me. He had just passed a miniature cape that juts out a little way from the regular curve of the beach when, somewhat to my surprise, instead of turning and coming back he swam towards the land and splashed his way ashore. For a moment he stood there bending over something, then he straightened up and set off at a run towards the house. Not having moved from the veranda I could not see what it was that he had found, but it flashed upon me that it might be my body. Moving swiftly in that direction I saw that I was right.

The tide was ebbing when Evans and Ankaret threw my corpse from the pier-head; so it had drifted only a few hundred yards, then caught on the spit of sand and been left just awash in the shallows. It was lying face upwards and while I cannot say I found its appearance pleasing, it was by no means as ugly a sight as I had expected. The eyes were wide and staring, the teeth clenched and the cheeks ruddy from congestion, but so far there were no signs of decomposition having set in.

Some minutes later Johnny reappeared with old Silvers and they came hurrying down to the place where the body lay. I could see that both of them were badly shaken and they exchanged only a few gruff sentences, mainly expressing their distress and complete puzzlement about how I could have met my death and been washed up on the beach in this way. Johnny then tried artificial respiration, but on realising the futility of his attempt gave it up.

It was he who suggested that my body should be put in the beach house—anyhow for the time being—as there would be less likelihood of Ankaret seeing them while they carried it there, should she be up and chance to look out of her bedroom window, than if they carried it all the way to the house.

The water-sodden clothes made it even heavier than it had been the previous night; so after staggering about fifty yards with it they had to put it down. But Silvers produced the bright idea that if they used a lounge chair as a stretcher that would make the job much easier, and after he had fetched one from the beach house they managed the remaining distance without having to take a rest. When they had laid the body on a sofa in the main room of the little pavilion they covered it with the table-cloth, then went up to the house. I accompanied them, now once more entirely absorbed in the drama of which my body was the focal point.

Silvers gave Johnny the number of Dr. Culver, our local G.P., and he telephoned to him to come at once; then, wisely circumventing the village constable, he reported the tragedy to police headquarters at Southampton. Meanwhile Silvers had collected the morning's post from the box and having looked through it said:

'There is a letter here, Sir, in the master's writing for Her Ladyship. It isn't stamped; so he must have put it in the box himself.'

Johnny took it with a frown. 'That's very queer. Surely his death can't have been anything but an accident. Yet he would hardly have left a letter for her like this unless he was going out for some special purpose and feared he might not come back. All right, Silvers, I'll take it up with me when I break the news to her. Do you know if she is awake?'

'I expect so, Sir.' Silvers glanced at the grandfather clock, which showed it to be just after half-past eight. 'Mrs. Silvers will be getting Her Ladyship's breakfast ready now. She has it in bed at a quarter to nine, and she is usually awake when Mildred takes in her tray.'

'You had better tell Mildred to stay put for a bit, then. I must get some clothes on, and I don't want her to butt in with breakfast just as I am breaking the news to her Ladyship.'

'Very good, Sir. And I'll tell Mrs. Silvers what has happened. We were both very attached to the master and I'm sure she will be terribly upset.'

As Silvers turned away Johnny walked through to the room that he always occupied when staying with us. It was one of those on the ground floor of the old bachelors' wing, the upper floor of which I had converted into a laboratory, for Evans. As quickly as he could he shaved and dressed, then, his face showing his reluctance to tackle the distasteful task before him, he went upstairs to Ankaret's room. In response to his knock, she called: 'Come in.'

She had, as usual by that hour, brushed her teeth and tidied her hair, and she was sitting up in bed with an open book on her lap. There were dark shadows under her grey eyes but otherwise she looked quite normal, and although she must have guessed that only the discovery of my death, or that of Evans's, could have brought Johnny up there, her voice was quite steady as she greeted him.

'Why, hello Johnny. I thought it was Mildred with my breakfast. You must be terribly steamed up about your row with Sue, if you couldn't wait till Giff gets downstairs to ask him to try to straighten things out for you with the Admiral. But the Prof must have kept Giff up so late that to avoid waking me he slept in his dressing-room. Go in and rouse him out.'

Ignoring her gesture towards the door leading to my dressing-room Johnny replied: 'I wish I could; but he's not there.'

'Not there!' she echoed. 'But he must be. He hasn't come through to have his bath yet. Unless—yes—he may have gone down for an early swim.'

'I'm afraid that's what he has done. At least . . .' Johnny hesitated, baulking unhappily at having to tell her the worst. But, seeing his evident emotion, she quickly took him up:

'Afraid! Why are you afraid?'

Johnny held out the letter to her. 'Giff went out during the night, fully dressed except for his smoking jacket. But he left this letter for you. Perhaps it may explain things.'

Taking the letter she ripped it open and appeared to run her eye swiftly over its contents. Then she dropped it, gave a

116

low cry and throwing herself sideways buried her face in the pillows.

Moving a step nearer to the bed, Johnny said softly: 'My dear. It's too frightful, I simply don't know what to say. I shall miss him terribly too. He was much more to me than an Uncle.'

Raising herself on one elbow, but still keeping her face turned away from him, she cried: 'It can't be true! It can't be true!'

'I'm afraid it is. It was I who found him. I went down for a swim and I hadn't been in the water more than a few minutes when I caught sight of his body. It had been washed up on that little point just below the place where the wood starts. I thought at first that he must have gone on to the landing-stage for something, then slipped and stunned himself as he fell in. But this letter . . .' Johnny hesitated again. 'His leaving it for you suggests that he knew he was going out to meet trouble. I didn't think Giff had an enemy in the world. By God, though, if someone did him in I'll see to it that they swing for it.'

'No, it wasn't that.' Ankaret suddenly turned and faced him. 'He took his own life. And it was my fault. I've been incredibly wicked and stupid. But I didn't mean any harm. I swear I didn't!'

While receiving the news she had put over a good act, and now she needed to act no longer. Her cry of self-accusation was genuine and it was perfectly natural that she should give free rein to her grief.

'D'you mean he committed suicide!' Johnny exclaimed. 'I'd never have believed it. Giff wasn't that sort of man.'

'He did,' she asserted, picking up the letter and offering it to him. 'You had better read this. It's all bound to come out sooner or later. Oh what can have possessed me to play the fool with Owen! Heaven knows, it was all innocent enough.'

Johnny began to read the letter but as he turned to the second page his eyes popped, and he exclaimed: 'God alive! Then the Prof's dead, too! Giff says here that he killed him. What a ghastly mess!'

Ankaret was now sitting up but her head was bowed and she had covered her face with her hands. 'Serve him right,'

117

she muttered angrily through her fingers. 'All this is as much his fault as it is mine; in fact more. Even if I did encourage him to flirt with me while I was bored with convalescing after my accident, I gave him no cause to boast about it. I don't wonder Giff was furious. But he should have known me better than to believe that I'd ever fall for anyone like the Prof. Oh what am I to do?'

'I'm afraid there is nothing you can do,' replied Johnny a little shortly. 'You had best stay here and let me take charge of everything.' He had finished reading the letter, and added: 'I think, too, that I'd better hang on to this. Showing it to the police right away may save a lot of trouble later. If we put all the cards on the table they'll treat what we say as in confidence and be much more discreet.'

'I won't see the police! I couldn't bear it,' Ankaret declared, still speaking through her fingers. 'I haven't got to, have I? The thought of Giff being . . . being gone is enough to drive me crazy, without having to submit to an inquisition by a lot of ghoulish strangers.'

Johnny's attitude had perceptibly hardened. As he put the letter in his pocket he said: 'Now that murder comes into the affair as well as suicide, I think it's pretty certain that the police will require a statement from you. But I'm sure they'll give you a chance to recover from the shock, and not insist on seeing you today. Anyhow, I'll do my best to head them off.'

She gave a great sigh, and murmured: 'Thank you, Johnny. I can't realise it yet. Please go now. I . . . I want to be left alone.'

Showing no reluctance, Johnny left the room, and hurried across the landing to the lab. As I entered it in his wake I saw at once that Evans had moved since I had last been there. He had managed to crawl a few feet towards the door; so he could not have been quite dead when Ankaret left him. But he was dead now. That was made clear by the way that Johnny, after kneeling for a moment to feel his heart, made an ugly grimace, stood up and walked out locking the door behind him.

As he went downstairs, Silvers was letting Dr. Culver in at the front door. Culver was a red-faced, middle-aged, rather untidy little man and far from being a shining light in his

118

profession. But he was quite sound about simple ills, he was our nearest G.P. and he and his father before him had looked after the family, so it had never even occurred to me to make a change.

Johnny introduced himself and in a few brief sentences gave the doctor a résumé of what had occurred. Culver blinked hard behind his pince-nez, muttered: 'Terrible; terrible!' several times, then accompanied Johnny up to the lab. After a cursory examination of Evans's body the doctor declared:

'Been dead several hours I should say. Judging by the degree of rigor mortis he probably died between three and five o'clock this morning. But one can't be at all certain without a more thorough examination, and I don't want to disturb the body any further before the police have seen it. Dear, dear! Poor fellow! He must have suffered a lot before he died. Please take me to Sir Gifford now.'

Down at the beach house he again made only a cursory examination. 'Heart. Could have been shock, but I suppose those tablets you tell me he swallowed killed him. Pity you've no idea what they were. But that is really immaterial. They must have been pretty potent and given him a heart attack within a few minutes of diving into the water. I should have thought that in his case rigor mortis would have been more advanced; it is hardly perceptible as yet. That is probably explained by the water still having the warmth it acquired during the summer.

'Well, there is no mystery for the police to solve here. That letter he left makes the whole affair only too distressingly transparent. I don't think they will worry you unduly. Where there is no question of bringing a criminal to justice they are generally very good about keeping private tragedies as quiet as they can. And it is not for them or us to attempt to assess Lady Ankaret's degree of responsibility. Women cannot be judged by the same standards as men. They are much more apt to become dominated by their emotions than is the case with our sex. I think I had better see her though, if only so that I can protect her from being badgered into making a statement before she has recovered from the shock. I expect, too, she will need a sedative, so I'll leave her a few of the pills I carry in my bag, until she can get some more made up.'

As I listened, I blessed the little man for his unquestioning acceptance of the situation at its face value, and his kindly consideration for Ankaret. Curiously enough it was not until he was walking back to the house with Johnny that I recalled once having helped him when in serious trouble.

His son, while a student at the London School of Medicine, had knocked down with his car, and killed, a child. In addition to the charge of manslaughter the police added one of dangerous driving, and as he had just left a cocktail party there was more than a suspicion that he had had one too many to drink.

For the defence it could be argued that it was twilight at the time, that the child had run out from behind a coffee stall, that the young man had a clean licence, and that he was habitually a sober type. But it was the sort of case in which if things went against the accused he was likely to get a really nasty sentence; so everything might hang on securing a tip-top barrister to defend him.

Culver's father had left him nothing but his practice and the small family property; so he could not possibly lay his hands on the thousand pounds needed to brief a leading K.C. to fight his boy's case. In his extremity he came to me. All he could offer as security for the loan was his practice and a promise to pay me back at the rate of two hundred a year; but knowing the modest circumstances in which he lived I felt that even that would prove a heavy burden on him. In consequence, I suggested that instead I should buy the field that adjoined his garden and a piece of woodland beyond it that he also owned. I didn't really want them, and he had the honesty to point out that they weren't worth the sum he needed. But his family had looked after mine for three generations, and the few hundreds capital I might drop meant no great sacrifice to me; so I eased his conscience by saying that when the Socialists were out the land might increase in value as a building site, and paid him the thousand for it.

In due course I had the satisfaction of learning that the money had not been wasted, as the boy escaped a prison sentence and later took his M.D. Having been occupied since with so many affairs the matter had slipped into the background of my mind; but now that it came back to me, I felt that if little Culver owed me anything he had, if unconsciously, now handsomely repaid it.

On reaching the house Culver went up to see Ankaret, while Johnny walked through the drawing-room to my library. Not wishing again to see Ankaret torn between the necessity to lie and her genuine grief, I followed the latter. Although it was only just half-past nine I assumed that, seeing what he had been through, he felt that he must get himself a drink; but I was wrong.

In the doorway he paused for a minute while he took a careful look round. Silvers, having been otherwise occupied, had not yet cleared up there so the glasses that Johnny and Ankaret had used were still on the bow-fronted cabinet in which the drinks were kept. Walking over to it he picked up Ankaret's glass, sniffed at it, and ascertained what it had contained by tasting the few drops that remained in it. He then went across to the desk and finding it locked stood there staring at it thoughtfully.

I watched him with considerable anxiety as it was evident that his suspicions had been aroused by something, although on what lines his mind was working I could not guess. But at that moment both his thoughts and mine were distracted by Silvers appearing in the doorway and saying:

'The police have just arrived, Sir.'

Hurrying out to the hall, Johnny greeted the two plain-clothes officers who stood there. The taller, a dark-haired sad-faced man, introduced himself as Inspector Mallet, and his younger, brisker-looking companion as Sergeant Haines. Then he said:

'I understand, Sir, that you reported an accidental death as having taken place here. I trust there are no grounds for supposing it to have been anything else, and that we shan't have to trouble you with our presence for long. Perhaps you would be good enough to give me particulars.'

Johnny made a wry grimace. 'Since I telephoned, Inspector, we have discovered that this is an even more terrible affair than I supposed. Apparently my uncle, Sir Gifford Hillary, had a quarrel with Professor Evans who was employed by him here, killed him, and then committed suicide.'

'That certainly is a terrible business,' the sad-faced Inspector agreed; and turning to his subordinate he added: 'You had better telephone for the squad, Jim.'

As the Sergeant went over to the instrument in the hall,

the Inspector asked: 'Who discovered the bodies, Sir?'

'I did,' Johnny told him.

'Then when the Sergeant's done, we had better take a look at them.'

Taking matters in their proper order, Johnny first led them down to the beach house. On the way he described how he had found my body, then said that Dr. Culver had already examined it and given the opinion that I had not died by drowning but owing to a heart-attack caused by some pills that I had taken just before throwing myself into the water.

The Inspector nodded. 'If Dr. Culver says that I don't doubt the police surgeon will agree with him. I've known him since I was a youngster on the beat, and I don't remember him ever having been proved wrong when giving evidence in a court case.'

His statement cheered me as I had feared that they might do an autopsy, in which case it would have emerged that I had not died as the result of an overdose of a dangerous drug, and the whole of Ankaret's cleverly thought out way of explaining my death would be brought into question. But it looked now as if there was a good chance of her clearing that dangerous hurdle.

After viewing my body, they returned to the house and went up to the laboratory. About the way in which Evans had met his death there could be no doubt whatever. His battered head and face told their own story, and nearby lay the steel rod with congealed blood and a few of his dark hairs still on it.

Pointing at it the Sergeant remarked: 'There's the instrument, all right; and it's probably smothered with Sir Gifford's fingerprints. When we are faced with having to find out who done it we don't often get a lead like that; yet here we're given it on a plate in a case that is plain sailing.'

'Maybe it's plain sailing, maybe not. Can't be certain as yet,' replied the Inspector with the caution bred of long habit. Then turning to Johnny, he asked: 'Have you any idea why they quarrelled, Sir?'

Johnny drew the letter from his pocket and handed it over. 'Sir Gifford left that in the hall letter-box before he went out to his death. It was found there this morning with the rest

122

of the post. I took it up to Lady Ankaret when I broke the news to her about her husband's death. When she had read it, she gave it to me. That is how I learned that Professor Evans was dead too. Naturally, the family will be most anxious to avoid a scandal. But I'm sure you gentlemen would soon uncover the truth, and that my showing you this right away will save everyone a lot of unpleasantness. I should be very grateful, though, if you would treat the matter with as much discretion as possible.'

Before replying, the Inspector read the letter, then handed it on to his colleague, and said to Johnny: 'Thank you, Sir. We always try to show our appreciation when people are frank with us, and this has saved us having to scratch our heads about a motive. In fact it seems to give us the whole unhappy story in a nutshell. I am afraid it will have to be put in as evidence at the inquest, but we can arrange to have it shown only to those concerned instead of read aloud. And, of course, your having produced it is going to make it unnecessary for the coroner to ask Lady Ankaret a number of embarrassing questions.'

On Johnny's face I could see the relief he felt at having done the right thing. Quite unwittingly, too, he had done exactly as Ankaret had wanted him to, by establishing her own story from the outset in the minds of the police. Inspector Mallet asked him:

'Were you, by any chance, aware, Sir, that Her Ladyship was having this affair with Professor Evans?'

Johnny promptly replied that he had not the least idea of it.

The Inspector shrugged. 'Ah well, I don't doubt the servants knew all about it; they are usually pretty quick at spotting anything of that sort that's going on. We may as well get downstairs now, and I'll take a few notes about the occupants of the household. Sorry to bother you, Sir, but we have to do that as part of the routine.'

All three of them spent the best part of the next hour in the drawing-room. There was one interruption owing to the arrival of the second police car from Southampton. It brought the police surgeon, a photographer, a finger-print man, and two constables in uniform. The Inspector told them where they would find the bodies and gave them the O.K. to go ahead; then he returned to his own business, which was asking Johnny a lot of apparently irrelevant questions while Sergeant Haines wrote down the replies.

I left them to it after the other police arrived, as I was much more concerned with what view the police surgeon might take of my body than with anything else.

Dr. Culver had waited to have a word with him; fortunately, he was both a youngish man and of the type that still shows some respect for its elders. Having invited Culver to view the two bodies with him, after making only a superficial check-up he accepted the older practitioner's opinion about them.

Later it was agreed with Mallet that the double inquest should be held on Monday morning at eleven o'clock, and the Inspector said that he hoped Lady Ankaret would then be sufficiently recovered to give evidence if the Coroner wished her to be called.

Culver replied that she might be, but he could not guarantee it. Then when the letter was mentioned it transpired that she had told him about it and its contents, and he proceeded to urge that as she could contribute nothing new to the enquiry, she should be spared the ordeal of having to appear at the inquest. Mallet said that he would not press for that if she was willing to make a statement to the police beforehand. Culver then promised that he would try to persuade her to do so, providing he considered her condition satisfactory.

These matters being settled, Culver told Johnny that he had given Ankaret a strong sedative and that for the next few hours she should not be disturbed. He added that when she asked for food she should be given only a light meal, and that he would come in again that evening.

What with Ankaret, Dr. Culver and the police, Johnny had not yet had a moment to attend to any other matters, let alone have any breakfast; but as soon as he had seen the doctor off, the thoughtful Silvers approached him and said:

'I've put some sandwiches in the dining-room for you, Sir, and half a bottle of champagne. It's past eleven o'clock, and with all the things you are having to attend to I felt that you really ought to have something to keep you going.'

Johnny smiled at the old boy appreciatively. 'Jolly good of

124

you, Silvers. This business seems to have robbed me of my appetite, but I could do with a glass of wine. First, though, I must telephone to Mr. Compton.'

Having got through to the office Johnny broke the news to James, then asked if he could tell him where Bill Wiltshire was staying for the week-end. I gathered that James did not know, but said that he would try to find out, and announced his intention of driving over to Longshot within the next hour or so. Johnny then went into the dining-room, ate some of the sandwiches and knocked back the pint of Louis Roederer '45.

He was still sitting there when the sad-faced Mallet came in to tell him that he had finished questioning the staff. He added that it had been only a formality and that none of them had heard anything during the night or been able to tell him anything beyond what he knew already; so there would now be no objection to Johnny calling in an undertaker to lay out the bodies, subject, of course, to their not being removed to a mortuary, so that they would be available for viewing by the Coroner's court when it met at the house on Monday.

At midday James Compton arrived. On his way he had picked up Eddie Arnold, my solicitor. Eddie was also a personal friend of mine of long standing, as we had joined the R.A.F. on the same day and done our training together. Johnny gave them particulars of what had happened, then the three of them held a gloom session during which I could not help being moved by the nice things they said of me and their sorrow that death had taken me from them.

When they got down to business it transpired that James had had notices issued cancelling the Board Meeting that had been arranged for Monday, and that his secretary had managed to trace Bill Wiltshire. The house at which Bill was staying for a week-end's shooting was near Winchester; so he could be expected to turn up sometime during the afternoon.

Eddie then said to Johnny: 'As you probably know, when old Hugo Wittling died last year Giff appointed you an executor and trustee in his place; the other is James here. May I take it that you are both agreeable to act?'

Their both having agreed, he went on:

125

'I haven't yet had a chance to turn up Giff's last will, but I can remember its principal provisions. He made it at the time of his marriage to Ankaret. She will have the enjoyment for life of both Longshot Hall and the income on his shares in Hillary-Comptons, after the present allowances have been paid out of it to his first wife and her children. Fortunately he had the forethought to insure against death duties, so Ankaret should still be in a position to keep the place up. It is fortunate, too, as far as the Company is concerned; for it means that the Board will not have to find a buyer for a large part of his holding, and they would have otherwise, as apart from that his estate will amount only to a few thousands. On Ankaret's death his boy, Harold, comes into the place and the Hillary-Compton shares, subject to certain provisions for his mother and sister, if still living. He is also the principal beneficiary, and will get such money as there is to come now after the legacies have been paid out. I can't recall details of them for the moment, but they were the usual sort of thing to old friends and servants, and I don't think their total was more than about fifteen hundred pounds.'

After a moment, he added: 'The will contains one rather unusual direction, though. Giff always had a terror that he might be buried alive. He told me that it originated in his having read while still a youngster an account of the removal of several hundred bodies from the Père La Chais cemetery in Paris. They wanted to run a railway embankment or something over that corner of the cemetery. Anyhow, when they dug up the half-rotted coffins they found to their horror that a score or more of the corpses had bent knees and raised hands with broken nails, showing that they had been buried while in a coma, and on coming round had striven to force their way out. I tried to persuade Giff to be cremated but he didn't like the idea. So he stipulated in his will that there should be no lead coffin, that the lid of the wooden one should not be screwed down, that air holes should be bored in its ends, and that the family grave, which consists of a brick vault, should not be closed down until seven days after his coffin had been lowered into it.'

Johnny gave a little shudder. 'What ghastly thoughts the discovery of those twisted bodies in the Père La Chaise cemetery conjures up.'

126

'I think most of them had been buried for over a century,' Eddie replied, 'and medical science has advanced so much since then that there is little chance of that sort of thing happening now. All the same, we must see to it that Giff's wishes are carried out.'

'The police have given us the O.K. to have the bodies prepared for burial,' Johnny informed him, 'but I haven't yet done anything about it, because I don't know the name of the family undertaker.'

'I can give you that,' volunteered James. 'I'll look up the number and ring them up myself.'

When he had done so, he and Eddie had a mournful drink with Johnny, then went out to their car to drive back to Southampton.

The next visitor was a reporter from a Southampton paper, who had somehow got on to the affair; but apart from a bare admission that Evans and I had died the previous night, Johnny refused to give him any information. In anticipation of being further importuned by the press, Johnny went into the drawing-room and had a word with Mallet, who was busily writing his report there. At his request the Inspector promised to give the uniformed constable posted on the front door orders that no press-men were to be admitted or allowed to question the servants.

As Johnny came out into the hall Silvers appeared to announce that lunch was ready and apologise that it would be cold, owing to Mrs. Silvers being too upset to cook anything. Johnny said he quite understood, and asked that trays should be sent in to the Inspector and the Sergeant; then, with his thoughts evidently on other matters, he munched his way through the food that had been set out for him. He was just finishing one of my beautiful Triomphe de Vienne pears with a most distressing lack of appreciation when Silvers came in to tell him that Mr. Fisher, the undertaker, was in the hall.

Mr. Fisher, soft-voiced and unobtrusive, agreed with Johnny that as I had no relatives living at a distance, who might be unable to attend the funeral if given less than forty-eight hours' notice, there was no reason why it should not take place on Tuesday morning. When informed of my special directions, he said:

'Quite so, Sir. On a number of occasions we've had similar instructions. You would be surprised how many people suffer from the same fear. Most of them, though, direct that the veins in their wrists shall be opened; as, of course, if the blood does not flow there can be no doubt whatever about their being dead. But perhaps Sir Gifford did not think of that. In which room do you wish the deceased gentlemen to be laid out, Sir?'

Naturally, when ringing up, James had said nothing of the circumstances in which Evans and myself were supposed to have died; so Johnny now had to take Mr. Fisher into his confidence. Thereupon the undertaker agreed that it would not be quite fitting for the two bodies to be placed side by side for the week-end, and suggested that a minimum of inconvenience would be caused to the household if each was prepared for burial where it was. Johnny saw nothing against this, so Mr. Fisher went out to his car to collect the man and woman assistants he had brought with him, and the three of them set about their gruesome business.

Having been on the go without intermission since half-past eight that morning, Johnny evidently felt that he was due for a short break, so he went through to his room and lay down on the bed. I drifted upstairs to see how Ankaret was faring. As orders had been given not to disturb her, she must have rung and ordered tea and toast, for a tray reposed on her bed table. But it looked as if she had eaten only one piece of toast, and the tea-cup, with a slice of lemon in it, was still half full. She was lying on her back and quite still, but I could see from her only partially closed eyes that she was not actually asleep, and her face looked ten years older. Apparently she was half comatose from the pills that Dr. Culver had given her; but I felt sure that she was still conscious.

Once more I was at a loose end, with nothing much to think about except my own situation. As far as I could judge, my state was exactly the same as it had become within a few moments of being murdered. I still had no feeling of being dead; my perceptions were every bit as acute as they had been then, and I was not possessed by the faintest urge to leave my present surroundings.

However, I felt no desire to remain with poor Ankaret. I

128

know well enough that others will maintain that she had brought all this upon herself; but, even if her mind was temporarily dulled by a drug, the half-formed thoughts drifting through it must still have been torture; so I could not bear the idea of staying there and contemplating in my own mind what she must be suffering.

On glancing out of the window I saw that it was a pleasant sunny afternoon; so I thought I would take a look round the garden. Getting there called for little effort; far less than it would have done had I still been hampered by a body. I simply floated out of the window, and drifted round the corner of the house, gradually losing height until I settled at my usual six-feet-above-ground level on the little square of lawn beyond Ankaret's rose garden.

For about half an hour I made just the same sort of round that I usually did on Sunday mornings, and sometimes on summer evenings, admiring a group of blossoms here, planning some small alteration there, or noting a dead branch on a tree or shrub that ought to be cut off. In September the weeds are always at their worst and, knowing that old Eagers now had more than his work cut out to cope with such a large garden, I took no particular notice of them till I reached the asparagus bed. The fern there was almost hidden in a jungle of unwelcome herbage which had sprung up, making the whole patch one solid mass of greenery.

Momentarily quite forgetting both that it was a Saturday and that I could no longer communicate with any human being, I decided that I must tell Eagers to do something about it. As I had not so far seen him during my tour I went straight to the potting shed. He was not there, and I was brought back to my new state with a jerk by the thought that on hearing about my death he had probably considered it fitting to cease work for the day. But the shed was still open and inside Smuts, our garden cat, was enjoying a feed of fish-heads.

Suddenly Smuts stopped eating and turned her face towards the doorway in which I was poised. Her black back arched in terror, she gave a furious hiss and next moment, in one bound, disappeared through the open window. Her action told me plainly that, although I was invisible to humans, I could be seen by creatures having extra sensory perception;

so I was still, in a sense, a being of this world. I wondered how long I was meant to continue as one.

*   *   *   *

My papa-in-law arrived in time for tea. He had been sent over in a chauffeur-driven Rolls by the friend with whom he had expected to spend the week-end. Silvers carried in the heavy, expensive, but old-fashioned cases, guns, shooting-stick and other impedimenta without which His Lordship never travelled on such occasions; then went to rouse Johnny.

The Rt. Honourable the Earl had evidently been informed only of the bare facts of my sudden death. As he listened to Johnny's account of the previous night's happenings his face became redder, his pale blue eyes more protuberant and his exclamations of amazement and horror more frequent. When Johnny had done he said jerkily:

'Extraordinary business! Of course, this letter of Giff's to Ankaret leaves no loop-hole for surmise. All the same, I don't understand it. Giff was an even-tempered chap. Not like him to go off the deep end, whatever the provocation. I'm different. If I'd learned that some feller had assaulted my wife, I might have beaten his brains in. But I can't see Giff doing that. Another thing: Ankaret's upbringing was very different from her mother's. Gels are much more sophisticated these days. Even if she had the bad taste to fool around with that little Welshman I'd have thought she'd have no trouble at all in keeping him at arm's length. She ought not to have had to call Giff in to do that. It isn't the first time, either, that she's had a little fun on the side. But she adored Giff, and he knew that she had a bit of a weakness for setting her cap at other fellers; so why the frenzy on this occasion? That makes it all the more extraordinary.'

'It certainly does,' Johnny nodded. 'Two of his oldest friends, James Compton and Eddie Arnold, who were here this morning both said that they had never known Giff to lose his temper really badly, and we all agreed that he was the very last man we would have expected to commit suicide.'

130

His Lordship grunted. 'One doesn't expect that of anyone who is normal, and no one could question Giff's sanity. But a man's sanity has no bearing on a case like this. It's courage that counts, and Giff had plenty of that. Hang it all, he had committed murder! Think what would have happened if he let himself be arrested! Weeks, months perhaps, cooped up in a cell being badgered by a lot of lawyers. The trial, an appeal, then at the end of it all Jack Ketch putting a rope round his neck. No, no; thank God he had the guts to commit hara-kiri while he had the chance.'

'It needs still more guts to face the music,' Johnny argued. 'And I would have betted on Giff doing that. Arnold was saying this morning that on a plea of intense provocation Giff might have got off with a ten-year sentence. Allowing for reduction for good conduct he would have been a free man again while still under fifty. No jury could have failed to recommend him to mercy if Ankaret had gone into the box and testified to the assault mentioned in the letter; or better still have gone the whole hog and sworn that Evans had raped her.'

'Oh, I haven't a doubt that she would have told any lie to save Giff! But d'you think he'd have let her?' Bill Wiltshire's voice rang with scorn. 'Think of the press, and all the filthy publicity that would have been given to the trial. He would never have allowed Ankaret to be dragged through the gutter for the edification of every Tom, Dick and Harry who get a cheap thrill out of cases like this. No; apart from the fact of such a well-balanced chap as Giff having suddenly gone insane with rage, everything is explained by his letter. I suppose even the mildest men are liable to that sort of black-out at times. Anyhow, once he realised that he had killed the Welshman, to my mind he did the right and proper thing.'

Johnny shrugged. 'Perhaps I'm prejudiced against the idea of taking one's own life; and I still find it hard to believe that Giff would have taken his. But we'll get nowhere by arguing about it further. I'm very glad you have turned up, though, and can take charge of things here now, because I'm only on forty-eight hours and must get back to London this evening. I would have telephoned for an extension if it wasn't for a rather tricky paper that I'm devilling on which should be in by tomorrow night. But I'll get leave so that I can come down for the inquest on Monday and stay over Tuesday for the funeral.'

On that they separated, Johnny to pack his bag and Bill going upstairs to see Ankaret. I hung about in the hall, wondering what to do with myself, till Johnny appeared with his suit-case; then I followed him out to the garage. It had just occurred to me that if I really were earth-bound I was probably tied by some law outside human comprehension to the neighbourhood in which I had met my physical end; so it would be interesting to test that out and see if I could leave it. In consequence, when Johnny got into the driver's seat of his Standard Eight I settled myself beside him.

As he put in the clutch I metaphorically held my breath, wondering if I should be drawn out through the back of the car in the same way that I had been drawn back to earth when I had attempted to rise above the roof level of the house. But I felt no pull whatever. As the car sped forward down the drive the essential 'I' moved with it.

As it was Saturday evening, even when we had by-passed Southampton and got on to the main London road there was comparatively little traffic, so we made good going. The weather was still fine and although I was condemned to silence, the tints of autumn on the trees and the sight of the pleasant countryside enabled me to enjoy the run.

We had left Longshot soon after five and by a quarter to eight were crossing Wimbledon Common. I was just wondering how best to amuse myself in London for the evening when I got a surprise. Half-way down Putney Hill, instead of going straight on towards the High Street and the bridge, Johnny turned off to the left between two big blocks of flats and ran on through several streets of medium-sized houses. I could only assume that he meant to call on a friend; but he seemed rather uncertain of his way, as he had to stop to consult the relevant page of a large-scale book-map of the London area. Two minutes later he pulled up outside one of a row of semi-detached villas, probably built in Edward VII's reign.

I had no intention of spying on Johnny, but when he got out I instinctively followed him up the short garden path. His ring was answered by a smartly-dressed young woman of

132

about twenty and, to my astonishment, I recognised her as my daughter.

*　　*　　*　　*

Evidently that morning, at some moment when my attention had been distracted, Eddie Arnold had discussed with Johnny the question of informing my first wife of my death; Eddie must have mentioned where she lived and Johnny volunteered to call in there as it was on his way up to London. Of course, I knew perfectly well that Edith and the children lived in Putney, as I had written to them there from time to time for years, but I had never been to the house and had not noticed the name of the street as Johnny turned into it. Moreover, I must confess that since having been violently ejected from my body I had not given them a thought.

Johnny had never met Christobel; so he proceeded to introduce himself. She had opened the door to him with a frown on her pretty, rather plump face but when he told her who he was she brightened and said:

'As a matter of fact we are just in the middle of supper; but we'll all be thrilled to meet a long-lost cousin. Do come in.'

'Thanks, but I can only stay a moment.' Johnny hesitated. 'To tell the truth this isn't a social visit. I've just driven up from Longshot and the family solicitor asked me to look in.'

Christobel's expression changed to a pout. 'How disappointing. I wondered why you were looking so serious.'

'It is a serious matter. Perhaps, instead of springing it on all of you at once, it would be best if I told you about it; then you could break it to your mother.'

At this clear indication by Johnny that he was the bearer of bad news, her brown eyes grew as round as saucers, and she exclaimed:

'For heaven's sake don't tell me that Pa has gone broke! That would be too much! But we can't stand here on the doorstep exhibiting ourselves to the neighbours. Come into the lounge. Whatever it is I can take it.'

Leaving Johnny to shut the front door, she turned with a flurry of skirts and led him down a short passage to a room at the back of the house. It looked out on a pocket-handker-chief-sized garden, but the view was partially obscured on

133

the hall side by a one-storied portion of the house that jutted out into it, and was evidently the kitchen quarters.

Had I entered that room in Timbuktu I think it would still have reminded me of Edith. No doubt its furnishings resembled those of countless others, also termed lounges, that had gradually evolved from the drawing-rooms of more spacious Edwardian days; but Edith had been my only intimate contact with that section of the middle classes which is utterly devoid of taste. For individual pieces, whether antique or modern, she had no use at all; her soul craved suites, the more expensive the better, as turned out by the hundred for the nouveau-riche by the big stores in Tottenham Court Road. She had no sense of space and crowded things in on the principle of 'the more the better', loading every piece with valueless and often hideous ornaments. The carpet swore at the curtains and on the walls hung pictures of 'The Soul's Awakening' type, in wide-margined gilt frames.

I recalled the battles I had had with her in my endeavours to restrain her from making a nightmare of our first home. Although I had had to give way to her about a walnut bedroom suite, on which she had set her heart, I had managed to save face with my own friends in the furnishing of our downstairs rooms. But here she had been free to do her worst.

Turning to face Johnny, Christobel asked in a flippant tone designed to show her youthful cynicism: 'Now, give us the works!'

No longer inclined to mince matters, he replied: 'Your father is dead. He died quite unexpectedly last night.'

'So that's it.' She did not turn a hair of her 'urchin crop' which I was old-fashioned enough to dislike.

'I'm afraid there will be a lot of unpleasant publicity connected with his death,' Johnny went on. 'You see, he took his own life; and the reason for his doing so was because he had just killed another man who was living in the house.'

At that my hard-boiled young daughter's eyelashes did flutter, but not on account of the imminence of tears. She simply gasped: 'Well I'm damned. I'd never have thought it of him.'

'Neither would I,' replied Johnny tartly. 'But there appears to be no disputing the fact that that is what he did. Please tell

134

your mother and brother, and convey my sympathy to them. The inquest is on Monday and the funeral on Tuesday morning. Now, if you will excuse me, I must be on my way.'

Apparently still too overcome by surprise to ask him any questions, she accompanied him to the front door. There she flashed him a sudden smile and said: 'Thanks for letting us know. Do come and pay us a proper visit some time.' Then she closed the door after him and stood for a moment irresolute in the narrow hall.

Now much intrigued to learn what the reactions of my ex-wife and son would be, instead of following Johnny I remained beside Christobel. After blowing the rather pudgy nose which was the worst feature of her otherwise attractively youthful face, she opened a door at the side of the hall which gave on to a small dining-room. Edith and Harold were sitting at an oval table eating cutlets and mashed potatoes.

The years had not been very kind to Edith. In her youth she had been a voluptuous blonde, but rinses had failed to keep the colour in her hair and her face had become distinctly fleshy. Really beautiful women owe their looks to bone formation and that alone gives lasting charm to the outline of their features. Ankaret, for example, if she had lived to be ninety, could not fail to mature to the end as a most handsome old lady. But such bone structures are not often met with. The great majority of pretty girls are, alas, doomed as their age advances to fight a losing battle against the contours of their faces becoming ever more disenchanting. Edith had proved no exception, and I noted, too, that she was now wearing a hearing aid. Even in her youth she had been a little deaf, and I was sorry to see that this trouble of hers had evidently become worse.

In Harold, at eighteen, I could take little pride. He was very tall but narrow-shouldered, sallow-complexioned, and, his sight being poor, he wore heavy tortoise-shell-rimmed spectacles. His appearance was not improved by the untidiness of his clothes and his unbrushed hair, a big lock of which he always let hang down over his forehead. That he was my son I had no doubt whatever. He even had a slight resemblance to me physically; but mentally, we were poles apart. His two gifts, a flair for figures—which, at his own wish, had caused me earlier that year to arrange for him to be apprenticed to a good firm of chartered accountants—and an appreciation of classical music, were both interests which I lacked the ability to share; and I had long since given up as hopeless all attempts to win his affection. He had erected a barrier that I could not penetrate, based, I suppose, on resentment of the fact that I had left his mother.

But, that apart, he lacked all sense of the joy of life. At his age, without being vicious, I had been quite a scamp, whereas he had a slightly sneering attitude towards any form of riotous living. At times, when I had been with him, I had not been able to prevent filtering through my mind the old story of the Colonel asking a Subaltern who was both a teetotaller and a notorious prude about women: 'Do you eat hay?' Much surprised the Subaltern had replied: 'No, Sir.' Upon which the Colonel had retorted: 'Then you are not a fit companion for man or beast.' To my shame, that was the way I felt about Harold.

As Christobel entered the room her mother looked up and asked: 'What was it, dear?'

The girl made no move to resume her place at table, and replied by another question: 'Mummy, you've always told us that Pa was the one man in your life. Did you really love him very deeply?'

Edith's slightly-sagging face took on the expression of the righteous and forgiving martyr. 'Of course, dear. But what a funny thing to ask in the middle of dinner.'

'Does he still mean very much to you,' Christobel persisted.

'Yes, child! Naturally! He was your father.' Edith's voice now held a faintly testy note. 'Come and sit down and finish your cutlet.'

For the first time Christobel showed traces of emotion; then she blurted out: 'Well, I'm sorry, darling, but Pa's had it. That was Wing Commander Norton. He's a sort of cousin, isn't he? Pa's solicitor asked him to call and tell us that there has been a frightful bust-up at Langshot. Apparently Pa killed another man last night then committed suicide.'

Edith dropped her fork with a clatter. 'Oh!' she exclaimed, her face twisting into a grimace. 'No; no! It can't be true!'

Harold jumped to his feet and snapped at his sister: 'Couldn't you have broken it a bit more gently.' Then he ran round to his mother, who had closed her eyes, pressed one hand to her ample bosom, and looked as though she were about to faint.

The brother and sister began to speculate on the cause of the tragedy at Longshot, but were cut short by Edith's standing up, leaning on Harold's shoulder and murmuring: 'Take me to my room, dear; take me to my room.'

Between them they got her upstairs, where she lay down on her bed, now weeping copiously. After providing her with aspirins, lavender water, and a supply of handkerchiefs, they made a few awkward efforts to comfort her, then drew the window curtains and went downstairs to finish their interrupted meal.

Christobel pushed aside the remains of the now cold cutlet, cut herself a large slice of treacle tart and, as she began hurriedly to eat it, remarked: 'I must buck up, or I'll be late meeting Archie, and he hates having to wait to go in until after the last programme's started.'

'I'd have thought you might have stayed in tonight.' Harold gave a disapproving sniff. 'After all, even if he had no time for us, he was our father.'

'Don't be stuffy,' she chided him. 'You know jolly well you'd be going out somewhere yourself if you weren't stony-broke. Having just learnt that Pa is dead wouldn't stop you.'

He gave a sour smile. 'I suppose you're right. This last month of the quarter always gets me down. I wonder how he would have liked to have to stay at home night after night for want of a few bob to go to a concert or a political meeting.'

'You can listen to the wireless, and you've got your records. If you didn't spend so much on them and drinking beer with your Left-wing friends you wouldn't be so hard up towards the end of every quarter.'

'Hang it all, why shouldn't I?' he protested, brushing the dangling lock away from over his right eye. 'And no one could accuse me of extravagance. It's just that in these days a hundred a year goes nowhere.'

'You're telling me!' Christobel took a quick drink of water.

'Oh you! For a girl it's very different. There are always plenty of chaps ready to take you places and pay for your fun.'

'Perhaps; but I have to watch every penny all the same.

137

You've no idea what clothes cost, and hair-do's and make-up stuff. I'm just as hard put to it on my hundred a year as you are on yours.'

'Ah, but you have a hundred plus.'

'Plus what?'

'Plus the asset of your sex. Having spent your hundred on dolling yourself up you are all set. The plus is letting your boy-friends maul you about a bit in exchange for giving you a darned good time.'

'Harold!' Her voice was sharp. 'Don't be disgusting! How dare you speak of me as though I were a tart.'

He shrugged. 'I didn't intend to imply that you would go the whole hog for money. But I'll bet all your kisses aren't given for love. Don't think I'm blaming you, either. I'd do the same if I were in your place. What is more, if you had met some really rich playboy and gone to bed with him for what you could get out of it, to my mind that would have been Pa's fault. There he was, always beefing about his super tax and allowing his daughter less than half the wages earned by a shop girl. Still, now the mean old so-and-so is dead, things should be a lot better for us.'

'I wouldn't count on that,' Christobel shook her head. 'You know how crazy he was about the bitch. I'll bet that she and her noble relatives have got their claws on everything, including the kitchen sink.'

Harold's mouth drew into a snarl. 'By God, if he has left the bitch everything I'll fight her in the courts.'

'Will you?' His sister gave him an amused look. 'And where is the money to pay the lawyers to come from, eh? Besides, you are only eighteen, so still a minor. Mummy is the only person who could start an action on our behalf; and you know how spineless she is. We'd never be able to persuade her to, even if there's a case; and I don't suppose there is one. It's hardly likely that Pa would have failed to make provision for her allowance, and ours, to be continued; and I shouldn't think we'd be legally entitled to demand more.'

'But hang it all!' Dismay mingled with the anger on Harold's sallow face. 'Even if you are right about yourself and Mother, I must come into something. I'm the new Baronet. Surely I'll get some cash with the title.'

At that Christobel began to laugh. 'Of course,' she giggled 'You are Sir Harold now. Somehow that part of it hadn't struck me, and it will take quite a bit of getting used to.'

'I don't see what's so funny about it,' he said sullenly.

'You wouldn't; and apart from being able to swank, I doubt if it will do you much good.' Standing up she added: 'I must beat it. And while I am on my way to sell myself to my rich admirer, Sir Harold Hillary, Bart., can do the washing up.'

For that crack, I must say, I liked my daughter quite a bit better; but it was followed by a sordid little incident.

'Hi!' he called as she made to leave the room. 'I did it last Saturday. It's your turn; and you haven't paid me yet for doing it the Saturday before that.'

After fumbling in her bag she fished out a half-crown and threw it on the table. 'Here you are, then. At a bob a night that puts me sixpence in credit.'

As he picked it up, she turned in the doorway. 'I may be pretty late. Archie said he might take me somewhere to dance for a bit after the flick. If he does I'll probably bring him in for a cup of coffee when I get home; so if you hear us don't come blundering downstairs thinking it's burglars. Night-night.'

When she had gone, he walked round the table to the fire-place and gave his reflection in the mirror of the over-mantel a long, appraising look; then, his tone expressing evident self-satisfaction, he said several times: 'Sir Harold Hillary. Sir Harold Hillary.'

Leaving him to it, I moved upstairs to Edith's room. She was no longer lying down, but kneeling beside her bed praying; or rather murmuring a sort of soliloquy addressed to God the words of which were quite loud enough to hear. I suppose I ought not to have listened, but her half-hysterical spate of pleas, excuses and lamentations was such an indictment of myself that I remained there for quite a long time, almost as a form of penance. There were frequent repetitions in what she said, but the gist of it ran something like this:

'Oh Lord, do let everything be all right. Don't let Giff have forgotten us, or have killed himself owing to financial troubles. I did my best to be a good wife to him. I know I haven't brought up the children very well; but I did the best I could for them on the money. Oh Lord please let there be a will and us be in it. I know Giff would have meant to provide for us. He wasn't a bad man, only selfish; and he couldn't help being a snob. That was his father's fault. Perhaps I ought not to have married him. I know he was above my class, but I loved him and I thought he loved me. Oh Lord, don't let our allowances be cut off. Even as things are it's a constant struggle. Ever since Giff left us I've had to scrape and save. If the allowances are cut off I don't know what we'll do. My own little bit won't be nearly enough to keep this house going. If it were only myself it wouldn't matter so much. I could just manage in a tiny flat. But there are the children. Please help me to look after them and continue to give them a home. Harold is too young to go out into the world, and I couldn't help it that he and his father never got on together. He is a good boy really, and it was only his not being able to understand that Giff had so many important things to see to that he couldn't give much time to us. Giff would have been different if it hadn't been for Lady A. But I bear her no malice. Please believe that. He had left me before he met her, so I really have no cause to complain. It's all my fault for not having been clever enough to hold him. If I had, Harold would soon be going up to Cambridge, and Christobel would have been presented at Court two years ago. But I'm not complaining about that. I only ask that we will be able to go on as we are. Oh please Lord let things be all right, so that we get the allowances just the same.'

On and on she went, poor woman, showing no particular sorrow about my death but generously seeking to excuse me having left her, and my lack of interest in the children, and desperately concerned about their future. That her worst fears were groundless, as she would soon learn from my will, did not make her present distress any the less harrowing. At length, feeling that I could bear the sound of it no longer, I drifted from the room.

Outside on the landing faint strains of classical music came down to me by a steep little stairway leading to the upper floor of the house; so it was evident that under the gables there 'Sir Harold' had his quarters, and was consoling himself for being confined to his home through lack of funds by playing his gramophone. That hardship did not seem to me a very great one, but all the same, having moved down to the lounge I settled myself for a really serious think.

The children's attitude to my death and Edith's gabbled prayers had weighed me down with an appalling sense of guilt. It was vain for me to argue with myself that I was not responsible for the characters of my son and daughter; for had I brought them up they might have become very different people. On the other hand, that did not apply to Edith, and by going back to the beginning I tried to assess how far I was really responsible for her broken and, since we had separated, dreary, financially-harassed existence.

We had met in the early thirties and, such are the trivialities upon which our fates hang, it is most unlikely that we should ever have met at all had I not when at Cambridge taken up tennis in preference to any other sport. Her brother Tom was also a keen tennis man. Apart from that we had little in common and I did not even have any particular liking for him. But we had both made up our minds to see Wimbledon week that year and he invited me to stay for it at his home in South London. As, for me, the alternative would have been an hotel, I accepted.

The Wilks—that was their name—lived in one of those large Victorian houses, each having its own short carriage drive and two acres or more of garden behind it, that used to abound in the wealthier suburbs of London. Most of them have since been pulled down, to make way for blocks of flats, or turned into small schools, nursing homes and boarding houses, but in the thirties quite a number of them were still serving their original purpose. That of the Wilks was on Tulse Hill, and unexpectedly pleasant I found it.

The family consisted of father, mother, three sons and three daughters. Mr. Wilks was the London agent for a Lancashire cotton firm, but we did not see much of him; perhaps because he was already beginning to feel the effects of the cancer that carried him, and a good part of his income, off not long afterwards. The mother was one of those fat, good-natured women who believed in piling people's plates high with food and did not seem to mind in the least if her children turned the house upside down in the process of enjoying themselves. The sons and daughters were much of an age, ranging from eighteen to twenty-six, Edith being the middle of the three girls, and three years older than my-self. They had a host of friends who were always rushing in and out, or staying at a moment's notice to lunch or dinner, both of which were movable feasts depending on the convenience of the majority. In fact the place was a cheerful Bedlam.

That, of course, was why I liked it. At Longshot I had been brought up as an only child, and although I had been allowed to have a friend to stay now and then in the holidays, life in my father's house never varied in its decorous routine. I, my school-friends, and the children of our few scattered neighbours could get as dirty as we liked in garden, fields and ponds, but we always had to appear clean, tidy and punctually at meals. No shouting indoors or practical jokes were per-mitted, much less riotous games of hide-and-seek during which young men and women squeezed themselves under the beds or into the wardrobes of their elders.

The fact that the Wilks did not normally change for dinner, had numerous customs that seemed strange to me, and spoke with a slightly Cockney accent did not in the least detract from my enjoyment, and during the hectic fortnight I spent with them it was not at all surprising that I should have more or less fallen for Edith.

I say 'more or less' because it was no question of a grand passion—anyhow on my part. It was simply a case of pro-pinquity. Attracted by her blue eyes, golden hair, abundant health and ready laughter, I attached myself to her from the first evening. How large a part the fact that I was the heir to a Baronetcy and a considerable fortune played with her, I shall never know; but she was certainly not a clever and designing woman by nature, so I think it only fair to assume that she was equally attracted to me physically. Anyhow, she accepted me as her special cavalier with unconcealed pleasure, and we were soon seeking opportunities to be alone together. It was that which led to my undoing.

On the afternoon of my last Sunday at the Wilks's she took me up to an old play-room at the top of the house. We both knew that to see her collection of stuffed animals was only an excuse, as we had already indulged in several bouts of kissing and cuddling in secluded corners of the garden. The door was hardly closed behind us before we were two very over-heated young people clasped tightly in each other's arms.

I did not actually seduce her, but during the hour that followed things did not stop far short of that. Anyway, when I left on the Monday morning, although not a word had been said about marriage, I felt that I had definitely committed myself.

That, of course, was before World War II had practically eliminated class distinctions as far as the sexes were concerned. In those days the traditions of behaviour current before World War I still governed most decently-brought-up young men. It was accepted that any young woman with whom one could scrape acquaintance in a park, a dance hall or any public place was fair game, and that if she allowed herself to be seduced a 'gentleman' was under no obligation to marry her. But any unmarried girl to whom one had been formally introduced was definitely taboo. In Victorian times many a man was caught by the sister of a friend allowing him to do no more than kiss her in a conservatory, and while by my young days things had to go a lot further than that before there was any talk of putting up the banns, it was still recognised that playing such games as I had with Edith in the old play-room could be taken by the girl as a clear indication that the young man wanted to marry her.

Now, thank goodness, girls and boys of all classes have been educated to speak out to one another frankly about these matters and, both parties being willing, can indulge in such pastimes without necessarily being committed for life to a partner with whom they have nothing in common but a sexual attraction that may burn itself out in a few months.

I have since learned that even in my day many of my contemporaries did not abide by the current rules; so perhaps, owing to lack of experience, I behaved as a simpleton and could have wriggled out of it had I wished at the price of some twinges of conscience; but the fact is it never occurred to me to do so. I should add I have not the least reason to suppose that Edith deliberately trapped me, and such a thought never even crossed my mind. I accepted the situation as quite natural and assumed similar ones determined the futures of most young men of my kind.

This may all sound as if I was not the least in love with

143

Edith, but that was far from being the case. I am now simply reviewing the affair in retrospect; but, at the time, my over-heated imagination was rarely free from visions of my lovely blonde divinity and my arms felt a positive physical ache to hold her once more in one of those embraces to which she responded so passionately. In consequence, when the Wilks invited me down later that summer to stay at a house they had taken at Paignton, I accepted with alacrity. Down there in Devonshire we found more opportunities for hectic love-making, and from my visit I returned engaged.

Naturally the next step was for Edith to come and stay at Longshot Hall. It was then that the first shadow fell on our romance. She simply did not fit and, even blinded by passion as I was, I could not help being aware of it. My father received her most kindly and as long as she was with us showed not the least trace of his disappointment at my choice. But the night after she had gone, he tackled me about it.

Without beating about the bush he told me that he considered Edith entirely unsuitable as a wife for me, and begged me to break off our engagement. Then he said the sort of thing that so many parents before and since must have said to their children in similar circumstances—that even in the best of marriages the honeymoon relationship cannot be re-tained indefinitely, and that for lasting happiness, putting all question of class apart, common interests and a similarity of outlook are absolutely essential. He added that, regrettable as it might be to have to break one's word, it was far better to do so than to condemn oneself to years of bickering that ended in the squalor of the divorce court.

He put it to me, too, that although it requires much more courage to jilt a girl than tamely to allow oneself to drift into a marriage the outcome of which is foredoomed, it was, in such circumstances, up to a man to face the music, not only for his own future happiness but because he was also re-sponsible for that of the weaker partner—the girl who had temporarily aroused his passion and, in the nature of things, was probably even more blinded by passion than he was himself.

How right my father was all older people know, and the really awful thing is that after Edith's stay at Longshot, at such times as I forced myself to think of my engagement dispassionately I knew that he was right. Yet, partly owing to a continuance of the physical bewitchment she exercised over me, and partly because I could not screw up the moral courage required to inflict such an abominable hurt upon her, I refused to do as he wished, and pushed these doubts about the future into the back of my mind. At the end of the following term I came down from Cambridge, and we were married a few weeks after Christmas.

It had always been intended that I should go into the family business and this necessitated living near Southampton. Edith had never been allowed to know of my father's opposition to the match and once he had withdrawn it—stipulating only that after the marriage I must not expect him to have anything to do with the Wilks—he behaved very generously towards us. He bought me a pleasant little property not far from Longshot and gave me a thousand pounds towards furnishing the house. The excitement of getting ready our home, the wedding, and the honeymoon occupied my mind to the exclusion of all pessimistic thoughts during those winter months, and Edith and I were as happy together as any pair of newly-weds could be when we took possession of Monksfield Grange in the early spring.

But that state of things did not last long. Edith had never hunted, nor shot, nor fished and she set her face firmly against taking up any of these pastimes. She did play about for a while in the garden, but the only kind of flowers she really liked were the sort that arrive wrapped in Cellophane from a florist's shop, and after the first summer she abandoned even the pretence that she enjoyed growing things. The Wilks were not uncharitable people but their idea of benevolence began and ended with sending cheques annually to certain London hospitals and taking a stall at the local Church Bazaar. Helping to run the Women's Institute, visiting sick cottagers, reading to the elderly bedridden poor, and other such good works to which most women of any position in the country consider it incumbent on them to devote a certain amount of time, were entirely foreign to Edith. By way of defence she declared that she thought it wrong to go poking one's nose into other people's private lives; but the fact of the matter was that not having been brought up to talk to labouring people as fellow human beings it embarrassed her horribly,

145

apart from giving them orders, to have anything to do with them at all.

Our neighbours, of course, all came to call, and welcomed Edith among them as my wife. But they soon took her measure and, while it never reached a point where they omitted to ask us occasionally to dinner or consistently refused our invitations, she proved incapable of making a single woman friend among them, and to the end they never came to regard her as one of themselves. They could not be blamed for that; neither could she. It was simply that she was a fish out of water, and lacked the ability to adapt herself to new surroundings.

The sort of life she really hankered after was a flat in Kensington, plenty of afternoon bridge, frequent meals out at restaurants, theatres, cinemas, and an occasional day at the races. It is greatly to her credit that she rarely grumbled and never attempted to nag me into changing our way of life. And, of course, the coming of the children provided her with a new, enthralling interest. But, despite the consolation she found in them, with every year that passed it became increasingly apparent that she loathed the country, and everything connected with it, more and more.

As I have stated earlier, very soon after the war broke out I joined the R.A.F. I must now admit that this eagerness to get into uniform was not solely inspired by a red-hot patriotism. Had I been forced to give a reason for my action at the time, I would have said it was, and honestly believed that to be so. But later I realised that subconsciously I had in part at least been impelled by the desire to get away from Edith.

My escape to freedom brought to a head the sore of discontent with my marriage that had long been secretly festering at the back of my mind. In 1940 I was only twenty-seven; so the best part of my life still lay before me. I decided without haste but absolutely definitely that I would not waste another day longer than I had to on Edith and I wrote asking her to give me a divorce.

At first she refused, but when she found that I was adamant in my determination not to return to her, and perhaps influenced a little by the lure of being able to live once again, after the war, in her beloved London, she gave in. It took some time to arrange but I gave her grounds, agreed to allow her five hundred a year free of tax, to give her custody of the children and to pay for their education. Well before I returned from India everything had been settled. She had left the Grange, which lay uncomfortably close to Southampton's bomb alley, and taken the children down to furnished lodgings in Torquay. I had never seen her again until this evening. Now, as I thought of these things in the lounge below her bedroom, I felt compelled to face the awful question: had I been justified in leaving her?

It was now pitch dark in there, as I knew from the distinct change in the appearance of my surroundings; for I had already learned that although in my new state I could see in the dark, the effect of darkness was in the nature of a dimming, which limited my range of vision and made nearby things seem as though seen only by twilight. Again my glance roved over the collection of gaudy, tasteless knick-knacks that so perfectly expressed Edith's personality, and here and there I noticed one which by recalling fresh memories of our past together gave me a fresh tweak of conscience.

Unquestionably I should have followed my father's advice, and broken with her before it was too late. But the fact was that I hadn't. I had in all solemnity, on oath in church, taken her for better or worse till death us should part. After that what right had I to repudiate her? She, although forced by me to live in uncongenial surroundings, had kept her part of the bargain, and without undue complaint. Had I allowed my material welfare and personal preference for life in the country to weigh more with me than her happiness? It seemed that I had; for by some sacrifice of income I could have got a job in London, and still retained my seat on the Board of the firm. Should we then have been drawn closer together and achieved contentment? When in my twenties and thirties I had been far from averse to theatres, parties and night-clubs; and, as making friends came very easily to me, although I should have seen much less of some of my old ones I should probably have made new ones among Edith's acquaintances; so a move to London might have turned our marriage into a success. Yet I had been too selfish for the idea of tearing up my own roots even to cross my mind.

Against that it could be argued that the marital doctrines of the Christian Church are entirely contrary to human nature.

147

Man is by habit a polygamous animal. Every other religion and every people of whom we have any historical knowledge have freely recognised that, and no contortions of reasoning have ever produced a convincing argument that he was meant to be anything else. Nearly all non-Christian women, and a vast number of Christian ones as well, are still the playthings of many men or get only a share in one. So why should we accept the arbitrary ruling that a woman like Edith is entitled to the sole rights over one man for the whole of his adult life.

Again, it cannot be denied that while women are restricted in their sexual lives by the urge to make a home and secure a permanent protector for their children, they are by nature also polyandrous. Edith was only a little over thirty when we agreed that she should divorce me, and still good-looking. She could easily have found a second husband had she cared to look out for one. That she had not done so was no fault of mine.

Yet the fact remained that she hadn't; so both by the law of the land, and by the moral precepts in which we had both been reared, I still remained responsible for her. The question was had I fulfilled my obligations?

Legally I had; for after deducting tax, the allowance I made her and the cost of the children's education had taken a good third of my net income during the years before my father died. But morally I hadn't; for while I had since enjoyed a life of comparative luxury myself I had left her to battle on her own against the increased cost of living, and a constant prey to anxiety about how to make both ends meet. True, I had not realised the straits to which she had been put until an hour or so ago; but I ought to have done so, and should have had I not been too occupied with my own affairs to give the matter a thought. I knew that she had about three hundred a year of her own, and when I had agreed to allow her five hundred, I had felt that eight hundred should be ample for her to keep herself and the children in reasonable comfort. But that had been thirteen years ago. My income had more than trebled since, but hers had not, although its purchasing power had shrunk to far less than its original value.

That she had never asked me to increase her allowance now seemed like heaping coals of fire upon my head; and in one

matter I felt particularly guilty. When the children had left
school, no longer having to pay their fees, but giving them a
hundred a year apiece instead, had made me several hundred
a year better off. Instead of cheerfully pocketing that surplus
I ought to have turned it over to Edith.

This matter of school fees having brought my thoughts to
the children, I began to consider my treatment of them. When
I rushed into the war, and left home for an R.A.F. training
camp, they were aged only four and two respectively. On my
return from India I wrote to Edith saying that I would like
to see them. She replied that she had no objection, but they
were still too young to travel alone, and our divorce having
been so recent it would cause her too much pain to meet me
with them; moreover, even if she could find someone to send
in her place she was not prepared to let them go to either
Southampton or London as long as the war and danger from
air raids continued.

The obvious answer was that I should have gone down to
Torquay.

Of course I meant to, but I was up to my eyes picking up
all the threads again at Hillary-Comptons. So I put it off until
I should be a little less busy. Soon afterwards we were asked
to double our output of craft in preparation for the Normandy
landings; then my father fell ill and I had to take on much
of his work as well as my own. What with one thing and
another I never got down to Torquay.

In consequence I did not see the children again until 1946,
after Edith had leased this house and moved with them up
to London. By that time Christobel was ten and Harold eight
—about as difficult an age as could be for a father to meet
again two children who had forgotten even what he looked
like. Edith had decided that the meeting would be less awkward if she did not appear; so they were duly delivered to me
at the Berkeley, where I gave them lunch, and afterwards I
took them to the circus.

They were pop-eyed with curiosity at seeing me and maintained a disconcerting stare throughout the meal. I did my
best to initiate conversation but I fear there must have been
a horribly false ring about my hearty jollity. Their replies
were mostly whispered monosyllables and during the afternoon the only spontaneous remark by either came from

Harold, who asked me just before the time came for them to be collected:

'Why don't you come home and live with Mummy?'

I replied that when he was older he would understand; and after their departure almost collapsed with relief that the ordeal was over.

Nevertheless, during the next three years I screwed myself up from time to time to repeat the operation, with theatres or cinemas in lieu of the circus, as a blessed escape from having to make stilted conversation with them for the greater part of our meetings.

I would have liked to have them down to Longshot, in the hope that being with them for several days at a stretch, and in different surroundings, would enable me to break through their reserve; but I didn't, because I was afraid of upsetting our staff. That sounds a poor reason, I suppose; but from the war onwards it has been extremely difficult to find servants who are prepared to live in such isolated spots. Up till 1949 my father—with whom I had gone back to live after my return from India—and I had had to make do with his old valet, who was then in his seventies, and an elderly, cantankerous cook named Mrs. Beagle. As our two women helps from the village worked only till midday most of the extra work entailed by two children coming to stay would have fallen on her; and, as it was, whenever she was asked to do anything at all out of the ordinary she always complained that she was being 'put upon'. I disliked her so much that if she had given notice I would not personally have minded, but for the last few years of his life my father was a semi-invalid, and for his sake I did not feel that I dared take the risk of our being left cookless.

The year of 1949/50 was a more than usually busy one for me. My father's death entailed a great deal of extra work winding up his estate; then I met and became engaged to Ankaret, which led to my leaving Longshot for a time while it was thoroughly done up. As I was divorced we were married at a registry office, then after lunch with a few intimate friends we went straight off on our honeymoon. To have asked the children to such a wedding would, I felt, have been a great mistake, but I had, of course, told Ankaret all about them, and after she had had ample time to settle in at

150

Longshot I asked her if she would mind if we had them to stay.

She agreed at once and I am sure had every intention of trying to make friends with them; but they proved impossible. Christobel, then fifteen, looked older than her years and was a precocious piece. On the second night of their stay Ankaret and I had a long-standing date for drinks before dinner with one of our neighbours, but when we arrived we learned that our host had suddenly been taken ill so the party was off. In consequence we were back at Longshot an hour before the children expected us, and a pretty scene we found there.

My well-grown young daughter was in our bedroom with a good part of Ankaret's trousseau scattered about her. At the moment of our entry she was parading herself before the mirror in an evening dress by Balmain that Ankaret particularly cherished, and when sharply reprimanded by me she had the effrontery to say that as she and her school-friends often swapped clothes she had been hoping that Ankaret would lend her some of hers during her stay, and was trying on a few to see which would suit her.

Ankaret kept her temper very well, but she was not unnaturally annoyed, particularly as when bringing up the children Edith had, apparently, slipped back into the Wilks's tradition that a bath once or twice a week was quite enough for anyone; so all the clothes that Christobel had tried on had to be sent to the cleaners.

Between ourselves we excused this piece of licence as a manifestation of adolescence; but worse was to follow. A few days after the children left Ankaret discovered that a bottle of her most expensive scent and four pairs of nylons were missing. I did not take the matter up with Edith because I knew how greatly it would upset her, but there was little margin for doubt about where these aids to glamour had gone.

Harold made himself an equally unwelcome guest in an even more unpleasant way. Although only thirteen he was already a budding intellectual—of the type that I find particularly repulsive. The Wilks, like most people of their class, were True Blue Conservatives so, presumably from sheer contrariness, Harold was in the process of becoming a Red Hot Communist. His conversation was still stilted, but he lost no opportunity of showing his disapproval of all that Longshot stood for; and now and again, with the callowness of extreme youth, burst into long diatribes, lifted almost verbatim from the books he was reading, on what a much better place the world would be when all sources of production and distribution were controlled by the workers. Bored as we were with his ill-digested cant, we put up with it and even paid him the compliment of trying to reason seriously with him until the night before he left. During dinner he launched an attack on British aristocracy, stigmatising them en bloc as worthless parasites, and it was perfectly clear that he was gunning for Ankaret. I shut him up by saying that the sooner he looked up the lists of the sons of peers who had given their lives fighting in the last two wars, and started to read the history of his country instead of a lot of subversive lies by the enemies of it, the sooner he would deserve the food that he was eating.

By tacit agreement we never asked the children to Longshot again, and I certainly cannot blame Ankaret for not having suggested that we should do so. I dropped back into my previous routine of sacrificing one of my evenings every three or four months when I happened to be in London to taking them out, and so matters had continued until I had, so unexpectedly, met my death.

Of the two of them I preferred the girl. She was hard as nails, her mind was mediocre, and her pert manners grated on me; but she at least showed a zest for living. Harold's one redeeming feature seemed to be his attachment to his mother; and no doubt it was his long-nurtured grievance that it was she who should have been the mistress of Longshot Hall, and in due course have become Lady Hillary, which had led to his antagonism to the upper classes—as represented in his mind by my father and myself—and to his hatred of Ankaret. But by any standard he was a poor fish, and I marvelled that even with a woman of Edith's limitations I could have begotten such a son.

But the question I now had to face was would they have been two quite different people had I carried out my full responsibilities as a parent to them?

Undoubtedly they would have if I had continued to make a home for them with Edith as, when I first asked her for a divorce, she had begged me to do. It was incontestable that

152

their outlook and manners would have been coloured to some extent by my own, and those of the country gentry who would have continued to form our social circle. The talk they would have heard and the books I should have given them to read while their minds were forming could not have failed to prove a life-long influence. They might not have turned out to be good or kindly people, but at least they would have possessed the asset of some culture; Christobel would have developed a better sense of moral values, and Harold not become an embryo traitor to his country.

Even had I not gone back to Edith I could still have exerted a considerable influence on the formation of their characters, had I kept in closer touch with them. War or no war, on my return from India I ought to have gone down to Torquay every few weeks for a couple of nights. When they came to live in London, instead of giving them only a few hours of my time I ought to have had them to stay with me every holiday for a few nights in an hotel. Again, had I bothered to exert myself I could have had them with me at Longshot by arranging to put them up at the village inn, bought them fishing rods and ponies and taught them to enjoy the countryside. They would then have accepted Ankaret much more readily. She would, I am sure, have smoothed away Christobel's gaucheries and later presented her at Court. And, of course, instead of jumping at the chance to get Harold into a firm of accountants shortly after his eighteenth birthday, I should have sent him to follow in the steps of several generations of Hillarys at Cambridge.

Instead I had left them to grow up as best they could, with no one to guide them other than their well-meaning but weak and sadly limited mother. Still worse, although I could well have afforded to be more generous, I had deprived them of many of the joys of youth by condemning them to make do on a pittance.

When I had fixed a hundred a year each as their allowance, I had been thinking in terms of my own youth, but I now recalled what one of my friend's sons had told me not long ago. He had assured me that if one took a girl out for the evening in London these days there was little change out of a tenner, and that if it was to be a real celebration with champagne for dinner and at a night-club afterwards, it could easily run one into twenty pounds. That the thought of Harold had not crossed my mind in this connection was hardly surprising, but all the same it was an indication how the cost of even more modest pleasures must have gone up.

That, too, must apply to the expenses of a girl who made any pretence of maintaining a smart appearance, and I wondered now how Christobel could look so well turned out as she did on her money. She, of course, could have been earning money for herself by now, but it was much my fault as anyone's that she was not. I ought to have insisted two or three years ago that she should train for some career, but I had never bothered to do so; and as, like her mother, she was lazy by nature, she had never done anything about it for herself.

So there it was. Partly through a mean instinct to keep as much of my income as I reasonably could for my own enjoyment, and even more from lack of thought for them, I had allowed three people for whom I was responsible to be harassed for years by financial worries, and deprived them of much happiness.

As I sat there, filled with shame at these thoughts, it occurred to me that perhaps it was by no mere chance that Johnny had brought me to Edith's house that night. Although I had now been dead for over twenty-four hours, there was still no indication that I was about to enter another sphere of consciousness. Quite possibly, then, what I was now experiencing could be explained by the old belief in Purgatory. Perhaps, before I could be allowed to pass on, I should see myself as others to whom I had done harm had seen me, and be harrowed by contrition for all my faults.

With that unhappy surmise in mind my thoughts again became vague and wandering until they ceased to flow. But, as a result of my past indifference of my family's welfare, before the night was out I was to suffer still deeper shame.

* * * *

I was roused by the opening of the door, and Christobel's voice saying: 'Stay where you are for a minute, while I put on the fire.'

By the light from the hall-way she crossed the room, switched on the three bars of the electric fire, and when it was

154

glowing fully called softly over her shoulder: 'You can come in now. This will give enough light to save you from tripping over anything.'

Closing the door behind him a man came into the room—presumably Archie. He was considerably older than I should have expected, and much nearer to my age than to hers. As he took off his overcoat I saw that he was wearing a dinner jacket; so it looked as though Christobel's story to Harold that she was going to a cinema was because she did not trust him and wished for reasons of her own to mislead her mother, and that actually she had gone straight up to the West End to dance and sup. It had struck me that she looked very smartly turned out for the pictures and possibly a visit to some local night-spot afterwards. A glance at the clock showed me that it was a quarter to four, and no local place would have kept open till near that hour.

Archie was a tallish man, rather red in the face and with thinning hair. Christobel seemed to be carrying her drink pretty well but it was obvious that he had knocked back quite a bit more than was good for him and, slurring his words a little, he said rather peevishly:

'I do wish you'd have let me take you to . . . to the flat.'

'No thanks,' she replied with a shake of her head. 'Not at this time of night, and have the porter recognise me coming out. Besides, I loathe having to get up and dress again.'

He gave an anxious glance at the ceiling. 'You're quite sure no one'll hear us?'

'No, darling, not a chance of it.' She threw herself down on the chesterfield at full length, and added: 'Even if Mother is awake, without her hearing aid she is as deaf as a post; and my kid brother is right at the top of the house.'

She had not taken her feet from the floor; so as she lay there invitingly her knees were on a level with her chin. Swaying slightly he stood looking down on her with an appreciative leer.

'Come on,' she said. 'What are you waiting for?'

At that, he plumped down beside her, took her in his arms and gave her a long rich kiss. But after a moment she pushed him away and asked:

'How about that hat in Josette's window that you were going to buy me?'

155

'Oh, come on,' he protested. 'It's only . . . only the other day I paid your hairdresser's bill for you.'

'I know that.' She gave him a quick kiss on the nose. 'But you like me to dress well, and it's over a fortnight since you gave me a present. Please don't be a meanie.'

Sitting up he got out his pocket book and with fumbling fingers extracted some pound notes. 'Here you are, then. It was a fiver, wasn't it?'

'That's right. Thank you, my poppet.' Taking the notes she performed the age-old gesture of pulling up her skirt and stuffing them into the top of her stocking.

Again he bent over her, then said in a tone that implied no insult: 'You know the truth is that you're a . . . a damned expensive gol . . . gold-digging little bitch.'

'Am I?' she laughed up at him. 'Anyway you've no cause to complain. You know that I always give you jolly good value for your money.'

I slunk away then, out through the passage and the front door to the street. It was the final humiliation, and that Harold should have foreseen the possibility of just such a situation added to its bitterness. Through my neglect of her, I had been brought to witness my daughter in the act of prostituting herself to a drunken man.

6

Sunday 11th September

Heedless of where I was going, I moved through a few silent residential streets instinctively taking a downhill direction and some ten minutes later arrived at the north bank of the Thames. Turning right, I made my way along the embankment until I reached Putney Bridge. There I remained for well over an hour, again contemplating my strange and unhappy condition.

Johnny and James Campbell had been perfectly right in their assessment of my attitude to suicide. In spite of Bill Wiltshire's view, that in certain circumstances it was the decent thing to do, I don't think I could ever have brought myself to take my own life; yet, so miserable was I from the experiences of the past night that, had I still been alive, I really believe I would seriously have considered throwing myself off the bridge into the river. But as I was already dead, to do so offered no escape from the thoughts that tormented me.

The sky over London is never dark, but gradually it lightened to the east until the street lamps were dimmed and the outline of Fulham Palace became clear in a new day. I had nothing to do and nowhere to go; but I decided that I must make an effort to rouse myself from the slough of despondency into which I had fallen, and that the best way to do so would be to make use of my extraordinary asset of invisibility. By it I could enter houses unseen and listen to the most intimate conversations. That at least offered a prospect of taking my mind off my own worries.

Crossing the bridge I proceeded towards London. As it was a Sunday morning the streets were still deserted, except for an occasional night-hawk taxi crawling home and a few groups of young people on bicycles making an early start for a day in the country.

The district that I entered was a mean and shabby one. The main street was lined with poor shops and the gutters were littered with refuse from rows of stalls that had stood there for a Saturday market. In the side turning solid rows of low, flat-topped, mid-Victorian houses faced one another. Each had a pillared portico, and at one time they had no doubt been small family residences for respectable head clerks, small tradesmen and widows with modest incomes; but they had fallen into a sad state of destitution and were now either tenements or cheap lodging houses.

I entered several and their interiors only added to my depression, yet somehow I felt forced to continue my investigations. Behind the grubby curtains I found a squalor which I had hardly realised existed. Few of the families had more than two rooms and sometimes numbered as many as six people. The greater part of them were still asleep; the grown-ups huddled under dirty coverlets in narrow beds, and often in the same room an old woman or children stretched out on palliasses on the floor. Among them were quite a number of negroes and others of obviously foreign origin.

In recent times many of the worst slums in the old East End have been demolished and replaced by big blocks of modern workers' flats; so a large part of the very poor have established new slum areas in Notting Hill and down there in Walham Green. Consequently, I knew that I was looking at what is called the 'submerged tenth'—the ne'er-do-wells, the petty crooks and near down-and-outs—that form a social sore in every great city, and for which no Government, given the best will in the world, can do very much. But all the same I was appalled by what I saw.

That must not be taken to imply that I became a sudden convert to Socialism. It is my firm conviction that although the honest Socialists—and there are many of them—have as their ideal the redistribution of wealth so that poverty shall be eliminated, the means by which they would attempt to do so are hopelessly impracticable. The results of increasing taxation on the better-off and the restriction of private enterprise could lead only to a general reduction of the standard of living over the whole country, and, eventually, to wide-spread unemployment. As has already been shown by a Labour Government, the additional revenue obtained from increased taxation does not go to bettering the lot of the very poor, but is squandered in paying the vast non-productive bureaucracy necessary to administer nationalised industries and maintain controls. Moreover as the prosperity of the country decreased so too would the amount received from taxes, with the final result that the Government itself would face bankruptcy, and be compelled to stop the payment of pensions, food subsidies, health benefits and all the other measures of social security which the people now enjoy as citizens of the Welfare State.

No, I was certainly not converted to Socialism; but there came into my mind the saying of Christ that: 'It is easier for a camel to pass through the eye of a needle than for a rich man to enter the Kingdom of Heaven.' And I had been a rich man.

Again I wondered if I was in Purgatory, and that, just as I had been shown the results of my selfishness towards my family, so I had now been directed here in order that I might see the appalling conditions in which many of my fellow human beings had been living while I, without giving them or their like a thought, must often have driven past these very houses in my big car, on my way into London and to a lunch, the price of which would have fed a whole family for a week.

I was jerked out of this fresh cause for heart-searching by a new and rather diverting experience. It was in a house crowded with negroes. In one carpetless room on the second floor, furnished only with a truckle bed, a single cupboard, a wash-stand and two chairs, a dusky couple had already woken. The woman, a beautifully healthy young animal clad only in an incredibly filthy kimono which she had left hanging open in front, was cooking up some mess on a gas ring; the man was sitting propped up in bed plucking chords from a home-made guitar and softly crooning a cheerful little ditty. I had entered by the window and was comforting myself somewhat with the thought that even the direst poverty could not prevent young people getting some joy out of life, when he glanced in my direction.

Suddenly his eyes began to roll in terror. Letting out a blood-curdling yell, he leapt from his bed, dashed for the door, wrenched it open and fled shouting downstairs. The only possible explanation was that he had seen me as a ghost, and it was interesting to know that physically sensitive human beings could do so as well as animals. But, more important at the moment, the sight of the whites of his eyes rolling ludicrously in his coal-black face, then of his flailing legs beneath the flying tail of his shirt as he bolted for the door, were just the things needed to restore my sense of humour.

Deciding that I had done quite enough slumming, I moved north-eastward at a walking pace, heading roughly in the direction of Hyde Park; but the mean streets seemed endless and by the time I reached the Queen's Gate area there were many more people about. Quite a few were entering a Church for early service, the Sunday papers were being delivered, and every few minutes I noticed the curtains of a window being drawn back.

The rows of one-time private mansions in the pleasant tree-lined streets and squares of this district had also been transformed, but in their case into private hotels and spacious apartments having anything from five to ten rooms. Here and there, too, whole rows had been demolished to make way for big blocks of luxury flats.

Like Don Cleofas in Le Sage's tale, after he had rescued the demon Asmodeus from imprisonment in a bottle by a sorcerer, roofs were no longer a shield to the privacy of any home I chose to examine, and during the next few hours I entered fifty or more, leaving each with a different emotion. There is no truer saying than that 'one half of the world does not know how the other half lives', and, applicable as it was to myself and the slums I had visited that morning, it also proved far more so than I would ever have suspected about these people many of whom were of my own social standing.

Most of them, of course, were behaving quite normally, but on average they seemed no happier than the poor wretches who had to struggle for existence some three miles to the south-west in Walham Green. A pair of, presumably, newly-weds, whom I surprised in an upper maisonnette, balanced out the cheerful negro couple whose morning I had inadvertently spoilt; but I was also the invisible witness of several grim little scenes.

In one flat I saw a youngish night porter who had just come off duty slap and jeer at a middle-aged woman who was

160

paying him to make love to her. In another, over breakfast, a despotic-looking uncle was deriving sadistic enjoyment from outlining the penalties he meant to inflict upon his school-boy nephew if the youngster did not get a better report at the end of the term which was due to start the following week. In a third a girl of about twenty-six, who was dressing in the bedroom of a white-haired man with the benign expression of a bishop, said to him. 'If you want me to spend another night with you, you'll have to make it better worth my while. Fifteen quid isn't good enough for letting you use me as a human pincushion.' In a fourth, again over breakfast. a hard-faced mother was laying the law down to her grown-up son, and telling him that unless he broke off his engagement she would cut off his allowance.

I saw a pretty girl take a shot of dope, and a young man beating himself with a dog-whip in front of a crucifix. A well-known barrister, whom I happened to know by sight, was refusing his wife's plea to dissociate himself from a group of fraudulent company promoters because he was able to avoid paying income tax on the big fees they were handing him in cash; while another man was saying to his wife that next time he went up to Manchester and his boss wanted her to sleep with him she had better let him, as that might lead to promotion; whereas her continued refusal might mean the sack, and where then would they find the money to keep their boys at an expensive prep school.

The worst thing I saw was a nurse torturing a small boy. She was making him stand in a steaming bath that was too hot for him. As he moaned and whimpered, lifting first one foot then the other, and struggled to get out, she kept on pushing him back, and saying: 'That'll teach you to tell tales to your mother about me speaking to gentlemen in the Park. Do it again, you spoiled little brat, and I'll push you under head and all. Then it won't be you who comes into your snooty Lord-papa's title.'

I would have given anything to be able to intervene, but I was incapable even of acting as a cooling draught of air which might have lowered by a fraction the temperature of the hot water in which the poor child was being forced to stand.

Another half dozen random visits revealed only people

snoozing or reading in bed; couples mildly bickering or cheerfully making plans for the day. Out of my half-hundred rather reprehensible snoopings into the lives of the better off, I had found nothing really to intrigue, and quite a lot to disgust, me. Although I could no longer talk to anyone, I felt a sudden craving for the companionship of someone that I knew and cared about. My thoughts turned to Johnny; so I set off for Westminster.

It was eleven o'clock by the time I arrived at the great block of Government offices that stretch from Whitehall to St. James's Park, and not only house several Ministries but also accommodate such departments as those of the Lord Privy Seal and Ministers without Portfolio. During the war the offices of the War Cabinet had also been situated in it, and it was no secret that a range of rooms on the ground floor overlooking the park had been converted into a flat in which Sir Winston Churchill lived for the greater part of the conflict. It was far less vulnerable to bombing than the old Georgian residence No. 10 Downing Street; and living there had enabled him to send, with a minimum of delay, for any of his Planning Staff, as it had occupied the basement beneath the flat.

Johnny had told me that the Joint Planners no longer devilled like troglodytes in the basement, but that it had been retained more or less in its war-time state and that little parties of distinguished visitors from overseas were now frequently taken round it. Assuming that the offices of the Planners would not have been moved very far I decided to begin my search for Johnny in the vicinity of the old ones, and as I entered the spacious hall I found that one of these parties had just arrived.

It consisted of four Americans and a Canadian couple. They were being received by the elderly custodian, and as he was examining their credentials I decided that it would be interesting to join them.

Leading the way down two flights of stone stairs, the old gentleman said in a soft voice: 'We are now about to enter the famous fortress basement from which the High Direction of the war was conducted. In addition to the four storeys of stone and steel building above it, a four-feet deep layer of concrete was inserted between it and Sir Winston's flat and the offices of his secretaries on the ground floor. It was

162

guarded by a special company of armed Home Guards who examined all passes, sentries supplied by the Brigade of Guards were posted on its entrances, and it had an internal garrison of Royal Marines, which also acted as servants to the Officers of the Joint Planning Staff who worked here under General Lord Ismay.

'As well as being bomb-proof it was gas-proof, air-conditioned, had its own electric light plant and was provisioned to withstand a siege. In it was the terminal of the Atlantic Telephone on which the Prime Minister had all his talks with President Roosevelt. Its telephone system was connected by deep-laid lines to all the principal cities and Command Headquarters of the Kingdom; so that, in the event of invasion, had every telephone exchange in London been knocked out by bombs operations could still have been conducted from here and from G.H.Q. Home Forces, which occupied a similarly-fortified basement adjacent to this one. If the Germans had decided to sacrifice an Airborne Division by dropping it on Whitehall with the object of attempting to destroy the nerve centres of the Government, this underground fortress would have closed up like a clam, with the War Cabinet and the Chiefs of Staff Organisation inside it, and they could have continued to direct the war overseas without the least apprehension, while the enemy parachutists were being mopped up by the troops under the command of G.O.C. London District.'

On entering the basement I saw that it was very like the lower regions of a battleship, and the humming of the air-conditioning plant added to the similarity. It consisted of a long, narrow corridor with a maze of shorter ones opening out of it. Along the ceiling and upper walls of them all ran innumerable white-painted pipes and wires. Every few feet a plywood door gave on to a room in most of which there were three or four desks, or, in the smaller ones, a single iron bed. On the doors of the latter were stencilled the names of the men who had occupied them: Sir Edward Bridges, Mr. Attlee, General Ismay, Mr. Brendan Bracken, Lord Beaverbrook, General Hollis, Sir John Anderson, Mr. Morrison, Sir Desmond Morton, and so on.

Our elderly guide explained that while Cabinet meetings had normally continued to be held at 10 Downing Street in the day-time, at night the War Cabinet had met in a room down here to which he took us. The sleeping cabins had been used by the P.M.'s principal assistants permanantly, and occasionally by Ministers who preferred to remain there rather than go home on nights when there were severe air-raids.

He showed us then the rooms of the Joint Planners, in each of which teams of three—sailor, soldier and airman—had worked together; the meeting room of the Chiefs of Staff; the map room, with its long range of different-coloured telephones, in which every conceivable piece of information available concerning our forces, their dispositions, and those of the enemy could be obtained at a glance; and finally Sir Winston Churchill's quarters. These consisted of a bedroom, a work-room and a private dining-room just large enough to seat four people. On the worst nights of the blitz his staff had persuaded him to sleep there, and in any emergency he would only have had to walk downstairs from his flat to continue fighting the war from there uninterrupted.

When we emerged from this intriguing tour I set about trying to find Johnny. As it was a Sunday few people were moving about in the long corridors and most of the first-floor rooms were deserted; moreover, as they had no maps on their walls it seemed probable that the men in them were Civil Servants. The second floor, perhaps because it is further removed from the noise and dust of the street, is the one in all Government offices where the bigwigs have their quarters. The rooms there were larger and much loftier; most of them containing big conference tables as well as handsome desks. I did not expect to find Johnny in these august surroundings, and had looked into a few of the rooms only out of curiosity, when I found myself in that of Sir Charles. He had evidently arrived only a few minutes ahead of me; and, as I gathered from his remarks to a young man for whom he had rung, had come in for an hour before lunch to sign some documents and look through the overnight Foreign Office telegrams.

I wondered if he had yet learned of my death, and thought it probable that he had as, even if it had not got into the London Saturday evening papers, it was certain to have been in those of that morning.

My own feelings apart, as I looked again at his tall, still youthful figure, thatch of white hair, and kind smile through the thick-lensed glasses, I felt sorry for him on account of it; for it had blown sky-high the plan on which he must have pinned considerable hopes.

I thought that probably he would try to get someone else to play the rôle he had designed for me—if not on account of E-boats then in connection with some other now redundant type of Naval craft—but that would take time, and it might not be easy to find a ship-builder regularly receiving Government contracts who, like myself, happened also to be air-minded, so sufficiently unprejudiced to view the problems as I had, and would agree to sacrifice both his Company's interests and, perhaps, the friendship of a number of die-hard sailors.

It was certainly bad luck for Sir Charles that my death should have occurred just at that time, and in circumstances which had not the remotest connection with our secret talk. Somehow it would not have seemed quite so bad if I had been murdered by someone who had found out our intentions —perhaps a Russian agent who had orders to do his utmost to prevent Britain going over to a New Look armaments programme, or a crazy young Naval officer holding the fanatical belief that our country could be saved only by the maintenance of the Old Look with more and bigger aircraft-carriers.

No doubt that is just the sort of way the events of which I am the central character would have developed had this been a Dennis Wheatley thriller; but, as far as Sir Charles's plans were concerned, once I was dead, who had killed me and why could have no bearing on the situation. It was only a, perhaps silly, feeling on my part that had I been done in with the object of wrecking his plans I could at least have counted my life given, in a sense, for what I believed to be the good of my country; whereas I had lost it as a result of an absurd misunderstanding between my wife, who loved me, and her passion-crazed admirer whom she did not love. There could certainly have been few more futile reasons for having one's life cut short, but I could only accept the fact that our existence while on earth, and its termination, does appear to be governed by just such pointless stupidities.

Leaving Sir Charles to his Sunday morning chore I moved up to the third floor and there struck lucky. The first room

I entered was a typists' pool. Most of the machines had their covers on, but two young women were busily tapping away there. Beyond it was a range of rooms each containing three or four desks, about one in three of which were occupied by men either writing or reading papers. They were all in civilian clothes, but the maps on the walls of the rooms told me that these must be offices of the Joint Planning Staff. Johnny was not among them, but I ran him to earth a few minutes later on the opposite side of the corridor.

He was in a fair-sized room that had no desks in it but an oval table and a number of elbow chairs. On the table there were a score or more of folders which at first sight looked like those used to contain magazines in a club reading room, and this evidently was a reading room, but the material in it was of the highest secrecy.

Each folder had its contents stencilled in large letters on its cover, and glancing at them I read some of the titles: 'MINUTES OF MEETINGS AT S.H.A.P.E., MINUTES OF THE CHIEFS OF STAFF, FOREIGN OFFICE TELE-GRAMS, MINUTES OF N.A.T.O. MEETINGS, JOINT INTELLIGENCE COMMITTEE, MINUTES OF DEPUTY CHIEFS OF STAFF, NORTH WESTERN ARMY GROUP INTELLIGENCE, MINUTES OF S.E.A.T.O. MEETINGS, EXTRACTS FROM CABINET MEETINGS, MINUTES OF U.N.O. MEETINGS, MINUTES OF DISARMAMENT CONFERENCE, MINUTES OF DEFENCE COMMITTEE.'

In addition there were another score or so of stencilled papers without covers, and reports printed on light blue paper, some of which I saw, as they were picked up and scanned by Johnny and his companions, ran to fifty of more pages in length. These had such titles as: Project Saucepan. New Assessment of Persian Oil. Operation Teasing. Report of ex-Naval Attaché Moscow. Bases in Malaya. Exercise Show-down. Enemy Propaganda in India. The War Potential of Turkey. Relative values of Light and Heavy Armoured Vehicles. British Cargo Tonnage State. Treaty between U.S.S.R. and Afghanistan. Potential of Norway to Wage War. The Underground in Czechoslovakia. Finding from recent Thermo-Nuclear Tests in the U.S.A.' and so on.

I felt that had I been left there for a month with nothing else to do I could not have mastered this mass of fascinating secret information, let alone the fresh material with which it would be supplemented from day to day; but Johnny and the two chaps who were with him in the room picked up and scanned through a dozen papers apiece quite casually in the course of the next half hour.

It occurred to me that in my present strange state I might make a marvellous spy if I could get to Moscow and locate some similar foom which must exist somewhere in the Kremlin. But on second thoughts I realised that such an idea was hopelessly impracticable. In the first place, with the restrictions which seemed to be imposed upon my movements it would take me quite a time to get there and back; in the second I could not read Russian; in the third, even if I could have done so, I was incapable of turning over pages for myself, so could read only such matter as was open to my gaze; and lastly I had no means of communicating to anybody anything that I might learn.

Nevertheless, I read over Johnny's shoulder with great interest the minutes and papers through which he was glancing, and even in that short time I was struck by one thing. Again and again Members of Parliament and the press attack the Government for not doing this and that, but there is a logical explanation for their apparent remissness which they cannot give in their own defence for reasons of national security.

In addition to the stimulating effect of these assessments of Britain's problems which I was reading, being again in Johnny's presence comforted me greatly. After my incredibly distressing morning it was unbelievably good to be with someone whom one had every reason to believe to be an inherently decent person. No doubt many of the people I had seen reading the Sunday papers in bed or getting their breakfasts were equally likeable, but I did not know them, whereas I did know Johnny.

There was something most commendable about his acceptance with enthusiasm of this extraordinarily arduous job, which debarred him for two years from the flying that he loved and might easily make a hash of his service career if he failed to handle it competently; of his entire lack of bitterness that his wealthy grandfather should not even have mentioned him in his will, and of the unfailing good humour with

167

which from his lazy blue eyes he regarded the doings of others. I don't think he was quite brilliant enough ever to get right to the top, but he had brains, a pleasant wit and, above all, integrity. Just to be with him gave one a sense of well-being and security. I would to God that he had been my son.

At about half past twelve Johnny left the reading room, went to his own office, collected from his desk a typescript which he locked into a brief-case, then descended to the ground floor in the old-fashioned lift. I accompanied him, and together we crossed Horse Guards Parade, passed beneath the arch of the ancient palace, and a few minutes later reached the Air Ministry in Whitehall Gardens. There we ascended in a swift modern elevator to the second floor and entered a room the door of which was labelled: 'Air Commodore Benthorpe, C.B.E., D.S.O., Director of Plans.'

A girl there greeted Johnny with a friendly smile, lifted one of the telephones on her desk and said: 'Wing Commander Norton to see you, Sir,' then laid it down and told Johnny: 'Master will see you; go right in, Wing Commander.'

In the adjacent room a small, thick-set, almost bald Air Commodore was sitting at a desk loaded with stacks of papers. Giving a swift nod he motioned Johnny to a chair and asked: 'Well, what's cooking over the way, Norton?'

'Nothing much, Sir,' Johnny replied. 'The Yugoslavian situation is not developing too well for us, and President Nehru is letting down the side again by encouraging the Afghans to accept neutrality. I came over only to give you this paper on atomic bases in the Arctic, and to ask for forty-eight hours' special leave from tomorrow morning owing to the death of my uncle, Sir Gifford Hillary. It is not only to attend his funeral but I may have quite a bit to do as one of his executors.'

The D of Plans nodded. 'Yes, I saw about his death in this morning's paper. I'm sorry, Norton. I gather that he was in the R.A.F. during the war, and a good chap. It's a sad business that his private affairs should have got into such a tangle. Fill in a form and I'll see to it that your leave is all right. There is one thing, though. We can't let that paper on air support for S.E.A.T.O. stand over for another week, and I understand that the G. Ones have not yet had your draft of it.'

168

'I have a luncheon date, Sir, which will go on for most of the afternoon,' Johnny replied, 'but I thought I would come in and finish it off this evening, if that's all right by you?'

'Certainly; by all means do that,' the Air Commodore nodded again. 'As long as it's in the hands of the G. Ones by tomorrow morning; then they should be able to let me have it by Tuesday. I'm sorry about your uncle. If you need an extra few days to get on with sorting out his affairs I don't doubt we shall be able to manage for that long without you.'

Having thanked him, Johnny left the Air Ministry, walked back to Whitehall, turned dŏwn it and halted at the bus stop on the corner of Parliament Square. My hour in his familiar company had done a lot to cheer me up; but now that he was evidently going to his luncheon appointment I felt that watching people eat, drink, and talk without being able to join in might bring about a return of my depression; so I decided against accompanying him. Yet, when he had jumped on to a bus, I was inclined to regret my decision, as I was at a complete loss what to do with myself.

That very fact suddenly struck me as interesting. The previous evening I had been taken all unsuspecting to see my family and early that morning impelled to witness the horrors of the slums. Since then my movements had been governed more and more by my own free will, and now I no longer had an urge to go anywhere. Was it possible that I had passed through two stages; the first to compel me to realise the evils with my selfishness had contributed to bringing about, and the second to show me the futility of interesting myself further in the doings of the still living? If so, I was now presumably in the clear and ready to leave earth.

The trouble was, though, that I still had not the faintest idea how to set about it and, apart from having no physical body, I felt as much one of the living as ever.

Poised as I was at the bottom of Whitehall, I found my gaze fixed on Westminster Abbey. It occurred to me then that it might be the portal through which I could receive my release. Whether one believed in the rituals of the Church or not, one could not deny the goodness of Christ, and His original teachings upon which the Church had been founded. Again, such Temples erected in His name had long been hallowed by

169

the prayers of countless men and women of high principles and upright life. Surely if there were anywhere in which a lost soul like myself could hope to be rested it must be in such a place.

Crossing the square I passed into the twilight depths of the lofty building. As it was the lunch hour the morning services were over and comparatively few sightseers were doing the rounds of the famous monuments. Advancing to the front row of chairs before the high altar, I lowered myself to the level of a kneeling position and began to pray.

For a long time I prayed with all the earnestness I could muster, beseeching forgiveness for the ill that I had done to others, and begging for release. But nothing happened; not even the faintest whisper of counsel to me.

No doubt because I had been roused before four o'clock that morning by Christobel returning home, I felt a great weariness stealing over me. Then I fell into the equivalent of sleep.

* * * *

When I woke nothing had changed, except that there were more people making the tour of the ancient edifice. For a time I remained where I was contemplating, a little bitterly I fear, the complete failure of my latest experiment. Apparently, for me at all events, there was nothing to hope for from the Christian God. Later I modified that view a little as it seemed at least possible that He intended me to expiate my sins by remaining for a considerable while longer in Purgatory before He would accept my repentance as sincere.

On that assumption there was a chance that I might hasten matters if I faced the music; so I tried to think of people that I had sinned against with the idea of seeking them out and deliberately harrowing myself by contemplating the injury I had done them.

But in that I came up against a brick wall. Like most people, I had undoubtedly been guilty of many small unkindnesses but they had been of such a minor nature that they had passed out of my mind. I had committed no serious crime and had been cursed neither with a malicious nature nor violent temper. I had, of course, indulged my natural appetites pretty freely, but I had never considered that to be a sin; as, regarded logically, if the Power that had created man had not intended that he should enjoy himself when he had the chance, by eating, drinking and making merry with the opposite sex, It would not have given him such desires. Search my conscience as I would, therefore, I could find nothing other than my neglect of my family, and having had more than my share of the good things of life while others were starving, with which to reproach myself.

More than ever puzzled at my state, and filled with angry frustration, I left the Abbey. Big Ben showed the time to be half-past five and it was a pleasant sunny afternoon with just a touch of approaching autumn in the air. Once more I was beset by an appalling loneliness, so I made up my mind to seek out a few old friends and see how they were faring.

My first choice was John and Alice Collier. He was my stock-broker, and they lived in a pleasant house up at Hampstead. Instinctively I made for the taxi-rank on the slope up to Westminster Bridge; but I had not covered a dozen yards before I realised that I was incapable of giving the driver directions; so, short of exhausting myself by moving for the best part of two hours at a walking pace, I must go by bus.

When one with the right number came along I impelled myself upwards, passed through a window, and settled on its upper deck. Having let it carry me up to Hampstead, I got off and drifted under my own steam the last half mile to the Colliers' house.

It was set back a little way from the road in its own garden, and as I went up the path I was cheered quite a lot by the memory of the many jolly evenings I had spent there and the thought of seeing John and Alice again, even though I could not talk to them.

Passing through the front door I crossed the hall to the drawing-room at the back of the house, thinking that the most likely place to find them at this hour on a Sunday. They were not there. Instead a strange couple were in possession. The man, a seedy-looking individual with a walrus moustache and a large paunch, was lying on the sofa; he was in his shirt-sleeves and wore no collar. The woman was seated close by in an arm-chair, knitting; she was somewhat cleaner, but her wispy grey hair looked as if it could do with a wash.

After my first surprise I realised that, the school term not having yet begun, John and Alice must still be down at Angmering with the children at the bungalow they had taken for the summer; and that these people were caretakers.

Much disappointed I made my way back to the main road and got on a bus that took me to Regent Street. At the last stop before Piccadilly Circus I left it and went up Vigo Street to the back entrance of Albany. It was there I meant to take my next call, and one Laurie Bullingdon, if at home, was to be the unwitting object of my attentions.

Laurie was another very old friend of mine, and one of the finest people I had ever met. While still a young man he had come into a considerable fortune and apart from serving for a few years in the Guards—and of course rejoining for the period of the war—he had never done anything. But no one ever blamed him for that because he was always doing things for other people—including lending them money which he rarely got back.

Apart from the fact that he dressed extremely well, collected beautifully-bound books, and loved to give the friends who went to dine with him the finest wines obtainable, he was not extravagant personally. Those tastes were typical of the man; for he detested this hustling modern world and quite clearly ought to have lived a century and a half ago. It was therefore most fitting that he should live in Albany, that strange enchanting relic of Regency days—probably the first flats ever built in London but still lying hidden and unchanged between Vigo Street and Piccadilly—in which the Bucks and Bloods had held their bachelor revels.

His 'set' as the flats are called was a ground-floor one on the right near the Piccadilly end of the covered way. When I came to it I saw him through the filmy curtain of the sitting-room seated at his desk. Having no need to enter by way of the stone-flagged hall I went straight in through the broad window.

The two main rooms of each set are beautifully proportioned and much loftier than those of modern flats; so they lend themselves admirably to housing a collection of books.

172

There were shelves from floor to ceiling and when I had last been there, some six months before, each wall, with its serried rows of gilt-tooled morocco, vellum and calf bound volumes, had formed a warm, subdued background. Now, much to my surprise, more than half the shelves were empty.

Turning towards Laurie I saw that he was not writing at his desk but simply leaning forward staring with taut expressionless face at some sheets of foolscap that lay upon it. Looking over his shoulder, I took in the grim fact that they conveyed. He had got out a statement of his financial position, and he was insolvent to the tune of several thousand pounds.

One sheet showed his annual commitments. Had these been limited to his personal expenses he would still have been comfortably solvent, but they included many hundreds of pounds in allowances to relatives, and several hundreds more to charities which, presumably, he had been paying for years and had not been able to bring himself to reduce. Income Tax and Super Tax had caught up with him, and now formed a liability more than four times as great as all the others put together.

Poor Laurie. One may say that according to present-day standards he had been reprehensibly unbusiness-like in handling his affairs, that he had been a fool to keep on giving away money for the benefit of the poor when he contributed so much in taxes to their care by the Welfare State, and that when he went to Carey Street the law would undoubtedly call him to account for having piled up debts that he could not pay. Yet he had done the very thing that I had failed to do, and this was his reward.

Sadly I left this simple, kind and generous man to brood unhappily over the plight to which he had reduced himself. More at a loss than ever to comprehend the strange laws by which humans were, presumably, expected to conduct their lives, I went out through the courtyard entrance to Piccadilly.

By this time it was close on eight o'clock, so it seemed probable that by then Johnny would be finishing his paper and shortly be returning to his rooms in Earls Court. I knew that he went up and down from them to his office every day by Underground, so he would have to go out there to collect his suit-case and car if he meant to drive down to Longshot that

173

night; and I wanted to go with him in order to attend my own inquest in the morning. Accordingly I went to Piccadilly Tube Station, drifted down the moving stair, took a train to Earls Court, and propelled myself round the corner into Nevern Square, where Johnny had his rooms.

Apart from breakfast, which was provided for him by the comfortable body who owned the house, he fed out; so he had only two rooms and a bathroom on the second floor, but they were roomy and comfortable ones. I floated up to his sitting-room and, finding that he was not yet back, settled myself there.

It was past nine when he returned. Going straight to a cupboard he got out a full bottle of whisky and put it in his brief-case. I wondered why in the world he should feel it necessary to take his own drink to Longshot; but that was not his intention. Instead of starting to pack his suit-case he went downstairs out of the house and round the corner to the station. I kept beside him and we got into a west-bound tube. At Hammersmith he got out and I followed him through several streets until we reached an old-fashioned, rather dingy block of flats. There was no lift and he plodded up three flights of stone stairs, then rang a bell beside a door the upper half of which had hideous panels of coloured glass let into it.

The door was opened by a young woman in a négligée. She was blonde, blue-eyed and, I should think, still on the right side of thirty. Raising a pair of skilfully-pencilled eyebrows, she exclaimed:

'Well I never! Fancy it being you! It's such weeks since you've been to see me I thought you'd been posted out of London—or else given me the go-by.'

'No.' Johnny gave her a friendly grin and, evidently feeling it best to tell the truth and shame the devil, added: 'As a matter of fact, Daisy, I've become engaged to be married. That's why I stopped going to the Club or making dates to spend Sunday evenings with you here.'

Daisy's eyes narrowed slightly. 'So that's it, eh! Why are you honouring me this evening, then? I suppose your girl's got scruples, and you can't wait for the wedding night; so you thought you'd work it off on me. If that's the case you'd better think again.'

'It's not that,' Johnny assured her. 'But we've had a quarrel and I'm feeling pretty browned off about it. I thought I'd take a chance I might find you alone, and that you would let me spend an hour just chin-wagging with you to cheer myself up. I've brought along a bottle of Scotch in case you were short of liquor.'

Her big generous mouth broke into a smile and she said: 'If that's the case, come right in, Big Boy. It's a bit of a laugh, though, that by turning shirty your fiancée has driven you to spend your evening with a tart. I bet she'd be livid if she knew.'

'I've told you before not to speak of yourself like that,' he said severely, as he followed her inside. 'You're not a tart. You haven't a tart's mentality.'

She shrugged. 'What's the difference, ducks? No girl who isn't kept by her family can earn a decent living just by dancing near-nude six nights a week in Cabaret. There always has to be a steady in the background to ante-up the rent cheque. And if I happen to meet someone in the Club that I take a fancy to who says "What about it?" Well, why not? I've never made any pretence of being the faithful kind.'

'I know that; but you don't go to bed with every Tom, Dick and Harry, or lie and cheat like lots of girls who are much better placed than you are. The fact is, Daisy, that you're a darn good sort and wouldn't accept money at all if you didn't have to. So stop talking nonsense.'

She threw an arm round his shoulders and kissed him lightly on the cheek. 'You're nice, Johnny. It's good to see you again. You're a real gentleman, I always did say.'

'Nonsense!' He gave her a friendly pat on the behind, then went into the kitchen to fetch a couple of glasses and a syphon. As he poured out the drinks I looked round Daisy's living-room with considerable surprise; it seemed to have been furnished by two persons with about as strongly contrasting interests as one could find.

A big divan piled with none too clean cushions and several gaudy dolls was pure cabaret girl, but above it in a long glass frame hung an original Egyptian papyrus depicting the weighing of the heart of a dead person against the Feather of Truth before the god Osiris. Photographs of film stars

175

alternated on the walls with pictures of Karnak, Abydos and other Temples on the Nile, while on two occasional tables cheap china souvenirs of seaside holidays in England jostled amulets and little idols retrieved from the ancient past. Later I was to learn the explanation of this strange medley.

Meanwhile Johnny and Daisy had settled themselves on the divan, and she was asking him about his quarrel with Sue. Naturally he refrained from giving her any details, and simply said that they had come to loggerheads over a question that concerned his job. Then he told her that he had been greatly upset by another matter, and asked her if she had seen any mention of my death in the papers.

She had, but apparently it had been only a brief announcement and she had not connected it with him, so he said: 'Well, it's a shocking business, but it's all bound to come out, so I may as well tell you about it.' And during the next quarter of an hour he gave her an account of the double tragedy.

Daisy's blue eyes grew ever rounder with excitement as he proceeded and she interrupted him only now and again to ask him to elucidate a point. When he had done, she exclaimed:

'My! What a business! That Lady Ankaret must have been off her chump to go after the little Professor when she had a nice fellow like your uncle for her husband.'

Johnny nodded. 'I don't think she's quite normal where men are concerned. And I'm convinced that she knows more about how my uncle met his death than she will admit.'

'Really!' Daisy's blue eyes popped again. 'What makes you think that?'

'One or two little things that I must keep to myself for the moment. I'm hoping that something may come out at the inquest tomorrow morning. Anyhow, I'm sure we haven't got to the bottom of the matter yet. My Uncle Giff wasn't the type of man to commit suicide, and I mean to do my damnedest to clear his name of such a stigma if I can.'

For a few moments they were silent then he said: 'Daisy, you are psychic, aren't you?'

'Yes, dear.' She inclined her blonde head. 'But why do you ask? I gave that sort of thing up ages ago. At one time I used to tell people's fortunes, but they're misfortunes mostly, and several times I hit the nail on the head. It scared me

176

stiff, it did, but I don't think it right to lie to people about the future one sees for them. That's why I gave it up. Pour me another drink, there's a duck.'

Johnny refilled their glasses and enquired: 'How did you come to find out that you had psychic powers in the first place?'

'I was born that way. My old Mum was a real wow at it. Besides being fey herself she learnt no end of things by studying under an Egyptian mystic when she was out there and Dad was doing his excavating. I was only a kid then, and when we came home she kept us all by telling fortunes for a living, until Dad drank himself to death.'

After pausing to take a drink Daisy went on: 'He came of a good family, you know, and was ever so clever; but he just couldn't keep off the bottle. Mum worshipped the ground he walked on and his death broke her up. It broke up our home too. She put me and my sister to a dancing school, then went into a decline and died herself.'

'I know; you told me once before. I mean about your losing both your father and mother when you were only ten. That was a rotten break.' Johnny looked his sympathy; and it crossed my mind, as it had once or twice on previous occasions, that for a normally impassive man he had an unusual ability for conveying his feelings in a look.

Daisy shrugged. 'Oh, I'm not one to complain. It would have been nice to have been brought up at a posh school; and I might have been if Dad hadn't taken to the bottle. But nothing really matters if your health keeps good. That's what I always say.'

'I was wondering,' Johnny said after a moment, 'if you could help me to get at the truth about my Uncle's death. I believe there have been cases in which occultists have helped the police to get a line on a murderer. Do you think that if I brought you something belonging to Uncle Giff—something he had been wearing at the time of his death—you might be able to tell me if he really committed suicide or was killed by someone else?'

'Mother could have done that,' Daisy replied with conviction. 'You only had to give her a ring or a glove, or something, and she'd describe the person it belonged to, then tell you the state of mind they'd been in when they last wore it.

177

Whether I could, I don't know. I used to do a bit of that sort of thing at one time, and it was really queer how I'd get a picture of someone I'd never seen. I'll try if you like, but you mustn't be disappointed if I don't get anything at all. Anyway, if your uncle was murdered I wouldn't be able to describe the fellow that did him in. At best I'd only be able to tell you if he was frightened when he died, or in a temper, or just sort of quiet and resigned.'

'All the same, I'd be very grateful if you'd have a cut at it,' Johnny told her. 'The funeral is on Tuesday morning; so I can get back to London early in the evening. How about my coming in for a drink with you before you have to go to the Club?'

'Fine, ducks. Do that and I'd be glad to oblige. That will be much better than after the show, too, because I'll be nice and rested; and there's nothing like a rest beforehand for getting results.'

Daisy's agreement to try her hand at psychic detection was anything but welcome to me. I thought it most unlikely that she would get anywhere near the truth, but there was always the chance that she might provide Johnny with a new line for his dangerous speculations; and, grateful as I was to him for his laudable desire to clear my name, I would much rather that my friends should have been left with the belief that I had committed suicide than that he should unearth some bit of evidence which might lead the police to conclude that I had been murdered. As things were Ankaret had only to sit tight and say nothing, but few people can maintain a convincing structure of lies in the face of long and skilful questioning. A full investigation might well end in her being brought to trial, and even the thought of that happening filled me with acute distress.

For some half-hour longer Johnny and Daisy sat on talking together, but mainly about the doings of friends of hers in the same floor show, and other subjects which held no interest for me. Then he said:

'I think I ought to be getting along now, as I've got to make an early start in the morning.' And a few minutes later he took his departure.

Now I knew for certain that he did not intend to drive down to Longshot that night, there was no particular point in my leaving with him; so I thought I would stay on for a while with Daisy. As she had openly confessed to living, at least in part, on her immoral earnings, in spite of Johnny's protests to the contrary, she was unquestionably a superior type of whore; but all the same, she was a most likable young woman, and at heart a very much better one than most of the people into whose private lives I had had a peep during that long day. Moreover she radiated such warmth and cheerfulness that I felt happier in her presence than at any time since I had died.

When Johnny had gone she tidied up the room, washed the glasses, then threw off the loose négligée she was wearing and began to practice some complicated dance steps. Now that she had on only her undies I saw that as well as a pretty face she had a lovely figure, and I thoroughly enjoyed watching her antics. I also derived some amusement from thinking how surprised she would be if she knew that she had an unseen audience for her private cabaret show.

It was this thought which gave me the idea that, as she was supposed to be psychic, if I could will it strongly enough, I might make her realise my presence and, possibly, even communicate with her. But just as I started to make the attempt she ceased her pirouetting and high-kicking and went into her bedroom. Unwilling now to give up the chance of trying out my new project, I followed. As she sat down at her dressing-table, I took up a position just by the window, so that I could still see her face, and focussing on it I willed her to look up and see me.

She did not take long to brush her hair and put cream on her face, so I was able only to get in a few minutes' concentration before she stood up and went into the bedroom. As soon as she came back I tried again, but she showed not the least indication that she was in any way affected, and began to take off her undies. Still I kept on silently throwing out the command: 'Look at me! Look at me! Look at me!' with all the force I could muster.

Suddenly she turned her head and stared in my direction. She showed no fright but a frown of annoyance appeared on her pretty face. I felt certain then that I had now done the trick and that she could see me. A second later she confirmed my belief by demanding sharply:

179

'What do *you* want?'

Greatly elated I essayed the next step and formed in my brain the words. 'Please tell me if you can how long I am likely to remain earth-bound.'

To my amazement she replied at once: 'You're not earth-bound, you're dreaming, silly; and just trying to get a cheap thrill by watching me undress. I've often seen night-walkers like you. Go on! Hop it. Get back to bed.'

7

Monday 12th September

On the Monday morning I was aroused to renewed consciousness of my problems by the shrilling of an alarm clock. It came from Johnny's bedroom, and he had evidently set it to ensure his waking in time to make an early start for Longshot. I was next door in his sitting-room, to which I had returned after my exciting but abortive contact with Daisy.

Disregarding her command to 'hop it', I had flung a dozen telepathic questions at her, imploring her to tell me more about my state; but, to my distress and chagrin, she had ignored them, jumped into bed and switched out the light. For a quarter of an hour or more I had remained there endeavouring to induce her to answer, but it was no good; she had turned her face to the wall and, apparently, shut her consciousness against me.

At length, abandoning the attempt, I had spent a long time drifting about the streets, heedless of where I was going, while I puzzled over this new development. It is an ancient and widely accepted belief that when asleep people's egos leave their bodies, and that dreams recalled on waking are jumbled, telescoped memories of the ego's experiences while away from its physical habitation. If that were so, it was perfectly understandable that psychics, like Daisy, should from time to time see the ethereal forms of sleeping people; but I simply could not accept her belief that my own was such a case. I had then been out of my body for over forty-eight hours and two doctors had definitely pronounced me dead; so dead I must be. Desperately weary after my long depressing day, I had made my way back to Johnny's rooms.

Emerging from his bedroom, Johnny switched on an electric kettle, made himself a pot of tea and had a snack breakfast of some fruit. Half an hour later he threw a few things into a blue canvas suit-case, then he got out a large old-fashioned brown leather one, made certain that it was empty and carried both of them downstairs. As I followed I wondered why he should be taking an empty suit-case to Longshot. I was to learn in due course.

It was still only a little after six o'clock when he collected his car from the garage and we set out. Our journey was uneventful and we reached Longshot just before nine.

When we arrived Silvers was already carrying extra chairs into the dining-room in preparation for the inquest. Shortly afterwards Inspector Mallet and Sergeant Haines put in an appearance. Then Bill Wiltshire came downstairs and handed the Inspector some folded sheets of foolscap.

'This is a signed statement by my daughter,' he said. 'Dr. Culver came again yesterday evening and gave it as his opinion that if she were made to attend the inquest a complete breakdown might result; so in his presence I wrote this out at her dictation. If you wish to question her after you've read it, she'll see you. But I hope that won't be necessary.'

With a word of thanks Mallet took the statement into the drawing-room and sat down to read it. Anxiously I peered over his shoulder while he did so, and was greatly relieved to see that Ankaret had made no dangerous elaborations to her story, but given it briefly point by point exactly as it had already been established by the forged letter.

After reading it the Inspector handed it to Haines, and told Bill that, at the present stage, he did not think it would be necessary for him to trouble Ankaret.

By this time a number of reporters had gathered in the hall and, standing a little apart from them, an elderly couple of not very prosperous appearance. The woman was in rusty black and the man wearing a black tie with an obviously ready-made suit. As they looked a little nervously about them Silvers came over to my father-in-law and told him in a low voice that they were Mr. and Mrs. Evans, Owen's parents.

Bill at once went up to them, condoled with them on their loss and, on learning that they had travelled from Wales through the night in order to attend the inquest, offered them breakfast. They said they had already had a meal at Southampton station, so he led them through to my library where they could wait instead of among the crowd, and insisted on providing Mr. Evans with a stiff whisky and soda.

Naturally they were much distressed by the death of their son; and as they believed him to have risen to a position of some importance and even greater promise, the cutting short of his career had proved an added blow to them. Mrs. Evans was peevishly resentful, and although her husband did his best to check her, frankly expressed her opinion that 'it all came of poor Owen coming to live in a big house like this and getting hisself mixed up with rich people who were no better than they should be'.

Bill might well have informed her that it all came of her son having made immoral advances to his daughter; but, with the good manners natural to him, he confined himself to remarking that, wherever the fault might lie, the tragedy had also robbed him, if not of a son, of a son-in-law for whom he had had a great affection.

The sense of *noblesse oblige* which had led him to take special care of the bereaved couple was not put to further strain, for while they were talking the jurymen had arrived and soon afterwards Silvers came in to announce that the Coroner was about to open the proceedings.

They proved much less sensational than I had expected. Johnny gave evidence of the finding of the bodies. Silvers followed and told of the letter, which was believed to have been written by myself, that he had found among the post in the letter-box and passed on to Johnny. It was produced and its contents naturally led to an increased tempo in the scribbling of the journalists, but the little flutter it caused subsided again when Dr. Culver gave particulars of the causes of death in dry medical terms. The police surgeon confirmed his findings and Inspector Mallet made a brief statement to the effect that the police had been called in without delay, had made a full investigation and were satisfied with the evidence given.

The Coroner then informed the jury that Lady Ankaret was still suffering too severely from shock to attend but that he had received a statement from her in which, while she maintained that her friendship with Evans had been entirely innocent, she substantiated that having had to confess to her husband that Evans was so violently in love with her that he had assaulted her had been the cause of the quarrel that had led to the death of both. He added that in the circumstances he felt it unnecessary to call further evidence.

The jury was then taken to the laboratory and the beach pavilion for formal inspection of the bodies. On their return they retired to consider their verdicts. They remained closeted for barely ten minutes and when the public were re-admitted the verdicts, now a foregone conclusion, were given: in Evans's case that he had died of severe injuries inflicted by myself, and in mine that I had taken my own life by an over-dose of a dangerous drug while the balance of my mind was disturbed.

No breath of suspicion about the dark doings that had really taken place at Longshot Hall the previous Friday night had fallen on Ankaret, and that cheered me greatly. Now, apart from my own still-veiled future, my only worry was over Johnny's quarrel with Sue, but soon after the Coroner's court rose, that too showed signs of being disposed of.

Bill had just been making arrangements for the Evans to have their son's body removed to the mortuary in Southampton that afternoon, and as I watched him escort them out to their taxi the telephone rang. Johnny went to answer it and when he realised who the caller was I saw his face light up. His 'Hello, darling!' told me that it must be Sue, and evidently she had decided to have a further explanation with him. Moving nearer, I heard him arrange to pick her up at a cross-roads near her home that evening, and then try to persuade her to let him give her dinner at The Master Builder's at Buckler's Hard.

The sitting of the court had occupied most of the morning and the last of the people who had come to attend it were now moving off. Inspector Mallet told Bill and Johnny that he hoped not to have to trouble them further, then he and his men took their departure. Bill went upstairs to tell Ankaret the findings of the court, then joined Johnny in my room for a drink. By the time they had finished it Silvers announced lunch.

Over the meal they talked about the morning's doings for a while, then Johnny asked when Ankaret would be fit to leave her room.

'The poor gel's still pretty low,' her father replied, so I

184

don't think she'll be up to coming down this evening; but she told me that she means to attend the funeral tomorrow morning.'

'I see,' said Johnny. 'Well, immediately after the funeral I'll have to get back to London, so if she's set on remaining up in her room I'd be glad if you'd ask her to let me have Giff's keys. As one of his executors I've naturally got to go into his affairs, so I want to collect the papers that are in his desk.'

'Right,' Bill responded cheerfully, 'I'll go up and ask her for them directly we've finished lunch.'

'It's two o'clock already,' Johnny demurred, 'and by then she may have settled down for a nap. I don't want you to disturb her unnecessarily, and as I was up at crack of dawn this morning I mean to have a sleep myself this afternoon. But I shall be going out about six and it's quite on the cards that I won't be back until late, so I'd like to have them by five o'clock. If you ask her for them when her tea is taken up that will be quite time enough.'

Bill shook his sandy head. 'No; to kick my heels in this place now for the rest of the day would give my the willies. When we've had our glass of port I mean to drive over to old Frothy Massingham's and as you're going to be out I'll probably stay to dinner; so I'll see her before I go.'

Some twenty minutes later he went up to Ankaret, but returned almost at once to report that the police had asked for my keys on Sunday; so she had sent them down by Mildred, and they had not yet been returned.

When I had heard Johnny ask Bill to get my keys for him I had felt no uneasiness, as I had taken it for granted that Ankaret would have slipped downstairs at the first reasonably safe opportunity to remove those incriminating trial forgeries from my desk, or at the latest have collected them some time during the previous night. But it looked now as if she had neglected to do so. Why otherwise had she lied about the police having my keys. And I felt sure she had. I could think of no point during their investigation at which they might have needed them, and had been there they would have asked Bill or Johnny to ask Ankaret for them, not sent a message up to her by a young servant girl.

Had I had any blood to chill, the thought of those damn-

185

able papers still being in my desk would have chilled it; and had I had arms I could have shaken Ankaret till her teeth rattled for her incredible folly in having failed to destroy the one thing which might yet bring her to the gallows. The cause of her remissness I could only guess at, but I had little doubt that it was another manifestation of that peculiarly female refusal to play for safety by prompt action which had so infuriated Evans when she could not be hurried into helping him dispose of my body.

As the last time she was supposed to have seen me was when I had left her to go to the lab with Evans, and Johnny had come upon her at my desk hours later, she could not deny having had my keys; so this story that she had passed them on to the police was simply an expedient to gain a little time. But it must soon be blown. Johnny had only to telephone Mallet and he would learn that she had lied to him. Anxiously I watched his face, on tenterhooks to learn his reaction; but it seemed that he was, at the moment, too tired immediately to pick up the implications.

Smothering a yawn he said: 'Oh well, it doesn't matter. Later I'll phone Mallet and ask him to put them in the post. They'll get here in the morning and I'll have ample time to collect the stuff in Giff's desk before the funeral.'

Then, turning, he crossed the hall and went down the passage under the laboratory to his room.

My mind, too, was again fagged out; so as Bill left the house, to go off in my car presumably, I went into the little library and settled myself there.

Later I learned that my mind had been blacked out for close on an hour, when a slight sound roused me. As my consciousness flooded back I saw that Ankaret was within a yard of me and just about to unlock my desk.

There were dark shadows under her big eyes and her face looked drawn, but her fine features, serene brow and the aureole of Titian hair curling down on to the shoulders of her turquoise blue dressing-gown still made her the most beautiful living thing that I had ever seen. That she had unwittingly brought about my death through indulging in a stupid peccadillo weighed nothing with me. I felt only relief and joy that this lovely being, whose faults I so well under-stood, should at last have seen the red light. Evidently she

186

had learnt from her father that he was going out, and that Johnny meant to sleep, so had determined to take this last opportunity to destroy those damning examples of her skilful penmanship.

As she unlocked the desk and rolled up its top the door, which she had closed behind her, was suddenly thrown open. Johnny stood there carrying the brown leather suit-case in his right hand.

He smiled at her, but his smile was by no means a friendly one as he said: 'Then you did lie about having given those keys to the police. I thought as much; so I decided to put off my sleep for a while in the hope of catching you out. And by jove I have—red-handed!'

Taken by surprise as she was, Ankaret did not lose her nerve; and no one who knew the desparate stakes for which she was now forced to play could have failed to admire the way she met Johnny's challenge.

After a first faint start she remained quite still for a moment, then slowly turned towards him, and said quietly: 'Aren't you being quite unnecessarily offensive?'

'I don't think so,' Johnny retorted, closing the door behind him and setting down the suit-case. 'The fact that you told a deliberate lie about these keys when I asked for them frees me from the obligation to mince my words with you. Why did you lie about them?'

'Because I did not wish to part with them, of course.'

'But you must have known that as one of Giff's executors I have a legal right to them.'

She gave him a faintly mocking smile. 'Certainly I knew that; but you should be old enough by now, Johnny, to know that women don't set the same value as men on technicalities of that kind, and seldom allow them to interfere with their own wishes.'

'No doubt you are right there. But why did you try to fool me into the belief that you had not got them? And what are you doing here now, while you believed me to be asleep. That's what I want to know.

'Then you must continue to want. My actions are my own private affair and nothing to do with you.'

'Oh yes they are!' Johnny countered quickly. 'Quite apart from my being one of Giff's executors I was closer to him than his own son. The fact that on the night he died you came down from your room at near midnight to rummage in his desk gave me the idea that you know more about how he met his death than you have told any of us yet; and catching you here in such circumstances again this afternoon has convinced me of it. I never have subscribed to this belief that Giff committed suicide. He wasn't that sort of chap. And I am determined to find out the real facts about his death.'

Ankaret shrugged her slim shoulders a shade disdainfully. 'My dear Johnny, no one would doubt your capabilities as an airman but by assuming the rôle of a detective you make yourself ridiculous.'

'There is nothing ridiculous about trying to find out the truth.'

'The professionals have already investigated everything there is to investigate about this frightful business, and pronounced themselves satisfied. No one is better qualified than I am to sympathise with you . . . our awful loss; but you really must not let yourself get carried away with wild ideas about it, and act like a small boy who has been reading too many shockers late at night.'

Johnny lit a cigarette and said quietly: 'Listen, Ankaret; nothing will ever convince me that Giff took his own life. Some time on Friday night he went out for some definite purpose; probably to meet somebody who was trying to blackmail either him or you. Anyhow your behaviour has given me very good reason to believe that you knew that he was going, why he went, and who he was going to meet. Come clean with me and, providing you are no more responsible for his death than you would have us believe at the moment, I promise I'll do my utmost to protect you.'

'Really!' Ankaret's apparent indignation was so excellently acted that one could hardly believe it was not real, as she stormed at him. 'How dare you offer me your protection! I think you must be out of your mind! But if you are determined to play the amateur sleuth, go ahead. I couldn't care less.'

'I will.' Johnny's face hardened, and picking up the suitcase he dumped it on a chair and opened it. 'As a first move I mean to relieve you of further temptation to make off with any of the papers in this desk. I shall take them back to

London with me and tomorrow evening I'll go through them with a tooth-comb. If I don't find some clue to Giff's death among them I'll make you an abject apology; but I've a thundering big hunch that one or more of them is going to lead me somewhere.'

As he began to throw the contents of the desk higgledy-piggledy into the empty case, Ankaret made an instinctive gesture to stop him. But, evidently realising the futility of such an attempt, she checked it and now white to the lips but with her head held high walked out of the room.

She had put up a magnificent fight but lost it, and I could have wept for her at the thought of what she must be feeling. Through her aloof indifference of playing for safety when she had the chance, she had jeopardised the whole fabric of defence which she had built up with such skill. She knew, as I knew, that Johnny had now secured proof that she was an accessory to my murder.

*   *   *   *

When Johnny had cleared the whole contents of the desk into the suit-case he carried it through to his room. As I followed, I wondered if his urge to get at the truth would lead him to take a first quick look through the papers at once and, perhaps, within the next hour come upon the dynamite with which to blow my beloved Ankaret sky-high that very evening. But the case was full almost to the brim with receipted bills, estimates, legal agreements, account books and scores of private letters that had accumulated over many years; and, evidently, tired as he was, he thought the mass too great even to glance through at the moment.

Having locked the case he took off his shoes, undid his tie and collar, and lay down on the bed for his belated nap. As soon as he had closed his eyes I left him and went up to Ankaret.

I found her seated in front of her dressing-table. She was sitting quite still staring into her mirror. Her lovely face was more drawn than ever. After a moment she quoted to herself in a low voice the famous line from Hamlet:

' "To be or not to be. That is the question?" '

Then she looked down at her right hand. It had been

closed about something, and as she opened her fingers I saw to my horror that it was a small bottle of veronal tablets. She was contemplating suicide.

For me it was easy to read her thoughts. It could be only a matter of time now, a few hours perhaps, a day or two at the most, before Johnny would know that she had forged the letter on which was based the accepted explanation of my death. Why, I then did not know, but for some time past there had been a coldness between them. As he bore her no love but had been so devoted to me, it seemed hardly likely that he would show her mercy and keep her secret. If he took her forgeries to the police what possible explanation could she offer to account for them? Under hours of questioning she must eventually break down, or at least be trapped into admissions which would give them a clue to the truth. They would turn the whole house upside down. There could be no hiding Evans's death ray machine, and she must reckon on my having examined it before it was used upon me; so my finger-prints would be on it.

Whether they would ever find out enough to link it with the crime and reconstruct the full sequence of events, it was impossible to say. But even if they could not prove her to be a murderess they would have a clear case against her as an accessory.

That would mean a long prison sentence; years of soul-shattering confinement, revolting food, a hard bed and being herded with the most vicious and debased women in the country. Appalling thought! Could she possibly face it? And then, when she came out, her looks gone and her life ruined.

Slowly she unscrewed the bottle top, shook a tablet into her left hand, put it in her mouth, threw back her head and swallowed it.

As I watched her my mind was in a turmoil. Johnny and my other friends had been right in their belief that I thought it wrong to take one's own life. My immediate instinct was to exert all my will-power in an attempt to stop her. Yet on second thoughts I checked myself. Had I the right to do so? It was her life, not mine. And, even if I possessed the power to intervene, should I be using it in her best interests. Was it not kinder to let her slip away in a drug-induced sleep, than attempt to make her face years of misery?

190

Even as I hesitated she suddenly spoke aloud:

'No! I'll be damned if I do!' And swiftly screwing on the top of the bottle she threw it back into an open drawer.

Probably the decision had never lain with me, but now that it had, beyond question, been taken out of my hands, my mind was momentarily submerged by a wave of relief.

Getting up from the dressing-table, she went over to her bed and lay down upon it. For a while she remained with her grey eyes wide open, staring at the ceiling. Then the one tablet she had swallowed began to take effect. Her long eyelashes fluttered once or twice and she fell asleep.

The two scenes to which I had been a silent witness during the past half hour had played the very devil with my emotions and I decided that a tour of the garden would be the best thing to quieten my agitated mind; so I drifted down to it.

The wonderful long hot spell we had had was at last breaking up. There had been several thunder-storms in the past few days and although the afternoon was fine I guessed that the chill of autumn could now be felt by living people. Insensible to it I wended my way along the familiar paths and borders, then went down to the beach, and so whiled away the best part of two hours before returning to the house.

Ankaret had evidently been woken by Mildred's bringing up her tea and was now sitting up in bed reading. Her absorbed expression and the crumb-covered plate on the tea-tray implied that she had temporarily shrugged off her anxieties; so reassured about her I went down to Johnny.

I found him changing into a clean shirt and generally sprucing himself up. When he had done he checked the suit-case that held all my papers to see that both the locks on it were fast; then as he left the room he locked the door behind him and pocketed the key. I accompanied him out to the garage and into his car.

Had anyone else shown such determination to ferret out the truth about my death, highly proper, and altruistic as their activities might be, on account of the danger into which they were bringing Ankaret I should have felt a very definite antagonism towards them. But I had no such feelings towards Johnny. Knowing that all he was doing was out of love for me, even his lying in wait for Ankaret that afternoon and high-handed treatment of her when he caught her, made

191

no difference to my affection for him. Both of them had a bigger place in my heart than any other person in the world; so while I was infinitely more concerned about the dire peril in which Ankaret now stood I was still anxious that the rift I had unwittingly brought about in Johnny's romance should be mended, and I wanted to learn for myself how far Sue had gone towards changing her mind.

We reached the rendezvous outside Beaulieu well before time and Sue, having been brought up in a family that respected the clock, arrived punctually. As Johnny threw open the door of the car for her I slipped over to the back seat; but she did not get in at once, and I took the chance to have a good long look at her. Normally, of course, one rarely really studies another person's face, because it is rude to stare, but I was able to take advantage of my invisibility.

She was a small decidedly plump young person with a mop of thick dark short curls. Her brows were level, her eyes brown, her nose short and her mouth seductively full. I have no doubt she used similar beauty preparations to all the other girls of her class and generation, but I felt sure that the rich colouring of her lips and cheeks owed more to good red blood than make-up. No one who was not in love with her would have classed her as a beauty, but she was pretty, healthy, vivacious, and in short, as I had said to Ankaret on the last night of my life, just the sort of piece with whom a wicked old boy, given the chance, would have chosen to have a romp.

But that thought brought back to me Ankaret's reply. For the first time I noticed the more delicate edition of the Admiral's 'battleship chin' of which she had spoken, and at the moment Sue's brown eyes, fixed unwaveringly on Johnny's, held more than a hint of hardness.

While I was studying her she had said in answer to his eager greeting: 'I must be frank with you, Johnny. This is only a—well, call it a conference if you like. I haven't altered my opinion about Daddy's being right, but I've never spent a more bloody week-end; so I know now that I'm much too fond of you to let you go without another try to see each other's point of view. But unless you feel that we can reach some sort of compromise it's not much good our talking.'

'That's fair enough,' he agreed. 'But need we start our

192

argument here and now? Couldn't we forget the whole thing for an hour or two while we enjoy a jolly dinner together just as we used to, then talk matters over afterwards?'

I admired his tactics, and with very little persuasion she agreed to his suggestion. After she had settled herself in the car and Johnny had let in the clutch there fell an awkward silence between them for some moments; but she broke it by asking him about the inquest, and that set him off.

Having brought her up to date with events at Longshot till lunch time, he added: 'All the same it's my belief that someone has pulled the wool over the eyes of the police, and that the verdict given by the Coroner's court is far from being the right one.'

'What leads you to suppose that?' she asked in surprise.

'Because I am convinced that Giff did not commit suicide.'

'As all the evidence points to his having done so, why should you believe otherwise?'

'Because I know that the motive ascribed to him is a false one.'

There was a doubt in Sue's voice, as she said: 'Even knowing him as intimately as you did, I don't see how you can judge the extent to which his mind might have become unbalanced if he was suddenly given reason to believe that Ankaret had been unfaithful to him.'

'Ah, but that's just it! Pure chance put me in a position to assess just how he would react to such a situation.' Johnny hesitated a second, then went on. 'Listen, Sue. I'm damnably worried about this thing and want to get it off my chest, but you must not breathe a word about it to anyone, because what I am going to say is highly slanderous. And quite apart from that, should it get about it might prejudice the case if there is one. I've no particular love for Ankaret, but if she is brought to trial I would hate to think that I'd helped to damn her before she even enters the court.'

'You know that you can trust me, Johnny,' Sue said quietly.

'Of course I do, darling. Well, this is the gist of it. About a year ago, as I think I've told you, I was sent as an observer to the Army of the Rhine during a big exercise they carried out. The idea was that a certain number of R.A.F. officers like myself should get some idea of the needs and difficulties of the Army during active operations. On the Divisional Staff to which I was attached there was a Captain named Desmond Chawton; very good looking, quite a clever chap, but a bit of a play-boy. One of his friends told me that he had been to Eton and Oxford and was very well blessed with this world's goods.

'The evening after the exercise was over a few of us went out to dinner, and as the party broke up Chawton offered to run me back to the Officers' Club. On the way we chatted of this and that, and I happened to mention that I was Giff's nephew. At that he grinned and asked: "How is the lovely Ankaret? I used to know her well before she married. I suppose she's still kicking up her pretty heels with some lucky devil in the South of France every winter?"

'In fairness to him I should mention that this was late at night and we'd both had our fill of good liquor. All the same he had no earthly right to say such a thing, even if it were true, and very naturally I was pretty nettled at what I then believed to be a wicked slander on Giff's wife. I said so very bluntly, and told him that he must apologise, and give me his promise that he would never say such a thing about Ankaret in the future.

'At first he pretended that I had misunderstood him, and he meant no more than that Ankaret had always been a girl who enjoyed having a good time. Being a bit tight I refused to accept that, and rather pompously insisted that he should admit to having said a disgraceful thing about her quite unwarrantably.

'In turn he got on his high horse. He brought the car to a standstill, and said: "All right then; since you're so set on having the truth, here it is. I didn't seduce Ankaret, but I came in first wicket down, and I can tell you her bowling was pretty terrific even in those days. She was only just over eighteen and I was a subaltern at Aldershot. She had no proper home and used to move around from one set of relatives to another every few weeks. Between visits she used to wangle a night or two to spend with me at some unfrequented little country pub. By jove! I wish I could have that affair over again; it really was something while it lasted. But after a few months she tired of me and went off for her romps with a young intellectual in the Foreign Office. I went abroad as A.D.C. to the Governor of Cyprus soon afterwards,

194

so I lost track of her for some years; but I met her again the winter before last in the South of France, and I know for a fact that while she was there she was sleeping most nights with a good-looking Spanish Marquis."

' "What reason have you for being so certain of that?" I asked.

' "Because she told me so, of course," he retorted. "Women like Ankaret have no secrets from the lovers of their youth. We dined together one night and took mutual delight in swopping happy memories. She told me then all about her marriage to Sir Gifford Hillary and how fond she was of him; but how she simply had to let off her superfluous steam with some other chap at least once a year. I really am terribly sorry if I've upset you by telling you all this, but I thought that everyone in our sort of circle knew that she was the next thing to a nympho."

' "Perhaps they do," I replied. "But I certainly did not, and I'm sure my uncle would be terribly upset if he learned how she is deceiving him when she is abroad."

' "Oh, you're quite wrong there!" he exclaimed. "Sir Gifford knows perfectly well that she is periodically unfaithful to him. She told me so. She said that one reason she was so happy with him was because he understood her, and made allowances for the desperate urge she felt to go off the rails now and then. And there is no earthly reason why she should have lied to me about that." '

Johnny paused for a moment. 'So you see the set up. Ankaret's glands have been her undoing. Some women are like that. Poor old Giff loved her to distraction, and it's clear from what she said to Chawton that Giff preferred to put up with the torture of knowing that she was taking lovers on the side when she felt an urge that way rather than cut her out of his life altogether. Now do you get what I am driving at?'

Sue nodded. 'Yes; it could hardly be clearer. If your uncle has been playing the complaisant husband for years it's unthinkable that on learning that she was having an affair with the Welsh Professor he would have gone beserk and beaten the poor little devil to death.'

'You've said it, sweetie. But if Giff didn't kill the Prof, who did? And with Giff's alleged motive for committing suicide burst wide open, who killed him? It looks to me as if there must be have been a third man, presumably another of Ankaret's lovers, who killed them both. God alone knows what really happened, but of one thing I'm certain: Ankaret holds the key to the mystery, and I believe I've got hold of the means to make her talk.'

He told Sue then how he had twice come upon Ankaret rummaging in my desk, and now had its contents locked safely away in a suit-case in his room.

Naturally she was tremendously intrigued, and they were still absorbed in their speculations about the tragedy at Longshot when we drew up at Buckler's Hard.

The double row of ancient cottages with a broad green between sloping down to a bend in the Beaulieu River makes it one of the beauty spots of South Hampshire. In the old days many fine ships were built there, some by my own forebears, and several that fought under Nelson at Trafalgar. The only big building in the hamlet, at the far end on the left-hand side, is now an hotel, and it is called The Master Builder's, because it was once the residence of the dockyard superintendent. The little restaurant there is one of the best for many miles around, as not only is its charm preserved by old prints and ship's furnishings, but it provides excellent cooking and a good cellar. I had enjoyed many a pleasant evening there, but now being debarred from gastronomic delights I did not accompany Johnny and Sue inside.

Instead I drifted down to the river and surveyed with an expert's eye the lines of the numerous fine yachts which were moored there. Then as twilight fell I returned up the slope and kept watch on the door of the inn so that I should not miss the lovers when they came out.

In due course they emerged, and turning into the garden walked over to a bench at its far end where they sat down. It was dark now, but I could see their faces well enough to guess that the latter part of their dinner must have been somewhat marred by thoughts of the explanation they were about to have.

It was Sue who opened the matter by saying: 'Well, come on; let's get it over.'

'All right,' Johnny agreed. 'I think the best thing would be for you to state the case you have against me.'

Sue did so, and I thought very lucidly. 'It's this. According to Daddy, when you had your board meeting your uncle disclosed a lot of Top Secret information which could have come only from you. That is a Service matter so it effects me only as throwing grave doubt on your integrity. The thing that really shocked me so badly was the object with which you gave away these matters. It was to aid your uncle in a plot to bring about the disbandment of the Royal Navy, and afterwards you admitted to me yourself that you would like to see that happen.'

'O.K. Let's take first things first. I have already given you my word that I did not brief Griff on his proposal. It came to me as a bomb-shell, just as much as it did to the others. I was under the impression that when last we met you had accepted my assurance about that.'

'I did; at least to the extent that you did not actually write out his proposal for him or know that he was going to make it. But he must have got his information from you. During the past year you have seen a lot of him, and must have talked to him pretty freely about what an atomic war would be like. Naturally men in your position don't discuss such matters with every Tom, Dick and Harry, but they do among their own kind whom they regard as safe. I know that, because I've often heard some of our Naval friends speak of things to Daddy that they would not dream of mentioning outside a house like ours.'

'To some extent you are right about that,' Johnny admitted. 'But talking in general terms, in the sort of circumstances you have in mind, is very different from disclosing Top Secret information. Giff never tried to pump me; such a thought would never have entered his head. And I swear by my love for you Sue that he never had from me the stuff he spouted at that meeting.'

'Where else could he have got it, then, seeing that these secrets are known only to a very limited number of people?'

'I haven't an idea; but it must have been from someone pretty high up, because he knew about trends of policy that have not yet even come my way.'

'Very well; I'll take your word that you didn't brief him even unconsciously; so that disposes of that. But you backed his proposal, and made it clear to me that you are a hundred per cent in favour of this frightful idea of scrapping the Navy.'

197

Johnny sighed. 'I did, my dear; and much as I love you I can't go back on that. I wouldn't be honest if I even led you to believe that I am prepared to compromise about it. You see, the nation is up against it in the matter of money and the Services in the matter of men. The balance of Trade having gone against us big economies must be effected, and it is just a question of deciding which forms of sacrifice will be least prejudicial to our safety.

'The number of men in the Navy today is fifty per cent greater than it was in 1936; it is the only one of the three Services which will not accept a material reduction in manpower over the next few years and the only one which is increasing rather than reducing its demands for money. The increase in man-power has no relation to the number of ships it could send to sea. On the contrary, they would look a miserable sight compared to the Fleet of the 1930's, and, of course, the fact that two-thirds of the chaps now dressed as sailors are not sailors at all. They are either airmen or technicians, and would be of far more value if they were redeployed into only slightly different jobs with the Air Force proper.

'If that could be done there would be no more building of these fantastically costly aircraft carriers, and all the smaller craft which are needed to protect them. Those in commission could be paid off and the saving would be immense.

'Then there is the question of the strictly nautical—cruisers, destroyers, and so on. I'll admit that they have a certain use in a cold war, for showing the flag in foreign ports; but if we spent the cost of their upkeep in radio programmes for the Arab and Asiatic nations, aimed at countering Soviet propaganda, we would get infinitely better value for our money.'

'So you would have us hand the seas over to the Russians without firing a shot?' Sue challenged him.

'No,' he replied promptly. 'But if the thing lasted long enough for there to be any sea war at all our shots should come from aircraft and guided missile sites. Even in the last war the big ships hardly dared to show their bows out from harbour from fear of being bombed or torpedoed from the air, and, if the Russians were fools enough to send their

198

Fleet into the North Sea, sending it to the bottom would be a piece of cake.

'I hate to disillusion you, Sue, but nine-tenths of the ships that the Navy has in commission are already as much out of date as Roman galleys would have been in Nelson's time. As for the new types they are building, to my mind it is simply chucking money down the drain; because the only way we can now hope to cut our cloth according to our needs is to scrap all the most expensive weapons and methods of waging war which are unlikely to be brought into use during a brief, violent conflict dominated by the use of thermo-nuclear missiles. And, of course, the proposed reduction in personnel makes it more imperative than ever that every possible man should be allocated to the units which will have to do the fighting.'

'Our sailors have always done their share, and more, of that.' Sue protested, 'so why pick on the Navy?'

'Because it is now our least valuable arm,' Johnny replied patiently. 'Its ships cost enormous sums to build and maintain, and it ties up a higher percentage of technicians than either of the other Services. Thermo-nuclear development must be maintained and increased if possible. The Army cannot be cut much further owing to our commitments on the Continent and overseas. The brunt of any future war must be borne by the R.A.F. So what have we left? Only the Navy, and it is a luxury we can no longer afford.'

'I don't agree. Daddy says the Fleet Carriers now form our first line of battle; and that as there can be no guarantee about it being a short war it is absolutely vital that we should keep on building more and better small ships for convoy protection.'

'I know all that, darling; I've heard it argued a thousand times, but what it comes down to is a question of priorities; and can you honestly say that your father is in a position to judge such matters?'

'Of course he is; he would never have reached such high rank otherwise, and with all his years of service he must know far more about these problems than you do.'

'Now listen, Sue. Everyone knows that your father was a fine sailor, and I have a great admiration for him as a man; but he has been out of the Service for several years. In these

199

days new developments occur with terrifying swiftness. The atom has entirely changed all our conceptions of warfare. Only a very limited number of people have the faintest idea of what is likely to happen if there is a blow-up. By pure chance I am one of them, whereas your father has long since ceased to have access to Top Secret matters. You must admit that's true.'

'Yes,' Sue agreed, 'I suppose it is.'

'Very well, then. In fairness to me you've got to keep your father's views out of this. And even if he were right it doesn't alter the situation. I've given you my word that I had no hand in Giff's plot to sabotage the Navy; but it is my considered opinion, based on the very latest appreciations of what the next war will be like, that for the safety of our country the Navy must sacrifice itself and rest upon its past glories. That being so, it is my positive duty to throw any little weight that I may have into working towards what is called the New Look, which amounts to merging all three Services into one that has few, if any, ships.'

For a moment Sue was silent, then she said: 'I'd never try to come between you and your conscience, Johnny. Since you consider that your duty, that's what you must do. All the same I feel this makes an awful breach between us.'

'Oh come, darling!' He reached out and took her hand. 'Don't think I don't understand your feelings. You wouldn't be you if you'd just taken it as a matter of course; and it was a piece of really bad luck for both of us that we should have been driven into discussing the issue at all. But since we've had to, I think you'll agree now that your resentment has nothing personal in it, and is really the outcome of loyalty and affection for the things you have been brought up to admire.'

Sue had not withdrawn her hand, and she nodded. 'I suppose it is really.'

'Then surely you're not going to let sentiment for something impersonal weigh with you more than all we mean to one another? I've been nearly crazy with worry since we quarrelled. You do still love me, Sue, don't you?'

'Of—of course I do,' she gulped, now very near to tears.

'Oh my sweet, bless you for that! Don't cry, darling. Please, please let's forget all this and never say another word about it. Let's think of nothing but one another and be wonderfully happy together as we were before.'

In response she lifted her face and turned towards him. Next moment they were in each other's arms.

This happy outcome of their meeting took one load off my mind, and feeling that to linger there longer would be unwarrantable spying on them, I returned to the car to wait with as much patience as I could muster until Johnny should convey me back to Longshot.

As I expected, the wait proved a lengthy one and it was made the less supportable by my no longer having anything to keep my mind off gloomy speculations about what might happen to Ankaret once Johnny had gone through my papers. The only hope for her now seemed to be in his deciding against handing her forgeries over to the police. If she refused to talk, without professional aid he would still be unable to prove that she had known anything about either of the murders until after they had been committed, and it did not seem to have occurred to him that she might have played an active part in them. It was therefore possible that, rather than expose the family to the scandal that her trial as an accessory would bring about, he might show her mercy. It was too, I could only suppose, some such line of reasoning which at the critical moment had determined her against putting an end to herself.

At last the lovers, all unsuspicious of my presence, rejoined me, and we set off towards Sue's home. Johnny pulled up on the corner from which he had collected her, and after a prolonged succession of good-night kisses they tore themselves apart. Humming cheerfully to himself now he headed the car south-east. As we ran onward I took no particular notice of the glow in the sky ahead; for I knew that it was caused by the escape jet of the huge oil refinery at Fawley, which can be seen for many miles around. But when we drew nearer to Longshot I saw that the glow was brighter over a spot that lay well to the west of Fawley and that it had an angry reddish tinge. After another mile the truth flashed upon me. My old home was on fire.

Johnny realised it at the same moment. Jamming his foot down on the accelerator he proceeded to take risks on the corners that he would never normally have done. Fortunately the lodge gates were open and to the accompaniment of loud blasts of the horn the car shot through them. Half way up the drive we rounded a group of ancient trees and could see the house clearly. It was the east wing that was on fire and tongues of flame were leaping up from a gaping hole in its roof.

Three fire engines were already on the spot and a fourth came clanging up behind us. Jumping from the car Johnny ran in through the front door, and I sped close behind him. Dead I might be, but I was still fond of the old place, and to my great relief I saw that the main building was still unaffected. As three fire engines were already in action it looked as if there would be a good chance of confining the fire to the bachelor wing, which contained only the extra spare bedrooms and the laboratory above them.

Two big hoses snaked through the hall, but there was no one in it; so Johnny ran out of the garden entrance to the terrace. To the left on the lawn below it a crowd was gathered: firemen, police, local people and most of the household. I could see now that the seat of the fire was about half way along the wing. The crowd was watching the hoses being played on it.

After a few minutes Johnny found Bill. He was in his shirt-sleeves and the grime on his face showed that he had been fire fighting. Struggling to get back his breath, Johnny gasped:

'How did this happen? How did it start?'

'God alone knows!' Bill replied, mopping his soot-streaked brow. 'I got back from old Frothy's a little before eleven to find the ground floor well ablaze. Silvers and a few people from the farm across the fields were fighting the fire as well as they could with extinguishers and buckets. I took charge, of course, but there wasn't much we could do. Fortunately Silvers had had the sense to telephone not only the local fire brigade but Southampton, Lymington and several other places round about.

'You see, by the time he came on the scene the fire already had a good hold and he realised that it was not going to be easy to put out. We might have succeeded in localising the fire if it had been discovered earlier; but soon after I got here it penetrated to the upper floor, and I think the Professor must have had a lot of inflammable chemicals there.

Anyhow, the whole middle of the wing had become a raging furnace before the firemen could get their first hose into action.'

After looking about him for a few moments Johnny spotted Silvers, and moving over to him said, 'I gather it was you who discovered the fire, Silvers. Have you any idea what caused it?'

Silvers shook his grey head. 'No, Sir. I've no idea at all; but it started in your bedroom. We do know that much. Perhaps you left a cigarette burning there, or something.'

'I'm sure I didn't,' Johnny replied promptly. 'Did you manage to get into the room before the fire spread?'

'Oh no, Sir; the whole corridor was full of dense black smoke when I opened the door from the main hall that leads to the bedrooms; so I shut it again immediately. But young Belton, our chauffeur, did. It was he who discovered the fire, not me.

'He's courting young Ellen Sykes, over at the farm, and he was crossing the garden on his way back to his rooms over the stables when he noticed a red glow coming from the window of your bedroom. When he realised it was fire he ran up to the house and shouted for me, but as you and his Lordship were both out to dinner I had taken the opportunity to go down to the local. Getting no reply he ran back and finding the window open scrambled into the room. He did his best to put the fire out and burnt his hands quite badly; so they have taken him off to the Cottage Hospital.

'When it proved too much for him he made a fresh effort to get help. Mildred had gone to bed but Mrs. Silvers was still up listening to the wireless. He sent her off to fetch the Sykes from the farm, then collapsed in our sitting room. Mr. Sykes and his boys got here only just before I did, and of course I telephoned the fire brigade at once. But all we could do by then was to try to keep the fire in check until they got here. It's a terrible business, Sir, terrible. Still, I think there's some hope now that they will save the main building.'

'Where is Lady Ankaret?' Johnny enquired.

'I can't say for certain, Sir. Mrs. Silvers went up and told her about the fire; so she came down and helped carry buckets of water out here to throw through the windows until the firemen got the first hose going. I haven't seen her since. But she was wearing only a coat over her night-things, so I expect she will have gone in to put some more clothes on.'

With a curt nod Johnny left Silvers and strode towards the garden entrance. In the hall a few wisps of smoke were curling up from under the door to the corridor, but there were no signs of immediate danger. After a hesitant glance at the stairway he turned and walked into the drawing-room. It was empty so he marched through it to my sanctum. Ankaret was sitting there alone, in an arm-chair. She had on a pair of slacks and a pull-over, and loosely draped over her shoulders her mink coat. Beside her on a small table stood a syphon and a bottle of brandy. In her right hand she held a glass, and the colour of the liquor in it showed her drink to be a stiff one.

'Hello, Johnny!' she greeted him with her Gioconda smile. 'Come to save me from the flames?'

'No.' His voice was hard but level. 'I came to ask you to whom I should apply for compensation for my bits and pieces that have by now gone up in smoke.'

She shrugged. 'To the insurance people, I suppose. I imagine that Giff's policy would have covered guests' clothing.'

'On the contrary,' he said harshly. 'I think that I should send the bill to you.'

Her smile broadened. 'Darling Johnny; you are really quite coming on in your new rôle of detective, aren't you?'

'No. If I'd been any good at it I would never have left that suit-case in a place where by climbing in through the window you could start a fire to burn it.'

Ankaret took a long pull at her drink. 'I'm sorry, Johnny, but I just had to. You see, there were papers in it that Giff would have been terribly distressed for anyone but myself to see.'

'And I can guess what sort of papers they were,' he told her angrily. 'Does the name Desmond Chawton mean anything to you?'

Her face suddenly became a mask. 'Yes; he is an old friend of mine. Why?'

'Because about a year ago I met him in Germany, and one night we got rather tight together. But not too tight for him to know what he was talking about. The amount he had drunk had loosened him up just enough for him to tell me a lot about you. From then on I realised that Giff had had a rotten deal. He was brave enough and clever enough to put a good face on it, so that he appeared to be happy with you; but all the time he must have been suffering the tortures of the damned. He adored you too much to give you up, although he knew that you were being consistently unfaithful to him.'

'You've got things all wrong, Johnny!' Ankaret's cry was one of genuine pain. 'I swear you have!'

'Oh no I haven't,' he retorted. 'How about the Spanish Marquis and all the rest of them? You've no more moral sense than an animal. As an intelligent human being you could have found ways to keep your lusts in check; but you wouldn't even try. Instead you gave free rein to your lechery, until it led to Giff's death. And now you have added arson to your other crimes. I haven't a doubt that those papers you have destroyed would have enabled me to put you and your latest lover in the dock at the Old Bailey. And if I can get a new line on what really took place here last Friday night I'll do it yet.'

Ankaret was very pale, but she had recovered her poise. After tossing back what remained of her brandy and soda, she said:

'You are tilting at windmills, Johnny. I haven't got a new lover, and if poor Giff were still alive he would be the first to tell you to stop trying to pin his death on me. But what's the odds. Go on trying if you will. I don't give a damn. The only thing which might have ever given anyone a clue to the truth about this awful business is now a handful of ash. You've missed the boat!'

8

Tuesday 13th September

By two o'clock in the morning the fire had been got under control. One engine remained and its crew continued to play their hose on the smouldering embers; the others departed, as did the locals and all but two of the police. Johnny was provided with a pair of my pyjamas and my toilet things and accommodated in the second double spare room, next to Bill; then the household went belatedly to bed.

The hall was in a fine mess, for muddy boots and hoses had been dragged through it, but that could soon be cleared up; and the only serious damage to the main block was in the dining-room, where a lot of water had come through the ceiling. On the other hand the wing beyond it had been rendered completely untenable. Three of the rooms on the ground floor had been gutted and left exposed to the sky when the floor of the lab and its glass roof fell in; so whether Ankaret had intended it or not she had killed two birds with one stone. Somewhere among the charred debris lay not only my papers, but also the twisted remains of the death ray machine. No one now would be able to deduce from it the secret of Evans's discovery and that eliminated the possibility of even remote speculations upon the use to which he might have put it.

I remained down in my library, and was ready enough to black out for a few hours when the others went to bed, but I was roused early by the clatter of pails coming through to me from the main hall. Silvers and our helps who come in daily from the village were mopping up and putting the place right as far as possible in readiness for my funeral.

At about half-past nine Johnny drove off in his car. I wondered where he was off to; but on his return, an hour and a half later, he was wearing a topper and a morning coat, so it was obvious that to hire suitable kit for the occasion he had driven in to Southampton.

The funeral had been timed for twelve o'clock to enable anyone coming from London for it to get down that morning, and shortly before midday those who were going to follow the hearse began to arrive at the house. Among them were Edith, Christobel and Harold, James Compton and the rest of my co-directors, Eddie Arnold, the Admiral and Dr. Culver. Meanwhile my body had been brought up from the beach house and its flower-covered coffin put into the hearse.

Bill had naturally taken charge of the arrangements and when everything was ready went up to fetch Ankaret. She bowed to the others as he escorted her out to the first car but I could not see her face, as she was heavily veiled. The church was about two miles away; and when we got there I was surprised to see the number of people who had assembled, for many of whom there was not room in the building. Of course I had a lot of friends in the neighbourhood and, the works having been closed for the day, a large number of my employees were present; but there were also many strangers. I imagine that news of the fire on top of the tragedy at Longshot had brought a lot of them there from morbid curiosity.

I have always hated long funeral addresses myself, so I was glad for everybody's sake that the Vicar made no attempt to preach. He said only a few dignified words about the infinite mercy of God assuring our seeing our loved ones again in a happier future. The coffin was then carried from the packed church and the principal mourners followed it to the graveside.

In the churchyard there are a number of graves of past Hillarys and the one in current use had been made for my grandfather. It consisted of a brick vault about ten feet deep and wide enough to take two coffins side by side. There were so far five coffins in it, the topmost being that of my father. Mine was lowered into the space beside his while the Vicar recited the classic line: 'earth to earth, ashes to ashes, dust to dust,' then it came to rest with a gentle bump on the one below it.

As it did so I saw its lid shift just a fraction sideways. Slight as the movement was, it struck a chord in my mind. In view of the fact that my spirit was very definitely not imprisoned in my body, during the past three days I had not given another thought to the special clause in my will about which

207

Eddie Arnold had told my executors on Saturday morning. But evidently my wishes were being faithfully carried out. The lid could only have moved because it was not screwed down; although I had not noticed them there would be air-holes in the sides of the coffin, and the great stone slab which closed the vault would not be replaced over it until my body had been down there for a week.

Those instructions had been drafted by me when making my first will and, like several other clauses, simply carried forward when I had remade it on marrying Ankaret. They were really a hang-over from childhood fears by which I had been badly haunted, and in recent years I had attached little importance to them. In fact I cannot recall the matter having even entered my thoughts. But as I now looked down into the grave my old horror at the idea of being buried alive re-turned to me, and I was momentarily conscious of an inex-pressible relief at the thought that the essential me was safely outside it.

The crowd respectfully drew back for the principal mourners to reach their cars and I returned to the house with them. Bill shepherded them into the drawing-room, where sandwiches and drinks had been set out, and apologised to the visitors that the fire had made it too difficult to give them a proper lunch. Ankaret, still keeping her veil down, took a chair apart in one of the windows and did not address a word to anyone. The others, respecting her grief, forbore from ap-proaching her and made low-voiced conversation. When they had refreshed themselves, Eddie took my will from his brief-case and read it to them.

Most of those present were already aware of its contents, and Edith's face showed that she was quite content with the provision which I had made for her; but Christobel looked sulky and Harold could scarcely contain his rage when, on questioning Eddie, he learned that he would come in only for about seven thousand until on Ankaret's death the Hall with its contents and my holding in Hillary-Comptons would revert to him. However, suicide or no suicide, there could be no question about my sanity when I had made the will, as Eddie, a trifle acidly, pointed out; thereby promptly squashing any thoughts of contesting it that the new Baronet might have been harbouring.

By half-past two the proceedings were completed, and Bill saw the members of my family who were returning to London to their car. Johnny was also about to leave but James Compton followed him out into the hall, stopped him and then beckoned over Bill who had just re-entered it.

'Look,' he said to them, 'I know this does not seem a very appropriate moment, but I think we ought to have a chat about the affairs of the Company. That is why I brought Sir Tuke back with me. It was he who raised the matter, and I knew you wouldn't mind his being present at the reading of the will as he is such an old friend of the family. He rang me up this morning to point out that it is now a week since the Admiralty contract for those two E-boats was handed to him. Normally, if it hadn't been for Giff's unexpected opposition, we should have sent an acceptance on Friday. Then this frightful business of his death scotched our having the further board meeting we had planned for yesterday. The people at the Ministry of Supply will think we are beginning to fall down on our job if they don't hear from us in a day or two now; so I felt that the Admiral was right in his suggestion that, as three of us had to return to the house, anyhow, and he could join us, we ought to take the opportunity to see if we can't get nearer to a decision.'

Johnny glanced at his watch. 'I have an appointment in London at six o'clock that I particularly want to keep; but I quite agree with what you say, so I'll put off starting for half an hour.'

'Good,' said James. 'Then I'll fetch Sir Tuke. I know that if Lady Ankaret seemed fit enough and Eddie could get her on her own he wanted to give her an idea how she will stand financially. He'll be glad of the chance to do that while we are talking things over.'

The four men gathered in the half-dismantled dining-room. James took the head of the table and it was decided without argument that at the next full meeting of the board he should be elected to succeed me as Chairman of the Company. Then he said:

'Well, gentlemen, there is only one matter we have to discuss here and now, and you all know what it is.'

Admiral Waldron followed him up quickly. 'I trust no discussion will be necessary. I am no believer in mincing

209

words. Regrettable as it is, we must accept the verdict of the Coroner's jury—that poor Gifford took his life while the balance of his mind was disturbed. The tragedy occurred on Friday night—only a few hours after he had placed his extraordinary proposal before us. How can we doubt now that for some reason unknown to us he had already become abnormal? All we are called on to do is to expunge from our minds the memory of our last meeting and send an acceptance of the contract.'

James shook his head. 'I can't agree with you there. I mean about Giff's already being out of his mind at the time of our meeting. His proposal raised an unexpected and unprecedented issue; but whatever may have happened afterwards, he was as sane as I am when he made it.'

'Since you think that, I have no desire to argue the point,' the Admiral rejoined. 'I put it forward only because I feel it to be a reasonable explanation of what I considered at the time to be a mental aberration. Anyhow, distressed as I am by Gifford's death, I sincerely trust that this last crazy idea of his has died with him. What's your view, Wiltshire?'

'What, me?' Bill sat back and thrust his hands into his trousers pockets. 'Well, we're all supposed to be business men, aren't we? To be honest I thought it a bit crazy myself. Anyhow as far as the interests of the firm are concerned, I agree with you that we'd best forget it.'

'And you, Norton?' the Admiral—continuing to take the chairmanship out of James's hands—shot at Johnny.

'I don't think it was in the least a crazy idea,' Johnny replied quietly. 'Even if I am alone in doing so, when it is put to the meeting I shall again vote for it.'

'Ha!' exclaimed the Admiral. 'I might have expected as much. It confirms my belief that you put Gifford up to it.'

The muscles about Johnny's mouth tightened. 'You have no right to imply that, Sir! As I have already told you, there is not the slightest foundation for any such belief.'

'Oh yes there is!' the Admiral shot back. 'No mere acquaintance would ever have disclosed to Gifford the matters he used as ammunition in his endeavour to win us over to his point of view.'

'Then it must have been some old friend who has now

become a high-up, and whom he met recently again in London. I give you my word that I had no hand in it whatsoever.'

'I suggest, Sir Tuke,' James put in, 'that you should accept that, and endeavour to view the question more objectively. As far as the Company is concerned it is neither here nor there where Giff got his information. What does concern us is that it had the ring of truth, and that on account of it he proposed that we should sacrifice the Company's financial interests in order to make a patriotic gesture. The point still at issue is: are we prepared to do so?'

The Admiral's cheeks went a shade deeper red. 'Patriotic gesture, my foot! On the contrary, if I hadn't known Gifford for what he was I'd have believed that the Communists had got at him. His proposal was nothing less than sabotage.'

'I don't agree,' James replied firmly. 'Since last Friday I've thought a lot about all Giff said, and I am more convinced than ever that he was right.'

Finding himself up against much greater opposition than he had expected, the Admiral quickly shifted his ground, and said in a much milder tone: 'Are you quite sure, Compton, that you are not being influenced by sentiment? I mean, in view of your life-long association with Gifford and affection for him, it would be quite understandable if you felt a moral obligation to carry out his last wishes regarding the interests of the Company.'

James shook his head. 'No; it's not that. If you remember, it was I who suggested that we should take the week-end to think it over. I went home full of it and stayed up very late on Friday night milling over the pros and cons with myself. When I woke up on Saturday morning I no longer had any doubts. I had already taken the decision to vote with Giff when the board met again on Monday, and that was some hours before I knew that he was dead.'

After pausing for a moment, James went on. 'But since you have raised the question of moral obligations, there is one that I feel we should consider. As you know, Norton and myself have been appointed executors of Giff's will and trustees of his estate. Under the will Lady Ankaret comes into a life-interest in his holdings in Hillary-Comptons, so for all practical purposes she is now the largest individual shareholder in the Company. As her trustees Norton and I have the

211

legal right to decide what shall be done without consulting her. But if we reject this Admiralty contract it may well have an adverse effect on the value of our shares and in due course on the dividends she will receive from her holding. Therefore, in my view, we have anyhow a moral obligation to put the matter to her and hear what she has to say before taking a final decision. Do you agree, Norton?'

'I do,' replied Johnny promptly. 'Each of us is free to risk the depreciation of our own shares if we wish; but as trustees it would not be right for us to jeopardise her sole source of income without her being a party to it.'

'I entirely agree,' the Admiral supplemented. 'Since you are responsible to her it is clearly your duty to obtain her views. The trouble is, though, that we ought to send a reply to the Ministry of Supply by tomorrow at the latest; and with Gifford's body scarcely an hour out of the house we can't possibly ask her to join us. It simply wouldn't be decent at such a time to involve her in our controversy, or submit her to lengthy explanations about an intricate subject of which she knows nothing.'

'Oh but she does,' Johnny informed him. 'She knows all about it. I was talking to her about it on Friday night.'

'What!' Sir Tuke's blue eyes popped with angry amazement. 'And you have the face to sit there and admit it! You must have taken leave of your senses. How can you possibly deny any longer that it was you who briefed Gifford, when you openly confess to such a breach of security as having discussed Top Secret matters with his wife?'

Johnny held up a hand in protest. 'No, no, Sir. You've got me all wrong. I'm afraid I expressed myself badly. When I got back from dining with you on Friday night I found Ankaret downstairs. She told me that Giff was up in the laboratory with Evans and had left word that they were not to be disturbed. I had wanted to ask him to ring you up first thing in the morning and give you his personal assurance that I had had nothing to do with his proposal to reject the contract. As I looked so glum when I learned that I could not see him, she asked me what was worrying me, and I told her that I had had a row with you over a proposition that Giff had put up to the board that afternoon. I assure you I said no more than that. It was then she said that she knew all about it; and that from what Giff had told her, I could hardly be surprised that you had taken umbrage at our wanting to scrap the Navy.'

'There!' barked the Admiral, glancing at the others. 'You see; while trying to explain away his talk with Ankaret he inadvertently admits that he was associated with Gifford's proposal.'

'Damn it, I did not!' retorted Johnny angrily. 'All I did was to back it after he had made it, and I still do. If you have seen the morning papers, you'll know that after months of arguing that great, hulking, useless battleship *Vanguard* is to be laid up, and . . .'

'How dare you!' roared the Admiral.

'Gentlemen, gentlemen!' protested James; but Johnny would not now be stopped.

'I was about to say that in Lord Mountbatten we at last have a First Sea Lord who is capable of viewing our strategic requirements as a whole; and that there are many younger officers in the Navy who, without being in the least disloyal to their Service, realise the necessity for its conversion into mainly a land-based Air Arm; and that it is people like you, many of whom are still serving, who, with their ill-informed conceptions and out-worn prejudices by opposing all change, are endangering the future of the country.'

The putting into moth-balls of H.M.S. *Vanguard* was one of the many matters that Sir Charles had mentioned to me during our long talk. Apparently Lord Mountbatten had been pressing to be allowed to effect this great economy, and secure her complement of sixteen hundred odd officers and men for more essential purposes, ever since he had become Chief of Naval Staff; but so great had the opposition been that a huge sum had been expended on her complete reconditioning before he could get his way.

At the time I had been endeavouring to absorb so many facts and figures that I had thought no more about it. But it struck me now that perhaps Mountbatten might be the one man who could effect some satisfactory compromise which would make the New Look acceptable to his own Service.

In view of the tradition he had inherited from his great sailor father and his own life-long devotion to the Navy, it seemed, on the face of things, unthinkable that he would even listen to any proposal for disestablishing it. On the other hand as Chief of Combined Operations he had been created a Vice-Admiral, a Lieutenant-General, and an Air Marshal in the same Gazette. And later, as Supreme Commander South East Asia, he had directed the combined operations of great sea, land and air forces until they achieved a brilliant victory in the vastest of all our theatres of war.

Because he had fought to disencumber his Service of this hugely expensive strategically obsolete vessel, it did not follow that he would be prepared to scrap the aircraft carriers and smaller ships; but it did show practical good sense and considerable moral courage, and it could at least be taken as an indication that he would give reasonable consideration to any proposals for further readjustments of our war potential to greater advantage.

Whether Sir Charles had approached him direct on the proposal to merge the three Services I had, of course, no idea. But even if they had had preliminary talks and he had not shown himself entirely averse to it, enormous opposition remained to be encountered and to overcome it by ordinary methods would mean the loss of invaluable time. In any case, it was obvious that Sir Charles's object in making use of me had been to save that time by provoking a crisis which would force the Navy to a show-down; and naturally he would never have placed Mountbatten in a false position by informing him of his intention to do that.

But the fact remained that the new First Sea Lord had more experience than any other Service Chief of the operational needs of all three Services, and should be able to adjudicate between them with a greater degree of fairness. So there did seem some hope that, whether the rejection of the E-boat contract played any part in the matter or not, he might prove the keystone in the building of the bridge upon which our new and better structure of defence could be based.

While these thoughts had been racing through my brain, James and Bill had succeeded in quelling the outbursts of the enraged sailor and airman. Johnny had been induced to apologise to the Admiral, and the Admiral had been told that his aspersions on Johnny's integrity were quite unwarrantable. The two of them subsided into hostile silence when James said:

214

'We are all agreed that it would be most unfitting to drag Lady Ankaret into our discussions here and now; but that she should be consulted. The point we have to settle is, bearing in mind that the matter is now urgent, when can that be done?'

It was Bill who for once put forth a constructive idea and solved their difficulty. 'As three clear days have now elapsed since Giff's death,' he said, 'she is over the worst of the shock. Naturally she did not feel like exchanging platitudes with Giff's first wife and those awful children of his, but she is quite up to having this thing put before her and taking a decision. As you know, I voted with Giff for his proposal on Friday and against it this morning. I still feel there is a lot to be said for both sides; so you can trust me to put both to her fairly. How about my having a chat with her this evening, giving her the night to think it over, then letting you know tomorrow morning what she feels about it?'

'Couldn't be better,' James nodded. 'In that case I'll call a formal meeting of the board in our offices, and when you have made your report we will decide on our reply to the Ministry of Supply. What time shall we make it?'

'I must spend tonight in London,' Johnny announced, 'and I ought to be back at my job tomorrow. But in the circumstances I'm sure my master won't cut up rough if I take an extra morning off. The earlier you can make it the better, though. I don't mind at what hour I start, but I'd like to be back in my office early in the afternoon.'

'Shall we say nine-thirty, then?' James's suggestion was greeted by a series of nods from the others, and, standing up, they all filed out of the room.

Ankaret was standing in the hall, her heavy veil now thrown back. She had just said good-bye to Eddie, and was on the point of going upstairs.

It was at that moment that Silvers emerged from the baize door leading to the servants' quarters. Going up to Johnny he smiled and said:

'I've some good news for you, Sir. When young Belton found his efforts to put out the fire in your room unavailing, he must have decided to save what he could before retreating through the window. I suppose the burns on his hands made it too painful for him to hang on to it for long and a minute or

215

two later he dropped it. But he succeeded in rescuing your suit-case. One of the men who is clearing up found it in the shrubbery, and I've just put it in your car.'

*   *   *   *

It is pointless for me to attempt to describe the feelings of Ankaret, Johnny and myself. To all three of us Silvers's innocently cheerful announcement spelt an immediate resumption of the shattering emotions that had swept over us the previous afternoon. Ankaret knew that once more her life hung only by a thread; Johnny could now be more confident than ever that he would shortly achieve the triumph of which he thought she had robbed him; I, after the bitter things they had said to one another while the fire was still raging, felt greater fear than ever that he would force her to pay the extreme penalty.

She had been about to go up to her room. At Silvers's last words, as though she had received a physical blow, she stumbled on the first stair. Believing her stagger to have been caused by an ordinary mis-step, James hurried forward to help her. But, swiftly recovering, she waved him back, drew herself up to her full height and, turning her enigmatic smile on Johnny, said:

'They say that it is better to be born lucky than rich. I thought that once; but now I'm not so certain.'

Yet, as it transpired, she was cavilling at Fortune before the fickle goddess had deserted her. Johnny murmured an inaudible reply. As she went upstairs the others exchanged a chorus of farewells, then I followed him round to the garage.

There a totally unexpected surprise awaited us. On the back seat of his car reposed a suit-case; but we had all jumped to a wrong conclusion. Instead of it being the old brown leather one into which he had put the papers, it was the smart blue canvas case he always used for week-ends.

As his glance fell on it he swore profanely; whereas I felt the sort of sensation that, had I had a body, would have been expressed by delighted laughter.

Five minutes earlier I had hesitated whether to follow Johnny or remain with Ankaret. Now I was no longer in doubt about which course to pursue. Ankaret had seen that blue canvas case of Johnny's a score of times. She must have realised that he had brought the brown one only as an extra in which to collect the papers from my desk. As soon as she could think up an excuse to send for Silvers she would ask him casually, in the course of talking to him on some other matter, which of Wing Commander Norton's cases had been saved. Silvers's reply would bring her the blessed knowledge that her awful fears were groundless, and that, after all, her defences had not been breached.

The appointment that Johnny was so set on keeping in London was, I knew, with Daisy; and they had planned that evening to try out her psychic powers in the hope that, while holding an object which had belonged to me, she would be able to furnish some pointers to the manner in which I had met my death. Naturally I was most keen to witness this experiment and now I was free to accompany Johnny without suffering constant anxiety on Ankaret's account.

That Bill would give her a reasonably unbiased account of the dispute that rent the Hillary-Compton Board, I felt fairly confident; but even if he didn't I had already told her a few hours before my death enough about its origin for her to form an independent judgement. And I had no doubt at all how she would react. Avarice had never been one of Ankaret's vices, and even had money weighed with her there was no question of the Company's risking bankruptcy; at worst her income might be some hundreds less for a few years. She was highly patriotic; so had fully approved, and even applauded, the line I had taken. Lastly, while she was beating Evans to death she had proclaimed aloud her deep love for me. Therefore it was as good as a certainty that she would inform her trustees that she wished them to use her shares to overcome the opposition of the Admiral.

Twenty minutes after leaving Longshot, Johnny pulled up in front of a men's outfitters in Southampton. Taking a large cardboard box from the back of the car, he carried it inside. When he came out again a quarter of an hour later, he had changed from his hired funeral plumage and was dressed once more in his own grey lounge suit. As we left Southampton it began to rain, so the journey was rather a depressing one; but we arrived soon after six o'clock outside the dreary block of flats where Daisy lived.

Having climbed the stone stairs, Johnny rang her bell; and as he did so I could hear her singing to herself inside. Throwing open the door, she greeted him cheerfully, then explained:

'My! What *have* you been up to? You look like something the cat left on the mat. Come in and I'll fix you a drink.'

It was true enough that Johnny looked about all in. The previous day he had been up at five and had not got to bed till near three in the morning. On top of that he had had the unhappy duty of attending my funeral, his secret struggle with Ankaret, the row with the Admiral and the long drive up from Longshot.

Leading him into her strangely-furnished but friendly room, Daisy gave him a stiff whisky and soda. While he drank it he explained his haggard looks by telling her about the fire, but not its cause, and when she asked him if, as he had hoped, the inquest had thrown any fresh light on my death, he shook his head.

'No; as the police appear to be satisfied that it was suicide the inquest could have hardly been duller; it was just a routine business. But I'm not satisfied. Far from it. One or two things that happened yesterday made me more convinced than ever that foul play of some kind was at the bottom of my uncle's death. So I still want your help. In fact I'm counting on it to give me a new line.'

'I wouldn't do that, dear,' she replied rather dubiously. 'It's ages since I've tried my hand at what my Mum used to call psychomatry, so I'm right out of practice. And even if the spirits are propitious, as the saying is, I'd be lucky if I could get more than a jumbled impression of the sort of man your uncle was. Still, I'll do my best for you if you've brought me something he was wearing when he died.'

'Here you are.' Johnny produced from his inner pocket a black evening tie. It was crumpled and soiled from having been in the water, and evidently he must have managed to get hold of it somehow after my body had been prepared for burial.

Taking it from him Daisy ran it slowly to and fro a few times between her smooth pointed fingers, then she said: 'If you don't mind, ducks, I'd rather you weren't with me while I work on it. You see, it's easier to get the 'fluence when one's alone. I tell you what. I'm down to my last packet of cigs. Slip out and get me some at the pub on the corner,

218

there's a dear. You needn't stay away long. Either I'll get something or know it's no go within ten minutes.'

Johnny stood up at once. 'Right! I'll get you another bottle of Scotch at the same time.'

'Thanks a lot.' She gave him her ready smile, then fished in her bag and handed him her latch key. 'Here, take this, so that you can let yourself in. If when you get back you find me lying on the divan with a dopey look on my face, and muttering, you'll know I'm getting something. Don't disturb me but just sit down quiet in the arm-chair. Your being here won't interfere once I've made a contact.'

When he had gone she smoothed out the tie, held it length-wise across her forehead then tied the two ends in a knot at the back of her golden hair. Lying down on the divan she relaxed and closed her eyes.

For a while I watched her, as I wanted to see whether she would get any results on her own; but she remained so still that after a time I felt sure that her efforts were proving futile. By then, as Johnny was due back shortly, and I might never again be given such a favourable opportunity to make con-tact with her, I decided that I must not let it slip; so I willed her to realise my presence.

Almost at once she opened her blue eyes, sat up, stared at me for a moment, then exclaimed: 'Oh it's you, dreaming again. You must be having a nap before dinner.'

In my mind I formed the words. 'I am not dreaming. I am Johnny's uncle; the man you were trying to find out about.'

She gave me a puzzled look and stammered: 'No . . . no. You can't be.'

'I am,' I insisted. 'I'm Gifford Hillary.'

'No you're not,' she snorted firmly. 'You can't be. He is dead.'

'Yes, of course I'm dead.' I endeavoured to thrust con-viction on her; and our strange conversation, audible only on her part, continued more or less as follows:

'Why should you think I'm not?' I asked.

'Because I don't see you as a dead person.'

'I can't help that. Two doctors declared me dead three days ago, so I must be.'

'Yes; if you were who you say you are. But you're not.'

'What can possibly lead you to suppose that I am someone

other than Gifford Hillary, and attempting to impersonate him?'

'Because he is dead and you are only dreaming.'

'I would to God you were right. But dreams don't go on for the best part of four days.'

'They may as far as the dreamer is concerned, even if in fact they occupy only a few minutes.'

'Look; today is Tuesday, isn't it?'

'That's right.'

'Well, for me this dream, as you call it, started on Friday night. In actual time that is, not dream time.'

'In your present state you're not capable of judging actual time. What you really mean is that when you started to dream your mind went back to Friday night, and in your dream you have been reliving the past few days.'

'I can't accept that. This is too utterly unlike any dream I've ever had. What is more, your idea that I am not Gifford Hillary is positively absurd. If I were not how could I possibly be aware of all his interests, thoughts and emotions?'

'You might if you had been a great pal of his. Perhaps his death came as a great shock to you. That could explain your having identified yourself with the tragedy in a dream and believing yourself to be him.'

'It would not explain my knowing how he died, and all the circumstances that led up to his death.'

'It could if you had been there at the time.'

'I was. I tell you I am him.'

'Nonsense. You are only imagining that because his death upset you. Stop pestering me, and go back to your body.'

'I can't. It is buried and as dead as a doornail.'

'Not a bit of it. The odds are that you are one of Sir Gifford's rich friends; so you're probably snoozing in a comfortable study or a Club arm-chair.'

'Damn it! If you don't believe me, Johnny will. Anyhow I want you to give him a message. Tell him that he is right in believing that I did not commit suicide, and that my death was an accident. But it happened through a misunderstanding and no one was to blame; so I am very anxious that no one concerned in it should be convicted for concealing their knowledge and, perhaps, be sent to prison. To ferret out the truth now can do me no good and may do several innocent

220

people a lot of harm; so I want him to drop the whole business.'

Daisy suddenly came to her feet. Her eyes narrowed and the expression on her pretty face was a strange mixture of fear, anger, and repulsion.

'So that's your game, is it?' she said in a low tense voice. 'Sir Gifford is dead; so you can't be him. But you are pretending to be because you were concerned in his death. Perhaps, even, you were his murderer and are now afraid of being found out. Anyhow, you are one of those people who have learned the secret of sending your mind out of your body at will. You must know that Johnny is already on your track, and you thought that by this trick you could get me to persuade him to stop trying to find out the truth. But it hasn't worked. You are evil, evil, evil; and by this sign I abjure you to leave this place.'

As she raised her hand I shot at her the thought: 'Tell Johnny I know that Belton saved the wrong suit-case.'

Even as I spoke she cried: 'Avaunt thee Satan!' and made the sign of the cross three times.

Presumably because I was not, as she supposed, an evil person who had acquired occult powers, her abjuration had no effect upon me whatever. But seemingly it did have the effect of raising a barrier between myself and her consciousness, as her eyes ceased to focus on me; and, although during the scene that followed I made several attempts to break through it, she clearly remained oblivious of my continued presence.

Her reaction on believing that she had rid herself of me was to turn away, collapse on the divan, and burst into tears. A few minutes later Johnny returned to find her still weeping and semi-hysterical. Having dumped the cigarettes and bottle of whisky in a chair, he strove to comfort her and get her to tell him what had happened.

At first she was capable only of incoherent mutterings between her sobs; but Johnny soon quieted her and after he had provided her with a drink she said:

'I've had a horrible experience; horrible. It was no fault of yours, Johnny; I've only myself to blame for having laid myself open to it. But it just goes to show how right I was to give up meddling with the occult.'

'But what happened?' he persisted. 'Did you have a vision and actually see my uncle murdered or something?'

'No; an apparition appeared to me. At first I thought it was just a person who had left his body in a dream. That often happens. My Mum used to call them night-walkers, and she was so psychic that she was always seeing them all over the place. I'm not bothered by them often, only now and again. But I'd seen this one before. That was on Sunday night; soon after you left me. I was undressing when he appeared and I thought he was just trying to get a cheap thrill; so I told him to get back to bed and I put out the light and shut my mind against him.'

'What did he do this evening to upset you so?'

'He declared he was your uncle.'

'Lord alive! Do you really mean to say that you have just been talking to Uncle Giff's ghost?'

'No. I knew right away that he couldn't be. You see, the apparition of a dead person is quite different from that of one who still has a body to go back to. This one had, and I told him so. But he continued to insist that he had been dead for four days and that he was Sir Gifford Hillary.'

Johnny drew a quick breath. 'What an extraordinary business. Do go on.'

'Well, I took the line then that he must be someone who had been very closely connected with your uncle, and very upset by his death. So in a dream he was imagining that he was your uncle. He wouldn't have that, and then the truth came out.'

'How? Did he admit to having had something to do with Uncle Giff's death?'

'No; but, all the same, I bet he had. In fact I wouldn't be surprised if he was your uncle's murderer. He stuck to his guns about being Sir Gifford, and said he wanted me to give you a message. It was to the effect that he had not committed suicide, but had died owing to an accident which wasn't anybody's fault. Someone knows all about it, and if the truth does come out he is afraid they will get into serious trouble for having concealed what they know from the police. On that account he wanted me to persuade you to throw your hand in and let sleeping dogs lie. You can see for yourself, just as I did, how that gave the whole show away.'

'I'm sorry, but I don't.' Johnny shook his head.

'Why, he was trying to protect himself, of course.'

'Oh come! People can't control their dreams; much less deliberately use them to appear to someone who is awake with the object of influencing events in their own favour.'

'Some people can. My Mum once told me that when she was studying under that mystic in Egypt he told her that anyone could if they had the guts to train themselves for long enough. Of course it's much more common out East than it is here, because they go in for developing their psychic powers more than we do. But there are people all over the world who can do it. If you had read as many books on the occult as I have you'd know that to have been proved over and over again.'

'You think then that this chap appeared to you with the deliberate intention of getting me to abandon my investigation?'

Daisy nodded vigorously. 'I'm sure of it. Of course he wasn't a dream apparition in the ordinary sense, like I'd first thought. He was someone who knows how to throw himself into a trance and project his astral out of his body, then make it appear as a vision anywhere he wants. And to use his powers the way he has shows that he must be evil. It's horrible to find yourself in contact with the astral of an evil person, That's what scared and upset me so.'

'I can quite understand that,' Johnny sympathised. 'But I'm still a bit at sea on this question of apparitions. Why should the spirit take a different form if it comes from the body of a living person from that which it does if he is dead?'

'Because they are not the same thing,' Daisy replied at once. 'The thing that goes out in sleep, and can be sent out while in a trance by those who know how, is a person's double. Of course it has no substance, so occultists call it the etheric double; but it is semi-opaque to anyone who can see it and exactly like the body it has left behind—the same age and appearance even to the clothes the physical body had on when it left it.

'Occultists believe that our etheric doubles leave our bodies every night, and that mostly they rove about on the lower astral plane, meeting the doubles of friends and sometimes the spirits of the dead. But in some ways they are almost as limited as we are, and must return when their body wakes. It is supposed that they are attached to it by what is called the "silver cord". That's a sort of invisible telephone line that can be stretched indefinitely. Normally they go back into their body just before it is due to wake, but should some shock wake the sleeping body unexpectedly, they receive instant warnings by means of the silver cord and so are able to flash back to it extra quick. When the physical mind becomes conscious again after sleep it often holds mixed-up impressions of places and people. We call those dreams, but they are really a patchwork of memories brought back by the double of its doings during the night.'

'All that sounds reasonable enough,' Johnny commented, 'providing one accepts the premises on which it is based. Now what about the other kind of apparition?'

'That is a true spirit. It is the indestructible personality; the immortal soul; the conscience that is always present to tell a person if he is doing right or wrong. It leaves the body to return to a higher plane at the moment of death.'

'And what does that look like?'

'It can assume any form it chooses. But they don't often return to earth, and if they do they usually wish to be recognised by the person to whom they are appearing; so they take on a resemblance to the body they inhabited while here. Although if they die old and decrepit they often return looking as they were when in the prime of life.'

'But how can you tell the difference between an etheric double and a spirit?'

'A double has a grey appearance and its outline is like a living person's; whereas a spirit has severed all connection with the body and has become a being of light. It glows with a sort of gentle radiance.'

'Tell me, Daisy; are you speaking from personal experience or only what you believe to be the case?'

'Oh I know what I'm talking about'; she sounded slightly huffy. 'You can set your mind at rest on that. As I've already told you. I've seen plenty of night-walkers in my time. Spirits, of course, don't come so frequent; but both my Mum and Dad appeared to me after they were dead; Mum several times, and twice she brought with her my young brother who was taken off with croup when he was only five.'

After a moment's silence, Johnny said: 'All the same I can't help feeling that you may be mistaken in the present instance.'

'What makes you think so, ducks?'

'Well, for one thing, you have admitted that a spirit can take any form; so I don't see why Uncle Giff's should not have assumed that of his double. For another, what he said to you about it not being suicide but an accident, and his wanting to shield innocent people who might get into trouble if I kept on playing the detective, is typical of him. He was just the generous sort of chap who would have come back for such a purpose.'

She shook her head. 'You may be right about that. But in whatever form he appeared, if he had passed over he would have had that unmistakable glow radiating from him; and this one hadn't.'

'All the same, I'd like you to describe to me the apparition that you saw.'

Daisy obliged, and as she proceeded to give details of my physical appearance, Johnny's face showed an increasing excitement. When she had done, he said: 'The description fits; but there are plenty of men of his age and build. What was he wearing?'

'All cats are grey at night, and so are etheric doubles. One has to depend on instinct to guess at colours. But I'd say he had on a smoking jacket and a bow tie that was either very dark or black and that his trousers were black too. There was a rather queer thing I noticed about his trousers; at the sides they had a deeper streak running down them. It might have been a stripe like officers have on their dress pants, but it looked too narrow for that and more as if it was a double line of braid or something.'

'By Jove!' Johnny jumped to his feet. 'It was Uncle Giff, then! When I pulled him out of the water it struck me as strange that he should be wearing the sort of trousers that are made only to go with tails. They have a double stripe, you know, whereas those made to go with a dinner jacket have a single broader one.'

'I can't help that, dear. The apparition I saw was an etheric double, not a spirit. Really it was.'

Impatiently Johnny brushed her objection aside. 'Is there anything else you can remember? Have you told me everything he said to you?'

'Not quite. Just before I managed to get rid of him, he said, "Tell Johnny I know that Barton saved the wrong suit-case." '

'Belton, not Barton, must have been what he said.' Johnny pulled out his handkerchief and began to mop his brow. 'Snakes alive! That clinches it! No one but myself knows about that. This is terrific!'

Daisy stuck out her chin a little, and argued doggedly. 'A person who has the power to leave his body could. He might have been overlooking you.'

'No, no!' Johnny brought his mind, trained to assess chances, to bear on the evidence. 'That would make too many coincidences. Even if someone's etheric double was out of its body early in the afternoon, the odds against its having been at Longshot, observing me, are enormous. Then there are the trousers with the double braid; and the description of Uncle Giff that you've given me. You have said that a double always takes the form of the body which it has left; therefore it could tell you that it was Uncle Giff, but it couldn't assume his appearance. It was Uncle Giff you saw. I haven't a doubt of it.'

'Johnny, it can't have been! Your uncle has been dead four days, and I'll swear this was not his spirit.'

'Since you are so certain of that there must be some other explanation. You know much more about this sort of thing than I do. Think hard. See if you can think of one.'

For a few moments Daisy was silent, then she said: 'We still have no details about how your uncle died—or the Professor. It's all still shrouded in mystery. Perhaps your uncle isn't dead. Maybe he has succeeded in pulling the wool over your eyes. Perhaps it was he who killed the other fellow, and to save himself from the gallows dressed up his victim's body in his clothes, so that it was thought to be his.'

'No,' Johnny declared, 'that's right out of the question. Damn it all, it was I who fished the body out of the Solent. I couldn't possibly be mistaken about its being that of my uncle.'

She shrugged. 'I give up then. But I don't care what you

say. If it was your uncle that I saw tonight it was not his spirit. It was his etheric double. So he must still be alive.'

*   *   *   *

It can be imagined with what intense interest I followed these arguments and speculations, and the effect that Daisy's conclusion, spoken with such unshakable conviction, had on me. When, during our first brief contact, she had told me that I was dreaming, I had been so certain that I was not that I had immediately rejected her contention as absurd, putting it down to the sort of error into which an amateur medium might easily fall. But now that I had heard her reasons for her belief I felt compelled to give it serious consideration.

Could she possibly be right? I did not think so. All my limited experience of dreams weighed with me against the acceptance of such a belief. Yet I had never felt any change in my mentality which might have been taken as evidence that I was dead. My natural expectations that some power would waft me to a higher sphere had proved unfounded, and I had prayed in vain for guidance. I was still as deeply concerned for the welfare of my friends as I had ever been when I had had a body, and the fact that my movements continued to be limited to a little more than those of a living human being showed beyond question that I was, in any case, earth-bound. In short, my state bore no resemblance whatever to that of those beings of light whom Daisy had described when speaking of the spirits of the dead.

Against one statement of hers there was certainly no argument. She had said that a person who is dreaming is incapable of judging time. That being so it was at least possible that I was still in the middle of a long and agonising nightmare. At the thought that I might yet wake up in my comfortable bed with Ankaret beside me I was almost overcome by nostalgia. For me, at that moment, it would have been more truly heaven than entering any of the promised paradises of the world's religions. Yet, again, all that I knew of dreams debarred me from putting any real hope in such a joyous prospect. My own dreams, and those of everyone with whom I had ever discussed the subject, had been brief, muddled, illogical and often composed of a series of scenes having little relation to one another. Whereas this, if it were a dream, had already lasted longer than all the other dreams I had ever had in my life put together, had contained nothing absurd or fantastic and, broken only by lapses into unconsciousness, was complete in its continuity.

While I had been thinking on these lines, Johnny and Daisy had been continuing their argument, but doing little more than repeat themselves; so getting nowhere. My full attention was brought back to them by Johnny saying:

'You know there is a possible explanation for all this. It's so terrible that I can hardly bear to think of it. But just supposing . . . just supposing that Uncle Giff has been buried alive.'

The shock and horror with which his suggestion hit me beggars description. It was the very thing that had been the nightmare of my youth. Yet in an instant I realised that it could account for everything. Johnny had seen me dead and buried, but my etheric double was still free to roam the world and appear to people with psychic gifts, like Daisy. Had it not been for those words 'still free', which my mind had just formed, I think the thought would there and then have robbed me of my sanity. But a merciful Providence had spared me the awful torture of lying consciously entombed, and, realising that, I was able once more to turn my mind to the scene before me.

Daisy had given a little shudder and gasped: 'Oh Johnny! What an awful thought. I suppose it's possible. But no; that sort of thing doesn't happen in these days. The doctors have methods of doing things now that they didn't have in the past. They always make really certain that a person's gone before they sign the death certificate.'

'God knows I hope you're right!' Johnny muttered. 'All the same, the more I think of it the more the idea worries me. You see it's the only one that fits all the facts as we know them.'

'It is, if you are right about it being your uncle who appeared to me; but I don't believe you are, dear. I'd bet six dozen pairs of nylons against a smack on the behind that it was someone who was mixed up in your uncle's death, and has an axe to grind in putting a stop to your detecting.'

228

'It couldn't have been. There is too great a weight of evidence against that.'

'Honest, ducks, there isn't. The message he sent you was just the sort of thing he would have sent if he'd been what I think; and if he is a real "black" he may have psychic powers far beyond what's common. It's true that etheric doubles mostly appear as themselves and in the clothes their body is wearing. But if it was him that killed your uncle, he'd know what he looked like and how he was dressed, and he might have willed me to see him just as your uncle was a few minutes before his death. That would account for their descriptions tallying, and even for the double stripe on the trousers. See what I mean?'

'I do, Daisy. But I don't subscribe to it. Uncle Giff never dabbled in the occult, neither does Ankaret. I'd be sure to have heard of it if they had. The idea that he was killed by a black magician is much too far-fetched. And even that would not account for the message about the suit-case.'

'I've already told you that this "black" might have been overlooking you.'

'No. However great his supernatural powers his consciousness could not be in more than one place at a time; and the odds against its having been in one particular place at three o'clock this afternoon are fantastic. It is frightful to have to consider the alternative. But I've got to. And what is more I'll have to do something about it.'

'What can you do?'

'Damned if I know!' Johnny gave her a worried look. 'But we can't just leave things like this. Put into words it sounds about as hopeful as to enquire about life on Mars; but I suppose the best way to start would be for me to try to find out a bit more about the behaviour of etheric doubles.'

'There are plenty of books about that.'

'Maybe, but ninety per cent of those sort of books are bally-hoo written by cranks or crooks who don't really know anything.'

'You can't say that of the ancient writings. The priests of the old civilisations studied such things for hundreds of years. They were the scientists of those days, and they found out an awful lot; particularly the Egyptians. Not only the priests, but most of the better-off ones, spent a good part of their lives preparing for their deaths by building tombs for themselves and furnishing them. Being so taken up with the after life it stands to reason that they learned more than any other people about the supernatural. Lots of the papyrus they left have been translated; so you could read some of them.'

'No; that's no good. It might be if I had the time; but I dipped into one once and it would take me weeks to extract the sort of information I want from such a mass of gibberish. This thing is urgent; perhaps desperately so. I've got to get a better line on it right away.'

'Why not try the Society for Psychical Research, then?'

'Ah!' Johnny came quickly to his feet. 'That really is a good idea. May I use your telephone?'

'Of course, ducks.'

Johnny disappeared into her bedroom. He was away for quite a time, but when he came back he was smiling.

'That's fixed,' he told her. 'When I said that I wanted to consult someone about etheric doubles, the girl who answered the 'phone said would I write in and make an appointment. I pulled a fast one then by telling her that I was an R.A.F. officer on leave in London for only one night. By luck there is a meeting going on there at the moment, and being a good sort said she'd see what she could do. She got hold of a chap called Wilfred Tibitts who has agreed to see me in his flat in Tavistock Square at half-past nine this evening.'

Daisy returned his smile, but shook her head. 'I'm afraid you're wasting your time, Johnny. Still, perhaps a talk with an expert will convince you that your uncle really is dead, and so set your mind at rest.'

'I hope to God you're right,' he rejoined feelingly. 'And now, how about some dinner? We might go to the Clarendon. That would save us from getting stuck in a traffic jam up West.'

'O.K. by me, Johnny.' Daisy stood up. 'I'll get my things on. I won't be a jiffy.'

She was considerably longer than the word implied, but when she emerged from her bedroom she was, as they say, an 'eye-full'. Her clothes were just a shade too loud, and her make-up a trifle too obvious, to be in impeccable taste; but, all the same, she would have passed anywhere as a respectable film starlet and most men would have felt rather pleased to be seen with her.

That fine old coaching inn, the Clarendon on Hammersmith Broadway, still maintains an excellent restaurant, and although Johnny's thoughts obviously drifted from his pretty companion from time to time, they both made a very good meal. Afterwards he dropped her at Earls Court Station, garaged his car, and went on by tube to keep his appointment with Mr. Tibitts.

When Johnny rang the bell of a first-floor flat on the south side of Tavistock Square, it was answered by a short round man of about sixty. His head was bald except for wisps of grey hair above his ears, and his friendly grin was made a little alarming by front teeth which stood out like those of a rabbit.

'Come in,' he said. 'Come in. Pleased to meet you.'

'Thank you, Sir. It's very good of you to see me at such short notice.' Johnny returned the vigorous handshake and followed his new acquaintance down a high narrow passage into a lofty ill-proportioned room.

The houses in Tavistock Square had been built in late Georgian times to accommodate single well-to-do families, but the decline of the district had resulted in most of them being cut up into a number of apartments early in the present century, when the conversion of such mansions was still in its infancy. The big L-shaped drawing-room on the first floor, into a part of which Mr Tibitts led Johnny, had been partitioned off into three, with results which were architecturally disastrous. Nevertheless, crammed book-shelves on all four walls and two easy-chairs beside the fire-place made it far from uncomfortable.

'Now,' said Mr. Tibitts, having waved Johnny to one of the chairs. 'Let's hear about your trouble. I may as well tell you at once, though, that if you have children or a pregnant woman in the house you may be certain that they are at the bottom of it.'

Johnny looked distinctly puzzled, but Mr. Tibitts smiled genially and went on: 'The genuine poltergeist is very rare; in fact a very rare bird indeed. But if you are really being troubled by one nothing would give me greater pleasure than to investigate it.'

'I'm afraid there is some mistake,' Johnny murmured. 'The matter I wish to consult you about has nothing to do with poltergeists.'

'Oh dear!' The little man was clearly distressed. 'That's very disappointing. That fool of a girl in the office knows perfectly well that my special subject is poltergeists. Still, as you are here—if there is any other way that I can help you.'

'I'm sure you can.' Johnny waved a hand towards the serried rows of books. 'If you have read even half of these your knowledge of the supernatural must be immense.'

'So-so,' admitted Mr. Tibitts, 'so-so. The unknown, or the unexplained to be more accurate, has been my principal interest all my life. But the subject is vast and its ramifications are innumerable. I'm weak on werewolves, for example, and vampires. Central Europe is the place for them, and I've never been able to afford to go there.'

Johnny only half suppressed a smile. 'This is nothing so . . . so out of the ordinary as that. Four days ago my uncle died, and he has since twice appeared to a lady of my acquaintance.'

'Tell me about her. Is she a professional medium?'

'No. Her mother was, though; and she used to tell fortunes herself, but gave it up several years ago.'

Mr. Tibitt's protruding teeth thrust themselves out in a sudden grin. 'Don't trust her, my friend. Hysteria or trickery. Probably the latter. Women with just a smattering of psychic knowledge often get up to these games to impress their men friends. I've exposed scores of them, hundreds in my time. That is the function of the Society, you know. Some people believe that we are delighted to go and gape at any so-called manifestation, but that's not the case at all. Our aim is research and we conduct our investigations just as seriously as any other scientific body. In fact we spend most of our time unmasking fakes.'

'Are you then still a sceptic?' Johnny asked.

'No, no; far from it. No one who studies these matters with an open mind could possibly remain so for long. Mental telepathy for example is now a proven fact. Foreknowledge of coming events is another matter upon which there can no longer be any reasonable doubt. And in my opinion the evi_ dence for survival after death is overwhelming. But we have to sort out the wheat from the chaff, and unfortunately there is far more chaff than wheat.'

'What you say gives me all the more confidence in consulting you. But I don't think that in this case there can be any question of trickery. There is good reason to believe that the young woman concerned inherited a certain degree of psychic sensitivity. I have known her well for quite a time, and she has nothing to gain by deceiving me. In fact it was I who persuaded her, more or less against her will, to try to find out what had happened to my uncle.'

'I take it you mean whether he is happy in the beyond. Well, what results did she get—or tell you that she got?'

'He, or a form that resembled him in every particular, appeared to her. Personally, owing to certain messages this apparition sent me through her, I am convinced that it was my uncle. The puzzling part of the matter is that, although I saw him myself in a state that I believed to be death, and the doctors certified to be death, she saw him three days later as an etheric double.'

'Very interesting. Quite extraordinary in fact—that is if she is really capable of judging such matters.'

'She says she has often seen night-walkers, as she calls them, and that after the death of her mother and father she was several times visited by their spirits. So she ought to know the difference. That is, if there is one?'

'Oh, she is right about that. No one who has seen both could possibly mistake the double of a living person for his immortal spirit.'

'Perhaps you would be kind enough to explain to me about these supernatural qualities with which it seems we are all endowed. My friend said that the ancient Egyptians had got further than any other people in their investigations of such mysteries, and I don't doubt that you have read a lot of their writings on the subject.'

'I have; and very interesting they are. Your friend was right, of course, about their having made a scientific study of the occult. In fact no other people have ever been so greatly preoccupied with what would happen to them after they were dead. I would not say, though, that they had got further in penetrating the veil than ourselves.'

'Why should you think that?' Johnny enquired.

'Because they lacked the scientific instruments that we possess. They had no electrical appliances or infra-red photography with which to check results. Nevertheless their basic theory on the immortal attributes of man was sound, and has never been questioned all through the ages. I say basic because the truth, as we still believe it, must have been discovered in very ancient times, but as happens in all religions it later became distorted by many generations of priests. Or perhaps I should say over-elaborated by the hair-splitting which is a fault common to the theologians of all races.'

Mr. Tibitts began to fill a pipe, and went on: 'Anyone who tried to get at the underlying truth by reading the papyri of the middle and later dynasties would become hopelessly confused. By then they had divided the spiritual attributes of the personality into the Ka or Double, the Sáhu or Spirit Body, the Khaibit or Shadow, and the Khu or Spirit Soul. They complicated things even further by attributing a separate soul to the Ka, which they called the Ba, and maintaining that the Heart also had independent non-physical qualities.'

Johnny smiled. 'I'm glad that I didn't adopt my friend's suggestion and attempt to unravel the mysteries for myself.'

'You wouldn't have got far if you had.' Mr. Tibitt's rabbit teeth flashed in a responsive grin. 'What is more, as you are interested in etheric doubles you would have been sadly misled. In their anxiety to protect every non-physical attribute that they had from attack by evil forces they put up separate defences for them all. Having endowed the Ka with a soul they had to protect that, hence the little statues of themselves called Ka figures that they had buried with them in their tombs. The Ka figure was for the Ka soul to live in when it was compelled to leave the physical body at death. They believed too that it needed food and clothing and could make use of the etheric counterparts of such necessities when they were placed in the tomb with it. The funeral tests are full of exhortations to relatives to provide a plentitude of the good things of this life for the Ka of the deceased. Through many generations they must have wasted millions upon millions of pounds worth of goods in this way; because, of course, their theologians had led them into error about the continued existence of the Ka. When a person dies it ceases to exist.'

234

'Are you fully convinced about that?'

'Entirely. We cannot yet explain the Ka scientifically; but all of us are charged with electricity, and it is now believed that the Ka's function is that of a generator, which leaves the body in sleep and on its return recharges us so that we can undertake fresh activities. It is that which makes sleep imperative; for if we don't sleep, and give the Ka a chance to do its work, we run down. You will see for yourself that when the physical body is dead the Ka no longer has any function to perform. It is, for all practical purposes, a part of the physical body; so dies with it.'

'You said just now that in the earliest times the Egyptians got as near the facts as any people have ever done. If that is so, surely it would have been more in keeping with the natural progress of mankind for them to have become still more enlightened, rather than to have lost sight of the truth. After all, it isn't as though they fell into a state of barbarism; it was not until the later Pharaohs that they reached their highest peak of civilisation. Don't you think it possible that there may have been some foundation for their later beliefs?'

'No, in the light of modern knowledge I certainly don't. They were misled into over-elaboration of their beliefs by ambitious priests who were out to make a name for themselves. Theologians of all religions have been tarred with the same brush. Look how our own faith has been split into a score of different sects, all calling themselves Christians; and at the palpably absurd doctrines postulated by some of the early Fathers. They even disputed amongst themselves how many angels could stand on the point of a needle.

'The same sort of splitting up into sub-religions occurred in Egypt; so that some people worshipped Osiris as a man and others as a Bull, and others again identified him with the sun god Ra. By the time they finished they had associated every animal and natural phenomena with some aspect of the godhead, and each had its retinue of priests who declared that their brand of soft-soaping the gods offered the surest way of getting to heaven.'

Johnny smiled again. 'Yes, I quite see your point. How about their original faith, though? What was it exactly?'

'They believed in a Holy Trinity of Father, Mother and Son—Osiris, Isis and Horus—all of whom had lived on earth.

235

That Osiris had been murdered by his brother Set—the embodiment of evil in human form. And that they would be brought before Osiris to be judged by him when they were dead. They believed that their spirits were immortal and they knew that they had etheric doubles which left their bodies when they slept. That is a very brief résumé but it covers the essential points.'

'And modern students of the supernatural still subscribe to the belief that man has no other non-physical attributes than his spirit and his etheric double?'

Little Mr. Tibitts nodded.

'And that the one could not possibly be mistaken for the other?'

'That is so.'

'How, then, do you explain this appearance of my uncle's double in the face of such incontrovertible evidence that he is dead?'

'I don't. I don't believe it was your uncle's Ka that this young woman saw.'

'I am satisfied in my own mind that it could not have been anyone else's.'

'Then either your uncle is still alive, or, for some purpose of her own, the young woman is lying to you. As, from what you tell me, the first is outside the bounds of all reasonable probability, the second must be the answer.'

'I find that very difficult to believe,' Johnny said after a moment. 'You see, she had never seen my uncle, and she described him so accurately. Besides, his message to me contained a reference to a matter about which she could not possibly have known.'

'Ah!' Mr. Tibitts gave a chuckle. 'That is just the bait by which so many people who lack experience in such transactions allow themselves to be led up the garden path. You think you know what she knows and what she doesn't; but how can you be certain? How could you even start to prove that she never met your uncle? For all you really know she may have known him intimately, but kept it from you.'

'The odds are extraordinarily high against that. And she is a very honest, straightforward girl; the sort that couldn't be bothered to go in for trickery.'

'My friend,' the rabbit teeth flashed again. 'You must come

to see me some other evening and let me show you my case-book. You would be amazed, positively amazed, at the tricks the most innocent seeming people sometimes get up to. My investigations into poltergeists are crammed with examples. Children who have only just entered their teens are among the worst offenders. The way in which they succeed in hood-winking their parents into believing themselves the victims of a haunting is absolutely astonishing. I investigated a case at Letchworth only a couple of months ago, and . . .'

Now that Mr. Tibitts was launched on his favourite subject there was no stopping him, and the tales he had to tell were certainly a revelation to me. I had no idea that so many apparently normal people exercised in secret the most in-genious cunning to satisfy some strange quirk which obsessed their minds. For over an hour Johnny listened to him, asking only now and then a question on some point that might throw further light on his own problem; so it was well after eleven when he rose to go, although by ten he had already secured the information that he had come there to get.

Just off Tavistock Square he picked up a taxi, and it set him down before a brightly lit portal in a narrow turning on the Soho side of Oxford Street. The doorman touched his cap and a reception clerk in a dinner jacket gave him a smiling, 'Good evening, Wing Commander. Nice to see you again. It's quite a time since you've honoured us.' So I guessed at once that this must be the night-club at which Daisy worked.

Downstairs, on a square of brightly lit parquet at one side of the otherwise darkened room, the cabaret was in full swing. And there was Daisy, her admirable legs encased to the thighs in black fish-net stockings, doing her stuff with ten or a dozen other lovelies. The place was fairly full but there were still the usual few tables adjacent to the dance floor that had been kept free by the management for regular patrons. As Johnny came through the doorway the head waiter, recognising him, would have led him to one of them, but he said that he would prefer one of the banquettes at the far end of the room. Having been ensconced in one of the little alcoves that were almost in darkness, Johnny ordered Scotch and asked that as soon as the show was over Miss Williams should be told that he was there.

About ten minutes after the cabaret had ended Daisy, now

wearing a full-skirted dance frock of blue taffeta that rustled as she threaded her way between the close-packed chairs, joined him. As she sat down, she said:

'Johnny, I can't stay long, my steady's here. What is it you want to see me about? I suppose you're still worrying about what happened this evening?'

'Yes; I'm very worried indeed,' he told her. 'In fact I've never been more worried in all my life. The Physical Research chap I went to see bore out all you said; and I believe there really is a terrible possibility that my uncle has been buried alive.'

'No! No!' The ring in Daisy's voice conveyed her antipathy to even considering the idea. 'That couldn't have happened! It really couldn't.'

'It could, however unlikely it may seem. In fact it is the only logical conclusion if one accepts the premises that our bodies house intangible substances, and are not merely lumps of animated matter.'

'If they were I wouldn't ever have seen night-walkers or the spirits of my Mum and Dad, would I?'

'No; and that's just the point. Have you?'

She turned on him angrily. 'Are you suggesting that I'm a liar?'

'Not a deliberate liar. But are you absolutely sure that you haven't been imagining things?'

'If you'd been brought up in the sort of home I was, you'd know better than to talk such nonsense.'

'Daisy, my dear'—his tone, at first soothing, became very earnest—'this is terribly important. Are you prepared to swear to me that you told me the truth, the whole truth and nothing but the truth about the apparition that appeared to you this evening?'

'Yes, Johnny. Cross my heart, it happened just as I said. I wouldn't lie to you about such a thing, really I wouldn't.'

Johnny took a long pull at his whisky. 'Thanks, Daisy. I didn't really think you had. There are too many facets to this affair for either imagination or lies to account for them all. Still, I had to explore every possibility. And now I have there is only one thing for it. As soon as you can get away from here I want you to come with me to Scotland Yard.'

'Go to the police!' Daisy exclaimed. 'Whatever for?'

'Because we've got to get an order to exhume my uncle's body. Only the Home Secretary can give us that, and the police are the right channel through which to approach him.'

'Not likely. I won't! In all my life I've never been mixed up with the police, and I'm not going to start now.'

'Don't be childish, Daisy. Just because you work in a night-club, the police aren't going to try to frame you as being a member of a dope ring, or anything like that. This is a perfectly respectable legal issue.'

'I'm not childish!' she retorted indignantly. 'It's you who are acting silly. I think you must have gone out of your mind. Exhume your uncle's body indeed! I never heard of such a thing!'

'Then you don't read the papers; otherwise you would know that exhumations take place at least a dozen times a year. But, of course, the Home Secretary has to be given reasonable grounds before he will sign such an order. And that is where I require your help.'

'Well, you are not going to get it; and that's flat.'

'Listen, Daisy . . .'

'No. I'm not going to listen. I've already told you that my steady is here tonight. That's him, sitting at one of the floor-side tables smoking a long cigar. I can see he's getting impatient for me to join him, and I'm not going to risk my rent cheque just to hear you go all over this again for the umpteenth time.'

'But don't you see that if I go to Scotland Yard on my own with a story like this they'll think I've got bats in the belfry?'

'So you have! Why can't you be sensible and accept the explanation I gave you: that it was some evil person's double impersonating your uncle?'

'Because it's too far-fetched; and for several other good reasons. But if I state them on my own the police will take me for a nut. Besides, it wasn't I who saw the apparition. It was you. And it's essential that they should be given a first-hand account of it. That's why you must come and say your piece while I vouch for the other side of the story. They might think one of us was a lunatic but they can't suppose that of us both.'

Trembling with agitation, Daisy stood up. 'No Johnny, I

can't do it. If you want to go to the police, then go. But count me out. What's more, if they pull me in and question me I'll deny the whole thing.'

As she hurriedly left the table, she turned her head and threw at him over her shoulder: 'I mean that, Johnny! If I am questioned I'll swear to it that you're crackers, and that all you've said about me is just silly lies.'

9

Wednesday 14th September

FOR a while Johnny stayed on in the Club; but I could see that his thoughts were miles away from the square of parquet, now packed with dancers, and the dimly-lit tables at which parties were laughing together or couples discreetly making love.

It was about half an hour after midnight when, evidently having decided that any further appeal to Daisy would prove useless, he paid his bill, had the door porter get him a taxi and was driven in it back to his rooms. Setting his alarm for six o'clock he undressed and went to bed, while I settled down for the night in his sitting-room.

For the past six hours or more I had been so concerned with not missing a word that Johnny, Daisy or Mr. Tibitts said that I had had little chance to ponder their implications to myself, but now these flooded upon me with full force.

In the light of Mr. Tibitts's expert opinion it seemed no longer possible to doubt that Daisy was right about my being what the ancient Egyptians had called a Ka. That she believed the Ka she had seen to be that of some evil individual attempting to impersonate me was beside the point. Every fact about my own death and that of Evans's was known to me. No third man had been concerned in either, and Ankaret was the only living person who knew the whole truth. To suppose that she was a witch with powers to leave her body and assume my shape at will was palpably absurd. To me it had been self-evident from the first that Daisy's theory was right off the mark, and these factors entirely ruled it out. But she had seen a Ka, and the Ka was mine. Therefore, unless the conclusions of everyone who had made a serious study of the occult from the earliest ages to the present time were wrong, there was still life in my corpse.

It was a terrifying thought. To have had to regard myself

for the past four days as an earth-bound spirit had been bad enough; but this was infinitely worse. Now it was even conceivable that if the energy with which my Ka was imbued gave out, it might be forced back into my body. Swiftly, I thrust that horrifying idea from me.

But what of my future? Would Johnny succeed in getting my body exhumed? I thought it most unlikely. Even if he had been able to persuade Daisy to tell her story, the difficulty of inducing the Home Secretary to sign an exhumation order solely on the psychic evidence would be immense; and if Johnny went to the police without her support they would put him down as a liar or a lunatic.

But say he did, after all, manage to cajole or bully her into giving her help, and secured the order; what then?

If they removed my body from its coffin, would my Ka be able to get back into it? The possibility that it might opened up a whole new field of speculations. I saw at once that my return from the grave as a living person would start an endless chain of fresh complications; but now was no time to think of that, as the odds were all against my ever being called on to deal with them. It seemed as good as certain that I must continue as a Ka. But for how long?

The body and the Ka being so intimately connected, I judged it reasonable to suppose that as the body decayed so the Ka too would gradually become more nebulous. As against that I had felt not the least diminution in my powers of movement, or my faculties, since my Ka had left its body at the presumed moment of death.

What, though, if the Egyptians had been right after all about Kas having souls of their own, and I had become a Ba; so must wander the world in my present state for ever? Few conceptions could have been more depressing and I did not see how the immortality of the Egyptian Bas could have been rendered much more attractive by being given Ka figures in their tombs to live in.

Anyhow it seemed that Mr. Tibitts had been right about Egyptian families wasting their substance by filling the tombs of their relatives with food and clothes. I had so far felt no suggestion of hunger or thirst, and I continued to be insensible to changes of temperature. That argued that he had also been right in his contention that Kas had no separate immortality and ceased to exist when life left the body.

I could only pray that it was so. The undiminished vitality of my Ka could be explained by the fact that a body properly prepared for burial takes a long time to decompose, and mine could hardly have started to do so yet. This theory anyhow offered the comfort of believing that a limit was set to my ordeal. Waiting for my body to rot threatened to prove extremely wearisome, but at least I might hope . . .

In mid thought I checked myself. As long as there was life in my body it would not start to decompose; and Tibitts had definitely laid it down that to exist at all a Ka must be linked to a body with life in it.

Hopelessly confused, weary and depressed, I gave up and, shortly afterwards, drifted into merciful unconsciousness; coming to again only at the sound of Johnny running his bath.

Soon after seven we were on the way to Southampton. At The Bear in Esher he pulled up for breakfast; then we drove on through the slightly misty morning, arriving at the Hillary-Compton offices almost exactly at half-past nine.

In the board-room the other directors had already assembled, with the one exception of Bill, and were standing about making desultory conversation. Having greeted them Johnny joined James at the long window overlooking our yards and Southampton Water. Five, ten, fifteen minutes passed, and still no Bill. Little Toiller then came over to James and proposed that they should start without His Lordship.

'Not much point in that,' James replied. 'The Wing Commander and I are expecting a report from Lord Wiltshire; and we are not disposed to discuss the matter of the E-boats further until we've had it.'

'I took the opportunity to put one or two routine things on the agenda; so we might get on with those,' Toiller suggested.

'Oh well, in that case . . .' James walked towards the table and, leaving the Chair vacant, took his usual place on the right of it.

When the others were seated, Toiller gave a gentle cough and, as Secretary, opened the proceedings. In a slightly husky voice he spoke of my death, and on his motion they all stood up to render the usual homage of one minute's silence to my memory. As they sat down, he said:

'And now, gentlemen, our next business is to elect a new Chairman.'

James was the obvious choice, and the Admiral was much too honest to allow their difference of opinion over the E-boats to deflect him from doing the proper thing as the next senior director. He at once proposed James, Johnny seconded the motion and on a unanimous show of hands James was elected. He said a few words of thanks then moved round to take the chair at the head of the table.

Before he could sit down there came a knock at the door. It was half opened and his secretary put her head round its edge. 'Mr. Compton,' she said, 'I know you don't like to be disturbed while you're at a board meeting, but Lord Wiltshire is on the 'phone from Longshot, and he says it's urgent.'

'Put him through,' James told her and walked over to the side table on which stood the telephone extension.

Picking up the receiver he said: 'Hello!' then his jaw dropped slightly. After a moment he added: 'I'm sorry . . . terribly sorry. No, of course I understand about your not coming over. Yes, I'll tell the others. If there is any way in which I can help you have only to let me know.'

As he hung up, he turned towards his co-directors and said dully: 'It seems as if a curse has suddenly descended on Longshot. When Lady Ankaret's maid took her breakfast tray up about an hour ago she found her in a coma. All efforts to rouse her have failed. The doctor has just declared her to be dead.'

His news was greeted with exclamations of surprise and distress. For a moment I felt stunned by it, but only for a moment. A series of vivid pictures flashed through my mind and I had little doubt that they explained this new tragedy.

I saw Ankaret in the hall at Longshot, as I had last seen her. Silvers had just announced the saving of Johnny's suit-case by Belton. She had jumped to the conclusion that it was the one that held those damning trial forgeries of hers. Poor sweet, in her secret agitation she must have forgotten that he had two cases and that it might be the other. Or perhaps she had never realised that instead of his usual one suit-case he had, on this occasion, brought down two. In any case, she could never have later secured full particulars from Silvers, as I had expected she would; otherwise she would have known that she still had nothing to fear. She had simply accepted it as a certainty that within another twenty-four hours she would be called on to answer questions to which even her quick and subtle mind could provide no satisfactory answers; and that she must then pay the penalty for her own carelessness in not having destroyed those few sheets of paper while she had the chance.

I saw her again seated at her dressing-table with the phial of veronal tablets in her hand. Again I heard her say 'I'll be damned if I do' as she threw it back into the open drawer. But that had been before the fire; before she had had her show-down with Johnny; before he had accused her of starting it. That had been her last card. Not only had it, as she thought, failed her; but Johnny had told her bluntly that he knew of her immoralities, believed that by her indulgence in them she had condemned me to a life of mental torture, and that if he could get at the truth he would have no mercy on her.

Who could blame her if, after that, she had decided to make a painless end of herself?

I was conscious of a great sadness. She had been the love of my life and I of hers. For those who love profoundly sex is only a minor element in the human relationship; so Johnny's belief that it had meant so much to either of us was wrong. From each of her infidelities she had returned to me and made herself more adorable, and had I while still living been robbed of her I should have been utterly inconsolable. Even now, disembodied as I was, I became a prey to the most poignant grief at the thought that never again would I behold her radiant beauty or hear her laughter.

For a few moments there was a shocked silence. It was the Admiral who broke it by saying: 'What an awful thing. Who would have thought a week ago that both Gifford and his wife would be gone from us. Still, there it is. No good carrying on now. We must once more postpone our discussion; and I suppose Monday is about the earliest day that it would be practical to call another meeting.'

'It was you, Sir,' remarked Johnny quietly, 'who pressed

for a quick decision. Your view was that we ought not to hold up our reply to the Ministry of Supply for much longer, and I take it you still feel the same about that?'

'I do,' the Admiral nodded. 'But I don't see now how we can go ahead much before Monday.'

'Oh we can, and personally I should prefer to get things settled this morning. You see,' Johnny proceeded to explain, 'while I am in my present post there is no difficulty about me performing my proper functions as a director and coming down here for monthly meetings—or an occasional special one. But I can't keep on just taking time off, and during the past six days I've put in only a few hours at my office. Partly on account of Lady Ankaret's death and partly for reasons of my own, I intend to ask for a further forty-eight hours; so I can't possibly take another day off till the end of next week. Were it any other matter I would be content to leave it to the board to settle without me; but this is an exception.'

'I appreciate your difficulty; but we met this morning expecting that Wiltshire would be able to give you and Compton Lady Ankaret's view on how the voting power of her shares should be utilised. Now that is out of the question, how can you proceed without it?'

'Her death has deprived her of any say in the matter.'

'I am perfectly aware of that. Gifford's shares now pass to his boy Harold; but as he is a minor the position of Compton and yourself, as Trustees, remains unaltered. He is quite old enough to understand how the decision of the board is likely to affect his interests; but, unlike Ankaret, he will have no previous knowledge of the subject. In consequence, when you have explained the whole thing to him, it would hardly be fair to give him less than two or three days to think it over.'

Johnny looked across at James. 'I don't know how you feel, but we are under no legal obligation to consult Harold; and the moment I heard of Lady Ankaret's death I decided, for reasons that you will no doubt guess, that we should be wrong to do so.'

James nodded slowly. 'Yes. I see what you are driving at, and I am inclined to agree. I think we must take the responsibility of deciding for him.'

'Why?' barked the Admiral. 'Now that he has stepped into Ankaret's shoes there is no difference in their cases.'

'Oh yes there is,' Johnny disagreed. 'She was a woman of the world and competent to appreciate the far-reaching effects which might result from her decision; but one can't say the same for this youngster. What is more Giff loved her and respected her judgment; so I feel sure he would have wished us to consult her. But unfortunately he felt very differently about his son. The boy was a great disappointment to him. He told me himself that he never meant to take him into the business; so I am certain that he would have been most averse to our allowing him to have a possible decisive say in a matter of this kind.'

'I can substantiate that,' James added. 'Poor Giff and young Harold never saw eye to eye about anything.'

The Admiral's face had gone a shade redder, and he snapped at Johnny: 'I see now what's behind all this. You were ready enough to consult Ankaret, because you banked on sentiment's influencing her to back you in pushing through your plot. But now it is a question of the boy, you fear that his dislike of his father will cause him to side against you.'

'Put it that way if you like.' Johnny spoke coldly. 'Although that is not altogether fair. You are right in thinking that out of spite Harold is likely to go against any project favoured by his father. But there is more to it than that. I know from Giff that Harold has Communist leanings. That being so, in the interests of security it would be very wrong for us to discuss this matter with him.'

'Gifford's boy a Communist!' flared the Admiral. 'What rot! I don't believe it! And for you, young man, to talk about security after letting out God knows what to both Gifford and Ankaret! But you need say no more. It is plain to me that having first persuaded Gifford to aid you in your nefarious scheme, you have now wheedled Compton round into helping you put it over.'

Johnny had gone quite white. Clenching his fists, he cried: 'I have told you time and again, Sir, that there is not a shadow of foundation for such imputations. I resent them intensely. Either you will withdraw them or I'll sue you for slander.'

'Sue and be damned,' roared the Admiral, jumping to his feet. 'I've got a cannon worth ten of that. Do what you like. You and Compton control the votes to force this thing

247

through, so go to it. But you'll put me down as dissenting. And I'll call an Extraordinary General Meeting so that the shareholders can be informed how you have prejudiced the interests of the Company. As for bringing a case against me, you haven't a hope. No, not even if such matters were permitted to be discussed in open court. Gifford and Ankaret are both dead, so can no longer be persuaded by you to perjure themselves and deny that you disclosed Official Secrets to them. But I can have a case brought against you. This afternoon I'll go to London. I'll see the Security people and disclose the whole of this scandalous affair to them. Before you are a week older you shall face a Court Martial.'

*   *   *   *

When the Admiral, a short compact furious figure, had swept from the room, like the vortex of a cyclone, there was a long embarrassed silence. McFarlane, the Scots chief engineer, was by nature a taciturn man. He had hardly uttered a word since they had sat down to the table, and he continued to stare with expressionless face at the clean sheet of blotting-paper before him. Charles Toiller had been making frantic doodles on his; but he stopped, threw down his pencil, and said with a reproving shake of the head:

'That was very unpleasant; very unpleasant—I must say. To see two of our directors quarrel like that—most upsetting.'

'Wing Commander Norton acted under great provocation,' James said, coming to Johnny's defence. 'All the same it was bad policy to threaten the Admiral. He's the last man to take that sort of thing lying down.'

'You are right about that, Sir.' Old Toiller continued to shake his head. 'But Sir Tuke's bark has always been worse than his bite. I've known him since he was a young lieutenant, and there's not an ounce of malice in him. He'll soon calm down; and I don't think for a moment that he will do as he said.'

'I hope to God you're right,' Johnny muttered. 'It could do his beloved Navy no good, and it would be bound to do me a lot of harm. There are plenty of people who are always ready to bring out the old tag "There is no smoke without fire".'

248

'Well,' James coughed awkwardly, 'I'm sure the board has complete confidence in your integrity.' He looked at the others and added: 'Isn't that so, gentlemen?'

They both nodded, and McFarlane said: 'This is no affair of mine; but if the Wing Commander was not in earnest about bringing an action, he'd do no harm to his own prospects by making Sir Tuke aware of that.'

Johnny thanked the Scot for his sound advice, and added: 'If only my Uncle Gifford was still alive he could force the old boy to eat his words about me; but as he isn't it would simply be my word against Sir Tuke's. As he could not prove his accusations I'd probably get a verdict, but at what a price! At best I'd be exonerated only on a sort of non-proven basis, and the case would create such a stink that it would ruin my Service career. No; I've no intention of bringing one, but I can hardly run after him to tell him so.'

'I can, though,' said James. 'Not literally of course; but it's only mid-morning yet, and from what he said it's unlikely that he'll start for London until after lunch. As Toiller implied, there's quite a good chance that by then he'll have calmed down, and not go at all. Anyhow he'll have to go home to pack a bag. I'll give him to midday to cool off then telephone and ask him to see me. He can't refuse, and I'll do my best to straighten things out.'

'That's very good of you,' Johnny said gratefully. 'But I'm afraid he's hardly likely to be in an accommodating mood if you go to him straight from a board meeting that has just passed this resolution he is so set against.'

James rose to the occasion. 'All right. Let's not pass it then. Why shouldn't we write to the Ministry of Supply and say that, owing to the death of our late Chairman, until we have had a little time to sort things out we are in no position to make a definite acceptance of new contracts. That's a shocking libel on poor Giff, and on myself for that matter; but they are not to know that Giff's death has not left the finances of the Company in confusion. Anyway, it would enable me to tell Sir Tuke that as yet we have taken no decision, and are still considering his point of view.'

'That's it, Sir; that's it,' old Toiller agreed. 'Gaining a little time can do wonders in such matters. This laying up of *Vanguard* shows the way the wind is blowing, and if other moves are made in the same direction during the next week or two, we may then feel it unnecessary to take the drastic step by which Sir Gifford wanted to arouse public opinion.'

'I only hope you're right.' Johnny gave a sigh. 'Of course, the laying up of *Vanguard* had been on the tapis for months; but there have recently been certain indications that the Navy is now prepared to take a broader view of strategic priorities. My uncle was probably incited to make his proposal by the feeling that time was precious and, of course, it is. But it was his proposal, not mine. My only commitment is to back it whenever it comes before the board, because to do otherwise would be contrary to my convictions.'

Thus the matter was left. As the meeting broke up Johnny put through a telephone call to Whitehall. He apologised to his master for not having gone to his office that morning, told him of Ankaret's death and asked for a forty-eight-hour extension of leave; which was granted.

After a further conversation with James in private, during which they did little more than go over the ground already covered, Johnny went down to his car. As I now expected, as soon as he reached Southampton's city centre, he took the road to Longshot.

Sitting, invisible, beside him in the car I felt greatly distressed by his sad and worn appearance. The riddle of how I had died, and even more the idea that I might have been buried alive, must have played a great part in that; but now, in addition, he was faced with a major worry of his own. Unless James succeeded in calling the Admiral off, poor Johnny was going to have some very difficult explaining to do. Innocent he might be, and no one could prove him otherwise; but unless he could produce some plausible explanation to account for my having been in possession of so much Top Secret information, the weight of circumstantial evidence would incline everyone to believe that it was he who had given it to me. Then, on top of all that, by extraordinary ill-fortune, it chanced that the very man who had threatened to do his best to break him was the one he hoped to make his future father-in-law.

All this, although through no deliberate fault of mine, lay at my door; but badly as I felt about it, fate had placed it beyond my power to help him.

It was a little after midday when we arrived at Longshot. Silvers was hovering unhappily about the hall. He told Johnny that he would 'find His Lordship in the library'; so Johnny walked through to my old sanctum. Bill was sitting there slumped in an arm-chair. On a table beside him stood a cocktail glass and a glass jug a third full of pale amber liquid, which I had no doubt consisted of about one French to eight Gin.

His Lordship liked his Martinis very dry. He also liked a carefree existence. In fact I had never known a man who, despite constant financial difficulties, displayed a greater ability to glide gracefully out of trouble. He toiled not, neither did he spin; but somehow, the war apart, he had managed to idle away all but a fraction of his life in congenial company. Now that trouble had been thrust upon him he was, true to form, doing his best to ride it out on a liberal supply of Dry Martinis.

Having proffered his deepest sympathy to the bereaved parent, Johnny accepted a ration of the brew. As he took it Bill said:

'Terrible thing. And right on top of Giff, too. Can't remember ever having been so cut up in my life—except when I lost my wife. Poor gel. Of course I knew she was damned fond of Giff, but not this much. Still, it's obvious now that she felt she couldn't go on without him.'

I had very good reasons to suppose, and so had Johnny, that it was not solely on account of love for me that Ankaret had made an end of herself. Naturally he forbade from suggesting that, and said instead:

'From the little James Compton told us at the meeting I feared that might be the case. I suppose it is beyond doubt that she did, er—take her own life?'

'Oh yes. It was quite deliberate, too. I imagine she had been contemplating so for some days. She ordered a half bottle of champagne to drink with her dinner; then when her maid found her this morning she had a lot of Giff's love letters scattered over her bed, and an empty phial that had held veronal tablets still clutched in her hand.'

'Did she leave any . . . any note, or anything?' Johnny asked. He made his voice sound casual but I caught an eager glint in his eyes, which told me that, despite his own

251

anxieties, he was still as keen as ever to get on the track of the hypothetical 'Third Man' who he believed had murdered me.

Bill had picked up the jug to pour himself another drink. 'No,' he said, without looking up. 'Not as far as I know; but there's just a chance that the police may find something. Naturally I had to call them in. They sent out that same Inspector chap and his pal the Sergeant. Being cautious blokes they wouldn't give any definite opinion, and they are still up there routing round. In a clear case like this it seems all wrong they should be allowed to pry into poor Ankaret's private affairs, but I suppose it's their job to satisfy themselves that she really did, er—take an overdose.'

'I'll be staying here for the night,' Johnny announced, 'if that's all right by you? As one of Giff's trustees I've got to go through his papers. Unfortunately I had already removed the ones which were probably the most important from the lock-up top of his desk; and they were destroyed in the fire. But there are still the drawers underneath, and I expect he had some letter files somewhere.'

'Glad to have you,' Bill replied. 'I've already telephoned to old Frothy Massingham and asked myself to dinner. Felt I must get out of the place for a few hours somehow. But Silvers will look after you. You'd better have the same room you slept in the night of the fire. Anyhow, make yourself at home.'

'Thanks. And while I am here, if I can be of any help, you have only to let me know.'

At the idea of someone else taking on the tasks with which his daughter's death had landed him I could almost see Bill's somewhat sluggish mind rev up. 'Well,' he said, 'there will be the funeral arrangements as soon as the police let us know when we can hold it. Perhaps you'd see the undertakers for me, and the vicar. Then there are Ankaret's aunts and other relatives who will have to be informed. If I gave you a list of names you could send the telegrams off for me.'

Johnny smiled. 'All right, let's draft a telegram and make out a list, right away. I can fill in the time and date of the funeral when we know it.'

Having no interest in the matter I left them and floated upstairs to Ankaret.

252

A sheet had been pulled up over her face; so to any living person she would now have been only a still form lying in the centre of the bed. But on becoming a Ka I had soon realised the super-physical qualities that my new state gave me. Not only could I pass through solids at will but I could to some extent see through them. Just as my speed of movement was limited, so was the penetration of my vision. I could not see through brick walls, but if I concentrated on a closed cupboard I could make out its contents quite clearly, and the clothes people were wearing only blurred the outlines of their figures.

In consequence the linen sheet that covered Ankaret's face was no more a barrier to my sight than would have been a sheet of cellophane; and even through the thicker bed-clothes her slender form was visible. She looked completely calm and there was a faint suggestion of a smile about her lips, as though she was amused at having cheated the world of its chance to condemn her to years of misery. About that I could not help being happy for her, yet my emotions were sadly wrung at the thought that her loveliness must soon be stiff, cold and mottled with blotches; and that never again could we experience together the joys we had known in life.

Yet it was not only to gaze upon her that I had come there. I hoped that having been so well attuned in life we might still be linked in death; and that if, as in my case, her Ka had survived we might be able to see each other, and so be happily reunited.

In that I was disappointed. No nebulous figure hovered in the room, and some psychic sense told me that her body was completely empty. Yet I did not despair of meeting her later on. If her Ka did survive it might well be elsewhere at the moment. In fact there was every reason why it should be, for the room was so full of police that they were almost tumbling over one another; and she would have resented their presence, just as I did.

The Inspector was going through the drawers of her bed-side table; the Sergeant was examining her make-up things; a photographer was erecting his camera by the window; a finger-print expert was scattering powder on the knob of the door leading to the passage, and a fifth man was rummaging through her wardrobe.

Sick at heart I left them to it and went out into the garden. It was again a pleasant morning, and I thought it the most likely place in which I might find her; but though I drifted disconsolately about it and along the foreshore for the best part of two hours my search proved unavailing.

Re-entering the house about half-past two I found that Johnny had settled down to go through my remaining papers in earnest. He had emptied the drawers of my desk and found the letter files which I kept in the cupboard under the bookcase.

As he went through the files he was extracting a letter here and there and putting it aside. A glance at them told me that he was no longer seeking for evidence of Ankaret's complicity in my death, or at least not primarily. The letters were mostly from men I had met in the war, who had remained my friends and since risen to high rank. There were four Air Marshals and two Generals among them; and three Admirals of a slightly older generation who had been friends of my father.

He was, of course, hoping to find that I had been in intimate correspondence with one of them, and thus perhaps get a lead to who had given me my secret information. But the letters he had put aside contained nothing other than news of mutual friends and arrangements to meet socially; and I knew only too well that we would come upon nothing which would be of the least value to him. Being tired now from another early morning start, I went into the drawing-room and settled down for my equivalent of a nap.

I was roused by Johnny coming through the room, and saw from the clock on the mantelpiece that it was now nearly six. As he strode past to the hall I followed, and we were soon once more together in his car. He took the road to Beaulieu and pulled up on the corner where he had met Sue two nights before. About five minutes later, her pretty brown curls blown back a little from her forehead by the wind, she came walking briskly up the lane.

As a lover's greeting Johnny's was considerably below par. Urged on by his anxiety, before she had had time even to settle herself beside him, he abruptly enquired if her father was at home.

'No,' she replied, raising her eyebrows, 'why do you ask?'

He sighed. 'I'm sorry to say, Sue, that this morning I had another row with him.'

254

'Oh darling! You promised me faithfully that at the next board meeting you would keep your temper—so as not to make matters worse.'

'I know I did. But there's a limit to what even a saint could stand. He accused me of being a liar, a traitor and a crook. I couldn't just sit there and let that pass; so I told him that unless he took it back I'd sue him for slander.'

'What!' Sue gave a gasp. 'You threatened to bring an action against Daddy?'

'That's it. Of course, I didn't really mean to; and after he had stamped out of the room James Compton offered to pour oil on the troubled waters by letting him know that. James promised to get hold of him about midday; but he telephoned me at Longshot, just after I asked you to meet me here this evening, to say that he had been on to your home, and the woman who answered the 'phone had said that your father would not be in for lunch. Until a moment ago I was still hoping that James might have run him to earth at the Club in Southampton or somewhere.'

'If Mr. Compton had spoken to me I could have told him that he would have no luck. Daddy packed a suit-case before he left this morning. He is spending the night in London, and after the board meeting he meant to drive straight up.'

'So he intended to go to London anyway?'

'Yes; but what is there so surprising about that?'

Johnny gave her then a full account of the meeting and of the Admiral's final outburst. When he had done she asked:

'What will happen to you if Daddy does carry out his threat?'

'I'm hanged if I know.' Johnny sighed again. 'Uncle Giff could have cleared me in a single sentence. He would only have had to name the source from which he got the gen. But as he is dead there is no way in which I can prove my innocence. On the other hand nobody can possibly prove me to be guilty, because I'm not. Yet they will believe me to be. The circumstantial evidence is so damning. For a breach of security of this kind, an officer in my position of trust would be liable to be cashiered and receive a heavy prison sentence into the bargain. As the Court can't find me guilty it won't come to that. But the Air Ministry can retire an officer compulsorily at any time, simply by notifying him that Her

Majesty no longer has any use for his services. That is probably the line they will adopt.

'Alternatively if they have any doubts—although I can't see why they should have—they may decide against being quite so drastic. That would mean my being hoisted out of my present job and transferred to some God-forsaken post in a desert or a jungle where I'd no longer be a security risk. And of course, I'd be barred from any chance of further promotion. They would just let me work out my time in my present rank, then "goodbye Wing Commander Norton". It would be a jolly life for the next few years, wouldn't it?' Johnny ended bitterly. 'Trying to run some little off-the-map station with everyone whispering behind my back that I was the promising boyho who had blotted it because he couldn't keep his mouth shut.'

After a moment he went on: 'I've not much doubt that your father meant to do what he threatened; and if he did I'm afraid I'm all washed-up. By the time the Air Ministry are through with me I'll be little good to myself or anyone else; let alone a sweet person like you. I'm glad now that we haven't announced our engagement. At least you'll be spared from officious sympathy and unpleasant gossip through having broken it off. And that's what we've got to do.'

Sue turned her face to his and her little chin stuck out. 'We'll do no such thing! Johnny, you're mine. I love you and I mean to hang on to you. I wouldn't be worth having if I hesitated about that for an instant. What is more, if they retire you or order you abroad I'll marry you the very next day after they've told you their decision.'

'No, I can't let you. I love you much too much to allow you to sacrifice yourself.' Johnny's voice was firm, but I could see that Sue meant to fight him for all she was worth.

Feeling that it would be hardly decent to stand in while they faced this private crisis in their lives, I moved off some way along the ditch but kept a watch on the car as I did not want it to drive off without me. Nearly half an hour elapsed then, ignoring the fact that they were on the open road, they suddenly clutched one another in a violent embrace, and from the position of their heads it was obvious that they were kissing. That made me pretty confident that Sue had got the best of the argument; so, having given them a few minutes to murmur endearments, I returned and passed into the back of the car.

Johnny was just saying: 'I meant to break the bad news to you, than spend the rest of the evening in misery on my own. But since you are determined to see this thing through with me we had better cheer ourselves up with some dinner.'

'I don't feel like going to an inn,' Sue said, after a moment. 'Let's go home, and I'll knock up something.'

'Better not,' he replied a shade dubiously. 'If your old man returned unexpectedly, he would be absolutely furious with you.'

Sue gave an abrupt, defiant laugh. 'The odds are all against that. But if he did, who cares? The sooner he knows that I mean to nail my flag to the mast about this, the better. Even if he threw me out I'm not such a nit-wit that I couldn't find a job to keep myself until we can get married.'

Johnny kissed her again. 'You wouldn't have to, my sweet. I'd see to that.'

Ten minutes later they were in the kitchen of Sue's home. As the Admiral was away she had given the gardener's wife, who came in and cooked for them, an evening off and had meant to get her own dinner. Now, their cares temporarily forgotten, they romped like children playing at husband and wife—except for breaking off to exchange frequent kisses—while preparing themselves a little feast to be eaten off the kitchen table.

But their happy mood did not last long. Before they were through the bottle of champagne that Sue had looted from her father's cellar Johnny was replying only in monosyllables to her cheerful chatter. Giving him a swift sideways glance, she said:

'You are looking wretched, darling; and terribly worn out. The big blow-up having taken place only this morning, that can't account for it altogether. I suppose you are still worrying over the mystery surrounding your uncle's death. Have you managed to get a line yet on the wicked Lady Ankaret?'

Sue's question caused Johnny to realise that, not having seen her father since the board meeting, she still knew nothing of the latest tragedy at Longshot. He proceeded to tell her about it and what he believed to be the reason for Ankaret's suicide. Once launched on the subject he was soon led to that of myself.

Quite understandably he refrained from disclosing his previous relationship to Daisy, describing her simply as a professional dancer whom he had met soon after his return from Malaya and whom, knowing her to have psychic gifts, he had looked up again to consult.

I don't think Sue was deceived; but she was the sort of girl who would have had little respect for a chap who had not sowed his wild oats, and had enough confidence in herself not to be jealous of the past mistress of a man she had made up her mind to marry. Anyway she refrained from comment, and Johnny went on to describe in detail all that had occurred during his meeting with Daisy and with Mr. Tibitts.

Sue listened, her brown eyes at times wide with amazement, at others shadowed by doubt or disbelief. When he had done, she said:

'This can't be true, darling. It really can't. The very idea of your uncle having been buried alive is too horrible to contemplate. It will give me nightmares for a week but I simply don't believe it.'

Johnny's tale had taken long in telling, and they argued the pros and cons for a further half hour; so it was after half-past ten when he declared:

'Anyway, I can't stand this uncertainty any longer. Neither Daisy nor Tibitts were lying. I am convinced of that. And if they are right about this Ka business you see what that adds up to? Uncle Giff is lying there in his coffin; and he is still alive. If they are wrong, and he isn't, then I'll be able to sleep again. But I've got to find out.'

'You . . . you,' Sue stared at him in sudden terror, 'you don't mean that you are going to his grave?'

'Yes; that's just what I am going to do. That's the main reason why I telephoned for an extension of leave this morning. I meant to anyway, before I had the row with your father. I couldn't go another night with this awful doubt hanging over me.'

'No, Johnny! No! You mustn't! It's sacrilege or something. Anyhow there's a heavy penalty for anyone caught interfering with a body that's been buried.'

'I won't get caught. You needn't worry about that.'

'You might. And if you were I'm sure it would mean a prison sentence.'

Johnny stood up. 'I can't help that. I'm sorry I told you, Sue. I wouldn't have if I weren't half out of my mind already. But I'll be driven right out of it if I don't settle this thing once and for all. It's a "must", darling. If I don't I'll never have a quiet conscience again for the rest of my life.'

Sue too stood up. She had gone very pale but her voice was firm. 'All right, then; I'll come with you.'

'You'll do nothing of the sort!'

'Why not? Be sensible. You'll need someone to hold a torch while you unscrew the coffin lid.'

'No I won't. It's not screwed down. Uncle Giff left an instruction in his will that it was not to be, and that airholes were to be bored in the coffin itself.'

'What an extraordinary thing to do.'

'It seems that he always had a fear that he might be buried alive. I can't help feeling now that it may have been a premonition. It's that idea on top of all the rest which decided me this morning that I positively must find out.'

A new look of credulity came into her eyes. 'I believe you may be right, Johnny. Anyhow, I agree now that you must make sure. It . . . it's going to be a ghastly business. But I won't let you down. I mean I won't faint, or anything. I've never fainted in my life.'

'No, I'm sure you wouldn't. All the same I'm not taking you with me.'

'Yes you are.'

'No I'm not. You were right about it being a prison job, if one is caught. Do you think I'd let you expose yourself to that?'

'It's all the more reason I should come. Two of us would run less risk than one. I could keep *cave* while you are down in the grave.'

'Sue, I won't have it. Nothing will induce me to let you mix yourself up in this.'

'You can't stop me. I've got my own car. I'll catch you up before you've had time to get the lid off the coffin.'

That put Johnny in a fix. For another few minutes he pleaded with her to remain behind; but he could not shake her determination.

259

'Very well,' he conceded at last. 'But on one condition. You are to remain outside the churchyard and seated at the wheel of your car. If you see anyone about to take the path through the churchyard you will sound your horn, then beat it like hell. No pulling up a hundred yards up the road to creep back and find out what has happened to me. You'll drive straight home. Is that understood?'

She nodded. 'Yes. I'll agree to that.'

'Promise? No mental reservations now. On your word of honour.'

'You have it, Johnny.'

For a moment they eyed one another tensely, then he said: 'We had better not park our cars close together, just in case I am surprised and have to run for it. Anyone chasing me might spot the number of yours as you drove off. You had better pull into the road-side just by the lych-gate outside the church. That's the most likely direction from which any-one may approach. No one will be going out at this time of night; but there is just the chance that some late-comer might make his way home by the short cut across the churchyard to the village.'

'Why not put it off till the small hours of the morning? It would be less risky then.'

Johnny drew a hand over his eyes. 'I suppose you're right. But I'd rather not. It's days since I had a really long sleep, and I didn't get a wink last night from worrying. I just couldn't face sitting up for another three or four hours.'

'You could have a sleep here, and I'll wake you at, say, two o'clock.'

'No. I'm all keyed up now. I want to get the thing done and finished with. It's now eleven and everyone goes to bed early in these parts. Really the risk is negligible. By letting you come to keep *cave* for me and dispersing cars I'm only taking precautions against an outside chance. I'll drive on round the church and up the road that leads to the village. There is a cottage opposite the other entrance to the foot-path. I'll park a little short of that and come into the church-yard that way.'

'And afterwards?' Sue asked.

'As soon as I'm through I'll drive back past you. As you see me pass, start up and follow me back here. If anything does go wrong we separate. You'll already be on your way home, and I'll drive straight back to Longshot; but I'll telephone to let you know that I'm all right.'

With everything now settled, they went out to their cars. Sue's was only an ancient run-about, so after a quick embrace he saw her into hers and gave her a few minutes' start. I followed with him.

There was no moon and the night was dark, so favourable for this grim undertaking. As we covered the few miles at a steady pace I could hardly contain my impatience. My body had now been presumed dead for five days. Its intestines should be beginning to decompose. As the lid of the coffin was not fastened down ants might have got in and—horrible thought—be eating away the face. Anyway by this time the eyes should have sunk right back and hideous blotches have appeared on the skin. One glance at it would be enough to tell if the beliefs of the occultists were all moonshine, or if I was still tied by an invisible thread to the flesh that had been buried in the grave.

If I was, what then? But it would be time enough to wrestle with new problems when I knew. As with Johnny, the question that caused me such agitation at the moment was: what *should* we find there?

As we reached the valley bottom and approached the church it suddenly seemed to rear up, a black silhouette against the dark grey-black sky. Sue had drawn in her car near the lychgate as Johnny had directed, but he did not slacken speed as we passed it. Driving on and round the corner on which the church stood he ran up the hill beyond it a few hundred yards, then drew in to the side of the road and switched off his lights.

I had listened to his plan with some anxiety, for I knew a thing that evidently he did not. The cottage opposite the entrance to the footpath was that of Cowper, the village constable. But it had been beyond my power to warn Johnny that it would be safer to go in the other way. Now, my uneasiness was increased by seeing that a light was still burning in one of the upstairs windows of the cottage, which meant that Cowper or his wife was still awake. If Cowper was there and had heard the car draw up, he might look out and, seeing that its lights had been cut off, come to investigate.

The chances were against his actually catching Johnny interfering with my grave, but Johnny would have some awkward explaining to do if on returning to his car he found
Cowper waiting there to serve him with a chit for having
left it on the road with its lights out. I could only hope that
Cowper was already in bed and would soon decide to go to
sleep.

Taking a big torch from the car Johnny made his way up
the last forty yards of road, turned into the churchyard and
walked resolutely down its slope. Having been at my funeral
he knew roughly the whereabouts of the grave, but not its
exact position. It was one in a line of graves among a group of
tall ancient yews, and it was so dark there that he had to put
on his torch to find it. Having taken a wrong side path he had
to hunt about for several minutes before he got his bearings.
Then the beam of the torch fell upon the faded flowers of a
wreath. Hurrying forward he found the grave and shone the
torch full upon it.

In accordance with my instructions, the great stone slab
that sealed the vault had not yet been replaced. It was lying
tilted up on edge against another gravestone nearby. But the
vault itself had not been left exposed. Presumably, to keep
out the rain, or to hide the coffins in it from the sight of the
morbidly-curious, a large tarpaulin had been spread over the
aperture, and was held in place by a number of loose bricks
on its sides and corners.

After a glance at the floral tributes that had been set out
on either side of the grave, Johnny selected a harp that had
been propped up amongst them and fixed his torch into the
wires to that its beam fell on the tarpaulin. Quickly now he
threw aside the bricks from one side of it, then drew the free
half back.

The vault had been made to hold ten coffins, but, as yet,
there were only six in it; so those of my father and of myself,
which lay side by side, were nearly five feet below the level of
the ground. It was quite a drop, and once down there, anyone
other than a fit man, like Johnny, would have found it difficult to scramble out again.

The torch was not shining directly into the grave, and it
was so dark that he could not even see the coffins. With commendable prudence, instead of lowering himself then stretching

out a hand for the torch, he picked it up first and flashed it downwards to see how far he had to drop.

It was at that moment, as we both stared down at the two coffins—my father's dull and damp-stained from the years it had lain there, and mine still highly polished, its silver fittings as yet hardly tarnished—that the faint sound of footsteps made me turn and look up the path.

The perceptions of my Ka being above the physically normal, I knew that I must have heard them well before Johnny would; and my sight being better able to penetrate the darkness I saw, as he would not have been able to do, the outline of a figure coming towards us but still some distance off.

Desperately I tried to convey a warning to Johnny. In an agony of apprehension I heard the footsteps getting nearer. With all the mental strength of which I was capable I willed him to realise his danger. But my efforts were of no avail. For what seemed to me an age he continued to stand there shining his torch down into that accursed grave.

To my unutterable relief the person who was approaching kicked against a stone. Johnny heard it. In a second he had gone into action. Switching out his torch he thrust it into his coat pocket. Next moment he had pulled the nearest of the two turned-back corners of the tarpaulin back over the vault and kicked a brick on to it. In two swift strides he was across one of the banks of flowers and, kneeling down, fumbled frantically for the other corner. Ten precious seconds were lost before his fingers closed upon it in the darkness and he drew it over. Dragging a brick from beneath his right knee, he jerked it on to the corner.

But he was still kneeling there when the bulky figure of Constable Cowper emerged from behind one of the big yews. A torch flashed on and in a gruff voice the policeman demanded:

'What are you up to here?'

I have never admired Johnny more than at that moment. Most people would have cut and run, trusting to elude the constable among the gravestones and get away in the darkness. I certainly should have. But I suppose he realised in time that his car might be found and its number be taken before he could reach it; and that it was the capacity instantly to balance risks, required for handling aircraft at near supersonic speeds, which saved him in this instance.

Coming unhurriedly to his feet he replied: 'Can't you see for yourself? I was praying. Who are you?'

'I am an officer of the Hampshire County Police,' came the prompt answer. 'And who may you be?'

'I'm Wing Commander Norton; Sir Gifford Hillary's nephew.'

'Oh!' Cowper seemed a little taken back. Raising the beam of his torch a little he shone it on Johnny's face. I could see that it was covered with sweat; and, seeing the grisly undertaking he had been on the point of attempting, I did not wonder. But as they were standing at opposite ends of the grave and more than ten feet apart, the policeman might not have noticed that.

Lowering the torch again, he said more amiably: 'I recognise you now, Sir, as the Air Force gentleman who sometimes stays up at the Hall. But if I may say so, this is hardly the proper time to say a prayer at a grave-side.'

'Why not?' Johnny said sharply. 'There is no law against being in a churchyard after dark. And if I had come here to pray in the daytime I'd have had to risk the unpleasantness of passers-by who know about the tragedy stopping to gape at me.'

'There is that, Sir. And there's nothing illegal about your being here. But there is about interfering with a grave. Very much so.' Shining his torch down on the side of the tarpaulin from which Johnny had removed, and not had time to replace, the bricks, he went on:

'You wouldn't have been interfering with this one, would you, Sir?'

'Certainly not.'

'Well, someone has. Them bricks were all on the tarpaulin to hold it down all round, as they should be, when I passed this way to my tea just before six o'clock.'

'I've only been here about ten minutes, and the grave is exactly as I found it.'

'Then someone else must have moved the bricks,' Cowper said a shade lugubriously. 'It was an odd notion of Sir Gifford's, asking that the vault should be left open until a week after his burial; and not a very sensible one. Sexton

Watkins is a great talker when he gets down to the local, so everyone hereabouts knows of it. And there are some strange characters about. It's not so long ago that someone broke into a church just over the border, in Dorset, and defiled the altar. Cracked, of course; but, all the same, to my mind it's tempting Providence to leave a grave open for longer than need be.'

Johnny gave a slightly forced laugh, 'Well, anyway, I'm not a Satanist, Constable. You can set your mind at rest about that.'

'I didn't think you was, Sir.' Cowper paused for a moment. 'Still, I take it you've done what you came to do, and will be going home now?'

'I owe a great deal to my uncle; so I intended to make a half hour's vigil here.'

'Just as you wish, Sir. Then I'll stay around out of sight and see that nobody disturbs you.'

'Thanks very much,' Johnny replied with a heartiness he certainly could not have felt; and, as the policeman moved off into the darkness, he knelt down again.

I should like to think that he prayed for me, and it is very probable that he did. At all events with Cowper lurking somewhere on the far side of the yews, any further attempt by Johnny to get down into the vault was quite out of the question.

Some twenty minutes after Cowper had left him there came two sharp hoots on a motor horn, then the noise of a car starting up and the sound of its engine gradually fading away in the distance.

I had no doubt that it was Sue, and went forth to investigate. Her car had gone and the figure of a man was advancing up the path from the lych-gate. Cowper emerged from the shadows, and evidently knew him, as they exchanged a few words and a cheerful 'good night' before the late-comer went on his way.

Shortly afterwards Johnny came out from behind the yews, evidently feeling that he had spent long enough on the vigil that he had been forced to undertake in order to allay the constable's suspicions. As he turned on to the upward path Cowper unobtrusively intercepted him, and said:

'Would I be right, Sir, in supposing that to be your car, up by my cottage there?'

Johnny had no option but to admit it.

'In that case, Sir,' the policeman went on, 'I'm afraid I must put in a report. It's an offence, you know, to leave a car on the highway after dark without its lights on.'

'I know,' Johnny said wearily. 'I've had an awful lot to see to these past few days; so I'm a bit tired. I switched them off without thinking what I was doing.'

'That might happen to anyone, Sir; but I'll have to report it just the same.' Cowper fell into step with Johnny and they walked up the slope side by side. When they reached the car the policeman saw Johnny into it, then said:

'Don't you go worrying about Sir Gifford's grave, Sir. I suffer a bit from insomnia; so I'm a great one for making night patrols. I'll be out again at least once more tonight, and I'll give special attention to it not being further interfered with.'

That, I felt, must squash any hopes that Johnny might have entertained of returning later for another attempt to get a sight of my body without fear of interruption. In a gloomy silence, which was on my part enforced and on Johnny's natural, we drove back to the Hall.

As soon as Johnny got in, he telephoned Sue. Although everyone had gone to bed, he kept his voice low, as he said:

'That you, darling? . . No, I didn't manage to do all that I had hoped . . . Yes, I was interrupted and had a slight spot of bother. But I got out of it all right . . . No, don't worry your sweet self. I'm not going back . . . No, I promise you. I'm dropping with fatigue, anyway. Besides, I did succeed in getting a good look at the box. If things had been as I feared I feel sure the lid would have been displaced . . . Yes, by what's there trying to get out when the thing that was seen returned to it between spells of travelling. But it wasn't. There was no sign that there had been any activity at all; so I'm satisfied now . . . Yes, really. And if anything happens about the other business I'll let you know at once . . . Yes, I will. Thanks, darling, for your help tonight. There are darn' few girls who would be brave enough to insist on lending a hand on a job like that. Good night, my sweet. Sleep well. Bless you.'

When he had hung up, I watched him go slowly and wearily upstairs. He had said that he was satisfied. But I wasn't. I too had had a look down into that grave. And by

266

concentrating I could see through the coffin lid. Hair always continues to grow after death so I had not been surprised to see a five-days' growth of stubble on my chin. But my body had been as fresh and pink as on the night it had crumpled to the floor under the shock of Evans's death ray.

10

Thursday 15th September

THE following morning, expecting that the police would arrive at about half-past nine to continue their investigations into Ankaret's death, I went up to make another attempt to get into touch with her while the house was still quiet.

I was pleased to see that although they had turned her room topsy-turvy the previous day they had afterwards put everything back in good order. But when I concentrated my gaze on the still form beneath the bed-clothes I had a sudden unhappy feeling that I was again to suffer disappointment.

She had been dead for only a little over twenty-four hours; so to the normal eye her appearance had probably not yet altered, but to my super-sensitive sight it had. As I looked down on her still lovely face it seemed to me that the hollows below her high cheek-bones were more pronounced and that the shadows beneath her eyes had become darker.

I had now come to the conclusion that the truth must lie somewhere between the beliefs of the ancient Egyptians and the modern occultists: namely that while the former had been right in believing that the Ka lingered on after death of the body, the latter were also right in maintaining that it had no separate existence from it. In short, that the Ka disintegrated in direct relation to the decomposition of the physical form.

If I was right in that, and also right in thinking that Ankaret's body now showed signs of decomposition, then it meant that her Ka, unlike mine, had already begun to lose something of its potency. In consequence every hour that passed would decrease my chances of communicating with it.

Nevertheless I hovered by the bed and spent a good hour willing her to come to me. At the end of it I gave up. All along I had felt convinced that her body was now no more than an empty shell, and, pray as I might, not so much as a ripple in the ether indicated that any presence other than my own had entered the room.

It was now about a quarter past nine. Passing into Johnny's room I found that he had slept late and was only just getting up; so I went downstairs. The noble Earl was in the dining-room, making a hearty breakfast. For a while I hung about disconsolately. Then the police arrived; but only Sergeant Haines.

After asking Silvers a few questions—which presumably they had not thought of the day before—and writing the answers down in his note-book, he asked to see Bill. My father-in-law came out to him and was then informed that the inquest would be held next morning at ten-thirty; so, if he wished, he could make arrangements for the funeral to take place on the following day. The Sergeant added that the police were now satisfied as to the cause of death, so only formal evidence would be given at the inquest. He then took his departure.

As he walked out of the front door, Johnny came downstairs and, when they had exchanged 'good mornings', Bill said to him: 'Sergeant Haines has just been to let us know that the inquest is tomorrow, and that we can have the funeral on Saturday. I see no point in putting it off over the week-end, do you?'

Johnny shrugged. 'It's for you to say if that will be giving long enough notice to her relatives who may wish to attend it.'

'Oh I think so.' Bill was obviously anxious to get such an unpleasant business over. 'Most of 'em live in the Home Counties. It will be if you'd be kind enough to send those telegrams off as soon as you've had your breakfast.'

'I'll do that,' Johnny agreed; but as he was about to enter the dining-room a taxi drew up at the front door and Harold emerged from it.

The London evening papers of the night before would, of course, have carried the story of Ankaret's death, and with quite indecent haste he had arrived to claim his inheritance. To reach Longshot so early he must have got up at crack of dawn and caught the six thirty-three from Waterloo.

With a brevity which showed complete lack of feeling, he

269

condoled with Bill on Ankaret's death, and at once began to look about him, evidently assessing the value of the pictures and furniture which were now his property.

Bill's mouth tightened slightly, but with his unfailing courtesy enquired if Harold had yet had breakfast and, as he had not, asked Johnny to take him into the dining-room and give him some.

They were hardly seated before he began to bombard Johnny with questions. How much was his income likely to be? Did all the contents of the house now belong to him or were some of them Ankaret's? What was the present value of his holding in Hillary-Comptons? How many acres of land went with the house? He even asked if I had had a long-playing gramophone and a television set.

Johnny, I thought, showed remarkable patience in bearing with him and answering his questions to the best of his ability. But as I witnessed Harold's shameless exhibition of greed and eagerness to get his hands on my ex-assets my indignation grew until I could have slapped him. This gawky long-haired youth might be flesh of my flesh but, all the same, had I had the power to make another will I would have been greatly tempted to cut him out of it.

Such a possibility would have hardened into a certainty as he went on: 'Of course, I shall sell this place. No one but a fool would squander half his income keeping it up. And as the land runs down to the foreshore it must be pretty valuable. We ought to raise quite a packet by selling the whole estate as a building site.'

At this display of vandalism I was delighted to see Johnny's patience give out. 'That,' he said sharply, 'is a matter for myself and my co-trustee, Mr. Compton. All your affairs are in our hands until you are twenty-one.'

Harold stared at him, then replied truculently: 'It's your job, and his, to get for me the biggest income that you can. That's a trustee's duty. It's what they are for.'

'On the contrary,' retorted Johnny. 'Short of robbing a trust they can do with it what they like; and they are under no obligation other than to protect its capital from depreciation to the best of their ability. As far as I am concerned I shall do my best to carry out what I believe would have been your father's wishes. To sell Longshot would not have been one of tnem, and I am pretty confident that Mr. Compton will agree with me about that.'

How right he was! To have sold this gracious old family home, which had been built, furnished and cared for by several generations of our forebears, while there were still ample funds to support it would have been the act of a barbarian. The idea of its being turned over to demolition squads in order that rows of jerry-built bungalows might be erected on its site made me see red. I could take only small comfort in the thought that Johnny and James would protect it for the next three years, and hope that during them Harold might come under the influence of someone with a better appreciation than himself of real values. But that anyone so boorish and self-centred was likely to be loved or changed by a sensitive young woman seemed highly improbable.

Reduced to surly silence by Johnny's having poured cold water on his immediate hopes of turning Longshot into money, Harold concentrated on his food until, just as they were finishing their meal, Johnny said:

'May I ask what has brought you down here?'

'Why, to take possession, of course,' came the surprised answer. 'Ankaret was no friend of mine, and I'm hanged if I'll let her relatives have the run of the place for a moment longer than is necessary. What is more, I mean to tell old Wiltshire so.'

I squirmed at this further breach of good taste; but Johnny was more than a match for Harold. With a frosty smile, he said:

'Do you, now? I wouldn't if I were you, or you may regret it. You seem to have overlooked the fact that it is James Compton and myself who will decide what is to be done here. Lord Wiltshire is naturally greatly distressed by his daughter's death. He will leave here in his own good time and not before. Should you be so rude as to suggest his departure to him I'll get Longshot listed as an Ancient Monument. Then you will never be allowed to do anything with the property which might be detrimental to the house.'

Harold jumped to his feet, his face working with rage. 'You can't do that! Houses for the workers are more important than preserving old houses like this just because they were built a hundred and fifty years ago.'

'Stop talking claptrap,' Johnny admonished him, standing up and throwing his napkin on the table. 'You know very well that you don't give a damn for the workers. Most people would feel overwhelmed by their good fortune at coming into a lovely old place like this. All you are thinking of is to cash it in for as much money as you can get to spend on yourself.'

'Well, I've a right to if I wish, haven't I? I think you're being beastly. I bet you've got some private axe of your own to grind. But I won't stand for that. I'll consult a solicitor.'

Johnny gave a mirthless laugh. 'The best thing you can do is to ring up for a taxi and go home. Consult who you like. I don't give a damn. But get out of here. I've enough worries without having to put up with impudent young cubs like you.'

I don't think he would have shown his dislike and contempt for Harold quite so openly if worry had not already frayed his nerves to near breaking point. But he had never spoken a truer word, and within another minute he was given still further cause for anxiety about his own affairs. Silvers came in with a slip of paper on a silver salver and, presenting it to him, said:

'A telegram for you, Sir. I have just taken it down over the telephone from the Post Office.'

Johnny took the paper and, looking over his shoulder, I read:

Your leave cancelled. Stop. Report to me personally immediately on your return. Benthorpe.

There could be little doubt what that meant. On the previous afternoon the Admiral had done his worst, and the unfortunate Johnny was being recalled to answer his allegation.

Thrusting the paper into his pocket, Johnny glanced at Harold and said: 'I have urgent private affairs to attend to; so I shall be leaving shortly. If you wish to stay here to attend Lady Ankaret's funeral on Saturday, and in the meantime have a look round, ask Lord Wiltshire if he will be good enough to give you a bed for a couple of nights. You had then best go home and wait till you hear from Mr. Compton or myself. You are clearly to understand that you are to remove nothing from the house. If you can manage to behave yourself

272

like a gentleman, we may decide to increase your allowance; but if I hear that you have been in any way rude to Lady Ankaret's relatives or the servants, we certainly shall not.'

Silvers, of course, had already left the room and Johnny now followed him. He found Bill in the library. Although it was only half-past ten, His Lordship was measuring out with scrupulous care his first brew of very dry Martini. After all, he had nothing else to do and a head like a rock; so why shouldn't he. Johnny said to him:

'I've had a telegram recalling me to duty; so I've got to leave at once, but I'll try to get back for the funeral. Sorry not to be able to help you about the arrangements after all; but there it is. I'm sorry to tell you that that young bounder, Harold, may inflict himself on you for a couple of nights. But the place belongs to him now so one can hardly chuck him out. You might keep an eye on him though, and see that he doesn't make off with anything of value when he does leave. He's quite capable of it.'

Bill nodded. 'Poor old Giff. Fancy him producing a son who is such an outsider. Still, my own boy gives me no cause for parental pride. Sorry you've got to leave, Johnny, but it can't be helped. Care to join me in a snifter before you go?'

'No thanks. It's a bit early for me.' Johnny declined the offer with a smile.

Ten minutes later I was once more with him on the road to London. In all the years I had lived at Longshot I had never made the trip so frequently in so few days, and I was getting a little tired of it. But I was now greatly concerned for him and all my thoughts were centred on what sort of reception he would meet with when we arrived.

As the morning was fine we made the run in good time. Instead of going to his office he drove straight to the Air Ministry and at a quarter to two parked his car outside it. Going into the building he followed the same route as he had when I had accompanied him there on the previous Sunday. On pushing open the door labelled 'Air Commodore Ben-thorpe, Director of Plans' he came face to face with the same young woman seated behind her typewriter. Giving him a surprised look, she said:

'I thought you were on leave, Wing Commander.'

'So I was,' he replied. 'But I've been recalled.'

'Really!' she raised her eyebrows. 'I didn't see the telegram; and there is no particular flap on.'

Johnny smiled at her. 'There is always some sort of a flap going on in these parts. No doubt the P.A. sent it.'

'I suppose so.' She smiled back, showing two rows of excellent teeth. 'Did the Air Commodore ask you to report to him personally?'

'Yes. But at this hour I take it he's at lunch.'

'That's it,' she nodded. 'You might just as well have had your own before coming in. But perhaps you have?'

'No,' Johnny told her, with a light-heartedness that he could scarcely have been feeling. 'My reporting while still hungry is just a demonstration of my zeal for the Service.'

She showed her pretty teeth again in a laugh. 'Well, he won't be back till half-past two or a quarter to three; so you had better get some.'

'I will,' he said. 'I'll go down to the canteen. Perhaps you would be good enough to give me a buzz there when Master has returned and is ready to see me.'

'Yes, I'll do that, Wing Commander,' she agreed decorously.

Downstairs in the canteen Johnny did not make much of a lunch, and afterwards he remained at his table nervously chain smoking. It was past three before the summons came and he went up again to his Chief's office.

In the inner room, the short square-shouldered little Air Commodore was sitting behind his desk. On a chair nearby sat a tall heavy-featured Group Captain with a fluffy grey moustache. As Johnny entered his master came to the point at once.

'Good afternoon, Norton. I'm sorry that I had to recall you from leave in the middle of family troubles; but a very serious charge has been made against you.' He waved a hand towards his tall companion. 'I don't know if you know Group Captain Kenworthy; but he is the Assistant Provost Marshal, and he has been instructed to go into the matter.'

The Group Captain and Johnny exchanged polite nods, and the Air Commodore went on: 'The information was laid against you at the Admiralty, and passed to us first thing this morning. It is to the effect that you disclosed official secrets to your late uncle and to other persons. What have you to say about it?'

Johnny shrugged. 'That it's a mixture of moonshine and malice, Sir. From the start to finish it is utterly untrue. The whole thing emanates from the over-heated imagination of a retired Admiral who refuses to face facts, and will go to any lengths rather than see his own Service take second place to the Royal Air Force. I hope you will treat it as it deserves and throw it in the waste-paper basket.'

'No.' The Air Commodore tapped a finger on some sheets of foolscap that lay in front of him on his desk. 'We can't do that. These are not the ravings of a lunatic. The report is far too circumstantial. Perhaps I had better read it to you.'

He did as he proposed and it took a good ten minutes. The report was a perfectly fair one; but it contained full details of all that had occurred at the Hillary-Compton board meetings since I had launched my bomb-shell, and a very well-remembered account of my impromptu second speech to my co-directors, which made things look so bad for Johnny. When the Air Commodore had done he laid it down and said: 'Now! What have you to say?'

'All that about my uncle's proposal to refuse the contract for the E-boats is perfectly true, Sir. But I didn't brief him for the arguments he produced. I give you my word that I had never discussed such matters with him at any time.'

'Then who did?'

'I haven't an idea. I've been worrying myself to death about it. I've been through his papers to try to find out; but I've had no luck. I haven't a clue.'

'It's all very well to say that, Norton; but reading between the lines of this report you can see for yourself the sort of information to which your uncle had obtained access. There is an obvious reference to "Project Frying Pan", another to the results of "Exercise Drastic", and several to Future Operational Plans which are of the highest secrecy. There are less than fifty people in the whole country from which your uncle could have learned about things of that kind; and you are one of them.'

'I can't help that, Sir. I can only repeat that he did not get his information from me.'

'You had knowledge nearly a week ago that this extraordinary breach of security had taken place; why did you not report it immediately?'

275

For the first time Johnny appeared shaken. After hesitating a moment he faltered. 'I . . . I don't quite know, Sir. I suppose I ought to have. But it was my uncle. I had complete trust in him and . . .'

'That is a pretty damning imputation you've just made,' cut in the Air Commodore.

'I didn't mean it that way, Sir,' Johnny protested. 'And anyway, within a few hours of the board meeting he was dead.'

'That is no excuse for failing to report what he had said.'

There was a moment's silence, then the Air Commodore turned towards the Group Captain and shrugged. 'I'm afraid I have no alternative but to do as your department requests.'

The Group Captain stood up and addressed Johnny in formal tones: 'Wing Commander. It is my duty to place you under close arrest pending a full enquiry. Be good enough to come with me.'

*   *   *   *

Matters had gone even worse than I had feared—much worse. The fact that Johnny was under a liability to report any leakage of secret information that came to his knowledge had not occurred to me. That he had failed to do so meant his being found guilty on that charge, anyhow; and it might seriously prejudice a court against him when considering the more serious one. It was certain they would argue that, as the Admiral had accused him from the beginning of being the source of my information, had he been innocent he would have cleared himself of complicity by reporting the leakage at once. That he had not now made the case against him very black.

Most unfortunately, too, he had not kept his head in front of his seniors as well as he had when surprised by Constable Cowper. He had been flurried into saying that he 'trusted me', and the Air Commodore had pounced upon the admission as an indication of his guilt.

Poor Johnny. Even if, as no direct evidence could be brought against him, they gave him the benefit of the doubt, his career would be irretrievably ruined. And all because, in my eagerness to win over my co-directors, for a quarter of an hour I had let my tongue run away with me.

I could not help but feel that Sir Charles had been much to blame. Having taken me into his confidence he should have specified precisely what I could or could not divulge as an aid to getting my board to agree to his project. I suppose the fact of the matter was that he was used to attending conferences at which other officials, who were not privy to vital secrets, had to be persuaded to agree to measures by the disclosure of only limited knowledge of what lay behind them. No doubt, when he had given me powers of discretion, he had credited me with the same facility, not realising that I had had no experience of that sort of thing.

All the same, I could not exonerate myself from blame. My fatal pride in my powers of advocacy had carried me away. It was not the first time that had happened, and occasionally it had later caused me to look slightly foolish, but never before had it had such heart-rending results.

My grief and distress were made infinitely more acute by the knowledge that I was powerless to do anything about it. If only I could have come to life again in that room for two minutes I could have cleared Johnny completely. Even if I could somehow have got a message to Sir Charles, that this miscarriage of justice was about to take place, it is certain that he would at once have taken steps to exonerate Johnny from all blame. But in my state as a Ka I could do neither.

Yet, as I wrestled with this seemingly insoluble problem of how to get through to Johnny's superiors, it suddenly occurred to me that there was still one possibility. I had twice made contact with Daisy. If I could do so again I might get her to give Sir Charles a message from me. The fact that it came from the so-called 'spirit world' might amaze him; but it would make no difference, because he knew the truth.

Without a moment's delay, I passed through the Air Ministry window and descended to the street. Drifting quickly along to Parliament Square I turned the corner, entered Westminster Station and rode free of charge in the Underground to Hammersmith. Unjostled by pedestrians, I made my way to Daisy's flat, arriving there soon after half-past four.

To my annoyance she was not in, so I waited in her sitting-room with such patience as I could muster. After about a quarter of an hour I heard the key turn in the lock and in she came. To my relief she was alone; but she looked very different from when I had last seen her.

There was nothing of the glamour girl about her now except her pretty face and good figure. Her hair was scraped back and she had no make-up on; she was wearing an old soiled raincoat and shabby shoes, and was carrying a string bag filled with eatables.

It took me a moment to realise that her present sluttish appearance was due to her living a very different life from most other women. The Club at which she worked did not close till four in the morning, so it would be five before she got home and to sleep; and still later on the occasions when she brought a boy-friend back with her. Most days it would probably be two o'clock before she got up and cooked herself some breakfast. Then she had to tidy up her flat, so she would not get round to her morning's shopping until the late afternoon. Obviously she had just returned from shopping and she would soon set about preparing her lunch before dolling herself up for the evening.

I lost no time in concentrating on her but she walked right through me into the kitchen. Having hung up her old coat behind the door she set to work on her purchases. Among them were a chop, two tomatoes and some runner beans, and sitting down to the small table she began to slice the latter. I took up a position opposite her and started to call her by name over and over again.

She was humming cheerfully to herself and for a while she remained completely unaware of my presence. Then she appeared to become uneasy, stopped humming and glanced up at me several times. In spite of that the vague look in her blue eyes told me that she still had not seen me; but I felt that if I kept on willing her to do so she soon would.

Unfortunately, by then she had come to the end of her bean slicing and had also trimmed the chop; so she broke the beginnings of the rapport I was establishing between us by standing up, going to the stove, and putting her meal on to cook. Next she went into the bathroom, took down some lingerie that had been hanging up to dry over the bath and, carrying it back into the kitchen, began to iron it. Again I tried to compel her to see me but now she did not even glance up; so I came to the conclusion that I would have to wait until her mind was no longer fully engaged by some definite task.

As soon as her meal was cooked she sat down to it; so, feeling that the circumstances were now more propitious, I made another attempt. Almost at once she showed herself more receptive by again casting uneasy glances in my direction. Then her eyes widened, her hand holding the fork began to tremble, and she exclaimed:

'Go back! Go back from where you came!'

Instantly I threw out the thought: 'Don't be frightened, Daisy, I only want to talk to you.'

'I won't let you!' she cried, dropping her fork with a clatter on to her plate. 'I won't let you!'

'I must,' I insisted. 'It's terribly important.'

'No! No! Get out! I won't have you here!'

'Please!' I begged. 'For God's sake don't shut your mind to me as you did before. Johnny is in serious trouble and . . .'

Cutting across my thought, she broke into a shrill tirade: 'I don't believe you! You're evil! You're not Sir Gifford. You're someone from the Left. You thought to trick me last time; but you didn't succeed. I'll have nothing to do with you. Go from here! Go!'

Losing my temper I did the equivalent of shout at her. 'You little fool! You're deceiving yourself. I've done no harm to anyone, and I'll do none to you. But you *must* listen to me. Johnny's whole career is at stake. You have got to take a message from me to . . .'

'I won't!' she broke in. 'I won't! By appearing to me at all you've caused Johnny to worry himself silly, as it is. Go back where you belong.'

'The message is . . .' I began, in an attempt to force it on her. But she sprang to her feet, her eyes wide and glaring. As she raised her hand I willed her to lower it, but in vain. She swiftly made the sign of the Cross and cried loudly:

'Avaunt thee, Satan.'

As had happened before I felt no effect whatever; but her expression at once became relaxed, and dropping back into her chair she sat there panting slightly. The mysteries of the human mind are unfathomable, but there are many well-proven cases of faith working miracles. I could only suppose that her faith in that age-old conjuration was so strong that it enabled her to believe that she had driven me away.

After a few minutes she recovered sufficiently to go on with her meal and by the end of it, although I was still facing her, she had clearly dismissed me altogether from her mind; for as she began to wash up her dinner things she broke into a cheerful little song.

From my experience to date it looked as if her utterance of the conjuration was only a temporary defence; so that she could not prevent me from appearing to her again after, perhaps, an interval of a few hours. That idea led me to contemplate haunting her, in the hope of wearing her down to a state in which she would agree to take a message from me to Sir Charles as the price of freeing herself from me. But I soon saw two snags to entering on such a campaign. In the first place to break her will might take several days, and time was precious. In the second, there was nothing to prevent her taking the line of pronouncing her conjuration immediately every time I appeared; in which case I would get no further and tire of such a pointless conflict before she did.

For a while I remained miserably in her sitting-room, then another idea came to me. Daisy was by no means the only person with psychic powers among the vast population of London. Perhaps I could find someone else who would get a message to Sir Charles for me. The trouble about that was that, never having dabbled in psychic matters, I had no idea how to set about finding a medium.

Mr. Tibitts I dismissed at once as, from the long conversation he had held with Johnny, it had become clear to me that he was not psychic himself; he was simply an investigator and a debunker of hoaxes. From what he had said that also applied to the other members of the Society for Physical Research; so it would be a poor bet to go and hang about at their headquarters.

Then another idea came to me. It was a long shot, but there was just a chance that Sir Charles might be psychic. Or if he himself was not, one of his household might be. I admitted to myself that the odds against that were very long, but there was one point which carried considerable weight as I contemplated the matter. If, by spending the night bobbing about in scores of bedrooms at random, I succeeded in getting

280

through to a back-street medium or some comparatively humble person, the likelihood that either would have the courage to beard a Cabinet Minister in his office, and tell him that a ghost had appeared to them with a message for him, was decidedly remote. Whereas if I could show myself and convey my thoughts to one of Sir Charles's relations, servants or staff, it was certain they would tell him of it.

Slender as the hope might be of succeeding in this design, so desperately concerned was I to save Johnny that I clutched at it as a drowning man would a straw. Leaving Daisy's flat I made my way back to Westminster and hurried through King Charles' Street to Clive Steps. I was just about to turn left and enter the Ministry of Defence when I caught sight of Sir Charles. He must have just left it and, brief-case in hand, was on the edge of the broad pavement about to get into a car.

Checking my momentum I swerved in his direction and came up beside him. That neither he nor his chauffeur became aware of me was not in the least surprising; and, for the moment, I did not even attempt to make either of them realise my presence. Sir Charles got into the back of the car but did not drive off; so I concluded that he was waiting for someone to join him.

While I hovered nearby I was facing towards St. James's Park. It was a pleasant evening and considerable numbers of people were scattered about its grass and walks; for at this hour its usual contingent of idlers had been augmented by many business people crossing it on their way home from their offices. At the sight of them I felt a sudden pang of envy but my thoughts were soon otherwise engaged—and very busily. The sound of quick footsteps on the pavement behind me made me turn. Approaching from the direction of the private-garden entrance to No. 10 Downing Street was a tall slim man who appeared to be in his late fifties, and whom I would have recognised anywhere.

Having greeted Sir Charles with a cheerful good evening, he got in beside him, I joined them, and without further orders the chauffeur set the car in motion.

'It is very good of you to spare me an evening,' Sir Charles opened up.

'On the contrary,' replied his companion, 'it is a most

welcome change. I only wish I could come down to your cottage more frequently as I used to. It must be delightful there at this time of year. You have no idea how lucky you are to have such a retreat. I have to spend most of my nights these days in houses that are so full of people coming and going that they are more like railway stations.'

The car was a big one and had a plate-glass partition between the chauffeur and his passengers. Stretching out a long arm, Sir Charles closed the sliding panel in it, so that he and his companion could talk freely.

Never before have I been driven so swiftly out of London. That was not due to the pace of the car, which kept to quite a moderate speed, but to the extraordinary efficiency of the police. Every officer on point duty seemed to catch sight of the special number plate immediately, and without any fuss open the way when the lights were against it, or smooth its passage through congested traffic. Within twenty minutes it had passed out of the inner suburbs and with increased speed was heading down into Surrey.

Meanwhile, the talk of its passengers ranged over a score of subjects: the riots in Cyprus, the latest F.O. telegrams from our Ambassador in Moscow, the financial conference in Istanbul, the effect that the raising of United States tariffs might have on British trade, the take-over by Sir Gerald Templar as C.I.G.S., the dangerous situation which now faced the French in Morocco and Algiers, and a dozen other matters.

Many of the names they mentioned were unknown to me and the interchange of ideas between these two first-class brains was so swift that I had difficulty in following the drift of their conversation. Nevertheless it was, for me, a fascinating journey.

I was so occupied in trying to set a value on every word they uttered that I took scant notice of the direction in which we were going. But about half-past seven we passed through Farnham, and ten or twelve minutes later entered a woodland drive to pull up in front of a small country house, rather than a cottage, which from its long sloping roof looked as if it might have been designed by Sir Edward Lutyens a little before the First World War.

When the two passengers had got out, the chauffeur drove

282

the car away towards another, smaller building about a hundred yards off, in which no doubt he had his own quarters above the garage.

At the door of the house the arrivals were met by a plump woman of about forty-five. She was wearing an apron and had wispy reddish grey hair. Throwing up her hands in protest she said, with a strong foreign accent, to Sir Charles:

'Why did you not let me know you come tonight! That is bad of you, Sir. How do you expect me to make the good meals for your guest if you no notice of your coming have given?'

He favoured her with his boyish grin. 'Don't worry, Maria. My friend gets plenty of rich food, so he will enjoy a simple meal for a change. Make us one of your beautiful omelettes and some cheese straws. There is certain to be plenty of fruit from the garden to follow; on that we'll do very well.'

The woman turned towards the guest, whom she evidently knew. Bobbing to him like an old-fashioned continental servant she said with a mixture of respect and familiarity: '*Küss die hand, Excellenz*. Nice to see you again. I hope you are well. You forgive please this small meal.'

He smiled at her. 'Nothing could be nicer than one of your omelettes, Maria. I am already looking forward to it.'

'There is no hurry,' added Sir Charles. 'We shall take our drinks out in the garden; so in about an hour will do.'

The two men left their things in the hall and went through into a long, low sitting-room. From it, french windows led to a paved garden in the centre of which there was a large oblong lily pool. At its far end stood a small summer-house furnished with a swing hammock and a teak table and chairs. Maria brought in some ice, Sir Charles fixed the drinks and they carried them out there.

After two months of wonderful weather there had been some rain during the past few days, but now another fine spell seemed to have set in. The warmth of summer still lingered in the evening air, and the silence was broken only by the chirruping of birds in the surrounding woods. It certainly was a perfect spot for two public men burdened with great responsibilities, and perpetually harassed for decisions on one thing or another during every hour of their long working days, quietly to talk over their affairs.

As soon as they had settled down they got on to the subject of Egypt and the threat to the security of the vast British-built installations on the Suez Canal, owing to Colonel Nasser's having entered into friendly relations with the Iron Curtain countries in order to secure armaments from them. This was very much Sir Charles's province, and I would greatly have liked to listen to his views. But I felt that I ought to lose no further time in attempting to get through to him, so I had to give my thoughts entirely to willing him to see me.

For ten minutes or more I remained stationary in front of him, but he talked on without showing the slightest reaction. Moving round the table I spent a further ten minutes opposite his companion, but with equally barren results. So I had to conclude that if either of them were psychic, his mind was much too fully occupied at the moment for me to break in on it.

I knew that Sir Charles was a widower; but he had two daughters in their teens, and on the way down to the car I had hoped that one of them might, perhaps, prove a sensitive. As Maria had made no preparations for serving a dinner it was clear that they were either out for the evening or living elsewhere; so Maria herself became the next object of my attentions.

Leaving the garden for the house, I soon found her kitchen and set about tackling her. But I had been concentrating on her only for a few minutes when she left it and went into the sitting-room. After a quick glance out of the window at the two men on the far side of the lily pool, she picked up the telephone and dialled a number.

When she was answered she asked if Mr. Klinsky was in. There was a pause, presumably while Mr. Klinsky was being fetched, then she said: 'Is that you, Jan? It is Maria. He is here. And at last you have luck. He has brought his big friend with him. I give dinner to them in twenty minutes.'

Replacing the receiver she went through to a small dining-room and laid the table for two; then she returned to the kitchen and began to make the omelette. Recalling my recent experience with Daisy during her culinary operations I decided that to make a further attempt on Maria for the moment would be to tire myself to no purpose; so I took the opportunity to have a look round upstairs.

Apart from Maria's room there were only three bedrooms, and none of them had the appearance of being regularly lived in, so that settled the question of Sir Charles's daughters. They were not out but living elsewhere, and Maria was evidently the only permanent resident at the cottage.

Hearing her call to her master that the omelette was ready, I went down to the dining-room hoping that during the meal I might have better luck. But unlike Daisy, who had eaten alone, the thoughts of Sir Charles and his friend did not drift. They continued an animated conversation which blocked any chance of my impinging on the consciousness of either, even had both been sensitive to psychic phenomena. By the time Maria put the cheese straws on the table I had resigned myself to awaiting again a more favourable opportunity and, having ceased to concentrate, I was free to listen to what they were saying.

I had taken in the full import of only a few sentences when I realised that they were now deep in the controversy of the 'Old' and 'New' Looks; and that it was to tackle his visitor on the matter without fear of interruption that Sir Charles had brought him down to the cottage.

To them the arguments on both sides were too well known for either to need to go into any details, and I gathered that the visitor had already made it clear that he was not prepared to give an opinion on the present strategic value of the Royal Navy; so the discussion revolved mainly round the possibility of amalgamating the three Services into a Royal Defence Force. Sir Charles not only pressed for it, but argued that the Government might be called to account later if it delayed too long in taking this first step towards a general readjustment of forces rendered necessary by the introduction of thermo-nuclear weapons. The other pointed out that many adjustments were already taking place, that others had been agreed on, and that if any such sweeping reform was proposed without preparing the country for it the results might prove disastrous to the Government.

Having agreed about that, Sir Charles said with a smile that he had had a private plan for pushing public opinion in the right direction, but that unfortunately it had broken down;

so, in view of the urgency of the matter, he had felt that without further loss of time he must make an attempt to bring matters to a head through orthodox channels.

Seeing the wretched situation in which his 'private plan' had landed Johnny, I would have liked to curse him roundly for ever having departed from 'orthodox channels'; but it was no good crying over spilt milk, and I waited with deep interest to learn how the conversation would develop.

In that I was fated to be disappointed. At that very moment my glance was caught by a queer outline low down on the door which gave on to a short passage leading to the kitchen. To my sight it was like the shadow of a kneeling man whose head was on a level with the door knob. Marshalling my powers of concentration, I stared at the door and, sure enough, on the far side of it a man was kneeling down peering through the keyhole.

'Spy' was the word which instantly flashed through my brain. Here was the sort of situation which one read of in thrillers—the secluded cottage in the depths of a wood, the Minister of Defence entertaining privately the man who could aid or counter his efforts to revolutionise our entire defence policy, their free discussion of the most vital secrets over a bottle of wine and a good meal together, and the agent of a foreign power, who had somehow gained access to the house, eavesdropping in order to report their decisions to his pay-masters.

I had often enjoyed reading of such scenes, but always afterwards had the slightly cynical feeling that they never took place in real life. Yet here, incontestably, I was faced with one. The man beyond the door was listening at its keyhole. What possible reason could he have for doing so other than to obtain illicit possession of official secrets? Swiftly I passed through the door and stared down at him.

He had red hair and looked to be in his middle thirties. There was no suggestion about him of the suave ex-officer secret agent of fiction, who moves freely in the highest society, traps the wicked mistress of the enemy Chief-of-Staff into giving away the plans that have been confided to her and ends up with the soft arms of his own Ambassador's daughter round his neck. On the contrary, this fellow looked like a working man. His hands were rough, his suit ready-made and his heavy shoes unpolished. Yet his apparently lowly status made him no less of a menace; and it seemed much more likely that for active operations the Russians employed men of this sort rather than untrustworthy crooks who were capable of passing themselves off as ex-public-school men.

Once again the fact that I was both invisible and inaudible made it impossible for me to do anything. I could only hover there, an intensely worried spectator, while the spy alternately peered through the keyhole and listened to a discussion which might ultimately result in a complete change in the system of defence of the whole of the Western Powers.

Through the door I heard Sir Charles urging the importance of reaching a decision before the meeting of the Foreign Ministers at Geneva in October, and stressing how greatly the adoption of his proposals would strengthen our hand at the Conference. Then a sound behind me made me turn. The door at the other end of the short passage had opened and Maria stood framed in it.

'Hist!' she made the sharp warning noise from between her teeth and, frowning, beckoned to the kneeling man to come away. He turned to glance at her, but shook his head and once more applied his eye to the keyhole.

I was so agitated that I could no longer put such snatches of the conversation as I caught into their right context. But a few minutes later I gathered that something had been settled, as I heard Sir Charles say:

'Well, I'm glad we agree to that extent. I have brought down in my brief-case a copy of the report by the Committee of Inquiry and when you have read that I feel pretty confident that you will give me your full backing. Anyhow, that is as far as we can go for the moment. Now; how about some coffee?'

As the bell rang in the kitchen, the spy swiftly tiptoed back into it. Maria had already retreated, and a minute or two later re-emerged carrying the coffee tray. Having delivered it she rejoined her red-headed friend, who had perched himself on the kitchen table with his short legs dangling from it.

They exchanged several swift sentences in a foreign tongue. She was obviously upbraiding him and he was laughing at her. At the language they were speaking I could only guess. From her greeting to Sir Charles's friend I had naturally supposed her to be an Austrian; but now it seemed certain that she was a Czech, an Hungarian or, perhaps, even a Russian.

Now that I had a chance to study the man more closely I could see that he came of peasant stock, but had probably improved himself by education; and his quick dark eyes, on either side of a long thin nose, showed him to have plenty of shrewd intelligence. It occurred to me that he had a faint resemblance to Maria; so it was possible that they were members of the same family, and had been working together for a long time, or that he might have some hold over hr.e

When they had finished their argument, he produced a small glass bottle of colourless liquid from his waistcoat pocket. After holding it up to the light, he wagged his finger at her several times while evidently impressing upon her how it should be used, then thrust it into her hand.

She seemed loath to take it, and again they entered on an argument which was to me unintelligible gibberish. But several times he pointed to a big ginger cat that was sleeping on a rug in front of the fire-place.

At last she left him, went into the larder and returned with a saucer of milk. Into it she put a couple of drops of the liquid, then set the saucer down in front of the cat. It was a big, heavy animal, and even when she woke it by stroking its back it seemed too somnolent to be interested. Lifting the saucer a little so that it was within a few inches of the cat's face, she splashed the milk about gently with her finger. The cat's pink tongue came out. It gave two laps, was shaken with a violent convulsion, went rigid for a moment, then rolled over dead.

The man sitting on the table smiled and spread out his hands as if to say: 'You see how quick and simple it is.'

The woman shrugged resignedly, picked up the saucer and washed the remains of its contents carefully away in the kitchen sink.

With growing horror the meaning of the scene I had just witnessed dawned upon me. The Soviet Secret Service was said to be extremely efficient. They must have found out that Sir Charles was the key man in the battle to bring about the New Look, which would so enormously strengthen our power to defend ourselves in the event of Russian aggression. The killing of the cat had been a try-out. Maria was a pawn in the hands of Britain's enemies and had been ordered to murder her master.

* * * *

Appalled by the conclusion, I asked myself if I could possibly be right. From time to time Presidents and Ministers are assassinated on the Continent; but not in law-abiding England. One moment though. In 1923 Field Marshal Sir Henry Wilson had been shot dead in Eaton Square, and attempts had been made on the life of both Lloyd George and King Edward VIII. Moreover, during the past few years the Western Powers had lost several of their strongest supporters among the national leaders of the Near East through Communist-inspired assassinations. Why, if the dividend were deemed high enough, should the long arm of Moscow strike its secret blows repeatedly in the Moslem countries and refrain from doing so in Surrey?

The excellence of our Immigration and Police systems no doubt explained the general immunity enjoyed by our leading statesmen; and in London or while travelling each had the protection of a private detective specially trained to act as his bodyguard. But here there was not even a policeman within a mile, and as the murder was to be committed by poison no shots would alarm any neighbours. If the deed were done when Sir Charles was alone in the house with Maria many hours might pass before his death was discovered. The extremely capable organisation for which she was acting would have ample time to whisk her away to an airport, provide her with a forged passport, and on a pre-arranged passage get her out of the country.

The more I thought of it the more convinced I became that I was right. She had surreptitiously summoned the man Klinsky, before dinner; so he was living somewhere in the neighbourhood and evidently visited her frequently. Sir Charles had brought his brief-case with him and left it in the hall, so that was doubtless his custom. He would of, course, keep it locked, but Maria would have had many opportunities of taking an impression of its key when he was in his bath. The odds were that when he had finished looking through the papers in it he left it down in the sitting-room for the night. What could have been simpler than for Maria to telephone Klinsky and for him to pay the house a nocturnal visit for the purpose of photographing its contents? In that way his masters would have learnt all about the New Look and his resolve to press the Cabinet to agree to its adoption. Should Sir Charles be eliminated the interests opposed to it might secure a postponement of the issue for many months. For our enemies no man's life could pay a higher dividend. I could no longer doubt that I had stumbled on a plot to murder him.

What could I do? How could I save him? How get a warning to him? My only hope lay in finding someone like Daisy. There must be quite a number of people who possessed psychic powers equal to hers; but how was I to find one? Urged to it by my anxiety for Johnny, I had sought out Sir Charles in the hope that he, or someone close to him, might prove a medium; but I had known that to be an outside chance, and so far my efforts had got me nowhere.

As I racked my brain for a means of preventing Maria from accomplishing her nefarious design, I saw that Klinsky had picked up the dead cat and was preparing to depart. It flashed upon me that I ought to find out where he lived; so that if I could get a message through the police would be able to lay him by the heels or, perhaps, through him get a line on the whole of his section in the Soviet espionage network.

He and Maria exchanged a few more sentences in their own language, then, still carrying the cat, he slipped out through the back door. It was now dark outside; but I had no difficulty at all in following him, and he naturally had not the slightest suspicion that he was being shadowed.

Taking a path through the wood he followed it for about two hundred yards, then threw the dead cat into the bushes. A little further on the wood ended, and crossing a stile he stepped down into a lane. For another ten or fifteen minutes he walked on at a smart pace until he came to a cart-track and turned up it. At its end there was a house with a few outbuildings which I at first took to be a farm, but on closer inspection it proved to be only a fair-sized cottage of the sort inhabited by small-holders who keep pigs and poultry and cultivate a few acres.

Crossing the barnyard Klinsky pushed open the front door

and entered a narrow, lighted hall. At the sound of his arrival a door on the right was opened by a young woman of about nineteen. She was not bad-looking but had a heavy body, her hands were calloused with rough work, and her ill-dyed fair hair was none too tidy.

Giving him a reproachful look, she said: 'So there you are! I do think it was mean of you to insist on going down to the pub for a drink on the night I persuaded Mum and Dad to go to the pictures.'

He grinned at her and replied in heavily-accented English: 'We have plenty of time yet, little naughty one.'

'Not much,' she objected. 'They'll be back in half an hour.'

'Plenty of time,' he repeated, following her into a small untidy sitting-room. 'I soon show you.' Upon which he threw his arm round her, buried his mouth in her neck for a moment, then pushed her backwards on to the couch.

The situation needed little adding up. As I had judged, Klinsky came of peasant stock. With labour so short he would have had small difficulty in getting himself taken on as a helper for his board and keep and a bit over, and he had made the robust daughter of the place his mistress. What cover could have been better for a spy allocated the task of keeping Maria up to scratch and reporting all that could be learned about Sir Charles.

Leaving the unsavoury couple to indulge in their animal pro-pensities, I hastened back to Sir Charles's; but, to my fury, I took a wrong path in the wood and lost my way for some minutes, so something over an hour elapsed between my leaving the house and re-entering it.

Maria was in the kitchen and had just finished washing up the dinner things. Sir Charles and his companion had not moved from the dining-room and were still engrossed in talking, now about Mr. Butler's latest proposals for checking the drain on our gold and dollar reserves. Feeling that, at the moment, it would prove a waste of time to attempt a further effort to make either of them see me, I cast about for some less direct means of conveying a warning.

I then remembered Sir Charles's chauffeur; so I passed out of the window and round the bend of the drive to the building I had seen through the trees. As I expected, it was a garage with a flat over it. Upstairs in the living-room the chauffeur

—a dark, curly-haired young man—was sitting in his shirt-sleeves with one arm carelessly thrown round the shoulders of a skinny peevish-looking girl wearing an apron over her cotton dress, presumably his wife.

To my annoyance they were both watching television; and their idiotically-blank but absorbed expressions told me that I stood little chance of impinging on either of them. Nevertheless, I placed myself in front of the screen and did my best. It was no good; neither of their faces altered by as much as the flicker of an eyelid.

I was just about to leave them when a whining cry of 'Mum . . . ee!' penetrated through the voice of the comedian which was being thrown out by the television set.

'There's the child again,' said the man.

'Oh shut up,' replied the woman testily. 'I want to watch this bit. Isn't he a scream? She'll go off to sleep in a minute.'

As they settled down again I passed into the room from which the cry had come. The darkness there being no bar to my sight, I saw that in a cot beside a double bed a small girl of about four was sitting up. She had kicked off all her bed-clothes, was shivering with cold, and large tears were running down her cheeks. Unquestionably she saw me at once.

She stopped crying, her eyes grew round, for a moment she stared at me in silence; then she let out a piercing yell.

The door was flung open and her mother flounced into the room. 'Stop it, you wicked girl! Stop it,' she shrilled, 'or I'll give you something to shout about.'

'The man, Mummy; the man!' howled the child.

'What man? There's no man here 'cept your father.'

'I seed him come through the door.'

I was then beating a retreat through it, but I heard the mother exclaim: 'So it's lies you've started to tell now, is it? I'll teach you to tell wicked fibs to me, Miss!'

There came the sound of two sharp pats, rather than slaps, but they were followed by another outburst of yelling, and coming to the door the man protested:

'Oh let her be, Gloria. You'll only make her worse.'

At that moment the telephone shrilled, cutting through the combined noise made by the child and the loopy-looking man on the T.V. screen. The chauffeur answered it, reached for his tunic, and called to his wife:

292

'I've got to take the Big Shot back to town, dear.'

The child's yells had subsided into muffled sobs. Gloria came out of the bedroom, pulled its door to behind her, and complained: 'Oh, that's too bad! Their sort have no consideration for other people.'

The man shrugged. 'What's the use of belly-aching. Most chaps have to work harder than I do for less pay. Anyway I told you the odds were against me being able to stay the night.'

'Yes but I was hopin' you would. Why couldn't he have his own car sent down to fetch him?'

'Ask me another. Got something else to think about perhaps. There's places called Cyprus an' Egypt, you know; and how many votes it's going to cost him if 'is pal Butler slaps a bigger tax on cars.'

'Still, it's early yet, Bert. They might have let us see the telly programme out.'

'He's not going to his dowdy bed, don't you fret yourself. When he gets home there'll be a stack of red and green boxes, like I sometimes see in the boss's office, with all sorts of conundrums in them for him. I wouldn't have his job for a packet. Where the hell are my driving gloves?'

Gloria picked them up from behind the television set, handed them to him and enquired: 'And what about Sir C. Will he be going up with you?'

'Don't expect so. He likes a night in the country, whenever he can get it.'

'Then you may be down first thing to fetch him, and wanting breakfast?'

'I doubt it. Most like he'll do as he done when he brought Monty down here for the evening and sent me up with him. He'll drive himself up in the little Morris.'

They kissed perfunctorily and Bert ran downstairs. I accompanied him round to the house in the car, then got out. Almost as soon as he had rung the bell the front door opened, Sir Charles gave the chauffeur his instructions, then stood aside for his friend, who turned to him before entering the car and said:

'Thank you for this evening, Charles. It made a delightful break for me. I'll study that paper carefully and arrange for a Cabinet to be called to discuss it next week. Thursday

293

would be the best day, I think. We'll get Dickie to come along to it, and hear what he has to say.'

I knew that Earl Mountbatten's intimates always called him 'Dickie', so the reference was obviously to him. Although the part I had been designed to play in Sir Charles's battle for the co-ordination of our defences had broken down, it looked as if he was making very satisfactory progress without me.

When the car had driven off I followed him back into the house. Collecting his brief-case he took it into the sitting-room, unlocked a secretaire there and settled down to work. Not very hopefully I gave a little time to trying to attract his attention, but it was no good; so I went again to the flat over the garage.

It had occurred to me that psychic powers are said to run in families, and that the seventh child of a seventh child is always fey. There was no reason to suppose that Gloria was a seventh child and even less to suppose that she had herself had six children before her little daughter; but as the child had supernatural vision there was anyhow a chance that she had inherited it from her mother.

When I arrived the lights of the living room were out, and in the bedroom the extraordinarily ill-named Gloria was undressing. The child, I noted with relief, had sobbed herself to sleep. As Gloria took off her underclothes I studied her dispassionately. There is a lot to be said for a boyish figure, but I have always thought that in the nude there is something rather repulsive about a really skinny young woman. On all counts I felt sorry for Bert; but I had much more urgent matters to think of than his folly in having allowed this pretty-pretty brainless creature to inveigle him into marrying her. She might prove an instrument through which I could communicate with Sir Charles, and that was all that concerned me.

As soon as she was in bed I presented myself with all my consciousness and willed her to see me. She picked up a film magazine and began to flick through its pages. For ten minutes I kept it up, then she yawned, threw the paper aside and switched out the light. I remained at the foot of her bed, my gaze unwaveringly fixed upon her eyes, but after a moment she turned on to her side and drew the bed-clothes up.

Five minutes later she was giving vent to a gentle snore.

Angrily as I was at my waste of effort I tried to consider my next step as calmly as I could. To seek for a medium in the nearest village was the obvious course; but every attempt on each individual would cost time and loss of energy. I must pick my subjects carefully. Not that there was likely to be any outward clue indicating that one was more probably psychic than another; but it would more than double my chances of getting a warning to Sir Charles if I could contact some upper class neighbour of his, rather than a cottager who would be scared of going to see him.

One thing was certain; Maria had the poison, and had been given a practical demonstration of how quick and effective it could be. She might not use it until next time Sir Charles came down to his cottage, as that would give her a whole night in which to make her get-away. But if Klinsky realised that a delay of a week might now render the crime almost useless he would have pressed her to seize the present opportunity. It was, therefore, quite on the cards that she might give Sir Charles the poison with his breakfast in the morning. If I failed to find a means of warning him that night, within nine hours he might be dead.

11

Friday 16th September

NEVER have I spent such a desperate and exhausting night. For tension, and a call upon my ultimate resources of endurance, nothing I had experienced in the war approached it. One blank session after another occasionally interspersed with wild hopes that made the disappointment with which they ended only the more bitter.

There were, I found, quite a number of fair-sized houses situated in the same wood as Sir Charles's. Guided in the early stages by their lights I located and entered a number of them. In one I came upon a four at bridge. Assuming that their minds would be much too much on their game for any of them to become aware of me I was about to make a quick departure, but a fat elderly woman, wearing a lot of quite expensive jewellery, who was dummy at the time, suddenly exclaimed:

'I feel a presence!'

'Oh Eleanor!' protested a little dried-up shrimp of a man in a dinner jacket, who was probably her husband. 'You are always imagining things. Do please attend to the game.'

Eagerly I presented myself in front of her; but she looked over my head, and began to cast welcoming smiles at various places on the ceiling, while repeating several times: 'Dear Spirit, do come to us and tell us of yourself.'

Spirit, Ka or Hobgoblin, I would have done so only too gladly, but she proved incapable of either seeing me or receiving the thoughts that I attempted to force into her mind. Her companions became greatly annoyed with her and eventually browbeat her into giving some thought to the hand she was dealt for the next game; but she still insisted every now and again that she knew there was a presence in the room and that it wanted to communicate with her. There was, and it did, but after wasting a quarter of an hour in dead-lock I decided that I must seek a more promising channel.

If only animals could have talked my task would have been easy. At half a dozen houses, among the many I approached, dogs bayed dismally, then fell silent and shivered as I passed them. Cats, too, arched their backs and scurried from my path. Children seemed more sensitive to a psychic presence than grown-ups. As I invaded bedroom after bedroom during the early hours it was inevitable that I should blunder into a certain number of night-nurseries and some in which children were either awake through illness or restless.

In one a small boy with a bandaged head, with whom his mother was sitting up, asked who the man was who had just come through the window, and kept pointing at me; but his mother lacked his supernatural sight, and assuming he was delirious told him that I was a good angel come to make him well.

Twice slightly older children screamed on my appearing to them, but one tiny tot laughed and held out her arms, inviting me to play. The sight of her was like a draught of water in a wilderness. In spite of the frightful urgency of my quest I could not forbear from spending a few minutes with her; passing my hands which were visible to her gently over her head I willed her to become drowsy, soon she snuggled down in her cot and, still smiling, fell asleep.

Somewhere around two in the morning I wasted over twenty minutes on a drunk. I came upon him just as he had found his way back to his house after a late binge, and was trying to fit his latch key into the lock of the front door. Momentarily forgetful of my state, instinct prompted me to say: 'Can I help you?'

Turning, he bowed a little unsteadily and replied: 'Thanks a lot. Been birthday party. Champagne . . . whisky . . . don't mix. Silly of me. Locks . . . very tricky things.'

A moment later it penetrated to his bemused brain that he was not talking to another human being. His eyes bulged, he dropped his key, staggered back against the door and gasped:

'God help me! I've got 'em.'

I hastened to assure him that he had not.

He insisted that he had; said he had always feared that he would get DT's one day, but deserved it.

I sought to persuade him that I had nothing in common with acrobatic rats or pink elephants, and the most crazy argument that I have ever entered into ensued.

No man in his state could be expected to grasp the factors which even I could only assume enabled me to appear to him in mine. Yet I clung desperately to the hope that having at last found someone with whom I could exchange ideas I might succeed in inducing him to telephone Sir Charles, and, drunk as he was, relay a message from me which would at least make Maria's intended victim chary of eating any breakfast. But every sentence I threw out sent him off on a different track.

'Sir . . . Sir Charles,' he said. 'Pity his wife died. Nice woman. Met her once. I . . . I was running coconut-shy at . . . at a bazaar.

'Spies! Shoot 'em! Shoot the lot. Peace or war. Damn fool thing our . . . our Treason Act. Fuchs now . . . Fuchs ought to have been cast . . . sussested. Where hell's my key?'

I pointed it out to him. Stooping in an incredibly involved lurch he managed to scoop it up. Patiently I explained the situation all over again.

'Maria!' he cut in, as I mentioned her name. 'Knew a girl called Maria . . . once. Damned hot stuff. Picked her up in café . . . Barcelona. You ever go . . . Barcelona?'

There was lots more to it. Plenty of rambling reminiscences but no indication at all that he had grasped the story I was so anxious that he should tell over the telephone once he got into his house. My efforts to induce him to concentrate on letting himself in proved equally futile, and eventually he sat down on the door step. Time was flying and we were getting nowhere; so I reluctantly decided that I must leave him there.

It was about three hours later that I at last came upon a genuine psychic. I had spent the greater part of that time in the village and already done most of the more prosperous-looking houses in it when, at its far end, I came upon a small Georgian mansion set a little way back from the road. Advancing up the garden path I went in under the Adam fan-light.

Even in the dark I could see that the place had recently been redecorated. Up a few steps inside the door an archway supported by fluted pillars glistened with fresh white paint, as too did all the woodwork of the square hall and the charming semi-circular staircase at its far end.

Mounting to the first floor I entered a spacious bedroom, furnished in excellent taste and gay, to my eyes, with new hangings. In it were twin beds placed side by side. One was occupied by a youngish man who was fast asleep; the other by a woman who was wide awake. She looked to be in her middle twenties, was dark, striking looking in a slightly foreign way, and was lying on her back staring at the ceiling. As I hovered over her she saw me almost at once, and sitting up, said quite calmly:

'What do you want with me?'

Elated almost beyond belief at having found someone to whom I could give my message, I told her.

She seemed to take it in; so having asked her to warn Sir Charles I went on to give her a second message for him about Johnny's arrest, with the reason for it, and requesting him to intervene at once.

When I had done she stretched out a hand, shook her husband and said urgently:

'Wake Harree, *mio*! Wake! Here is a ghost who talks with me.'

'A what!' the man muttered sleepily, sitting up and rubbing his eyes.

'A ghost,' she repeated. 'What you call spirit. Look, 'e stands at the end of my bed.'

The young man stared straight at me, then shook his head. 'I can't see anything. You're imagining things, darling.'

'No, no! Crosses on my heart! I see 'im clearly.'

He switched on the bed-side light, brushed back his tousled hair and exclaimed triumphantly: 'There! You can see for yourself that you were mistaken.'

'But I see 'im still,' she protested. ' 'E is a big man, tall, an' wears a black bow-tie with a smoking jacket.'

'Really, my sweet; you're suffering from an hallucination.'

'Not at all. I have tell you before, Harree, that as a young girl I often see things. I am what you call psychic. This ghost 'e come here because 'e is much worried.'

'What about?' enquired Harry with a smile, evidently now deciding to humour her.

It was only then I realised that in my anxiety to get my messages through to her I had made a stupid blunder. I had overrated her capacity to take in my thoughts as swiftly as I transmitted them. In consequence she had received them only as a jumble. She thought that I was worried about an R.A.F. officer who had turned spy and was attempting to poison someone. She mispronounced Sir Charles's surname and that, added to the probability that they were newcomers to the district, caused it to fail to ring a bell with Harry. When he had heard her out he said:

'It doesn't make sense, darling. How long is it since you have seen a spook?'

'Seven years; eight per'aps,' she admitted. 'I was still at my convent. A poor servant girl there, she get put in the pood, as you say. She drown 'erself an' she come back to me.'

He shook his head. 'That's a long time ago, poppet. If there were anything here I'd see it too. Honestly, Lolla, you've been dreaming.'

'But I see 'im still, Harree. 'E is trying again to make 'iself understand. Now we talk though, I get less 'is meaning.'

'Your brain is overtired, darling, that's what it is. You've built up a fantasy in your mind owing to this wretched insomnia you suffer from. Still, we found one cure for that on our honeymoon, didn't we?'

With a smile he switched out the light, then scrambled from his bed into hers, took her in his arms and gave her a long passionate kiss on the mouth.

It was a bitter defeat, but I had to accept it.

By this time dawn had come. I tried another five houses in the village without success; then, not knowing how early Sir Charles would have his breakfast, and gnawed with anxiety about what might happen when he did, I decided to return to his cottage.

In my wanderings from house to house during the night I had come further from it than I thought, and as I could progress at no faster pace for any length of time than a quick walk, it was half past seven before I got there. Maria was in the kitchen and just about to take Sir Charles's breakfast up on a tray. I had intended to learn the best or worst by watching her prepare it, but having lost that chance I could now only accompany her upstairs, still sick with apprehension.

After knocking at his bedroom door she went in, set the tray down beside his bed, then drew the curtains. He was already awake and wished her a cheerful 'good morning'. As she returned his greeting, in her slightly guttural voice, I studied her face closely. It showed no sign of agitation and she left the room unhurriedly.

Quickly I switched my attention to Sir Charles and the breakfast tray. On it there was a pot of tea, some slices of toast, butter and a pear. I cursed myself for having delayed so long in the village. I had intended to return while he was still asleep, so as to be present at the moment of his waking as, if he was at all psychic, that would have given me a better chance than I had had the night before of getting through to him. But that forlorn hope was now gone. I could only wait on tenter-hooks to find out if he would be dead within the next few moments.

With what seemed to me maddening slowness he picked up a piece of toast, buttered it and took a bite. About the result of that I had no fears. A liquid poison could hardly have been inserted in either toast or butter. Neither could it in the pear. It was what might happen when he drank his tea that caused me to break out into a mental perspiration.

I could hear the clock ticking on the mantelpiece. As he slowly ate the toast another two age-long minutes went by. At last he picked up the tea-pot and poured himself a cup. It was pale golden in colour and looked very weak. He put two lumps of sugar in the cup and lifted it to his lips. Suddenly I realised that there was no milk on the tray, which would have been another vehicle for poison. Evidently the tea was fine China and he preferred not to destroy its bouquet by adding either milk or lemon.

He drank; but neither attempted to spit the liquid out nor was taken with an immediate seizure. My relief was unconveyable. Yet I still had to wait for some minutes to be certain that he had escaped, as the poison might have been tasteless and needed longer to take effect than it had had on a small animal like the cat.

Gradually my agitation subsided and my confidence increased. Without showing any sign of illness he finished his breakfast, then he jumped out of bed and spent five minutes

301

doing physical exercises. By then my mind was at rest—but only for the moment.

There were two good reasons why Maria should have refrained from attempting to poison him that morning. Firstly, he had had no cooked breakfast; so there had been nothing but the tea in which she could readily have put the poison, and, as no poison is entirely tasteless, the odds were that, detecting the unusual flavour, he would have spat it out before swallowing enough of it to kill him. Secondly, as a good part of his day was spent at meetings, at which he must usually be the most important person, if he did not arrive at his office when expected enquiries would be set on foot soon afterwards, and his death would probably be discovered by midday.

Evidently Maria meant to wait until he came down again for the night; she would be able to give him the poison in whatever she cooked for his dinner and have a clear twelve hours afterwards in which to make her get-away.

When, I wondered, would that be?

It was on the previous Sunday morning that I had seen him in his office, so it seemed probable that he had spent the Saturday night at some late conference or function. If so, that made it all the more likely that he would have kept the coming Saturday evening free so that he could come down here. If his daughters or a friend came with him that would be some protection; so, unless Maria was prepared to commit a double or triple murder, the presence of others in the house would both make it more difficult for her to administer the poison to him and, should she succeed, ensure the discovery of the crime much sooner. On the other hand, if he did come down alone Saturday was, for her, the most favourable night of all; with luck, up to nearly forty hours might elapse before the hue and cry started after her.

And today was Friday. Seeing the appalling handicap I was under in my efforts to get an intelligible warning to him, the time at my disposal was, once again, all too desperately short.

When he had bathed and dressed he went downstairs and collected his brief-case from the sitting-room. In the hall Maria was waiting to see him off. As he took his hat from her he confirmed my worst fears, by saying to her:

'Unless I telephone to the contrary I shall be down on Saturday evening. Don't get a lot of food in as there will be no one staying the week-end, and I shall be out to lunch on Sunday.'

Miserably, I wondered if he would still be alive for that meal.

Accompanying him round to the garage I got into the small Morris with him and we set off for London. For me the whole of the journey was a blank. My endeavours throughout the night had utterly exhausted me, and there was nothing further that I could attempt for the time being; so as soon as we were out of the drive, I closed my mental eyes and at once sank into oblivion.

I must have been roused by the slamming of the car door. On taking in my surroundings I saw that the Morris was drawn up in Storey's Gate facing towards St. James's Park, and that Sir Charles had already left it. A glance through its back windows showed his tall figure striding across the broad pavement towards the great bronze doors through which he had to pass to his office.

I followed at once, for I was still of the opinion that I stood a much better chance of getting a warning to him through somebody who could approach him without difficulty, than through some contact made at random.

Catching him up, I ascended with him in the lift to the second floor and, refreshed a little by my recent rest, set about making further endeavours to find someone who would react to my presence.

For over two hours I invaded room after room, presenting myself in turn to officers of the Joint Planning Staff, men clerks, girl typists and elderly messengers, willing them to see me.

In one case only did I meet with any response. A rather handsome man, with greying hair and a weatherbeaten face, whom I put down as probably a Captain R.N., suddenly sat back at his desk and said to his three companions who were also sitting at desks in the room:

'You know, chaps, if I did not know that it was only eleven o'clock in the morning, and that I was stone-cold sober, I'd be inclined to believe that I was bloody tight. I'd damn near take my oath that I can see a man's face standing out from that map of Palestine on the wall, there.'

'Eye strain, old boy; eye strain,' replied one of his companions, who had an airman's moustache. 'As long as we are in this dump it is part of the sentence that we should have to read round about fifty thousand words a day of mostly roneoed stuff or typescript. And you've been here for eighteen months, so what can you expect?'

'That's about it,' agreed the Naval type, taking off and wiping his spectacles. 'I'll have to get my oculist to ante up these; otherwise, when I do get to sea again, I'll not be able to tell the difference between a corvette and a Thames coal barge.'

The third man, whom I took to be the soldier of the party, grunted: 'You are darned lucky to be nearly through here, Jerry. I've had only three months of it, but I'd willingly drop a pip to get back into the open.'

'Oh no you wouldn't, Arthur,' remarked the fourth man, who had 'Foreign Office' written all over him. 'You'd just hate to be a major and back on the barrack square again. This is the forcing house for high command later on; and every bright little warrior who is posted here knows that he's darn lucky to be in it.'

The sailor put his specs on again and once more gave his mind to the papers on his desk. And that was that.

By midday I gave up. I was so tired from the strain of willing one person after another to see me that my powers of concentration were giving out. Moreover, during the past two and a half hours I had had a crack at nearly everyone in this small, select Ministry, so its possibilities seemed exhausted. Going out into the Park, I drifted down to the edge of the lake with the idea of resting there for a while before considering what my next move should be.

But I did not rest for long. Within two minutes of my arriving at the water's edge a pretty dark-haired girl leading a poodle walked briskly past me. Something about her bronzed good looks reminded me of Lolla, the foreign newly-wed wife, to whom I had succeeded in appearing early that morning. Instantly my brain again began to tick over.

Too late, I realised that accompanying Sir Charles to London had been the action of a half-wit. Only my extreme tiredness after a night of unflagging mental effort could excuse it. Having found a channel through which I could communicate I should, instead, have returned to that charming little Georgian mansion. Although Lolla had imperfectly understood me at the time, there was no reason at all why she should continue to do so. She had shown willingness, even eagerness, to receive my thoughts; so, unlike Daisy, there was no reason to suppose that she would drive me away if I appeared to her again. I had only to get her alone during a quiet hour of the afternoon and proceed with patience. If need be I could dictate my message to her word by word while she wrote it down.

Imbued with a new surge of energy at the simple means of discharging my terrible responsibility, I set off at once, passed down Great George Street and picked up a bus at Parliament Square which took me over the bridge to Waterloo. I was just in time to catch the twelve-twenty-seven for Farnham.

While in the train my weariness nearly caused me to black out again; but fear of being carried past my destination kept me sufficiently alert not to miss it, and soon after half-past one I was impelling myself swiftly down Farnham High Street.

It was not until I reached the main cross-roads in the little town that I was suddenly confronted with a new and annoying problem. I did not know the name of the village near which Sir Charles's cottage was situated. While accompanying him and his distinguished companion on their drive down the previous evening I had been too engrossed in listening to their conversation to take much notice of the route the car had followed. It was only by chance that I had recognised a stretch of it as the Farnham by-pass where it cuts through the edge of the town. After that the car had carried us another six or eight miles along a second-class road and then through a succession of twisting country lanes. And on the return journey that morning, for the whole way, my mind had been blacked out. Except for the belief that the village I wanted lay somewhere to the south, I had not a clue how to find it.

The afternoon proved as infuriating in its disappointments as had the preceding night. As an unseen passenger in lorries, tradesmen's vans and private cars, I must have covered scores of miles. In each I travelled for anything from five to twenty minutes probing the country to the south, west and east of the town.

As I was incapable of asking any of their drivers where they were going, only too often they took turnings which carried me over ground that I had already covered; so I had to get out, wait for another vehicle which was going in the opposite direction, leave that where the last had taken me off the route I wished to investigate, and pick up yet another in the hope that it would carry me the way I wanted to go.

In that part of the country, too, villages and well-wooded areas cut up into small private properties abound, and during the night I had been so absorbed in trying to find someone to whom I could convey a warning to Sir Charles that I had paid little attention to anything except people and their immediate surroundings. In consequence I may quite well have been carried through the village I was seeking without recognising it; and, as the little Georgian mansion was set some way back from the road, I might have failed to spot it easily when passing had my attention been caught for a moment by something on the opposite side of the road.

Anyway, there it was. After four long hours of searching, and having made fresh starts from Farnham at least half a dozen times, I had no more idea where Sir Charles's village lay than when I had first arrived in Farnham High Street.

Back there again, with the craving to allow my mind to sink into oblivion growing ever stronger, I forced myself to take a first step towards a half-formed resolution.

The germ of this new concept had first sprouted in my brain as a result of the ill-success that I had met with in the Ministry of Defence that morning. Hastily I had thrust it from me, and escape from having to contemplate it further accounted for a great part of my relief when, in the Park, the passing of a sun-tanned girl had recalled to me the contact I had made with Lolla. But as the afternoon had worn on, and I was becoming more and more despondent of my chances of finding her, the alternative to which failure to do so might compel me had begun to occupy an ever increasing place in my thoughts.

For a whole night and the best part of a day I had used my utmost endeavours to get to Sir Charles a warning of the fate that menaced him, and I had failed. There was now, at six o'clock in the evening, little more than another night and day to go; and there was no reason to suppose that the methods I was using would prove more successful in the next twenty-four hours than those through which I had striven in vain. Filled with trepidation at the thought of the course I contemplated, harassed with doubts about the possibility of accomplishing the aim I had in mind, and, as yet, far from decided on even attempting it, I took the next bus for Alton.

There I caught another which carried me a further ten miles to Basingstoke. The ancient town, which withstood a siege and held out for Charles I during the Great Rebellion, is on the Waterloo-Southampton line. Many of the fast trains stop there, and I felt pretty certain that the 6.30 down from Waterloo did so. By then it was nearly seven, so I thought I would not have long to wait, and I managed to keep my mind from fading out by reading the advertisements on the station platform.

Another disappointment awaited me. A little before half-past seven a train roared through the station, and I felt sure that it must be the express for which I had been waiting. But better luck, if one can call it luck, was on the way. A few minutes after the half hour the loud speaker announced a train that was about to leave from another platform for Southampton. It was slow, stopping at all stations and not due in until 8.39, but I was rather glad than otherwise as that postponed the decision I would have to take at the end of my journey. Crossing the lines I entered the nearest compartment and instantly gave up all further effort to think.

When consciousness returned to me the train was stationary, empty and unlit. For a moment I half feared, half hoped, that it had carried me on to some terminus further west; but on passing through its roof and looking about me I saw that it had been shunted into one of the innumerable sidings that fringe Southampton Dockyard.

Making for the nearest gate I passed the unsuspecting policeman and ten minutes later reached the town centre. The clock in the tower there showed it to be twenty minutes to eleven; so I had been 'out' for just on three hours. The buses were still running, so I took one to Totton; but from there on my progress was again handicapped. As during the afternoon, I had to use private vehicles and take a chance that they would continue moving in the direction I wanted to go. After three changes I got to within a couple of miles of Longshot. The last lap of my journey I did at my equivalent of a walk. At a little before midnight I entered the churchyard.

Except for most of the flowers in the wreaths at the sides of my grave now being dead, and that the bricks Johnny had moved from the tarpaulin had been replaced, it was exactly as I had last seen it with him two nights before. The tarpaulin that covered the vault made little material difference to my supernatural sight, and once more I stared down at the two coffins lying side by side in it—my father's, dull and mottled with streaks of whitish mould; my own, almost as garishly new as when it had been selected by the undertaker from his stock.

Concentrating my gaze I willed it to penetrate the lid of my coffin. During my bus ride from Farnham to Basingstoke, and again while on my way from Southampton to this hallowed but fearsome spot, I had hoped desperately that when I looked down at my body again I should see upon it clear indications that it had begun to decay. My hopes were vain. It appeared as fresh and firm as it had exactly a week ago, when, almost at this hour, Evans and Ankaret had thrown it into the Solent. Now, I admitted to myself that, all the time, I had felt certain that would be so.

For it to show no signs whatever of deterioration after a week was unnatural. But then mine had not been a natural death. It had not even been a violent one in the sense of having my head bashed in, or having received a knife thrust or a bullet through some vital part. Evans's death ray had, I could only now suppose, driven the electrons which vitalised my physical being out of it, causing an immediate suspension of animation, but otherwise doing my body no harm. Tibitts had said that the reason the Ka left the body during sleep was to act as an accumulator, so that when the Ka returned the body would be able to go about its business with renewed energy. If he were right, and I was right in believing that none of my vital organs had been harmed, should my Ka prove capable of re-entering my body it would at once restore my body to active life.

These thoughts, only half formed and each time repulsed with dread, had gnawed at me on and off during most of the day. But now they crystallised, and there was no escaping the awful conclusion to which they led. If I were prepared to go down into that grave I might yet save Sir Charles from being murdered and Johnny, whom I loved far better than my own son, from having his whole life ruined through my folly in letting my tongue run away with me.

To the possible repercussion which my resurrection might have in other quarters I gave no thought. During the past forty hours, the greater part of which had been passed under appalling strain, I had known only four hours of merciful oblivion. My recent three hours had restored to me only sufficient energy to continue on the path that I had been impelled to take when I had started out from Farnham. My brain refused even to consider any other but the major issue —should I or should I not take a step that made my mind reel with fear and horror but by which I might, perhaps, save one man from death and another from undeserved life-long shame.

Wrestling against all my instincts, I endeavoured to persuade myself that I really had little to fear. If I could not make my Ka re-enter my body, that was that. Neither I, nor either of those towards whom I felt so great a responsibility to help, would be any the better or worse off. If I could, there should be no difficulty about my arising from the grave. The lid of the coffin had not been screwed down. It was no great weight. All I would have to do was to push it aside, sit up and climb out of the vault. In the very worst event, should I find myself unable to raise the lid, then by the same way as my Ka had entered my body it would leave it, and, once again, no one concerned would be better or worse off than before.

For how long I argued with myself I have no idea; but at last I screwed up my courage to take the plunge. Passing through the tarpaulin I hovered immediately above my coffin. Some instinct told me how to proceed. Perhaps it was a memory of Genesis, and how, in the beginning, the Almighty had breathed into the nostrils of Adam to give him life. Lying along my body I laid the mouth of my Ka firmly against the nostrils, made mentally the motions of breathin deeply, and at the same time willed my Ka to become one with it.

A few moments passed during which I was not conscious of any change, then I felt the heart of my body start to beat below me; next second I blacked out completely.

*   *   *   *

When my brain began to function again it told me that I had just woken after an evil dream. The high spots of my experience during the past week ran through my mind like half a dozen snapshots, but it was just as though I had come out of a deep sleep during which I had had a nightmare.

Wondering what the time was I turned my head slightly in the direction where the window of my bedroom should have been to see if daylight was yet percolating through the cracks between the curtains. A Stygian darkness met my gaze, and the movement caused something soft to brush against my nose and forehead. Jumping to the conclusion that the top sheet had somehow got up over my face I moved again with the intention of throwing it off.

I was lying on my back with my hands crossed upon my chest. For some reason that I could not understand I felt terribly stiff and very tired. It was all I could do to raise my hands a few inches. They too brushed against the sheet, which lifted with them so easily that I was surprised not to feel the weight of other bed-clothes above it. Next moment the backs of my fingers encountered something hard and solid.

Memories of the past week, or my nightmare as I thought it, were now flooding back to me, although still in fragments lacking continuity. All were jumbled, but recent episodes were more numerous than ones that had taken place some days ago. Suddenly I saw again the detectives rummaging in Ankaret's room and her dead form on the bed.

My left hand jerked weakly in an instinctive gesture to stretch out, touch her and bring me reassurance that she was still alive and lying there beside me. Again the feeble gesture brought my knuckles into contact with something hard beyond the sheet. My elbow too struck some solid substance that had nothing of the yielding qualities of tender flesh. Simultaneously I again saw Johnny shining his torch down on to my coffin while he wondered if there could possibly still be life in me.

At that I panicked. I strove to thrust outward with all my limbs at once. All I could manage was one spasmodic wriggle. My toes, knees, hands, elbows and forehead were all brought up short by unyielding barriers beyond the sheet. Gasping, I dropped back.

It was true, then—true! I was in my coffin! No, it could not be. This was still part of my nightmare. But I was awake—wide awake. I was not in bed. The surface on which I lay was hard as a board. The sheet that covered me was a winding sheet. My beloved Ankaret was dead; and I—I had been buried alive.

I wonder that in the next few moments I did not go mad. Probably the thing which saved my reason was that like flashes of lightning in a thunderstorm, my stark terror was pierced now and then by further glimpses of my Ka's experiences while on its travels. In one I saw Tibitts and instantly recalled much of what he had said. In another I saw my Ka standing on the edge of the vault, and again in an instant, followed the way in which it had reasoned with itself.

It had reached the conclusion that once it was reunited with my body I should have no difficulty in pushing up the lid of the coffin and climbing out of the vault, and its grounds for believing that had been perfectly sound. Almost sobbing with thankfulness at this, to me no less than a divine revelation, I endeavoured to control the shudders which were running through me. It seemed that I had only to get a grip on myself and make one great effort, then I should be sitting up, once again breathing the fresh night air.

For some moments I lay quite still rallying my forces, then I thrust upward with all my might. The use of the word 'might' in this case applied to will, not the deed. Horror of horrors! My strength had gone from me. My state was much as it would have been had I just regained consciousness for the first time after a long and terrible illness. My traitor limbs made only the feeblest response to the command of my brain. Again my knuckles and forehead struck the heavy coffin lid, but so gently that they failed to raise it by even the fraction of an inch.

Panicking again, I beat upon it frantically; or rather made motions that had I had my full strength would have done so. But they were in fact little better than a wild fluttering of my hands, which did no more than rap against it. As they fell back at last upon my chest, still quivering but incapable of flapping upward any longer, a fresh wave of terror surged over me.

My Ka's reasoning had been logical enough according to theory; but in this case theory did not accord with fact. Tibitts was no doubt right in his contention that a Ka, on returning to its body after a few hours' normal sleep, recharged it with fresh energy; but mine had not been a normal sleep. Perhaps my Ka's failure to revitalise me fully was due to its over-long absence; or the fact that it had been violently expelled from my body, instead of leaving it in the ordinary routine way as I fell asleep. Whatever the cause it had failed to fulfil its proper function. I was as weak as a babe; and with ever-mounting terror I was brought face to face with the fact that I could no more lift my coffin lid than I could have had I had my full strength and ten tons of earth were weighing down upon it.

Yet there remained one hope. Before coming down into the grave my Ka had fortified its resolution to make the attempt on which it was set with the belief that, should it not succeed in re-animating my body, it would still be able to leave it again by the way it had got in.

Again I fought down my terror and lay for a while rallying my all too pitiful physical resources. I then began to breathe steadily and deeply, in through the mouth and forcing the air out through my nose. Instinctively I increased the tempo of my breathing until my heart was pounding furiously beneath my ribs. Desperately I willed my Ka to leave my body. My eyeballs ached with the strain. I felt as though my head was about to burst. But I did not lose consciousness. I felt no indication whatever that my state was about to change.

Having got back into its body my Ka refused to leave it. Perhaps it was now chained there by some power or law beyond my comprehension. At last my panting eased from the sheer inability of my lungs to continue to force air swiftly through my nostrils any longer.

312

Still gasping, and retching with sick fright, I was forced to recognise the terrible, awful, frightful, ghastly fate that had befallen me. I was alive; I was in my coffin, and I was trapped there.

12

Saturday 17th September

WITH my eyes wide open, but staring into impenetrable blackness, I wondered how long I would have to endure this terrible ordeal until I was released from it by complete and absolute death.

The atmosphere in the coffin had that horrid blend of coldness and stuffiness with which one meets in an unheated railway carriage packed with people that has long had its windows closed on a freezing winter's day. Each breath needed a conscious effort as it had to be drawn through the winding sheet, yet, had life depended on air alone there was an ample supply to keep me alive indefinitely.

That, of course, was due to the air holes which had been bored in my coffin in accordance with my instructions. Now, I cursed my folly for having inserted that clause in my will. Had I not done so I could have counted on death from suffocation, the agony of which would at least have been compensated for by its comparative quickness. As things were I was doomed to die of starvation.

Presumably as my animation had been suspended absolutely from that moment that Evans had loosed his death ray upon me, my tissues had hardly yet absorbed the fortifying vitamins contained in that last dinner which I had eaten so cheerfully with Ankaret. Moreover, I was no starveling. While by no means a glutton I had, within reason, indulged my good appetite and love of rich foods freely for many years past. Even though I was not burdened with much surplus fat, regarded simply as a warehouse my big healthy frame must contain a fine stock of those chemicals which kept life going; and had I been called on to play my part as a citizen in a medieval town withstanding a siege lasting many months, it was a very good bet that I should have remained capable of carrying on long after a big percentage of my fellow townsfolk had starved to death.

But that was really beside the point. For the maintenance of life liquids were far more necessary than solids. Men had often gone for three weeks or more without food, but the case of anyone who went without water for even three days would be desperate. And the awful thing was that one did not die of thirst. At least not until it had sent one mad.

That, then, was the fate to which I was condemned. In a few days thirst would drive me mad. But no; I should be mad long before that. The constant strain of having consciously to draw in each breath through the sheet, claustrophobia and anticipation of the agony inseparable from my final death throes would drive me insane before I began to suffer seriously from thirst. Perhaps within a few hours.

If so, I might still hope for a relatively swift escape. For madness was surely a state in which the mind refused any longer to put a true value on the circumstances of the person to whom it belonged. It could regard rags on the body as royal raiment or remain convinced that while eating mashed potatoes it was enjoying a dish of peacock's brains. Yet the body of a madman, despite its supernatural strength, did not become insensible to pain. I might imagine myself to be the Pharaoh Cheops entombed in the centre of the Great Pyramid, still by far the vastest monument ever raised by human hands. I might fool myself into believing that my winding sheet was a mummy's bands that I had managed to loosen in an effort to free my limbs from them. But I would still be buried alive, and be subject to the most ghastly physical torture before I finally expired.

Again, time is relative. Most people can recall how their school hours dragged; so that during an afternoon class ten minutes would often seem like half an hour. And contrari-wise, how an evening out with someone with whom one was in love, although lasting for six or seven hours, would seem to be over before it had properly begun.

How long it was since my Ka had re-entered my body I had not the faintest idea. It already seemed as though half the night must have passed, because such a great variety of fears, hopes, speculations, panic thoughts and awful apprehensions had in turn occupied my brain. Yet all of them might have sped through it in a few moments, and I doubted if in fact my mind had been again one with my body for more than ten minutes.

How long then, in terms of my own consciousness, was it going to take before either claustrophobia or thirst drove me mad? To me it might seem like days, or even weeks. A fresh fit of shuddering shook me.

For a time I prayed desperately, abjectly; begging God either to give me the strength to force my way out of my coffin, or by some means I had not yet thought of decree for me a swift end. Both prayers remained unanswered. A new attempt to raise the heavy lid above me showed me that my physical strength was still hopelessly unequal to the effort needed, and no sudden choking or heart stroke seized me giving promise of a convulsion that might carry me off.

I began, within the limitations of my weakness, to thresh about, in the hope that by exhausting such energy as remained to me I might die sooner. But very soon I was forced to abandon that idea for possibly accelerating my death. The quicker breathing necessitated by my exertions became a torture, and the bumping of my head against the sides of the coffin resulted only in giving me a headache.

It was as I lay still once more, painfully recovering from my latest exertions, that, like a sail seen by a shipwrecked mariner on a desert island, new hope flamed in my breast. Ankaret was to be buried on Saturday, and this was Friday night.

With that thought my attitude towards my ghastly situation instantly became reversed. Instead of doing anything I could to hasten my end I must conserve my energy by every means in my power. Somehow I must hang on to my sanity. I must fight the demons of fear with every ounce of will-power that I had left. If I could defeat panic and do nothing whatever but lie there breathing quietly for a few hours, I might yet be saved.

When the Vicar had conducted the first half of Ankaret's funeral service in the Church, her coffin would be carried out for the second part to be read over it as it was lowered into the grave. Some minutes before that the Sexton would make the vault ready by drawing back the cover from it. Owing to the air-holes in the coffin I could not fail to hear the tarpaulin scrape across the vault's brick edge. That would be the signal for me to begin to shout. Even if the Sexton happened to be as deaf as a post, the Vicar, the coffin bearers, or some of the mourners assembled round the grave's edge to witness the last rites were bound to hear my cries and come swiftly to my rescue.

Now, how I thanked God for those air-holes. I marvelled too at the wondrous ways of Providence; for had I not left instructions that they were to be drilled, I would already be suffering the excruciating tortures of slow suffocation and be dead long before morning. It seemed that those youthful nightmares in which I had feared that I might be buried alive had been sent to me on purpose; so that I could make provision against it. There was, then, a pattern in things after all. I recalled now my Ka's kneeling in Westminster Abbey and praying in vain to be rescued from its loneliness; and how I had later railed against God for ignoring my plea to be guided to a place where I might mingle with others who were dead. How wrong I had been to do so. He had known that my body was still in a state to receive my Ka back; and He meant me to live.

It was that thought 'He meant me to live' which now buoyed me up and gave me the courage to face the hours that I must pass imprisoned in that awful darkness.

My greatest concern was to make my breathing easier. Raising my hands a little till they were above my mouth I got a fold of the sheet between my fingers. To tear it was beyond the strength of my weakened arms, but I began to knead and scratch at it with my nails. Frequently I had to stop and rest owing to the feebleness of my wrists and fingers. How long it took I had no idea, but at last I succeeded in wearing a small hole in the material. Thrusting a finger through it, I exerted all the strength I could and tore a rent a few inches long. The relief was immediate. Gradually I drew long breaths of the cold air deep down into my lungs. After a few moments I forced both my hands, back to back, through the rent, clutched the torn edges of the sheet and tore them apart. By feeble pulling I was then able to free my face from it entirely.

My limbs showed no signs of regaining their strength, but the better air supply helped to clear my brain. Or, at least, no longer having to labour for each breath enabled me to think more coherently. Further scenes witnessed by my Ka during the past week now came back to me, and began to take their proper place in the sequence of events.

Normally when one wakes after a dream the impressions of it are vivid but soon forgotten unless one makes a deliberate effort to retain them in order to describe them to someone else. But in this case the process was reversed. My first memories of what had occurred had been vague and fragmentary, but as the night wore on they came back to me with increasing clarity until I could recall every detail of my Ka's experiences. Why that should have been I do not know. I can only suppose that it was because my Ka had not left my body in natural circumstances and to the conditions in which it returned enabled it to inform my physical brain of how it had been ejected and of all that had followed.

As I thought of the threat to Sir Charles's life I realised that it should now be in my power to save him. Ankaret's funeral would almost certainly take place, as had mine, in the morning. Even if it did not do so till the afternoon there would still be ample time to telephone a warning to him before he left his office.

At the same time, while telephoning to him, I should be able to get him to clear Johnny of the weighty charge made against him by Admiral Waldron and order his release from arrest. Perhaps, even, Johnny would be able to get down to Longshot that evening and join me in celebrating my resurrection.

Another thought on the strange workings of Providence came to me. It was through Ankaret's irresponsible encouragement of Evans that the little Welshman had all but killed me. Now, it was through her own death and funeral that I was to rejoin the living. Yet the knowledge that she was dead struck me with renewed force, and for a time I was once more overwhelmed with grief at my loss.

In an endeavour to assuage my misery I tried to turn my mind to other things. My reappearance in the world was going to require a lot of explaining, and there were many matters that would have to be straightened out. Amongst others Harold would have to be told that he was not 'Sir' Harold after all. As I imagined his angry disappointment I actually laughed in my grave.

318

The hollow sound was positively terrifying, and it brought me back with a jerk to the awful fact that I was, literally, not yet out of the wood. Thoughts can pass through a mind so swiftly that although it seemed to be hours since my Ka had re-entered my body, it might in reality be only about thirty minutes. The dawn I should not see was still probably hours away, and after it another six, or perhaps even nine, hours must somehow be got through before I could hope to be rescued. My real battle to hang on to my sanity still lay before me.

For some time I had been increasingly conscious of the cold. It now filled me with a new fear. As my movements were so restricted and the vitality of my body so low, I might die of cold before the hour of Ankaret's funeral.

In an endeavour to counter it I began to exercise such limbs as I could move a little. Again I thanked God for having led me to make special provisions about my burial in my will. Had I not done so I would have been encased in a satin-lined lead casket within the wood coffin and certainly dead from suffocation by now. But, that apart, whoever had measured me for my coffin had either not been told, or had forgotten to allow for, the fact that it was not to contain an inner casket. As a result of this oversight, instead of my body being wedged tightly against the wood it had an inch or two of free space all round.

That enabled me to stretch my legs, flex my toes, wriggle my hands down until they rested on my thighs, and even ease my position from time to time by turning slightly sideways. There then began a struggle between my continued weakness and my endeavours to do my utmost to keep my circulation going. Naturally I had made further attempts to lift the coffin lid, and tried using my knees instead of my hands, but the lid seemed to weigh a ton and I was utterly incapable of shifting it. All I could do was weakly to roll my head from side to side or stretch a limb occasionally, but to that I stuck with grim determination.

All further thoughts about how other people might be affected by my return from the grave, I put from me, because it had, once again, become a question of 'if' not 'when' I was rescued. I no longer dared to count on it. The seeping cold might finish what Evans had begun. Yet had I allowed

my mind to become vacant new fears and terrifying possibilities would swiftly have drifted into it, so to keep it occupied I began to say over silently all the poetry I could
remember.

I must have gone on like that for a long time; for I had
always been fond of poetry and, although far from word perfect, my repertoire was considerable; and I ran through most
of my favourite pieces twice. No doubt it was the cadences
that first soothed then lulled my overwrought mind. Without
realising what was happening, I fell asleep.

It was the sound of a loud bump immediately above my
head that awoke me. I had slept deeply and, opening my eyes
with a start, I stared up into inky blackness. For what,
unrealised by me, were now several incredibly precious minutes, I did not know where I was. My brain, bemused by
sleep, stumbled as through a fog, grasping at first only
physical essentials; that I was cold, that my limbs were
numbed, and that I was lying without a pillow on a hard
surface in complete darkness. It was another sound which
brought back to me with awful suddenness the fact that I was
in my coffin and how I had got there.

Somewhere above me I caught a sudden faint murmur. It
ceased and then came again almost at once. It had in fact
been only one word of two syllables pronounced simultaneously by a number of people and repeated after a very brief
interval. Yet even at a distance it was plainly recognisable.
A congregation had twice made the response 'Amen'.

Ankaret's funeral was taking place. I had slept while the
Sexton was drawing the tarpaulin cover aside from the vault.
Slept on while the Vicar had read the short second half of
the service at the grave-side. It was her coffin when lowered
bumping on mine that had aroused me. For the minutes
while the last paragraphs of the service were being pronounced
I had continued to lie there inactive, still half asleep. Only
at its very end had the truth crashed home into my comprehension. The opportunity for which I had striven so hard to
survive was almost gone. The crowd that had assembled about
the grave-side and stood there for a good five minutes must
now be moving away from it. My hope of life now hung by
a thread.

Galvanised by desperate fear I went into instant action.

At the same moment my hands shot upwards and I called for help. To my horror my voice, through having been unused for a week, was no more than a hoarse croak.

In vain I strove to force a shout. My mouth gaped open, the sinews of my throat contracted, but only guttural sounds emerged. My agonised cries were little louder than the mewings of a cat and could not possibly have been heard by the people now moving away from the grave-side.

Yet, as I thrust upward, it flashed upon me that during sleep my strength had returned. My muscles were stiff and severe pains were shooting through them; but in this frightful emergency I gave little heed to that. With unspeakable relief at the thought that it now needed only an effort to burst my way out of the coffin, using hands, knees and head, I made it. To my amazement and terror the lid refused to budge.

Suddenly the awful truth dawned upon me. Ankaret's coffin could have been lowered on to either my father's or mine. The funeral mutes had, for no particular reason, chosen to let it down on my side of the vault. She was now lying immediately above me and the weight of her coffin made it impossible for me to raise the lid of my own. My strength had returned to me too late, and I had slept through my one chance of getting myself rescued. This was the end. After a few hours of agony I must now die where I lay.

*   *   *   *

I was no exception to the rule which makes battling to survive a paramount instinct in man. I refused to accept the logical conclusion that there was no hope for me. As I croaked on my voice grew stronger. I shouted, raved, cursed, pleaded. Had I done so as loudly five minutes earlier I must have been heard. But those little holes in my coffin, while large enough to give me air, were too small to allow my shouts to be audible above ground level as more than muffled sounds. The Vicar must have closed his prayer book and with solemn mien be making his way to the vestry to disrobe. Bill, Ankaret's aunts and cousins, James Compton, the rest of my co-directors, and the other mourners would all now have left the grave by divergent paths across the churchyard to drive off in the cars that had brought them there.

Fighting down the instinct to go on shouting, I forced myself to become silent for a moment while I listened. After the reverberations of my yells in that closely-confined space the silence was almost stunning. It had that eerie quality which has been so aptly described as 'of the grave'.

I shuddered at the thought it conveyed. My sentence had not after all been suspended, but was confirmed. Up there, probably in the September sunshine, a score or more of people any one of whom would have dashed to my help had they known that I was alive were quietly walking off, thinking no doubt of their lunches, or perhaps their teas. I had lost my chance to make contact with them and it would never come again. No; never. Once more I was completely isolated from my fellow men and this time my isolation was final.

Yet, for as long as I can remember, I had always believed in the old adage that 'God helps those who help themselves'. By what seemed a miracle He had restored my strength to me. I suppose that having fallen into a natural sleep my Ka had, unrealised by me, again left my body, and fulfilled its normal function by returning as I woke to recharge it with new energy. In any case, although my limbs were cold and my movements still cramped, physically I felt as strong as I had ever been. Perhaps the feat of raising Ankaret's coffin as well as my own coffin lid was not now beyond me.

Bracing myself, I made the attempt, thrusting upwards with my knees. With frantic excitement I felt the weight above me yield. A faint streak of greyness appeared low down near my left leg between the coffin and its lid. I heaved again. The streak widened. Once more I heaved. The gap was now at least three inches wide. If only I could sustain and increase the pressure I might yet escape death by inches.

Yet, even as new hope flamed so brightly within me, I suddenly realised that my strivings were in vain. To free myself I must, somehow, overturn Ankaret's coffin sideways on to that of my father. To lift it even a foot or more was not enough, I could not possibly raise it on end with my knees alone, and keep it suspended in mid-air while I crawled out from beneath it.

To yield those few inches of grey daylight which I had gained by such tremendous exertion was one of the hardest things that I have ever done. But done it had to be. The hope of achieving freedom that way I now recognised as an illusion. To pursue it was as useless as butting one's head against a brick wall.

Slowly, with intense reluctance, I relaxed the pressure on my aching knees. I could have wept as that band of dim light narrowed and finally disappeared. It had seemed to link me again with life and joy and all the happy things I had ever known; yet I had had voluntarily to sever that link and once more condemn my eyes to unrelieved darkness.

For a time I lay still, rallying my strength for a fresh effort. Then, placing my hands palm upward, flat against the coffin lid above my head, I made it. Again, under the pressure I exerted the coffin lid lifted. Again I saw that blessed streak of grey daylight to my left, and now on a level with my head. The strain upon the muscles of my arms was agonising. It increased with every fraction of an inch that I forced upwards the grim weight that now held me prisoner. It was a torture equal to that of being stretched upon the rack; but to bear, and wilfully intensify, it offered the only possible alternative to suffering tortures still worse. More—in addition to lifting I had yet to throw Ankaret's coffin sideways before I could crawl out of my own.

Raising my right knee I placed it firmly against the coffin lid. Relaxing a little the pressure exerted by my left arm, I took the weight of the head end on my right. I was all set now for the final movement. Taking a deep breath, I threw every ounce of strength I had into one terrific heave, aimed at using my right knee and arm to tip Ankaret's coffin over on to that of my father. The band of daylight on my left swiftly widened to from two to four, six, eight inches. The strain seemed unbearable, yet it might not have been if I had paused then, holding up the weight but not striving to raise it further until I had recruited fresh strength. It was owing to my reasoning faculties having been submerged by terror, and the frantic urge to escape, that I made my fatal mistake.

The accursed thought came to me that by gripping the right edge of my coffin lid I should be better able to exert the leverage needed to turn Ankaret's coffin right over. Withdrawing my right hand from its place above my head, I made a swift grab at the raised edge of the coffin lid. I was not quick enough, and my movement was fouled by my finger-tips striking the brick side of the vault. My right knee and left arm proved insufficient to support the weight above me. My left arm crumpled; the upper part of the lid descended with a rush. My right hand was half in, half out of the coffin. Its palm was caught and crushed. A sickening stab of pain ran up my right arm. But that was not the worst. Frantically I strove to drag my hand free. I could not. It was trapped; gripped as in a vice between the coffin lid and the right-hand edge of the coffin. The agony became excruciating. I fainted.

For how long I was out, I had no means of judging. When I came to my brain was again bemused, and thoughts trickled back into it through a mist of pain. Once more I suffered the ghastly process of slowly becoming aware of the full horror of my situation. My right arm was bent round at an awkward angle and my hand caught palm upward on a level with my head. The hand itself had gone numb, but a pulsing ache throbbed through the muscles of my arm right up to the arm-pit.

As I remembered the opportunity of which sleep had robbed me tears trickled from my eyes. Then as I thought of the way in which the funeral party had left the grave-side before I could make myself heard by them, a ray of fresh hope suddenly illuminated my distraught mind.

When they left, the Sexton had not drawn the tarpaulin back over the vault. It was certain that he would return to do so before nightfall. I should hear him and my shouts would bring him to my rescue. Suffering as I was, there was no danger of my falling asleep a second time. There was another danger, though. My heart contracted as I thought of it. Unless my pain eased I might faint again. Yet another thought brought quick relief. Even if I did faint, while covering the vault he could not fail to see my fingers sticking out from the side of the coffin.

It was then I made a terrible discovery. My trapped palm held open the right side of the coffin near my head a good inch. A streak of grey twilight should show there. But it did not. I was once again enshrouded in the utter darkness of the pit. The Sexton must have come and re-covered the vault while I was lying unconscious. As Ankaret's coffin was on top of mine, in the deep shadow cast by it he had failed to see my fingers.

At this dashing of my final hope I lost all control of myself. Threshing about within the narrow limits of my prison, I screamed and shouted: 'Help! Help! Help! Let me out! I'm alive! Alive! Alive! Oh can't you hear me! Help! Help! Help!'

My voice, seeming unnaturally loud in that confined space, roared and rumbled, sometimes rising to a piercing shriek, but it only echoed back to me mockingly.

All the time I was shouting, my limbs were flailing in violent unco-ordinated movements. I kicked with my feet, banged on the coffin lid with my knees, hammered at it with my clenched left fist, and jerked at my imprisoned right hand. For as long as my strength lasted, I kept it up; but my voice grew husky and my limbs tired until they were capable of no more than feeble twitchings. At last, overcome with exhaustion, I fell silent and lay still once more.

My frantic efforts to free my hand had set all the nerves in it going again. The coffin lid was cutting like the edge of a door that was being forced shut into the upper part of my palm just below the fingers; the side of the coffin cut with equal force into the back of my hand. As I lay panting and sweating from my recent struggle I recalled having heard of people who when similarly trapped in some desperate situation had saved themselves by cutting off the limb by which they were held prisoner. For me to have done so in my case, had it been possible, could hardly have caused me greater agony. But it was not possible. I had no knife and, even had I had one, I was so cramped for room that I could not have used it effectively.

Yet, unless I could free my hand, there was not a particle of hope left for me. I wondered if by a superhuman effort I could tear my fingers off, or perhaps wriggle them until they were severed by the two edges of wood that cut into them so cruelly. If I succeeded there was the possibility that I would bleed to death, but that was a welcome thought compared to the other death that awaited me.

Nerving myself afresh, I made the attempt. Never had I believed that I could endure such agony. Perhaps I might have succeeded if it had been my fingers only that were caught, but the lower part of my hand was also trapped, and too thick for those terrible edges to cut through. The only result of my effort was that I again fainted.

When I came round I was conscious for the first time of thirst. My exertions had at least succeeded in temporarily warming me, but they, and the pain I was in, had caused me to break out in a profuse sweat. It was now dry and cold on my forehead, but my mouth felt hot, dry and parched. Again sheer terror seized upon my mind; and once more my limbs threshed convulsively.

After a time I once more got control of myself. Accepting the fact at last that all hope of either rescue or escape was gone, I faced up to a new problem. My extremity had purged me of all my old prejudices against committing suicide; and I began to consider how I might save myself from further torment by making a quick end of myself.

Again I cursed my folly in having ordered air-holes to be bored in my coffin. Had I not done so I might have been dead long since; yet, if only I had the strength of mind, I might perhaps manage to suffocate myself. Wriggling my left hand around, I got hold of the torn winding sheet, pulled it up as far as I could, and stuffed a wad of it into my mouth. As I could still breath through my nose the mouthful of sheet did no more than add to my discomfort. Firmly I gripped my nose between finger and thumb, and held on to it.

For some moments I felt no appreciable effect. Then a pulse began to hammer in my throat. I wanted to retch. My head felt as though the blood was being pumped into it until it would burst. I began to gasp internally. My eyes bulged. My lungs screamed at my brain for help. I could not go on. I let go my nose, spat out the sheet, and gulped in great draughts of stale chilly air.

My next thought was to open a vein so that I might bleed to death. Once more, I would have given every penny I possessed for a sharp implement; if not a knife a safety razor blade, or even a nail. That last thought spurred me to fresh action. I had no iron nail, but I had my own nails. Squeezing up my left hand I began to claw at the side of my neck hoping to open my jugular vein.

It was no use. I had always been rather proud of my hands, and had kept my nails well trimmed. Had I had more room for my arm I might have succeeded, but cramped and twisted as it was I could not drag my nails fiercely down my neck. All I could do was to scratch with them and their blunt edges refused to penetrate the skin. All they did was to split upon it and make a sore from which seeped only a little surface blood. When I realised the futility of continuing I broke down and wept unrestrainedly.

I think my tears eased the tension of my mind a little, although they could not relieve my pain. As my sobbing lessened I scoured such wits as I had left for some other means by which to blot out my consciousness for good. I could think of none; but it occurred to me that I might, perhaps, render myself unconscious for a time, and as with every hour I must grow weaker, any time which could be so gained would lessen that of my sufferings.

Accordingly, I began to bang my forehead against the coffin lid in an attempt to knock myself out. Once again, lack of free space strictly limited my action. I could not bash my head with any force against the lid, but had to do my best with a swing of something under three inches. Jerking my neck repeatedly I struck as hard as I could, all the time increasing the tempo of the movement.

Soon my head was aching intensely, my ears were singing, and waves of coloured lights waxed and waned in the darkness before my eyes. Suddenly I had the impression that I was about to leave my body. I redoubled my efforts until I was three parts stunned. But, alas, the loosening of my mind under the stimulus of unceasing self-inflicted pain resulted in the lessening of my physical control over the muscles of my neck. Before I was properly out my head ceased jerking with any force at all, then dropped back and lay limply rolling from side to side. I had added a blinding headache to my other ills but was still sufficiently conscious to know that even temporary escape was beyond me.

Yet there had been those few blessed moments when I had felt myself to be within an ace of freedom. Owing to the battering I had given my forehead it seemed to be opening and shutting. That, of course, was an illusion; but, near insane now from half a dozen simultaneous forms of suffering, the idea came to me that I might drive my spirit out through my head. Calling up all the will-power that I had left, I strove to do so.

In my delirium I no longer paid any regard to my newly-acquired knowledge of the occult, but reverted to the belief of a life-time: that man had only a body and a soul. That my Ka might go out on the waves of pain through my gaping head, while leaving my spirit still imprisoned in my flesh, did not occur to me. Yet I believe that is what happened.

I found myself in Daisy's flat. It was early evening, but she was not in shabby clothes or preparing her high-tea-lunch. Propped up with cushions, and wearing a most fetching négligée she was, lying on the divan in her sitting-room. Close beside her sat the dark, rather heavy-looking man whom she had joined after refusing to listen to Johnny any longer at her night club. She had referred to him as her 'rent cheque' and, as it transpired during their conversation, he had exercised the privilege of his position to make her telephone to her club and say that she could not appear that night because she had gone down with a sudden bout of 'flu; so would not be in till Monday.

He was now trying to persuade her to dress and pack a suitcase; so that he could take her in his car down to an hotel near Maidenhead, and they could spend a short week-end there. But she would not play.

She said there was too great a risk that someone who knew her would spot her, and that it might get to the manager of the club that she had bilked him. If it did she would get the sack; so the game was not worth the candle.

I was already endeavouring to make her see me; but the argument went on for quite a time, and her mind was entirely absorbed by it. Her friend tried to bribe her to accept the risk by the offer of a special present of twenty pounds, but she still dug her toes in, and said:

'No, ducks. Nothing doing. I like it where I am, and other jobs aren't so easy to get as you seem to think. Not jobs on the level, that is. And you know you wouldn't like me to have to let myself be messed about by some other fellow as part of what it takes to get a decent pay packet. After all, what's wrong with this place? It's nice and cosy here, and we won't have to get up before we want in the morning because the chamber-maid has got to make the bed, or something. You slip out and buy us a nice bottle of wine, and half a chicken or a cold lobster for our dinner.'

The man gave in, and as he stood up my hopes rose; but only to be dashed a minute later. Instead of leaving the room to do as Daisy suggested he walked across to the gramophone and put a record on. Until I could get her alone, with her mind in a receptive state, I knew I had little chance of making contact with her; and soon I had cause for a new worry. I became conscious that my Ka lacked the feeling of permanency that it had had during the week it had roved at will through London and the Home Counties. Slowly but perceptibly the strength seemed to be ebbing from it; yet for well over an hour it was compelled to hover there impotently, before Daisy's friend at last said that he would go out and get something for them to eat.

As soon as the front door had slammed behind him Daisy jumped up from the divan, walked straight through me, and went into the bathroom to powder her nose.

I should have known better than to follow her. However lax Daisy might be in her morals, she had the innate respectability of the British middle classes. Urged on by the knowledge that my still living body lay in the grave, I thought of nothing but my desperate need to be rescued, and saved from further torment at the earliest possible moment. Taking not the least notice of what she was doing I placed myself before her and positively forced my presence into her consciousness.

She started and went bright pink. Then her blue eyes blazed at the way I had outraged her sense of modesty.

'You beast!' she cried. 'You filthy-minded scum! How dare you come and play the Paul Pry on me when I'm paying a penny!'

Thoughts tumbled towards her in a torrent from my brain. 'Daisy, I didn't mean to. I swear I didn't; but I've been striving to catch your attention for the best part of two hours. Help me! You must! For God's sake help me! Telephone to Longshot. You only have to let people know. You needn't even give your name. I'm . . . don't! Stop! Please!'

That was as far as I managed to get. Now white with anger, she made the sign of the Cross and shouted: 'Avaunt thee Satan! Go! Unclean thing, go! Get back to Hell where you belong.'

Had she had the powers of an archangel her abjuration,

in this instance, could not have been more effective. I expect that she would have barred her consciousness against me anyhow, even if I had not so flagrantly infringed her particular code of decent behaviour. But I had been rushed into my blunder not only through the dominating urge to get help. It had also been, in part at least, because for the past hour I had known my Ka to be weakening. Now its last resources of will and energy had been used up in its desperate effort to get a hearing from Daisy. Under her curse, it seemed to wilt. I saw her only as through a thickening veil for another few moments. Then I found myself back in my coffin.

I was no longer delirious. Whether my Ka had actually journeyed to London and appeared to Daisy, or that had been only a figment of my distraught imagination, I had no means of judging; but my mind was again quite clear. I was still in great pain and now terribly weak. While I had been lying still the seeping cold had numbed me, yet my face burnt with fever. My tongue was thick and leathery in my mouth.

For the last time my mind sought wildly for any possible chance that I might have overlooked. I had laid it down in my will that the vault should not be sealed until a week after my funeral. The Sexton and his mates would then come again to my grave. But I had been buried on Tuesday and this was only Saturday night. Without water I could not possibly survive for another two and a half days. But how long would it be before I died? I made one last despairing effort to break out of my coffin, then fell back utterly exhausted. Soon afterwards I drifted into merciful oblivion.

13

Thursday 15th to Sunday 18th

BEFORE proceeding further it is necessary that I should give
an account of what happened to Johnny Norton after he had
been placed under close arrest.

Group Captain Kenworthy led him to the Provost Marshal's
department, where the formality of taking down particulars
was gone through; then into another room where there were
two Security Officers. After inviting Johnny to sit down and
giving him a cigarette the Group Captain told him that it
would help matters considerably if he were willing to answer
a few more questions about me, as that might give them a
new line of investigation and enable them to clear him of the
accusation that had been made against himself.

No doubt the suggestion was made in perfectly good faith;
but, fearing that he might be led to make statements which
would later prejudice his own case, Johnny very wisely replied
that, in view of the gravity of the charge, he was not prepared
to discuss the matter further until he had consulted a solicitor.

On that he was assured that he would be given every facility
to do so. The Group Captain then introduced one of the
others—a tall fair man—as Wing Commander Tinegate, and
said that he would be responsible for Johnny during the period
of his arrest. Tinegate took him down to the courtyard and
across to a waiting car with an R.A.F. driver.

Johnny suggested that they should go in his car wherever
they were going; but Tinegate was not agreeable to that. However, he did agree that it could not be left parked indefinitely
outside the Air Ministry, and also that Johnny should be
allowed to pick up some things from his rooms. Another
R.A.F. driver was procured to drive Johnny's car down to
Earls Court and leave it in the mews garage that he rented
behind Nevern Square. The Air Ministry car followed it with
Tinegate and Johnny. Having seen it garaged they drove

round the corner to the house and went upstairs. While Johnny packed a bag Tinegate waited in his sitting-room, then, when they came downstairs, he told his landlady that he would be away for a few days and they went out to the car. In it they were then driven down to the R.A.F. Depot at Uxbridge.

Tinegate was evidently familiar with that part of it in which officers awaiting courts martial are confined as, when the car pulled up in front of one of the many buildings, he took Johnny straight in past a sentry to a ground-floor corridor that had a number of rooms opening on to it. One was a sitting-room, quite comfortably furnished, and well supplied both with books and indoor games. The others were small bedrooms. Johnny was given the one at the far end of the corridor, and Tinegate took the one next door, leaving in it a suit-case he had brought with him in the car.

Back in the sitting-room he said that, as Johnny must know, in cases of close arrest an officer of equivalent rank had to remain with the prisoner during his period of detention; so they must pass some days in one another's company; that to discuss the charge with the prisoner was against regulations so no reference should be made to it; that any reasonable request by Johnny would be granted; and that he hoped they would get on well together.

Johnny thanked him, then asked to telephone to a solicitor. Tinegate agreed, and as Johnny had not got a solicitor of his own he took the sound step of getting on to my old friend Eddie Arnold in Southampton. Eddie said that he had an appointment at ten o'clock next morning which he could not possibly cut, but that he would catch the first train up to London after it, and come out to Uxbridge in the afternoon.

The two Wing Commanders then settled down in the sitting-room. Tinegate sent for drinks, and they had a desultory chat, mostly about their Service experiences and other officers whom they found to be mutual acquaintances. Dinner was brought in to them from the Mess on trays, and afterwards Johnny sat down to write a long letter to Sue while Tinegate read a novel. At about half-past ten they went to bed.

Next morning after breakfast Johnny asked to see the Commandant of the depot; adding that he had no complaint to make but wished to speak to him on a private matter.

Tinegate enquired if it was not something in which he

could help, and on being assured that it wasn't, summoned an orderly who fetched the Duty Officer of the day. He was duly given a message, but came back ten minutes later to say that the Station Commander had already left to attend an Air Ministry conference for ten o'clock; so Johnny would not be able to see him until his return.

Part of the morning was spent in exercise, but Tinegate must have found Johnny a dull and greatly preoccupied companion as they walked up and down the edge of the parade ground together, and have been heartily glad when it was time to go in for lunch.

Soon after two Eddie Arnold telephoned to say that he had been unavoidably detained so could not get out to Uxbridge till about six. A further enquiry for the Station Commander elicited the information that he was not yet back, and that when he went up to the Air Ministry he usually spent the day in London. So Tinegate was condemned to spend a good part of the afternoon walking, or sitting, again with his near-mute prisoner. Just before six, Eddie made his appearance and Tinegate left Johnny with him in the sitting-room.

As well as being my solicitor Eddie also acted for the Company, and James Compton had told him privately of the upset I had caused just before my 'death' by proposing that we should refuse the E-boat contract; so he already knew the background of Johnny's story. He was most sympathetic, accepted Johnny's assurance that he was innocent, and promised to do his utmost for him; but he could not, as Johnny had thought just possible, suggest any line of enquiry which might solve the mystery of where I had obtained my information.

Dinner was due to be served by the time they had finished their conference and, very decently, Tinegate asked Eddie if he would care to remain for it; so an extra tray was brought in and his cheerful presence helped for a time to dispel the uneasy atmosphere which had developed between the two Wing Commanders owing to Johnny's gloom and their un-natural relationship.

When Eddie had left them Tinegate again sent to enquire about the Station Commander; but he was still not back, so it now looked as if he had a dinner engagement. As Johnny insisted on seeing him that night Tinegate started on a new novel, while Johnny restlessly thumbed through a collection of old magazines.

It was nearly midnight before the Duty Officer appeared to say that the Station Commander had returned and would see Johnny. Tinegate accompanied him to the office, and there presented him to an elderly Group Captain, to whom he made his request. It was that he should be allowed out on parole for twenty-four hours, to attend to entirely personal affairs which were urgent and causing him great worry.

Tinegate immediately followed his request by saying that before the Station Commander gave a decision he would like a word with him alone. Johnny was taken into an adjoining room by the Duty Officer, and when he was brought back the Group Captain said to him:

'I would like to oblige you, but I'm told that you are under arrest in connection with a breach of the Official Secrets Act. That is a very serious matter. No doubt you've seen in the papers the frightful rumpus that is going on about Burgess and Maclean, and their having been allowed to get out of the country. I trust there is nothing in these charges against you; but that remains to be seen. And after all, you are an Airman. What is to prevent you pinching an aircraft from some flying club or other, and hopping across the Channel before morning? If that happened it would be the end of me. No, I'm sorry; but I can't risk it.'

To that there could be no answer, so Johnny returned with Tinegate to their quarters and they turned in for the night.

On Saturday the same routine was followed, except that it was not enlivened by a visit from Eddie and that Sue rang Johnny after lunch. But in spite of a long conversation with her he became even more gloomy and restless, while the unfortunate Tinegate became even more bored and wearied from having to remain constantly with him.

An hour or so after they had finished dinner that evening, Johnny suggested to Tinegate that they should go early to bed. Having yawned his head off while waiting for the Station Commander's return the previous night Tinegate readily agreed.

When Johnny had shut himself into his room he did not start to undress but sat down, and for the next half hour endeavoured to occupy his mind by scanning an evening paper. He then switched out the light.

Glancing at the illuminated dial of his wrist watch from time to time, he sat on there in the darkness until it was eleven o'clock; then getting up, he gently opened the door of his room and looked up into the corridor. No one was about, so he tiptoed down it to the sitting-room. Unlike the bedrooms and the lavatory, its windows had no bars. Cautiously putting his head out he saw that the sentry was at his post on the main door of the block. After a few minutes the man turned his back and marched off on his beat. As soon as he was out of sight round the corner, Johnny clambered through the window and, crossing the road, walked quickly through a gap between two other buildings.

There was, of course, no prison compound to have to get out of, as the courts-martial of officers were carried out at the depot only occasionally, but he had to find a place where he could scale the fence that surrounded the great establishment with little risk of being spotted by the few men who were still about. After some ten minutes of wandering among a maze of buildings he found a row of latrines which screened the fence from observation for about forty feet, and, going behind them, managed to scramble over. A quarter of an hour later he was in an almost empty tube train which took him direct to Earls Court. Walking quickly round to his garage, he got out his car, and it was still only a little after midnight when he set out for Longshot.

The fact of the matter was that when Johnny had telephoned to Sue after his abortive visit to my grave, and told her that he was satisfied, he had not been telling the truth. It will be recalled that, at my funeral, when my coffin was lowered into the vault it had bumped as it came to rest on the one below it, and its lid had shifted slightly. That was how, as an unseen spectator, I had learned that my instructions had been carried out about not screwing the lid down. Johnny had seen the coffin in the beam of his torch before being surprised by Constable Cowper long enough for his brain to register an impression that the lid had been moved.

While driving back to Longshot he had been tempted to sit up for a few hours then return and go down into the vault, but his narrow escape from having been caught in it and

335

arrested made him consider the factors in the situation with understandable caution.

The only reason for supposing that I might still be alive was the acceptance of occult theories which so far had not been supported by an atom of scientific proof; so, regarded logically and dispassionately, the odds against my being so were very long indeed. Moreover, the further he drove from the churchyard the more doubtful he became whether the lid of the coffin had really been moved or if he had been deceived by an optical illusion. Constable Cowper had said that he often went for night patrols and meant to give particular attention to the churchyard; and Johnny knew that if he were caught he would be liable to be sent to prison. In consequence he had decided that for the outside chance of finding me in a coma the risk of making another attempt that night was too high.

His promise to Sue that he would not had therefore been an honest one; but deep down in himself he was still not altogether happy about me and he had told her a white lie about that to keep her from worrying. Instinctively, too, he had not bound himself by any promise regarding the future. Next morning, while he was getting up, his doubts had strengthened, and he had begun to contemplate making another attempt to set his mind at rest during the very early hours of Friday, as pre-dawn seemed the least likely time for Constable Cowper to be out and about. But after breakfast the telegram recalling him to London arrived, and his arrest had followed.

For the greater part of Thursday he had been occupied with his own intensely worrying affairs but, even so, he had seen again intermittently all day a mental picture of my coffin, and had become convinced that the lid had been moved a little. It was this nagging thought that had caused him on the Friday morning to ask for an interview with the Station Commander.

During the day he had worried himself nearly silly with the thought of me, but had continued to pin his faith on the Station Commander's accepting his parole, so that he could go down to Longshot on the Friday night and settle his doubts once and for all. As that worthy had not returned until midnight Johnny's hopes had not been dashed until then; and up to that time he had not considered any possible alternative.

Again he spent a miserable night of heart-searching and self-reproach that he had not returned to the vault a few hours after Constable Cowper's arrival on the scene had forced him to leave it; but it had not been until the early hours of Saturday morning that he had begun seriously to consider breaking prison.

He knew that it should not be difficult to do so, as the officers occasionally detained at Uxbridge mostly faced charges only of drunkenness or peculation; so no very rigorous precautions were taken to guard them. All the same to break prison would make his own case infinitely worse; and by Saturday midday he was wondering if, should he succeed in reaching my grave, it would not be too late. I had by then been presumed dead for a week. Even if I had been buried while in a coma and during it my Ka had appeared to Daisy, the shifting of the coffin lid suggested that I had since come out of my coma, and had made an effort to rise from my grave, proved too weak to lift the heavy lid, and had soon after really died.

But, he continued to ask himself, would I necessarily have died? If I had remained in a coma from Friday night until anyhow Tuesday evening, when I had appeared to Daisy, might I not, after a brief rousing sometime during the next twenty-four hours, have fallen back into it and so still have life in my body after a further three or four days.

There was no one he could consult who possessed the authority to dispel his doubts on such a question. Tinegate or the Station Commander would have thought that his own troubles had unhinged his mind. He wished by then that he had taken Eddie into his confidence, although he thought it most unlikely that the lawyer would have put any credence in Daisy's visions. During the afternoon he had faced the fact that the responsibility was his and that there was no one with whom he could even share it. Either he must be harrowed all his life by the thought of the ghastly death to which he might have condemned me, or blacken his own case for a purpose he might never have able to reveal by breaking prison that night. To him, for having chosen the latter course, I can never be sufficiently grateful; but, for him, it has led to a situation far worse than the wrecking of his Service career.

So for his sake—and to some extent for my own—I could wish now that he had left me to suffer my final agony in my grave.

As there was little traffic on the road during the midnight hours he made the journey to Longshot in excellent time, arriving at the churchyard by half-past two in the morning. This time he left the car at the lych-gate, then walked swiftly up the slope to reconnoitre Constable Cowper's cottage. It was in complete darkness which gave Johnny good hope that Cowper was there and sound asleep. Turning back towards the church he made straight for my grave, pulled the tarpaulin back from over the vault and shone his torch down into it.

Ankaret's coffin had not been there at the time of his previous visit. Now it was on top of mine. He scrambled down into the vault and with some difficulty managed to drag her coffin across on to that of my father. It was not until he could shine his torch again, right on to my coffin, that he saw my fingers sticking out from its side.

His horror can be imagined. Kneeling on Ankaret's coffin he bent over, grasped the lid of mine and pulled it up sideways. Staring down at my body he took in the twisted limbs, the crushed hand red with clotted blood, the crimson sore on my neck where I had torn at my jugular vein and my forehead black and blue from the bashing I had given it. At first he thought I was dead, but he lifted my right arm and as the wounded hand came away from the coffin's edge I gave a deep groan.

Later, Johnny told me that never in his life had he heard anything so terrifying. But it was clear proof that I was still alive. His efforts to rouse me from my torpor produced only a fluttering of the eyelids and more groans. He could now have run up to Cowper's cottage to get help, but he had very good reasons for not doing so. Somehow he got my heavy body out of the vault on his own and laid it among Ankaret's comparatively-fresh floral tributes. Going down into the vault again, he replaced the lid of my coffin, lugged Ankaret's back on top of it, climbed out, pulled the tarpaulin across and replaced the bricks that he had had to move to roll it back.

Half carrying, half dragging me, he got me to the car, laid me on its back seat and wrapped a car rug round me. That done he immediately drove off, but only half a mile along the lane; then he pulled up on the grass verge to think out what he had best do. It took him about ten minutes to make up his mind. I was still less than half conscious, so had not yet realised what had happened or where I was, and when the car started into motion again I had no idea that I was being taken to Longshot Hall.

Johnny drove straight through into the old stable yard, got out, collected from the shed where it was kept the key of the spare garage, which he always used when he came to stay, unlocked its doors, and backed the car into it. Belton, who slept over the main garage at the far end of the yard, was the only person who might have heard him. But he knew that Belton was used to him putting his own car away late at night and sometimes getting it out very early in the morning.

Closing the garage doors, Johnny switched the light on, propped me up, and made a more careful examination of me. My hand had started to bleed again, but otherwise my injuries were only superficial and my heart, which had always been strong, was beating steadily. Reaching over for a first-aid pack from the dashboard shelf he got busy on my hand. As the iodine entered the wounds fresh stabs of pain brought me round. With a cry, I started up and stared about me.

'It's all right, Giff,' he said quickly. 'It's me, Johnny. There's nothing to be afraid of. I got you out—out of your coffin. Poor old chap, you must have been through Hell. But you're quite safe now.'

I could only nod weakly. I felt incredibly cold. A shiver ran through me and my teeth began to chatter.

As soon as he had finished bandaging my hand he drew the rug up to my chin, tucked it round me, and said: 'Stay still. Relax as much as you can. I'm going to the house to get something to warm you up. I shan't be long.'

I clutched at him with my left hand and croaked out my first words: 'Don't leave me! For God's sake don't leave me!'

'I must,' he insisted. 'You are safe, I tell you. If you go off into another coma I won't let them put you back. I swear I won't. But if I don't get some warmth into you pretty soon you are going to die of pneumonia.'

I made a feeble motion of assent and sank back.

By throwing small gravel at Silvers's window Johnny

339

brought him down to the back door of the house. The story he told the old butler was to the effect that, as my executor, he had to collect more of my papers; that he had meant to do so during the day, after attending Ankaret's funeral, but an urgent conference at the Ministry of Defence had made it impossible for him to get away; so he had had to make a night run instead. He added that he would get himself a drink, and perhaps a snack in the kitchen, before he left; then he had firmly refused Silvers's offer to get anything for him and sent the old boy back to bed.

Without the least suspicion that anything exceptional was afoot Silvers retired by way of the back stairs and as soon as he was out of sight Johnny nipped into the kitchen. Having put a kettle on to boil he padded lightly up the front staircase to my dressing-room. Still moving quietly, so as not to wake Bill Wiltshire, who was sleeping in a room just across the corridor, he spread my dressing-gown on the floor, flung on to it a lounge suit, a shirt, underclothes, shoes, socks, my hair brushes and a few other things, then tied the whole lot up in a bundle, and slipped downstairs with it.

In the hall he collected my heaviest overcoat and put it on over the raincoat he was wearing. When he got back to the kitchen the kettle was boiling. After getting the coffee percolator going he hunted round till he found a couple of Thermos flasks and a basket, then got milk from the frig and a basin of jellied soup that happened to be there. Leaving the kitchen again, he fetched a bottle of whisky and a bottle of brandy, both three-parts full, from the drinks cupboard in the library. Having filled the two flasks with a mixture of coffee, brandy and milk, he put all the oddments into the basket, snatched up the bundle, and hurried back to the garage.

He had not been away for more than a quarter of an hour and during it I had remained semi-conscious. My hand, head and throat ached savagely again, and between bouts of shivering I was seized with waves of panic; but there was light to see by and I could once more move my limbs freely; so I managed to fight them down.

We used part of the spare garage as a store for garden cushions, collapsible chairs, and so on, during the winter, and after my body had been removed from the beach pavilion,

340

Silvers must have collected them from it; for, as soon as Johnny had given me a few gulps from one of the flasks, he threw down alongside the car rubber lilo and proceeded to blow it up.

With his help I managed to stagger out and tumble on to it. Stripping me of my winding sheet he poured some of the whisky on to my chest and began to rub vigorously. Ignoring my groans he pounded and kneaded the flesh of my back, thighs, arms and legs for all he was worth, using the whisky as a friction until the bottle was empty. The treatment was harsh but effective.

By the time he had done, the rubbing with neat spirit had restored my circulation and something of my strength; so that I was able to sit up on my own and help him a little in getting me into clothes he had brought from my room.

During the latter stages of the operation he gave me a résumé of what had happened to himself, the events which had led to his coming to my rescue, and how he had got all the things from the house without arousing Silvers's suspicions. Finally he got me into the heavy overcoat, made a sling from a strip of the winding sheet for my injured hand, and helped me back into the car. Having put out the light, he opened the garage door and took his place beside me; then we drove off on the next stage of our extraordinary and tragic odyssey.

He had given me one of the flasks and put the bowl of jellied soup on my knees. As he had forgotten to bring a spoon I had to scoop up the soup with a piece of cardboard torn from the cover of a motoring map, but it slid down my parched throat like nectar, and the café-cognac completed the good work Johnny's massage had begun.

While I fed he gave me a more detailed account of his arrest and of how he had broken prison and got me out of the grave. I told him he need worry no more about being court-martialled and that it was the Minister of Defence himself who had given me my information.

It was this which brought into my still-far-from-orderly mind the threat to Sir Charles's life. As yet I had not even grasped what day of the week it was, but in broken sentences I told Johnny of the danger in which his Chief stood and how urgent it was that we should get a warning to him.

Johnny, of course, thought that the reaction to my escape

had already set in and that I had become delirious. Huskily I tried to persuade him to pull up at a telephone kiosk, but he put me off with soothing phrases, and I was still in too much pain to carry on an argument about anything for long.

On my complaining of my pain, he said: 'Stupid of me; I should have thought of that before,' and slowing down the car he got out the first aid kit to give me a couple of tablets. After a while they took effect, my pain eased and I fell asleep.

I was woken by being thrown forward with a jerk. Johnny had been driving fast through still almost deserted streets, and a milk-float emerging suddenly from a side turning had necessitated his braking hard. Dawn had come, but for the moment I did not recognise the shops and houses on either side of us; so I asked him where we were. He told me that we were just coming into Fulham and we began to talk again.

He was telling me about Daisy, and how she had refused to believe that the apparition she had seen was mine, when I told him that I had been present during his talks with her, and added that I had also listened in at his interview with Mr. Tibitts. For a moment he was astounded, but quickly admitted it was logical that my etheric double should have brought such memories back with it to my re-awakened mind. He asked me then, a little diffidently, if I knew that another coffin had been lowered on to mine.

I relieved him from the fear of having to break the news to me about Ankaret's death, and went on to say that during the week my Ka had been absent from my body it had been able to follow many of the doings of himself and the rest of my family.

He asked me then what had really occurred on the night that I was supposed to have committed suicide. I replied that it was too long a story to go into at the moment, and would have to wait until I was feeling less groggy. It was not, now that Ankaret was dead, that I had any objection to telling him; but, although my mind was much clearer since my sleep, it was still to some extent confused, and coherent thought was made difficult owing to the pains that insistently racked my head.

We had not fallen silent for long before we pulled up in Nevern Square. With Johnny's aid I was now just strong enough to walk. Getting upstairs was a slow and laborious business, but with one of my arms round his neck I managed it, and having lowered me into an arm-chair in the sitting-room he went down again to fetch up the other things from the car.

While he was away my thoughts again drifted to Sir Charles; so directly Johnny came back I said that we must telephone at once. He thought I meant in order to get Sir Charles to clear him of the charges made against him, and said that now I was safe there was no immediate hurry about that; the most important thing at the moment was to get me to bed.

The time was about a quarter-past six, and I had now gathered that it was Sunday morning; so I feared that Sir Charles was already dead. But if he was and we raised the alarm at once the police might get the woman who had poisoned him before she could leave the country. I told Johnny that; and although my sentences were still laboured I could see that he was a little shaken in his belief that my concern for Sir Charles was a fantasy of my brain due to the great stress it had been under.

After some further urging I persuaded him to ring up his office and find out Sir Charles's telephone number in the country. Somewhat reluctantly he got on to the Ministry switchboard and obtained the number. It was some time before we could get an answer from the cottage, and the lack of it increased my fears; but at last we did and Johnny handed me the receiver.

On my asking for Sir Charles, it was Maria who replied. From her heavy accent I had no doubt about that. She said that Sir Charles was not there. She had expected him the previous evening but he had not come down after all. It was often like that.

Greatly relieved, I replaced the receiver. That Maria had been speaking the truth, I was convinced. If she had put poison in his dinner she would have left the cottage hours ago. For the moment, by the grace of God, he had escaped; and he had said that he had a luncheon engagement. But he might go down there that evening; so it was imperative that I should get a warning to him sometime during the day.

This fresh effort had again brought me near exhaustion, but a long pull at the second flask of café-cognac revived me enough to help Johnny get my clothes off. When he had got

343

me into bed, and had just put the rest of the pain-killer tablets on the table beside it, he said:

'Look, Giff, I still feel that I'm in a pretty tricky spot. Say Sir Charles backs out and refuses to admit that he gave away official secrets to you. What happens then?'

'He won't,' I replied. 'He is not a dirty little careerist politician. I'm certain he would never allow one of his staff to be ruined to cover up something he had done himself.'

'I think you're right there,' Johnny agreed. 'But say there really is something in this extraordinary idea of yours, and he is murdered before he has a chance to exonerate me? Is there anyone else who could prove that it was he who gave you the gen?'

I nodded weakly. 'Yes. Get hold of Martin Emsworth at the Treasury. It was he who arranged my meeting with Sir Charles. We met on the evening of Wednesday the seventh at Martin's flat. Martin will be able to substantiate that, and the fact that we met in secret is proof enough that it was Sir Charles who put me up to the line I took at the board meeting on the following Friday.'

Johnny wrote down Emsworth's name in his pocket diary, then he wrote something else on a loose-leaf, tore it out and laid it on the bed-side table next to the pain-killers. I had just closed my eyes, but he shook me gently and said very earnestly:

'Listen, Giff. You must listen to me for a moment. This is terribly important.'

'All right. Go ahead,' I muttered, again trying to concentrate my attention.

He spoke slowly and distinctly. 'I hate to have to do it, but I've got to leave you now. It may have already been discovered that I've broken prison. If so there will be merry hell going on at Uxbridge. As they seem to regard me as another Maclean half the police in England will have been turned on to hunt for me, and nothing that I can do will save the poor devil who was responsible for my custody from getting a most frightful rocket. But for the past two days I have not been called till eight, and during the daytime it's an open camp; so if I beat it back right away there is still a sporting chance that no one will ever know that I left it. I wouldn't be able to reach my room without being spotted.

But I could say that I'd slipped out for an early morning stroll while the sentry's back was turned; and Tinegate wouldn't be such a fool as to report that. He's been very decent to me; so I'd like to save his bacon if I can. Understand?'

I nodded, and he went on: 'Now; about yourself. You are damned ill, and I ought to have sent for a doctor right away. But I didn't because I don't want you to talk to anyone before you are in a state to think more clearly. As far as I can judge the bones in your hand are not broken and you are in no immediate danger. If you stay put for forty-eight hours you should be sufficiently recovered to get about again.

'If you do get bad pains in your chest, though, you'll have to have a doctor; so I've written the name and telephone number of a local medico on that slip of paper. Should you find it imperative to call him in, your name is the same as mine and I brought you here after we had been in a car smash early this morning. Before I go I am also going to write a note for my landlady, Mrs. Burton. She won't be up yet, so I shall leave it on the sitting-room mantel-piece. In it I shall ask her to look after you until you are fit enough to get up and leave. If you call yourself by my name it will be easy for you to remember. I shall tell Mrs. B. that you are my uncle and that I was christened after you. So for the time being, anyway, you are John Norton senior. Is that clear?'

I looked up at him with a puzzled frown, and asked: 'Why all this mystery, Johnny?'

He gave a sad smile. 'I don't wonder that you are still a bit slow on the uptake after the ghastly time you have been through. This whole show is so utterly extraordinary that I can hardly believe it to be true myself yet. Still, we two know it is, and we have got to face facts. When you have had time to think a bit, you'll realise that the most frightful complications are bound to arise were it known that you have come back to life again; or rather, were never really dead.

'That is the reason why I want you to take a false name for the time being. It is the reason, too, why I mean to keep my mouth shut about where I went and what I did during the hours I took French leave from Uxbridge.

'You have put me in the clear now. When I write and ask Sir Charles to exonerate me I can say that you told me yourself immediately after the board meeting that you had got your information from him; and that I have kept mum about that so far because I didn't want to embarrass him and was expecting him to get me out of trouble himself as soon as he learned of my arrest. And if he fails me I've got your friend Emsworth to fall back on; with one or the other of them I'll be all right; so I won't have to drag you into it, and you don't have to worry about me any more.

'But you will have to do some hard thinking before you leave this house. You have got a suit of clothes, and I've put some money in the pocket of your jacket. Only about six pounds but that's all I had on me, and it will carry you on for a bit. I dragged Ankaret's coffin back over yours and replaced the tarpaulin, so nobody will ever know you left it. That is, unless you decide to tell them. It is our secret and you can rely on me to keep it.'

Suddenly he leant forward and kissed me on the forehead. 'Good-bye, Giff. The best of luck whatever happens. But to all the world you are dead. And I think the best thing you can do is to remain so.'

14

Sunday 18th September

When Johnny had gone I took two of the pain-killers and soon after fell asleep. Since then I have several times been the victim of the most frightful nightmares and, believing myself back in my coffin, woken screaming. But on this occasion I was spared that. On waking, a glance at the bed-side clock showed me that it was ten-past three. I had slept for over eight hours and nothing is so healing as sound sleep. My headache had gone, my neck no longer hurt, and there was only a dull ache in my hand; but my mind was far from being restored to normal.

Had it been I might have acted differently. My health had not been seriously impaired; so if I had stayed where I was for another day or two I might have gone out into the world under another name. It would have been hard to start life again from scratch at my age, but I was strongly built and by no means lacking in intelligence. With so many good jobs go-ing begging owing to full employment I could soon have got one without too many questions being asked; first as a casual labourer, then something better until I had saved enough to get abroad, perhaps to Germany, where shipbuilding of all kinds was booming and my experience would soon have com-manded a salary large enough to keep me in comfort.

But my brain was not normal. For seven days and nights my Ka had registered an almost continual succession of frightful doubts, acute anxieties and harrowing experiences; then for some twenty-seven hours I had lain imprisoned in my coffin. It is true that many of those hours must have been passed in spells of unconsciousness, but anyone need only imagine what it would be like to be buried alive for ten minutes to judge the mental strain I had been through.

My mind was lucid about some things but confused about others and events during the first few days after my presumed death had been pushed into its background by more recent occurrences. The succession of tragedies at Longshot now seemed to me to have happened months ago, and no longer to be of much importance; so despite Johnny's warning of the complications that I should be faced with if I resumed life as Sir Gifford Hillary, I hardly gave them a thought. On the other hand the problems which had confronted me when I forced my Ka back into my body were still fresh in my mind.

That of Johnny had been dealt with, but there remained that of Sir Charles. The recollection of the whole night and day that I had spent vainly trying to get a warning to him, and the fact that it had been mainly to do so that I had gone down into my grave, now drove out all other memories. By an act of Providence he had been prevented from going down to his cottage the previous night; but he might do so that evening or, perhaps, was already on his way there. Looking at the clock again I saw that it was twenty-past three. Galvanised into action by the thought that I had not a moment to lose, I got out of bed.

My long sleep had done me a power of good. I found that I could walk quite well without assistance; but when I went into the bathroom I received a terrible shock. As I saw my face in the mirror I did not recognise myself. That I had eight days' stubble on my chin was no surprise, but it was white. So was my hair—snow white; and my eyes were sunk back in my head, making me look like a corpse.

When I recovered a little from the shock I did my best to freshen up and tidy myself. As every minute counted I had to deny myself a bath, and my injured right hand put shaving out of the question; but with my left I splashed some cold water over my face and combed back my hair. Getting into my clothes was far from easy and with movement my hand again began to hurt. I could not get a collar or tie on, and had to leave the laces of my shoes undone; but by twenty to four I was on my way downstairs.

Out in the square I was lucky enough to pick up a cruising taxi. Its driver gave me an astonished look, and probably thought that I had escaped from an asylum; but as I stumbled in I shouted at him:

'Storey's Gate! Ministry of Defence! Quick! Double fare if you can get me there in fifteen minutes!'

From long habit he let in his clutch without argument.

As it was Sunday afternoon, he made it. I paid him off out of Johnny's money, and heard Big Ben chime four as I entered the building.

In the hall I was received by an elderly bald man wearing the blue serge uniform with gold crowns on its lapels of a Whitehall messenger. His pale blue eyes popped as they took me in, but before he could utter a word, I cried:

'I must see the Minister; and at once. It's very urgent.'

'Have you . . . have you an appointment?' he stammered.

'No,' I said sharply. 'But that doesn't matter. Is he here, or has he left for the country?'

The messenger cast a worried look towards a policeman who had been standing at the far end of the hall, but now approached with slow majestic tread, eyeing me dubiously.

'Come on!' I insisted. 'Is Sir Charles here or not?'

'I . . . I've only just come on duty,' faltered the messenger. 'I haven't seen him leave, but . . .' he looked appealingly at the policeman, who volunteered:

'He hasn't gone out this way; but he may be round at Downing Street or across at one of the Service Ministries. I expect he'll be leaving soon though, because his car's just driven up.'

'Thank God he hasn't gone yet!' I exclaimed. 'But wherever he is I've got to see him. It's terribly important. Please ring through to his office and find out where he is.'

As the two men continued to eye me askance, I went on hurriedly: 'Don't pay any regard to my appearance. I've been involved in a car smash. I expect I'm looking pretty ghastly but I know perfectly well what I am doing.'

'Quite, Sir, quite,' said the policeman soothingly. 'But all the same Ministers don't see people without their having appointments. Wouldn't it be best if you went home now and just dropped him a line?'

Ignoring him, I turned back to the messenger. 'If you don't ring through to Sir Charles's office at once I'll make an issue of it that will end by your getting the sack.'

The little bald man drew himself up. 'Threats won't get you

nowhere; and unpleasant things is likely to happen to them as makes them.'

'He's right, Sir,' the policeman added. 'Using threatening language to a government official in the course of his duty. I could charge you with that. But seeing you're ill I don't want to press matters unless you force me to. Be sensible now, and let me call you a taxi.'

The state I was in was so much against me that had the argument continued my chances of ever getting to Sir Charles would have been far from good. I might have persuaded them to let me see a secretary, who would probably have proved equally obdurate, or I might equally well have landed up in Cannon Row Police Station. As it was, matters were brought to a head with unexpected swiftness. Quick footsteps sounded on the broad stone stairs, and turning I saw Sir Charles coming down them on his way to his car.

Brushing past the messenger I took a couple of strides towards him, but I got no further. The policeman grabbed me by the arm.

Sir Charles came to a halt in the middle of the hall, and asked quietly: 'What's the trouble?'

'This man, Sir . . .' began the policeman.

'Trying to force 'is way in,' said the messenger simultaneously.

But I was more determined to be heard than either of them, and my cry drowned their voices; 'Sir Charles! I've got to see you! I must! I've been very ill, but I'm not out of my mind. Don't you recognise me? I'm Gifford Hillary.'

At the sound of the rumpus another policeman and two more messengers had appeared from somewhere. Sir Charles gave me a quick look through his thick-lensed glasses and said:

'No, you are not.' With a glance at the policeman who held me, he added. 'Have the poor fellow taken home, officer, unless he proves obstreperous.' Then he went on his way to the door.

'You heard,' said the policeman warningly. 'Come now, or . . .'

But I was shouting after Sir Charles. 'I am! We last met in Martin Emsworth's flat.'

At that, he halted and came back. After another look at

me, he said: 'You certainly resemble Sir Gifford, but I really can't believe . . .'

'I am he,' I cut in. 'But I've been very ill and my hair has gone white.'

He nodded; but the puzzled look remained on his face as he muttered: 'I still don't understand. I thought you were dead.'

'My death was reported in the press, but it was a mistake,' I told him. 'And you *must* give me a few minutes. Your own safety hangs on it.'

'Very well, then,' he said after a moment. 'Come up to my room.'

As I followed him up the short flight of broad stone steps, the policeman said: 'Wouldn't it be as well, Sir, if I came up and stood outside your door?'

Sir Charles turned and gave him his boyish smile. 'No thank you, officer. It is just possible that this gentleman is who he says he is, and if he isn't he doesn't look very formidable in his present state.'

We got into the small, slow, ancient lift which must have so astonished Americans like General Eisenhower when, during the war, they had been taken up in it to confer with the British Chiefs of Staff. At the second floor we got out. Sir Charles led me to his room, sat down at his desk and waved me to a chair.

I sank gratefully into it. Getting into my clothes, the journey from Earls Court, and the altercation in the hall had taken more out of me than I thought. My wretched hand now seemed to be on fire and sweat had broken out on my forehead. I knew that I must be running a temperature.

'Now,' he said. 'If you were shaved and properly dressed you would look like a twenty-year-older edition of Sir Gifford; but however ill a man might be I find it difficult to believe that he could age that much in the space of ten days. And someone might have told you about my meeting with Sir Gifford at Emsworth's flat. Above all Sir Gifford's death was not just reported in the ordinary way. Owing to the tragedy in which he was involved it was splashed all over the place; and the whole press doesn't often allow itself to be misled about matters of nation-wide interest. I warn you now that if I find that you have been wasting my time by trying to play some silly game, I shall hand you over to the police. But my impression is that you have a bee in your bonnet and ought to be under medical care. Anyhow, I want a lot more evidence before I am prepared to accept you as Sir Gifford Hillary.'

His attitude was perfectly understandable for, except to nod to, he had met me only once, and as I now looked such a scarecrow it was not at all surprising that he thought me to be some harmless lunatic. But as I gave him particulars of our meeting, his expression began to alter, and when I had finished about the E-boat business I mentioned the fact that he had put soda-water into his last liqueur brandy. Anyone who was giving a description of the meeting received from some-one else could hardly have known that, and it clinched matters.

'I'm satisfied,' he declared. 'I would have been anyway after you had been talking for a bit, as your voice hasn't changed. But you poor fellow, you look in the very devil of a state. What in the world has been happening to you?'

I told him that I still felt very weak and that it would be too much of an effort to go into that now; so if he didn't mind we would get down right away to the reason I had come to see him.

'Go ahead, then.' He waved a hand. 'Down in the hall you said something about being concerned for my safety.'

'I am. Very much so,' I replied. 'But first I'd like to deal with another matter. It's about Johnny Norton.'

He frowned. 'I don't think I know anyone of that name.'

'He is a nephew of mine and a Wing Commander on your Planning Staff. I mentioned him to you when we were at Emsworth's.'

'Oh yes, I remember now. But he hasn't been here very long so I haven't met him yet.' Suddenly Sir Charles straightened in his chair. 'Norton! Why, that is the chap I had a report about on Friday, in connection with a breach of the Official Secrets Act.'

'Exactly,' I commented dryly. 'He is now under close arrest at Uxbridge; and between us you and I are responsible.' I told him then about Sir Tuke Waldron's reactions at our board meeting, and how the Admiral had later laid an information against Johnny accusing him of having given me my facts and figures.

When I had done, Sir Charles said at once: 'I'm sorry; terribly sorry. But as I was asking you to do something for me which was entirely contrary to your own interests, I felt that it was only fair to give you the whole picture. I thought you would have realised that I was speaking in the strictest confidence, and that when I gave you discretion to use the gist of what I had said to win over your board, you would have confined yourself to a general statement. Still, it's too late to worry about that now, and as far as Norton is concerned you needn't give the matter another thought. I take entire responsibility. I will telephone before I leave here and arrange for his release. Now, tell me about this other business?'

'It is your cook-housekeeper,' I replied. 'In no circumstances must you eat another meal in that country cottage of yours before you have had her arrested. I have found out that she is a Russian agent and intends to poison you at the first opportunity.'

To my amazement he sat back and roared with laughter. As I stared at him indignantly he stopped, took off his spectacles, wiped them and said:

'I'm sorry, Hillary. I shouldn't have treated your fears for me so lightly. But really, you are talking the most utter nonsense. Old Maria is a Pole. She was driven from her country in nineteen thirty-nine, and hates the Russians more than the most blimpish Colonel Blimp in the country. She has been with me for close on ten years, and the idea that she intends to poison me is fantastic.'

'You may think so,' I retorted grimly. 'But there is such a thing as pressure being exerted on refugees from the countries behind the Iron Curtain. She probably has an old mother, or a husband, or a son, still in Poland whom she cares for much more than she does you; and has been told that they will be put through the loop unless she carries out the orders that she is given.'

He nodded. 'Yes; that sort of thing does happen. But I think it most unlikely in this case. Upon what do you base this extraordinary charge?'

I told him then how on Thursday night, soon after he had

arrived at his cottage with his distinguished guest, Maria had telephoned to Klinsky; how Klinsky, kneeling at the key-hole of the dining room door, had listened to their conversation, and how the poison had been tried out on the cat.

After staring at me for a moment, he shot out: 'How do you know all this?'

'Because I was a witness to it,' I replied. 'Of course, it was entirely by accident that I stumbled on this plot. I came down to your cottage because Norton had been arrested that afternoon and it was my intention to ask you to intervene on his behalf.'

'Then why didn't you do so?'

His question was the first snag I had met with in telling my story. If I had replied by stating the truth he would never have believed me; and if he once got the idea that I had only been imagining things it was certain that he would ignore my warning. He would pack me off to a private nursing-home, then drive down to the cottage and to his death. I had no alternative but to lie to him, and I said:

'Finding you to be engaged with such an important visitor I didn't feel that I could interrupt you.'

'He left quite early. Why didn't you wait until he had gone and come in to me then?'

I took refuge in a half-truth. 'Because I thought it important to find out where Klinsky lived. I followed him home and could not find my way back to your cottage afterwards.'

'Since you were so concerned about Norton, why didn't you come to see me here the following morning?'

The following morning I had been lying in my grave. I shuddered at the recollection, as I replied a little lamely: 'I have already told you that I have been ill—desperately ill. Between then and now it has been impossible for me to get here—or even to ring you up.'

He nodded. 'Yes, nobody could contest your assertion that you have been ill; and that is the root of the matter. Your brain has become temporarily unbalanced during your illness. Now you are recovering that is nothing to worry about. It often happens when people have been under a great nervous strain, and you will soon be all right again. But in the meantime you have been building up fantasies in your mind with Soviet agents and myself as the central theme. I suppose you must have been down at my cottage on Thursday night to know about Maria and that I took a certain person down to dine with me there. But it is quite impossible for you to have seen all the happenings that you say you did. You couldn't have done without being seen yourself. They are simply figments of your imagination.'

Just as I feared, he was set upon rejecting my testimony because I could not tell the truth, and if I failed to convince him of his danger he would be on his way down to the cottage as soon as he had got rid of me. A little bitterly I said:

'All right, then. If you choose to believe that Maria is an angel and that Klinsky is only a product of my disordered brain, how about this?' Then I repeated to him a disparaging remark about one of their colleagues that his guest had made while they were sitting at dinner.

He sat back and his blue eyes goggled at me through the thick lenses. After a moment he said: 'Damn it; if you overheard that you must have been there. All right. I'll not go down tonight, and I'll have M.I.5 put tabs on Maria. But there's a lot that I don't understand about this yet. I think you had better begin at the beginning, and tell me how it is that while everyone believes you to be dead you are still alive.'

My efforts to convince him of his danger had taken a lot out of me. I was again very tired and I had not so far had a chance to think out how I was to account for my resurrection; so I took refuge in the obvious gambit and muttered:

'I don't really know myself. As I told you, I have been very ill. For one thing, I was in a car smash. I lost my memory, and have been wandering for a week.'

'Oh come!' he protested. 'Things can't have been quite like that. When you came down to my cottage on Thursbay evening you played the part of an observer remarkably well, and your memory must have been perfectly sound then for it to register so clearly all that you saw and heard. If your mental collapse occurred last week-end that would account for your not being able to explain why all the papers reported your death. On the other hand if it occurred after your visit to my cottage that would explain your not having come here to warn me about Maria on Friday or Saturday. But you can't have it both ways.'

'I . . . I had more or less recovered by Thursday,' I stammered wearily. 'But afterwards I had a relapse.'

On Sir Charles's face there was now no trace of the famous school-boy grin, and even if he still reminded one of a white-crested owl, it was no longer a benevolent one. He said harshly:

'Hillary, you are lying to me. You are hiding something. I want the truth. If you had lost your memory you would not be here now. Where have you been during the past week? Why were you reported as dead when you were not?'

Racked with fever and pain as I was, my brain proved unequal to producing even a remotely plausible explanation; but it did grasp the fact that sooner or later a part, at least, of the truth must come out; so I explained desperately:

'Very well then! Since you insist, everyone was misled into believing me dead by my having fallen into a coma. On Tuesday last I was buried alive.'

'Buried alive!' he gasped, starting forward in his chair. 'Do . . . do you really mean that?'

'Look at me!' I retorted bitterly. 'Look at me. Just now you said I had aged twenty years in a week. Can you think of anything more likely to do that to a man?'

'Good God, how terrible!' he sank back in his chair. 'But how . . . how did you escape from your grave?'

'Norton was never quite satisfied that I was dead. The thought preyed on his mind until he felt that he must make certain. He came to the churchyard at night and got me out of my coffin.'

For a moment Sir Charles stared at me in silence, then he said: 'It must have been ghastly for you, Hillary. It just doesn't bear thinking about. For how long were you actually buried?'

That was a question which it was impossible for me to answer truthfully. I had given him incontestable proof that I had been at his cottage on Thursday night. If I told him that I had remained buried from Tuesday midday till Saturday midnight, and that it was not my physical self but my Ka that had been a silent witness to Maria poisoning the cat, and all the rest of it, he would never have believed me. I took what I felt to be the only possible course, and replied with a half-truth, back-dating my ordeal by two days.

'I was in the grave for thirty-six hours. Norton got me out on Wednesday night.'

At once he seized upon the weak point in my story. 'If that is so, where were you all Friday and Saturday? You had recovered sufficiently by Thursday evening to come down to my cottage, and you were perfectly sane then. Why didn't you come here to warn me about Maria the following morning?'

I was at the end of my tether. Grasping the arm of the chair with my good hand, I levered myself to my feet and cried in protest: 'Damn it all! I have warned you! Isn't that enough? As for the rest, I've been ill! I don't know! I've forgotten!'

Sir Charles got to his feet. Moving round the desk he took me by the arm and led me through a door into the next room. A youngish man was working there on some papers. He stood up as we came in, and Sir Charles said to him:

'Geoffrey, this is Sir Gifford Hillary. I want you to look after him for the next quarter of an hour or so. He is very ill, so don't let him leave you; otherwise he might injure himself.'

The young man pushed forward a chair and I sank into it. Sir Charles returned to his own room. My temperature had mounted while I was talking and my mind began to wander again. The young man shot me a covert look of interest then resumed his work. The quarter of an hour and more drifted by. I was not thinking of myself, but of Johnny, and that everything had been made all right for him and Sue, when a buzzer sounded on the desk. My silent companion stood up, opened the door and nodded. Then he said to me:

'Sir Charles would like to see you again now.'

Getting to my feet, I walked slowly forward. The door closed behind me. With Sir Charles there were now two other men. They were standing in a little group in front of the desk.

As I advanced, Sir Charles said: 'Please don't think I am ungrateful, Hillary, for the warning you have brought me. But as a Minister of the Crown—or for that matter as an ordinary citizen—there are certain things which it is obligatory on me to do.'

The bulkier of his companions stepped forward. He had

Detective Inspector written all over him, and he said gruffly:

'Sir Gifford Hillary. It is my duty to take you into custody in connection with your own signed confession to the murder of Professor Owen Evans.'

15

18th to 30th September

They took me down to Brixton Prison in an ambulance and put me to bed in the infirmary there. The doctors stuffed me full of M and B, so saved me from pneumonia, and I had a narrow escape from brain fever; but my good constitution and normally placid mind saved me. After three days I was pronounced out of danger.

During that time I was not allowed any visitors. For all of Monday and a good part of Tuesday I was under drugs, and such thoughts as I had were mostly nightmarish memories of the hours I had spent in my coffin. But by Wednesday I was able to think clearly again and that evening I faced up to the task of deliberating on how I could best endeavour to free myself from the deadly web in which I had become entangled.

Next morning a Detective Inspector Watkins came to see me and asked if I was willing to make a statement. I replied that I was not until I had consulted my solicitor.

He smiled and said he had expected that would be the case, and that a Mr. Arnold had notified them that he wished to see me as soon as I was up to receiving visitors; so they would let him know that he could come along that afternoon.

At about three o'clock Eddie arrived. The sight of my old friend cheered me a lot. His short plump figure and lively brown eyes still recalled the fine airman he had proved himself in the war, and I knew the good brain that lay under his broad forehead.

He could not conceal the shock he got at the first sight of my sunken cheeks and snow-white hair; but, quickly recovering, he took me by both hands and cried:

'Dear old Giff! What a wonderful thing to know that we have not lost you after all. I can't tell you how overjoyed I was when I first heard that you were still alive.'

I smiled rather ruefully. 'Thanks, Eddie. But the question now is can you manage to keep me so.'

'I know.' His forehead wrinkled as he sat down beside my bed. 'Of course, this frightful business of your having been buried alive gives the whole thing the flavour of one of Edgar Allan Poe's "Tales of Mystery and Imagination"; but there are certain basic facts connected with your presumed death that we can't get away from. I hope you haven't yet made a statement to the police?'

'No. I said I must consult you first.'

'Good I think we'll have to give them something, though. Innocent people rarely refuse to talk at all; so now you have had a chance to recover from the shock, and your mind is clear again, it would not be good policy just to dig your in and keep on saying "I don't remember". Unless, of course, that is the truth.'

'I remember everything only too damn well,' I admitted. 'But I am in favour of taking that line. If I do and say that I have had a complete black-out right from the beginning, you might get me off on a plea of insanity.'

He shook his head. 'I don't like it, Giff. As your friend I was delighted to find that you have come through this horrible experience so well; but as your solicitor I can't ignore the fact that you are now as sane as I am. The doctors can tell the symptoms of anyone who has recently been out of their mind for a week. You would never be able to pull that one on them. Besides, although you haven't made a statement to the police, I understand that you talked to Sir Charles.'

'I said nothing to him about what happened at Longshot on the night of the tragedy.'

'No; but you did about going to his cottage last Thursday evening. And by all accounts you were perfectly sane then. That makes it impossible for you to maintain that you have no idea what you have been up to all this time.'

'Am I bound,' I asked, 'by everything I said to Sir Charles?'

'Not necessarily. You are known to have been very ill when you saw him; so we could say you did not know what you were talking about. A judge would accept that and rule that it should not be admitted as evidence. But you must remember that he repeated to the police all that you said to him within a quarter of an hour of you saying it; so although we can prevent them from using it we can never expunge it from their minds, and if you go back on it they are less likely to believe anything else you may say. But don't put too much weight on that. The really important thing is that the statement we are about to put in should be as watertight as possible.'

I had asked the question because I had told Sir Charles that it was on Wednesday night that Johnny had got me out of my grave, and I had not definitely made up my mind—that is if I made any statement at all—whether to stick to that or tell the truth about it having been Saturday. As it was only by sticking to Wednesday that I could explain having been a witness to the events at Sir Charles's cottage the following night, I had already all but decided—should I find myself compelled to talk—to do so; and what Eddie had just said finally decided me on that course.

While I was silently settling this highly-important point, Eddie had been going on: 'I'm sure it would be best to wash out any idea of pleading insanity. If the crime of which you are accused had been committed after you had been buried alive that would be very different. Such a frightful experience might have driven anyone off their nut. But it wasn't. You were not put into your coffin until many hours after Evans was dead.'

Still clinging to the belief that my best hope lay in pretending that my mind had gone blank, I said: 'The ordeal I have been through might have robbed me of my memory.'

He shrugged. 'It might; but it hasn't. And unfortunately I am not the only person who knows that. The fact that we can prevent Sir Charles from testifying in court to what you told him makes no essential difference. Through him the police know that you were in full possession of your faculties when you were down at his cottage on Thursday night, and that was twenty-four hours after Johnny Norton had rescued you. As you still knew what you were up to then no one is ever going to believe that you have lost your memory since. The police are up against that sort of thing every day of their lives. They have ways and means of dealing with it; and it is a certainty that they would catch you out in no time. Honestly, Giff, I'm sure your best course would be to tell me the whole story of what led up to your killing Evans, and leave it to me to do my damnedest to save you from the worst by pleading extenuating circumstances.'

With a pale smile, I said: 'I didn't kill him. He killed me; or thought he had.'

Eddie's eyes opened wide. 'D'you really mean that?'

'Yes, that's the way it was. Cross my heart.'

'But . . . but,' he stammered, 'how about that letter? You confessed to killing him in it, and said you meant to commit suicide. Look here, old man, if I'm to be of any help you really must put me in the picture.'

He had convinced me now that to play dumb would not save me, and might even make my case worse. Tempted as I was by the idea, I had feared it might prove so; and, in consequence, during the past twenty-four hours I had thought out a story which, with a little luck, might be accepted.

It was obviously out of the question to tell them the truth. Evans's death ray machine had been totally destroyed in the fire, and nobody would believe that it had ever existed. Far less would they believe that while my body had remained inert, and dead enough to deceive the doctors, my Ka had been floating about observing all the major events which had followed on the tragedy. In planning my story I had had entirely to exclude the supernatural, and to bear in mind that I should have known nothing of events which had taken place between the Friday night when Evans 'killed' me and the Wednesday night when Johnny got me out of the grave— except for the main outline of events, which he would obviously have told me. To Eddie I said:

'All right. Here goes. I'll come to the letter in due course. On the seventh of this month, a Wednesday, I went to London. By a previously-made arrangement I met Sir Charles that evening at the flat of a mutual friend. We had a long discussion on future strategy; and having informed me that a contract to build two more E-boats was being offered to the Company he persuaded me to get my board to reject it.

'That, of course, is neither here nor there; except for the fact that on that Wednesday night I was away from Longshot and Evans seized on my absence to make a pass at Ankaret. And when I say a pass that does not adequately describe it. He got into her room after she had gone to bed and begged

362

her to let him sleep with her. When she tried to turn him out he tore her night-dress off and did his damnedest to rape her.

'I thought her manner a bit constrained when I got back on Thursday; but I knew nothing of what had happened until Friday evening. After we had had dinner together she asked me to give Evans the sack. Naturally I said I wouldn't unless she could give me a reason. Then it all came out. She admitted that while she had been laid up with her broken leg she had been so bored that she had entered on a mild flirtation with him; but nothing that could possibly justify his brutal attempt on her. She said that she had had the devil's own job to fight him off, and that nothing would induce her to stay another night in the house alone with him except for the servants.

'Well, I saw red. I don't mean with her. Of course it was silly of her to encourage him in the first place, and she ought at least to have formed some idea of the passion she was arousing in time to pour cold water on it before it came to a head; but you can be certain of one thing—she never had the faintest intention of taking a little runt like that as a lover. No. The thing that made me see red was the mental picture of Evans in my bed struggling to overcome Ankaret.

'Don't run away with the idea, though, that I meant to kill him. Such an idea never even entered my mind. You must know, Eddie, that I'm not that sort of chap. And when I say that I saw red you mustn't get the impression that I didn't know what I was doing. I mean only that I made up my mind that before sacking him I would give him a lesson it would take him a long time to forget.

'Outwardly I was perfectly calm. Having kissed Ankaret's tears away, I went up to Evans and suggested to him that as it was a nice night we should take a stroll on the beach while he told me what he had been working on recently in his lab. All unsuspecting he agreed, so out we went. My intention, of course, when I got him down by the beach pavilion was to give him a darn' good hiding. But things didn't pan out quite that way.

'When we reached the shore I told him that Ankaret had spilled the beans to me and exactly what I thought of him.

Like the little rat he was he squealed at that, and swore that she had led him to expect that she would give him all she had got, and was only waiting for the chance to do so. That led to a slanging match. For a few minutes we shouted abuse, calling one another every filthy name we could think of.

'Then I hit him. He staggered back against the veranda of the beach house. The edge of the boards caught him behind the knees and he went over on to them. I dived after him to yank him up and hit him again. But he was too quick for me. Rolling over he scrambled to his feet, grabbed up a folding chair and flung it at me. One of its wooden arms caught me a crack on the temple. I saw stars, then everything went black and I folded up.'

On that dramatic note I ended, feeling that I had told my story well, and waiting with interest for Eddie's reactions. They were not long in coming, and it was obvious that he believed me.

He let out a low whistle. 'What rotten luck! Fancy that little devil getting the better of you. But what happened then?'

I gave him a smile which I flatter myself was as enigmatic as one of Ankaret's. 'How should I know? From that moment my mind was a complete blank until some half hour after Johnny got me out of my coffin. About what followed, your guess is as good as mine; or nearly so.'

'But the letter,' he protested, 'How do you account for the letter?'

'I have a theory about that,' I told him. 'and in my own mind it amounts to a certainty. Of course, as both Evans and Ankaret are dead no one will ever learn the full truth about what happened after I was knocked out. But as I was so close to her, the way her mind worked, her character and her capabilities were an open book to me; so my speculations have probably brought me nearer to the truth than anyone else will ever get.'

'Let's hear them, Giff,' he said eagerly.

'Ankaret was the great love of my life and I was the great love of hers. You may perhaps have heard rumours that when she went abroad for winter holidays on her own she had affairs on the side. She did, but I knew about it and condoned them. Naturally that gave me a lot of pain when I first found out about it, but when I learned that they were entirely physical I accepted the situation, just as one might have on finding that one's wife was a victim of kleptomania, occasional bouts of secret drinking, or some other neurosis. The fact that I did so made her love me even more profoundly. Without me she would have drifted from man to man, and God only knows what would have been the end of her. But I was her sheet-anchor—the one person who brought out all that was best in her and gave her life some purpose. To appreciate the sort of shape events must have taken after Evans knocked me out, you must keep that central fact in mind.

'Now Evans. Consider the situation in which he found himself. Two nights before he had done his damnedest to force Ankaret and now, as he must have thought, he had killed me. If he reported to the police what he had done, what hope would he have had? He could plead self-defence, but could not prove that it was I who had attacked him and not he who had attacked me. Had our quarrel had some other cause he might have got away with manslaughter; but not in this case. There isn't a jury in the country that would have shown him mercy after Ankaret had gone into the box, as she would have done and described how he had tried to rape her. As he stood there on the beach looking down at my body he must almost have felt the hangman's rope round his neck.

'I haven't the least doubt that he decided that his only chance of not being convicted of murder lay in his making my death appear an accident. He must have carried my body to the end of the pier and pushed it off into the water.

'What happened next we shall never know. It is possible that Ankaret heard us shouting abuse at one another before I went for him, and came down from the house to try to intervene. If so she might have arrived in time actually to see him push me off the end of the pier. If that was not so, he must have been in a shocking state of nerves and funk when he got back to the house; so he may have broken down and confessed to her. Again, he must have known that she was expecting me to return shortly and go up to bed with her; so when I failed to return up she would institute a search and later, fearing I had met with an accident, call the police in. He seems, from what he said during our quarrel, to have believed quite mistakingly that she really had a soft spot for him; so fearing that he would not be able to stand up to questioning that night he may have told her the truth and begged her to take no action till the morning. Anyhow, one way or another Ankaret must have learned that he had killed me.

'Why she should have gone with him to the lab I have no idea; but by then she must have been seized with a fit of uncontrollable grief and rage at the thought that he had robbed her of me, grabbed up the steel rod and bashed his head in.'

Eddie gave me a puzzled look and asked: 'As you were to all intents and purposes dead, Giff, how is it that you know where and how he met his end?'

For a second I was caught off guard; but I recovered quickly enough to set his mind at rest by saying: 'Johnny Norton told me that had taken place, after he rescued me.'

'Of course,' he nodded. 'Stupid of me not to have realised that he would. Well, go on.'

'Next, then, we have to reconstruct Ankaret's reactions after she had done in Evans. Just think of what the poor girl was faced with when she recovered from her frenzy, believing my dead body to be somewhere out in the Solent and seeing the Prof's lying a bleeding mess on the floor. There could be no passing his death off as an accident, or suicide. He had been murdered; there was no escaping that. And only two people could have murdered him—she or myself.

'Most women would have collapsed and let matters take their course. But what would have happened if she had? It would probably have come out that she had been having an affair with Evans, and someone would have dug up all the dirt about her affairs in the South of France. Moreover she could not plead that she killed Evans in self-defence, because she had not just knocked him out, but had struck at him again and again until his head was a pulp. She must have known that she would be reviled as a sort of Messalina, who took lovers and had not stopped at murder when she wanted to get rid of one. It is pretty certain they would have hung her, or at least given her a life sentence, which for a girl like her would have been worse.

'That she did not collapse may seem surprising; but Ankaret came of a long line of tough aristocrats, most of whom had been born and bred to fight in England's wars and face up to every sort of dangerous situation. From them she had inherited tremendous guts. Once she had regained full control of herself she must have decided that the only way to save herself was to father Evans's death on me.

'After all, she believed me to be dead, who can blame her? She must have gone downstairs and . . .'

'Surely, Giff,' Eddie cut in, 'you are not going to suggest that Ankaret forged that letter?'

'I certainly am,' I assured him.

'No, old man; no. I've followed your theories so far with the greatest interest, and to me they sound quite plausible. Evans's having been scared into trying to cover up his crime in the way you suggest is entirely in keeping with human nature. Ankaret's killing of him afterwards is less so; although having regard for the great love she bore you it is by no means improbable. So far we would be on pretty sound ground but for one thing—the letter. And that blows the whole of the rest sky high. You couldn't have written it before he knocked you out, because the premises for what is in it did not exist, and to have fabricated them would have been completely pointless.'

'But I didn't write it; Ankaret did.'

He shook his head unhappily. 'I'm sorry, but you can't expect me, of all people, to swallow that. I know your writing as well as I know my own, and I naturally got in touch with the police as soon as I heard of your arrest. They have shown me all the exhibits in the case. Much as I should hate having to do it, if I were called on in court to identify the writing in that letter I would have to swear to it being yours.'

'Then you would be wrong. I tell you it was Ankaret who wrote it.'

'What possible proof can you advance in support of this extraordinary statement?'

'Unfortunately none; except that I know her to have been an expert forger.'

'Ankaret a forger! So's my Aunt Sally! Sorry, Giff, I didn't mean to be rude; but really, old man . . . Still, go ahead. What sort of things did she forge? Have you any examples of her work that you can produce? How many people can you bring to testify to this unusual activity of hers?'

I made a wry face. 'That's just the trouble. The only visual evidence we can produce lies in her drawings, which show the extraordinary ability she had for copying anything she set her mind to with minute exactness. She did have a scrap-book into which she copied the handwriting of a number of famous historical personages; but I haven't seen that for years, and I've no idea what she did with it. As for people knowing about this peculiar talent that she had, we are little better off; because she had no occasion to use it. Her father and brother might, but I doubt if anyone else would. It is ages since the subject has even been mentioned between us, but when we were first married she used to joke about it. I remember her saying once that one day she might have to forge a really big cheque to get me out of a mess. Poor darling, she little thought then that her gift would land me with my head in a noose.'

Eddie was looking extremely uncomfortable. After a moment, he said: 'If I were not a personal friend of yours, and you insisted on sticking to this line, I should tell you that you must get some other solicitor to conduct your case. As it is I'm much too fond of you to do that. But I implore you, Giff, to abandon all thought of basing your defence on the contention that Ankaret wrote that letter. I want to get the very best man I can to act as your counsel, and I had in mind Sir Bindon Buller; but no one approaching his eminence would accept the brief if he has to fight on such a wildly improbable assumption. Please let's forget all that we've said in the past three-quarters of an hour, and start again at the beginning.'

'That is all very well,' I replied. 'I greatly appreciate your loyalty, Eddie, and the last thing I want is to make things difficult for you. But you must see that the letter is the crucial factor in the whole issue. Apart from it, there is not one scrap of evidence against me. You have already agreed that my theory about Evans putting me in the Solent and Ankaret killing him afterwards is quite plausible. But whether that is accepted or not makes no material difference to my case, provided it can be proved that I did not write that letter. If I did not, the person who did would have done so only after he or she believed me to be dead, and with the object

368

of fastening the murder of Evans upon me. Ankaret alone could have had a motive for doing that, and to my knowledge she was capable of forging my writing. That is my case, and I mean to stand or fall by it.'

He nodded. 'Very well, Giff. If that's the way you feel there is no more to be said. Of course, you are dead right in your contention that if the letter could be proved a forgery that would put you in the clear. But I'm afraid it will be the devil's own job to get a jury to believe us. Naturally the last thing I would suggest is that you should confess to a crime you did not commit; but, to be honest, when I came here I was hoping you would instruct me to enter a plea of homicide committed under intense provocation. I think we might have got you off then with a ten-year sentence.'

'Ten years!' I gave a bitter laugh. 'No thanks! I have been too near death this past week to have any fear of a quick one. I prefer to gamble all against nothing. Get all the handwriting experts whose opinion is worth a damn to examine that letter against genuine examples of my writing. Have Ankaret's things at Longshot searched to see if you can dig up that historical scrap-book of hers, and collect all her drawings which are copies of others. Ask Bill and her brother Roc if they ever remember her forging anything. That's what I want you to do.'

'All right,' he agreed. 'I'll do my best about the letter. Now, how about the rest of this awful business. I'd be interested to hear your views, particularly on Ankaret's suicide. It has been generally assumed that she took her life during a fit of acute depression resulting from your death. But, accepting for the moment your theory that it was she who killed Evans, she might have done so for a very different reason. If she did, and we could prove it, that would immensely strengthen your case.'

If only Johnny had succeeded in retaining possession of Ankaret's trial forgeries nothing else would have been needed to prove my innocence; but, most unfortunately for me, he had been robbed of them by the fire that Ankaret had started. Still worse, he had never been aware of their existence; so he could not even testify to having seen them. It was only through my Ka that I knew them to have been among the papers he had taken from my desk, so all I could reply to Eddie was:

369

'I believe you may be right about that. From something Johnny Norton said to me when he was bringing me up to London I gathered that he knew about Ankaret's infidelities, and suspected that, owing to a love affair she was having with a man unknown to any of us, she was in part responsible for my death. That, of course, was simply speculation, and had no foundation in fact. But she may have made some slip; and, guessing that Johnny suspected her, feared that he was on the point of finding her out. If that was the case it is quite on the cards that rather than face the music she decided to quit. We will never know for certain, though; so there doesn't seem much point in pursuing the matter.'

'No; but all the same we'll produce it as a theory,' Eddie said quickly. 'Now that we are committed to basing our defence on the letter having been forged by Ankaret we can't afford to neglect anything which would help to bear that out. And fear of being charged with murder is a much stronger motive for suicide than the loss of a husband, however well beloved. Tell me, now, about Johnny Norton. His having pulled you out of your grave has no bearing on the case, but I am curious to know what led him to believe that you might not be dead.'

'I suppose it was a hunch more than anything,' I replied guardedly. 'He says that when he saw me put into my coffin I didn't look dead. Of course, he knew about my fear of being buried alive, and the air-holes and all that. The idea that those precautions might have been ordered by me as the outcome of a premonition occurred to him, and he could not rid himself of it. Eventually he decided that he had simply got to find out. He did and saved me from a most agonising death; so whatever may happen now I can never be sufficiently grateful to him.'

Eddie nodded. 'I take my hat off to him for his pluck in going to a graveyard and opening up a coffin in the middle of the night. In addition to all else it is, of course, a serious offence. I've no doubt that in view of the result I'll be able to get him off; but if you had been dead and he had been caught in the act, he would have got a prison sentence.'

'Do you mean to say that a case is being brought against him?' I cried in angry surprise.

370

'Yes. According to the law they had no option. The breach of the Official Secrets' Act charge against him was withdrawn on Monday; but the civil police took him over and preferred this charge of unlawfully interfering with a grave. But you don't have to worry about him. No court could possibly convict him for having gone to the rescue of a man whom he believed to have been buried alive, when it turned out that he was right.'

'Thank God for that! I would like to see him as soon as possible. Can you arrange for him to be allowed to come and visit me?'

As I asked the question I endeavoured to conceal my eagerness. I felt that I had done as well as could be expected with Eddie, and that I could now rely on him to instruct counsel for the defence on the lines which offered me my best chance of an acquittal. But it seemed to me of the utmost importance that I should have a talk with Johnny so that we could work out together exactly what each of us was going to say, and not contradict one another should he be called as a witness at my trial.

To my alarm Eddie shook his head. 'I'm afraid that is out of the question, Giff. The police won't allow you to have any visitors who are in any way connected with the case.'

On second thoughts I became easier in my mind. It was a sure thing that Johnny would not say anything to anyone about Daisy and how it was her seeing my Ka which had really determined him to come to my grave. He would confirm what I had said about his simply having a hunch about that I was not dead. He would confirm, too, that he had had his suspicions about Ankaret; and that would be all to the good. As for what had happened after he had rescued me, if our stories differed somewhat that could be put down to my version being incorrect owing to my mind not having fully recovered from the effects of my ordeal. Anyway, as I saw it then, no discrepancies in our accounts of my resurrection could have any bearing on the case against me for a murder committed in the previous week.

Eddie's next question to me was on that very subject, and to it I replied: 'When Johnny got me out of my coffin I was unconscious, and for many hours afterwards I regained consciousness only for short intervals; so naturally my memories

371

are fragmentary and confused, but this is more or less what happened.

'He took me back to Longshot and garaged the car with me in it. Evidently he realised at once that having come alive again I was liable to be charged with Evans's murder, and he wanted to give me a chance to recover before letting anyone else know about my resurrection. From the house he fetched things to revive me and plenty of warm clothes. Having brought me round and dressed me he gave me a couple of pain-killers and tucked me up in the back of the car, then left me to sleep.

'When I next came round it was mid-morning and we were on the road to London. He gave me some more pain-killers and I dozed off again. I woke when we pulled up outside his rooms in Nevern Square. He got me upstairs and put me to bed. It was while doing so that he told me about the deaths of Evans and Ankaret, and gave me an outline of what had been going on. Then he had to leave me because he had had an urgent summons to the Air Ministry. I slept again.

'About five o'clock he returned to pack a suit-case while another officer waited in his sitting-room. He had not wanted to trouble me with his own worries before, but he told me then about the accusation Sir Tuke Waldron had made against him, and that he had been placed under close arrest. I told him that I could get Sir Charles to clear him, and having enjoined me to stay where I was, off he went.

'But when he had gone I began to worry about him. You must remember that I had been out of my grave for only about fifteen hours. As I had slept for a great part of that time I was more or less recovered physically, but my mind was still far from normal. Sometime during our drive up to London Johnny had told me about the letter I was supposed to have written, but that, and Ankaret's death, all seemed to be a part of a prolonged nightmare and I had not yet grasped the fact that I was liable to be charged with Evans's murder. You see, as I was innocent it never occurred to me that I was in danger until I was actually arrested in Sir Charles's office on Sunday afternoon. On the other hand Johnny's arrest was fresh and clear in my mind, and I became obsessed with the thought that it was incumbent on me to waste not a moment in clearing him.

'In consequence I got up, dressed, telephoned Sir Charles's office and learned that he was on his way down to his cottage in the country. Johnny had left me money to give his land-lady to buy me food. I used some of it to go to Waterloo and take a train down to Farnham. From there I hitch-hiked out to the cottage.'

Having got so far in my blend of fact and fiction I told Eddie the truth about the events there which had been wit-nessed by my Ka, then went on:

'After I had shadowed Klinsky to the farmhouse, I meant to return to the cottage and warn Sir Charles of what was going on, but I lost my way in the wood and eventually struck the village two or three miles away from it. There I cadged a lift from a man with a car. He had just come out of a pub and no sooner had we set off than I realised that he had had several over the odds. About a mile outside the village he took a corner too fast and we came to grief in the ditch. Both of us struck our heads on the wind-screen and passed out.

'When I came to he was still inconscious and my right hand had somehow become a nasty mess. I managed to struggle out and stagger away in the darkness bent on getting help. But this last shock proved too much for my already-overburdened brain. It was then I lost my memory. I haven't the faintest idea where I was or what I was doing during Friday and Saturday. Probably I was wandering in the woods again or for most of the time lying unconscious in some barn or outhouse. It wasn't till Sunday morning that I found myself on the road between Thursley and Godalming. I had no idea what day it was and the one thing that had stuck in my mind was the urgency of warning Sir Charles that his house-keeper meant to poison him. I felt ravenously hungry, so I had a meal in the first wayside café I came to, went on to Godalming, caught the next train to London and took a taxi to the Ministry of Defence. You know the rest.'

As I finished I felt that I had put up a very good show. Johnny had given me the idea of saying that the injury to my hand had occurred in a car smash, and I had already told Sir Charles that it was having been in one that had caused me to lose my memory; so it fitted in excellently and enabled me to explain away the two days unaccounted for between my Ka's visit to his cottage and the actual night of my rescue.

Eddie took in all that part of my story without a murmur; then he set about drafting for the police a statement of my version of what had occurred. As soon as he had done, Inspector Watkins was called in, it was read over and I signed it. Then, when the Inspector had gone, Eddie said.

'There is one thing that still beats me, Giff. How on earth could the doctors have passed you for dead when you were not?'

I shrugged. 'Ask me another. Only Johnny seems to have had any doubts about the matter, and that was two days later, when he saw me put into my coffin. Still, there is one possible explanation. You may remember me telling you sometime or other that after I was shot down in Burma I was invalided back to India suffering from a wretched nervous disorder. As the British doctors failed to cope with it I went to an Indian, and he prescribed various exercises in Yoga. He taught me how to put myself into a self-induced trance, in order to rest my nervous system. I became quite good at it, and he said that I would make an excellent subject for attempting long comas, such as the Fakirs practise to disipline themselves. I can only suppose that when Evans knocked me out I passed into one instead of coming round, and that the doctors mistook my suspended animation for death.'

With a quick nod, Eddie said: 'I think you've got something there. Looking at it from their point of view, they would have been pretty astonished if they had found you alive when they had been told that you had been washed ashore after spending a night in the Solent. Their minds would have been further prejudiced, too, from knowing about the letter, in which it was said that you meant to take an overdose of some Indian heart dope as a prelude to committing suicide. I don't think doctors often make mistakes like that; but in your case, now you have told me about this coma business, it certainly seems that they had grounds for doing so.'

We talked on for another hour or so, and I think my insistence that the suicide letter had been forged by Ankaret eventually convinced Eddie that I was innocent; and that the events following my death must have taken more or less the pattern I had described.

374

Anyway, having promised to do his utmost for me, he left in a far more cheerful frame of mind than he had arrived. I, too, felt much more optimistic about my chances, for I had brought off a terrific *tour-de-force* in reconstruction, and succeeded in explaining away the almost inexplicable.

At least, I thought I had. I had yet to learn the terrifying thoroughness of a police investigation, which was utterly to destroy my house of cards; and the wrong but appalling conclusion they would come to as the result of it.

* * * *

Eddie Arnold has proved a true friend. Since that first talk we had in the prison infirmary he has worked night and day on my case. Sacrificing every other matter connected with his large and valuable practice he has been up and down between Longshot and Brixton a dozen times, interviewed scores of people, and spent many many hours with myself, with counsel and at Scotland Yard. But he has been fighting a losing battle.

The day following that on which I made my statement I was taken down to Southampton in a Black Maria, and formally charged before a magistrate. I pleaded not guilty and reserved my defence. After I had been committed for trial at Winchester Eddie accompanied me to Southampton prison and we had another long talk.

The first thing he asked me was if I were prepared to confirm absolutely definitely that it had been on the Wednesday night that Johnny had rescued me. Then he added:

'Before you answer me I ought to tell you that Johnny Norton has been questioned and he declares categorically that it was Saturday night; or, rather, during the early hours of Sunday morning.'

I pretended surprise, and replied: 'How very extraordinary. Worry over this wretched business must have addled his wits even more than it has mine. Anyhow, at least I am clear on that point I am prepared to take my oath that it was Wednesday.'

Eddie gave a couple of his vigorous nods. 'I felt sure you would be. It was obvious to me that Norton could not be right otherwise it would have been impossible for you to be down at Sir Charles's cottage on Thursday evening.'

That, of course, was the crux of the whole matter. Whether Johnny had succeeded in getting back undetected into camp early on Sunday morning, I did not know. But I did know that if he had he would wish to continue to protect Tinegate, if that were possible. Moreover, I had told him about my Ka's visit to Sir Charles's cottage, so I had counted on his realising that unless I said I had been there in my physical body I should never be believed. Finally, if he had said it was Wednesday nobody could have contradicted him, because that was the night on which he had actually been in the churchyard on his abortive attempt to find out if I was still alive; and, as far as I could see at that time, it made not a ha'p'orth of difference to his own case which night he said it was.

With those points in mind I had thought it a good bet that, although I had been prevented from tipping him off, he would spontaneously corroborate my statement. That he had not done so could, I felt, probably be put down to his having failed to appreciate that once my having visited the cottage in the flesh was called into question everything else would be. It was on that account that I had no alternative but to stick to my guns. But I asked with an anxiety that I did my best to conceal:

'Did he say anything about having consulted someone with psychic gifts on whether I was dead or alive, before he decided to go and find out for himself?'

'No; why? Did he?' Eddie replied.

I shook my head. 'Not as far as I know. It was just a thought that he might have; but I think I only imagined he had in one of my nightmares. Anyhow whether he did or not is immaterial.'

Eddie's innocent reply was, to me, far from immaterial. I knew by then that he was acting for Johnny as well as for myself, and it told me as plainly as an answer to a straight question could have done that Johnny had said nothing about my Ka. As matters stood my case seemed to me a pretty clear-cut one; but if he had brought the supernatural into it that would have upset the whole apple-cart, and I should have found myself up to my neck in a morass of lies and contradictions. My relief that he had kept his own counsel about that can be imagined.

During the three days that followed Eddie came to see me four or five times, and on two of his visits he brought that fat, hairy, dynamic and most eminent Q.C., Sir Bindon Bullock, with him.

Sir Bindon made no secret of the fact that he did not like the case on account of my insistence that the defence should be based on the letter having been forged by Ankaret. He would have much preferred me to plead that I had beaten Evans to death during a fit of insane jeolousy, and put my trust in him to get me off with a life sentence, or perhaps only seven years. But I dug my toes in and told him to take it or leave it.

That he did take it was, I have no doubt, on account of the immense publicity he would get out of the case. On the evening of my committal for trial banner headlines had appeared in the papers—

SIR GIFFORD HILLARY RETURNS FROM GRAVE— NOW ACCUSED OF MURDER

and although the police had so far refused to issue a statement the press was rife with speculation. When my trial came on and the full story broke there could be no doubt that it would prove a *cause célèbre*, and the temptation to be well in the centre of the limelight had proved irresistible to Sir Bindon.

I was still pretty groggy; so I was being treated with every consideration, and I had been put into a single-bed cubicle, so that I could consult with my legal advisers in private. Sir Bindon's bulk half filled the free space in the little room, and, seated on a chair which I felt might give way under his weight at any moment, he fired innumerable questions at me.

It was an exhausting business, but I stuck to my story in every particular and, I think, eventually persuaded him that it was the truth. Eddie studiously refrained from saying anything, for the time being, which might shake the great man's growing faith in me, but I knew that he was much more worried than he appeared to be.

He told me at one of our private sessions that there was a time when the beans would have to be spilled to counsel but for the moment he thought it best to leave well alone. Then in that, and other talks we had, he disclosed to me the many nasty hurdles which one by one would be erected against us by the prosecution.

From the servants at Longshot the police had verified the fact that Ankaret had been having an affair with Evans. Mildred had actually come upon them together in Ankaret's bedroom, so it was supposed that matters had gone further than I thought. That did not worry me as I knew that they hadn't; but the next item did.

They had found out about Ankaret's previous affairs, and from someone like Desmond Chawton that I had played the part of a complacent husband. That being so, they argued, why should I have been so enraged with Evans? I had not endeavoured to beat up any of Ankaret's other lovers, so why him? In the letter I was alleged to have written it was stated that she had confessed to flirting with him, then asked me to get rid of him. Surely, in view of her past, my normal reaction would have been to tell her that I would do so, but that she had brought his assault on herself. If so, I should have gone quite calmly to the lab with the intention only of giving him the sack; so it must have been some taunt he had flung at me while there which had caused me to go berserk and murder him.

Further doubt was cast upon my story that I had lured him down to the beach with the intention of thrashing him by the fact that as I was far the stronger it seemed unlikely that I should have come off worst in the encounter.

That might have been ill-luck; but I had said that he had thrown the chair at me, not struck me with it. The furnishings of the beach house at Longshot had been inspected. The chairs were of two kinds only; full length mattress-covered lounges —which were much too heavy and cumbersome for Evans to have picked up—and collapsible canvas and wood affairs; so it must have been to one of the latter that I had referred. Seized by a leg and wielded it could have made a moderately dangerous weapon, but thrown defensively, almost at random and on the spur of the moment, it was so light that it could have been knocked aside; so the odds were all against its having done me serious damage.

Johnny, Silvers, Dr. Culver, the Police Surgeon and the Undertaker's people had all been asked if they had noticed a cut, bruise or abrasion on either of my temples. None of them had.

That was a particulary nasty one.

Evans was a small man, while I was a large and heavy fellow. From the beach house to the end of the pier was a good hundred and twenty yards. Experiments with a dummy figure loaded to my weight and dragged by a man of Evans's size had shown that such a feat was possible only by most desperate efforts and with frequent rests.

When that point was put to me I remembered, only too well, how Evans had pleaded with and finally threatened Ankaret because her help was so essential to him in carrying my body downstairs; and how they had had to use a wheelbarrow to get it down to the beach. I ought to have said in my statement to the police that I had meant to give Evans a ducking so before going for him had lured him to the end of the pier. But it was too late to think of that now.

Why, they asked too, if he had dragged my body so far across the beach and over the rough planks of the pier had my clothes not sustained the smallest tear, or my face and limbs showed any trace of bruising—and the woman who had washed my corpse had declared that there was not a blemish on it.

The police had timed their experiment with the weighted dummy and the little man, and it had taken close on an hour. That ruled out my suggestion that, hearing the noise of the quarrel, Ankaret had come down to the beach at once and arrived just in time to see Evans pushing my body off the end of the pier. If she had heard nothing, would she not have gone up to bed and waited for me to join her there? Why, anyhow, should she have gone with Evans into the laboratory? Yet, if I was right about it being she who had killed him, she must have done so.

Why had my velvet smoking jacket been found in the labor-

379

atory? It would have been natural enough for me to take it off down by the beach house if I had intended to fight Evans. But its being found in the lab implied that I had taken it off before going for him there—and with the steel rod, instead of with my fists.

Was it really believable that Ankaret had beaten Evans to death? She had been a slender girlish woman weighing only seven stone ten. He, although small compared to myself had been a well set-up little man, and certainly no weakling. It was regarded as unlikely that she had laid him out with her first stroke as, had she done so, to inflect his other injuries she would then have had to prop him up, and it was highly improbable that her anger, however great, would have led her to such an act of vicious brutality against an unconscious body. Yet, if her first stroke had not knocked him out, surely, being so much the stronger, he would have been able to wrench the rod out of her hand overcome her.

Again, his head had received such a battering that the experts declared it impossible for a comparatively frail woman to have inflicted it unless abnormal strength had been lent her by madness. Admitting that Ankaret had possessed abnormal strength while carried away by a frenzy, was it conceivable that within an hour or so her brain would have been restored to the cold calculating calm needed to plan the letter, and her hand been under the absolute control required to forge it? The prosecution would argue that I could not have it both ways.

As my Ka had been a witness to the whole business, and this part of the theory I had advanced was an exact description of what had actually happened, it seemed hard that it should be disputed. But I had to admit that these arguments stood a good chance of being accepted by a jury.

On the question of the all-important letter I fared no better. Eddie collected from Longshot a score of Ankaret's beautiful drawings which were line perfect copies of famous originals, but it was argued that they were no proof at all that she was capable of forging handwriting; and, as I feared might prove the case, the historical scrap-book she had shown me years ago could not be found.

With Bill the police got in before Eddie had a chance to get at him. When questioned he said that Ankaret had been marvellous at copying anything, but he had never known her to go in for forgery. He had then hindered rather than helped by adding, with unconscious facetiousness, that as a little girl she had astonished everyone by being so good at her pot-hooks and hangers.

Ankaret's brother, Roc, was found to have left England for Africa at the beginning of the month with a Film Unit; so could not be got hold of.

The handwriting experts were equally unhelpful. The Scotland Yard specialist was ready and willing to go into the box and swear that the writing was mine. Of the best half-dozen outside men to whom Eddie submitted the letter with samples of my writing only two expressed any doubt about it, and neither of those was prepared to stake their reputation by appearing for the defence and declaring in court that the letter was a forgery.

Not content with a most thorough investigation of Evans's murder and my own presumed death, the police were also busily delving into the contradictory accounts given by Johnny and myself of his rescue of me, and the account I had given of my movement afterwards.

Apparently Johnny had succeeded in getting back unde-tected into the camp at Uxbridge early on Sunday morning; and, until he had been called on by the police to make a state-ment describing his rescue of me, no one had suspected that he had ever left it. That he had he was able to prove by his having knocked up Silvers in the middle of the night. But Silvers could only say he had collected some papers and made himself coffee in the kitchen. There was no evidence at all that I had been in the garage while he was in the house; or that it had been then that he had collected some of my clothes. He might equally well have taken them for me on the Wed-nesday night.

Again, he could produce no proof that it was on Sunday that I had spent some ten hours in his rooms, or that I had been in them after his arrest. As he had brought me there very early on Sunday morning and left again by six-thirty, and I had left during the quite of Sunday after noon, no one had seen either of us come or go.

That he had taken me there to recuperate I confirmed in my own statement; but I had said that we had arrived on Thursday at midday and that I had left again that evening. That we had not been seen arriving could be accounted for by Johnny having waited to smuggle me in until he had a good chance to do so unobserved. That Wing Commander Tinegate had not seen me when he had come there in the afternoon could be explained by his having remained in the sitting-room while Johnny packed his bag. The note that he had left on Saturday, on the sitting-room mantel-piece, for Mrs, Burton had not been dated; and as he had told her when leaving on Thursday with Tinegate that he did not expect to be back for some days, she had not been up there until Monday, when the police came to interview her. So it might have been there four days.

No one, apparently, had so far thought of checking up on the taxi that had taken me to the Ministry of Defence and, even if they did, I could say that my mind still not being fully recovered from my two days' black-out must have lapsed again after my arrival at Waterloo; so that unknown to myself I had gone down to Nevern Square with some vague idea of seeing Johnny, then realised that he would not be there and taken a taxi to Whitehall.

The police check on my own fictitious movements during Friday and Saturday had naturally produced nothing. No car ditched by its driver had been reported on the Thursday night within many miles of Sir Charles's cottage. But its driver might have recovered consciousness, succeeded in getting it out of the ditch and, if he had not had far to go, driven it home. Plausibility was given to such a theory by my having said that he was drunk. The accident could have sobered him enough to do so, and to realise that with his breath smelling strongly of drink he would be in for very serious trouble unless he could cover up his accident.

Neither the staffs at any of the cafés in Godalming nor at the station there recalled having seen a bedraggled figure answering to my description on Sunday morning; but that proved nothing. It was, however, thought surprising that during my visit to Sir Charles's cottage no one had even caught a glimpse of me, although the account I had given of the scenes that had taken place there showed that I must have moved freely about in it.

That, of course, remained the crux of the whole issue. If I had not been there, and been there on the Thursday night, how could I have possibly repeated to him a part of his conversation with his distinguished guest? For me to have been in league with Maria or Klinsky and had it from either of them was altogether too far fetched. For one thing, if I had, why should I have denounced them? For another, I was the last sort of person to have been a member of a Soviet spy ring. For a third my anxiety to get Sir Charles to clear Johnny provided a perfectly sound reason for my having gone down to the cottage.

As far as the date of my resurrection was concerned the evidence was, therefore, overwhelmingly in my favour. I was sorry to have to make Johnny appear a liar; but, as I saw it at the time, he had nothing to lose, whereas I had all to gain, for only so could I give a plausible explanation of having been at the cottage; and, had I failed to do so, my veracity on every point would at once have become suspect.

It was not until the end of the week that the line I had taken came back upon me like a boomerang.

Eddie, I could sense, was far from sanguine about my chances; but out of consideration for me he did his best to conceal that and on the whole succeeded very well. I was, therefore, considerably alarmed when on his ninth—or it may have been his tenth—visit, he arrived looking really gloomy.

Before I could ask him the reason he opened fire on me about my having taken up Yoga in India. Apparently the doctors had agreed that the best explanation for my having been accounted dead by two of their fraternity was that offered by myself; and Eddie wanted to know how often I had gone into self-induced comas; how frequently; for how long at any one time; the degree of completeness of suspended animation; if I had kept up the practice after leaving India; if I had ever fallen into one by accident, and so on.

Once the practice had cured my nervous disorder I had given it up, and as that was now some twelve years ago I was a little hazy about details, but I gave him such particulars as I could and told him that at the end of my training

I had been able to remain in a state of suspended animation for up to four hours at a stretch.

When I had done he shook his head and said sadly: 'I hate to have to tell you so, Giff, but our case has been going from bad to worse, and this Yoga business about puts the lid on it.'

'Why?' I asked. 'It has nothing whatever to do with how Evans met his death.'

'No; but it might have a very great deal to do with what happened afterwards.'

'Surely you are not suggesting that I put myself into a coma and had myself buried alive deliberately; are you?'

He shrugged. 'It had not occurred to me; but that, as I learned this afternoon, is exactly what the prosecution are suggesting.'

'Then they must be crazy!' I exclaimed. 'Any such idea is utterly fantastic!'

'Is it?' he eyed me gravely. 'Our line that Ankaret forged the letter has proved a complete wash-out. They are a hundred per cent convinced that you beat Evans to death with that steel rod. They are now of the opinion that afterwards, as the only chance of escaping from being hanged for murder, you decided to pretend that you were dead. They are going to suggest that after writing your suicide letter you fixed things so that you should be found apparently washed up on the beach in the morning; that it was your intention, after the doctors had assumed you to be dead, and you had been buried for a few hours, to emerge from your grave, a free man to start life again under another name.'

'No, Eddie; no!' I cried. 'That doesn't make sense. It is the wildest nonsense. Even if I had been able to fool Johnny and Silvers, and had succeeded in keeping it up for another two or three hours so as to get past the doctors, I couldn't have carried it through. Damn it, man, my body was lying in the beach house from early Saturday morning until midday Tuesday. Whatever Indian Fakirs may do, no European could have suspended his animation and gone without food or drink for all that time.'

Eddie shook his head. 'It is not suggested that you did, Giff. The prosecution believe that you had an accomplice who came by night, bringing you food and hot drinks to warm you up.'

I stared at him aghast. 'You . . . you don't mean they think that Johnny did that; then rescued me from my grave afterwards, knowing all the time that I was alive?'

He nodded. 'That is what they think. It is unbelievable that you could have remained in your grave from Tuesday midday till Saturday night withour succumbing to cold or pneumonia. For that, and other incontestable reasons, it is clear that Johnny has been lying about it being Saturday night that he rescued you. Why he should have done so, and still sticks to it, I don't know. But it was the fact that he lied about that which first made the police suspect the whole set-up.

'See how everything fits in,' Eddie went on, in swift bitter sentences that beat like a succession of hammer blows on my brain. 'Johnny was staying at Longshot the night of the murder. He dined with the Waldrons, but left their house earlier than he would have done owing to his having quarrelled after dinner with the Admiral. He must have arrived back at Longshot soon after you had killed Evans. Everyone knows how devoted Johnny is to you. He agreed to help you save your neck. Having plotted the business between you, he went to bed and you spent the night in the beach-house. Early in the morning you lay down at the water's edge and went into your first self-induced coma. He comes out as arranged and finds you. He suggests to Silvers that instead of taking your body up to the Hall they should put it in the beach-house, where it will be much easier for him to visit it later without being seen and questioned. The doctors make their examination and declare you dead. An hour or two later you come out of your coma. During the afternoon you lie there dozing. At night he comes to you with food and drink. In due course he tips you off when the body-washers will be coming to prepare you for burial. You then go into another coma. Through Sunday and Monday he keeps a watchful eye on you and brings you sustenance at intervals. On Tuesday he sees you into your coffin. As one of your executors he has seen to it that the clause in your will about the air-holes and the lid not being screwed down has been faithfully observed; so he knows you will be all right for a limited period.

'Why he did not get you out on Tuesday night we don't

yet know. Perhaps he got cold feet at the thought of what he had promised to do. It must have been lying there for twenty-four hours longer than you expected that turned your hair white. Anyhow, by Wednesday evening he must have known that if he left you there much longer you would be dead by morning. We know he went to the churchyard on that night because the village constable caught him there and sent him packing. He must have returned later, helped you out of your grave and taken you to Longshot. We have your own admission that, having procured clothes for you, on the Thursday he took you up to London, smuggled you into his rooms and hid you there. Why he broke prison to go down to Longshot again on Saturday night is another thing we do not know. But he could not have known then that you had already left his rooms. Probably you had told him before he left you on Thursday where he could find a wad of bearer bonds, or perhaps Ankaret's jewels, or something else which could be turned into ready money. Anyway, who can doubt that the final stage of the plan was for him to help you get abroad so that you could make a new life for yourself under another name.

'That it broke down was due in the first place to Johnny being arrested. In the second to your thirty-six hours in the tomb having proved too much for you. Your mind had become temporarily deranged. Instead of waiting where you were until he returned to you with a wallet full of bank-notes, you became obsessed by the idea that you must get Johnny cleared by Sir Charles. The fact that three days elapsed before you actually spoke to him is neither here nor there. By doing so you burst the whole outfit wide open, and put the rope round your neck.'

'You are wrong!' I cried desperately. 'Utterly and entirely wrong. I mean about the part Johnny has played in all this. Where is he? What has happened to him?'

Eddie spread out his hands in a helpless gesture. 'I didn't want to add to your worries, so I've kept it from you as long as I could. At the request of the police, the charge against him of unlawfully interfering with a grave was held over; but bail was refused and he has since been held as a material witness in your own case. He is here in Southampton prison. This morning he was charged with being an accessory to the murder of Evans, and having entered into a conspiracy with you to defeat the ends of justice. He's in this thing up to his neck, and I doubt if he'll get off with less than ten years.'

16

1st to 9th October

That night, when Eddie had gone, I knew the ultimate depths of despair. About my own fate I no longer cared; but the network of lies I had invented in an attempt to save myself had enmeshed the person whom, now that Ankaret was dead, I cared for more than anyone else in the world. And what a shameful return to make to poor Johnny for all the loyalty and courage he had shown in breaking one prison and risking a long sentence in another against the remote possibility that I might still be alive in my grave.

I felt so shattered that although Eddie stayed on with me for a while I could find little to say apart from reiterating my protests that Johnny was innocent. To have jobbed backwards and admitted that it had been on Saturday night that he had rescued me would have done no good; because I should not now be believed. They had proof that he had been in the churchyard on Wednesday night, and I had built up my own version of my resurrection too securely. Besides, the basis of the case the police were bringing against him was that, as I was capable of self-inducing comas at will, he had entered into a conspiracy with me from the beginning to succour me in secret while I was presumed dead, and later to rescue me. He had rescued me, and the date on which he had done so was not an essential point in the build-up which must bring about his ruin.

There were still a few minor discrepancies between the account Johnny had given the police and what they were able to prove; but, as Eddie gloomily pointed out, that was always so in murder trials. It was the weight of evidence which governed the verdict, and the case for the prosecution was overwhelming, both against me for murder and against Johnny for having afterwards endeavoured to prevent justice from taking its course.

When Eddie left me I continued to rack my poor brains for a way to save Johnny, but no ray of light came to relieve a darkness in my mind which was worse than it had suffered while in the tomb; but by morning I had taken a decision. Even though it stood no chance of being believed, I would prepare another statement, in which I would tell the truth, the whole truth, and nothing but the truth, about this extraordinary series of events of which I have been the victim.

My hand is mending well, but it will be many weeks yet before I can write with it again. In fact, I don't suppose I ever will, as I shall before then have been tried, convicted and hanged by the neck until dead. So the prison authorities allowed me to have a tape-recording machine sent in, and for the past eight or ten days I have been dictating steadily into it. This occupation has done a lot to keep my mind off the wretched fate that awaits me; and when I am gone I intend that a copy of it shall be sent to the Society of Psychical Reseach for they, at least, should find it interesting.

I have also been allowed to receive letters and a limited number of visitors. Many of the letters have touched me deeply. Those of Charles Toiller, Silvers, Dr. Culver, my personal secretary Jean Nicholls, and many of my employees at the works, particularly so. It is a big consolation to anyone situated like myself to know in this way that quite a lot of people will regret one's passing, and that many little acts of kindness, long since forgotten, that one has been able to do, are remembered.

Bill, as a material witness, has not been allowed to come to see me and his letter was typical of him. He had evidently learned from Eddie the line that my defence was to take; and, although he did not actually say it, reading between the lines I could see that he thought it a bit unsporting of me to try to father Evans's murder on Ankaret. I have no doubt that had he been in my shoes he would have kept his mouth shut, and taken his medicine with a good grace. How I wished as I read it that I had done so; for then poor Johnny might have escaped being involved. But it was too late now to do anything but continue to reproach myself about that. For the rest, Bill's letter displayed good honest affection for me, and the heart-felt hope that I would escape the worst.

Sir Charles also wrote to me, and his letter read as follows:

My dear Hillary,

The unhappy situation in which you are makes me all the more sensible of the obligation I am under to you; particularly as it was my action which led to your arrest. Yet I feel sure you will not hold that against me, as it was a duty that I could not shirk, and neither of us can doubt that even had I refrained from doing as I did your state was such that you must have fallen into the hands of the police before very long.

I would have visited you to express in person my gratitude for the warning you brought me but as I shall be called as a witness at your trial I am debarred from doing so. This letter must, therefore, serve for that and also to acquaint you with certain facts which I feel it is right that you should know.

Your well-intentioned efforts on my behalf, disappointing as it may be for you, but happily for me, had no basis in reality. Old Maria, as I told you, has been with me for many years and, as I expected, M.I.5's enquiries have shown her to be entirely beyond reproach. Jan Klinsky is her cousin, and he escaped from Poland only a few months ago. She had in fact told me of him, and that he had secured work on a nearby farm in order to be near her. But the welter of affairs that clutter the mind of a man in my position caused me temporarily to have forgotten his existence when you spoke of him to me.

It was, of course, culpable of her to admit him to the house clandestinely and allow him to spy upon me; but the explanation for her doing so is quite simple. Having learned from her that the distinguished guest who dined with me the night of your visit came occasionally to my cottage, Klinsky had expressed a quite natural curiosity to see the great man at close quarters. At the first opportunity, therefore, Maria telephoned him and indulged him in his wish.

He is however quite harmless and, in fact, such a fanatical anti-communist that he braved considerable dangers in making his escape from Poland. Moreover, fearing that he might be caught he brought with him a phial of poison, which he had determined to take rather than submit to capture. It was a small dose of this poison which you saw Maria give her cat. The animal was very old and had gone blind so she felt that

*the kindest thing was to make away with it. Had she men-
tioned the matter to me I should of course have had it put
down by a vet. But the frugal mind of the continental peasant
is naturally averse to seeing anyone spend a guinea unnecessarily, and Klinsky having offered to do the job for nothing
Maria agreed.*

*I must refer now to our long talk at Martin Emsworth's and
thank you again for the selfless and patriotic way in which
you agreed to abet my private design for making the nation
conscious of the necessity for a complete realignment of our
armed forces.*

*That events of such a tragic nature should have prevented
you from carrying out the ideas which I put to you is a matter
on which I will not dwell, except to offer you my deepest
sympathy. However, you will, I am sure, be pleased to learn
that despite the failure of our plan, factors which I could not
foresee at the time have since served much the same purpose
as its success would have done.*

*These last few weeks matters have moved with remarkable
rapidity. Early in September the public was hardly aware
that any controversy existed with regard to the future of the
armed forces. Now, at the end of the month, the whole question has been ventilated in the press with most satisfactory
results. A special post as co-ordinating head of the Chiefs of
Staff Committee is being created for Marshal of the Royal
Air Force Sir William Dickson, and the merging of all three
Services into one Defence Force has been openly canvassed;
while the Prime Minister has agreed that either myself, or
whoever he may appoint to succeed me as Minister of Defence, should in future exercise a much greater degree of
control over the Service Ministries and the Ministry of Supply.
Moreover it has been recognised that the maintenance of
reserves and war potential which could not be brought into
play during a five-day conflict are a waste of public money
and that wherever possible they should be translated into a
strong and efficient home defence emergency service. A major
reorganisation of this kind is bound to take time but it can
now be said with confidence that we are on the road to achieving
a 'New Look' which will give our country a far greater measure
of security.*

In conclusion please believe that my thoughts are with you

*in your present ordeal. The country can ill afford to lose men
like yourself, and it is my most earnest hope that you will
succeed in proving your innocence.*

Very sincerely yours.

So there it was. All I had done was to raise a mare's-nest,
and my doing so had played no inconsiderable part in landing
Johnny and myself behind bars. Yet, as I saw again in my
mind's eye Maria, Klinsky and the dead cat, I felt that I had
had sound grounds for the conclusion I had come to, and that
it would have been despicable of me to refrain from taking
the action that I had. At least I had not got Sir Charles's death
upon my conscience.

Harold also wrote to me. His was an awkward, ill-expressed
letter, conveying little except the one thing he could not
conceal—namely how aggrieved and uncomfortable he felt
at my having placed him in such a situation. He made a
half-hearted suggestion of coming to see me, but added rather
pathetically that as we had never really been friends it seemed
a bit late to start now.

Personally, I felt that a meeting in such exceptional circumstances was the one thing left which might possibly have
brought us together; and had he been in my shoes I should
certainly have made an immediate and spontaneous attempt
to prove that blood was thicker than water. But he more or
less implied that it was an unpleasant duty which he would
not seek to avoid if I wished him to observe it; and no good
could come of our meeting in that spirit.

I harboured no bitterness against him, but felt complete
indifference, and the only effect his letter had was to remind
me that, having returned from my grave, it was again in my
power to make a new will. He had been 'Sir' Harold for
nine days and soon enough now he would be Sir Harold again,
and for good; but I would see to it that he never had Longshot.

James Compton was my first visitor, and from the hour he
spent with me I derived great comfort. Dear James is one of
those honest God-fearing souls who prove a tower of strength
to their friends when in tribulation. It was not so much anything that either of us said but the warmth of true friendship,
tried and proved over many years, which radiated from him
to wrap me in a temporary contentment.

Actually we talked for most of the time about the affairs of the company. He, of course, could not know, neither could I tell him, that I had been an unseen presence at all the recent board meetings; so he gave me an account of the strife my last proposal had caused. I told him how I had obtained my information and showed him Sir Charles's letter. In view of its contents there was now obviously no point in penalising the Company; so we decided that the E-boat contract should be accepted with apologies for our delay in giving a definite answer. Some months must elapse before even the keels could be laid down; so the contract might well be cancelled—if the 'New Look' included a reduction in the establishment of small fighting ships—while the Government were committed to pay no more than a few thousand compensation. That sort of thing was far from uncommon in the armaments world, and anything they had to pay us would be a flea-bite compared to the huge cost of having entirely reconditioned *Vanguard* before laying her up.

James is far from being a demonstrative man but on leaving he took me by the shoulders, smiled anto my eyes and said: 'Fear nothing, Giff! Fear nothing! I know you are innocent and so does our Lord. Have faith in Him and just keep on thinking how the boys and girls in our yard will cheer you when you come back to us acquitted.'

It was true enough that I was innocent. But how I wished that I had James's simple faith to sustain me. Alas I had not, and was still uneasily endeavouring to resign myself to the worst.

My next visitor was Sir Tuke. He was as forthright as ever but he seemed to have aged quite a lot since I had last seen him. When I told him what James and I had decided about the E-boats he waved it aside and said wearily:

'Oh to hell with that; if we hadn't taken the blasted contract some other firm would have. Anyhow, I'd rather have had to come out of retirement to fight the Russians with my naked hands than have this happen.'

Although only a figure of speech, that told me how badly he must be feeling, and I said: 'Your attitude was quite understandable; it was just hard luck on Johnny that I was put out of circulation before I could tell you that he had had no hand in my proposals.'

'I know,' he nodded. 'I'd always liked him so it went against the grain to do what I did. Put it down to over-zealousness for my Service if you like, but I felt I had to. Still, that is all over now. I have made him my humble apologies—and that's a thing I have never done in my life to anyone else. It is this new trouble which is driving me to distraction.'

'Johnny is as innocent of that as he was of the other,' I assured him.

'Yes. I've just come from seeing him; and as both of you maintain that I naturally accept it. But what are the chances of his getting off? That's what I want to know.'

'None too good, I'm afraid. I am innocent too but I'd willingly perjure myself if that would save him. The trouble is that it wouldn't. There is nothing I can say which would clear him or even make his case better.'

'So I gathered from Arnold. And he says that if the jury find Johnny guilty, he'll get ten years. Just think of it, Gifford. Ten years!'

I refrained from remarking that I did not expect to escape hanging, as he went on: 'Even with good conduct he wouldn't get out under seven; and seven for him means seven for Sue.'

'She is determined to stand by him then?' I asked, although I already knew the answer.

'Yes. She nailed her flag to the mast the day he was arrested. Told me that if I didn't like it I could go jump in a pond. Game little devil.' The Admiral's blue eyes suddenly flashed. 'I'm proud of her, Gifford! Proud of her! Naturally I kicked at first. Couldn't tamely welcome a chap into the family who had betrayed Official Secrets. But directly I learned that he'd been cleared of that I sailed right in behind her. What else could I do?'

I nodded, and he went on: 'But seven years! Just think of the frustration these two youngsters must suffer in all that time. And what will he be like when he comes out, eh? There are not many men whose character could stand up to seven years with only jail-birds as their companions.'

In that I could at least offer him a little comfort, as I was able to say with conviction, 'I believe Johnny's would. Particularly if he has Sue to look forward to. In fact I'm sure of it. In some ways it is going to be worse for her than him.'

'You are right there,' he agreed. 'She insists on being present at the trial and that will be bad enough. Of course, I'll be with her; though I'd rather be in *Lion* again with Beatty at Jutland when all our ships were blowing up behind us. But it's the long haul afterwards, when all the excitement is over. That will be infinitely worse.'

We talked on for a while, and I did what I could to cheer him, though it was little enough. It was not until he was on the point of leaving that he said:

'I'm a self-centred old devil, Gifford. I've been talking of nothing but myself and my concern for Sue. All the same I'm sure you know how deeply I feel for you. Your father was my good friend and there is nothing that he could have done for you that I wouldn't, given the chance. The pity of it is that I know of no way to prove my willingness to help. Sue is of yet another generation so she's hardly had a chance to get to know you well; but all the same she said: "Give him my love, and tell him I know that he was much too fond of Johnny ever to have deliberately brought him into danger." Well; so long. We'll both be keeping our fingers crossed for you.'

My third and last visitor was Christobel. To my shame I must confess that I had tended to couple her with Harold and, after receiving his letter, if I had thought of her at all it had been with equal indifference.

We greeted one another rather awkwardly, then she plunged at once into what she had come to say: 'Mother meant to write to you but I decided that I'd like to come to see you; so instead I've brought you a message from her. We have always assumed that you are very rich, but Ankaret must have cost you a packet, and appearances are sometimes deceptive. Everyone knows that briefing the best barristers for a murder trial costs the earth. So Mother wanted me to tell you that if you are hard up for cash, she has a thousand pounds put by and that it's yours if you need it.'

I felt utterly abashed. All I could do was to exclaim: 'Oh my dear!' and the tears started to my eyes.

She saw them. Next moment her arms were round me and she cried. 'Don't worry, Daddy. Everything will be all right.'

The ice of long years was instantly broken. What we said for a time after that, I don't remember. I told her, of course, that I had ample funds; but that I could never be sufficiently grateful for her mother's offer, and how greatly I appreciated her having come to bring it to me; then, before we realised it, we had settled down to talk like old friends.

After a while she said: 'Isn't life strange? Just to think, Daddy, that you had to be accused of murder before I could look on you as anything but almost a stranger, and one I didn't care for much at that.'

'I'm afraid I'm the one to blame,' I admitted. 'I was too wrapped up in my own concerns to give much time to you when you were young; so naturally you grew away from me.'

She shrugged. 'It wasn't all your fault. You did make an effort now and then; but I resented your leaving us for Ankaret. And she was so lovely; so much everything I would have liked to be but knew I couldn't, that I was desperately jealous of her. That's why I made such a little bitch of myself when you asked Harold and me down to Longshot.'

'All the same, as I was older, I should have understood and made allowances. Anyway, there must have been some career that you would have liked to have taken up. I ought to have found out about that and done something for you instead of just leaving you to drift.'

'Oh I don't know,' she shrugged again. 'I don't think I was cut out for a career girl; any brains I have don't seem to run in that direction.'

Recalling the situation in which I had last seen her, I had to make a conscious effort to keep a trace of grimness out of my voice as I asked: 'In which direction do they run?'

'To having a good time,' she replied with unexpected frankness. 'I know I'm not a real smasher like Ankaret; but I've never had any difficulty about collecting men.'

'If that is your sole occupation don't you get a bit tired of it?' I enquired.

'To tell the truth I am.' Her eyes were shrewd and much older than they should have been as she admitted it, and went on: 'The trouble is that those who can afford to take a girl to the right sort of places all seem to be either middle-aged or boring; the nicest ones have no money, and drinking beer in pubs has never struck me as much fun.'

After a moment I asked: 'Isn't there something else you would like to try for a change. If you don't fancy office work, what about taking a job as a librarian or in a smart hat shop?'

She shook her head. 'No. I'm not at all that fond of books, and nothing would induce me to wear myself out all day, fetching and carrying hats for other women to try on. If I did do anything, I'd like it to be in the country.'

'Really!' I raised my eyebrows. 'I had no idea you were that sort of girl.'

'If you are thinking of me as a land-girl, I'm not,' she replied promptly. 'And if I had to look after horses I'd go cuckoo in a week. It's really that I'm utterly sick of London. I've had my fill of night-clubs, anyway as a regular amusement, and I'd love to get some good fresh air.'

'But if you don't care about the land or animals what could you do in the country?'

She hesitated a moment, then she laughed. 'It's silly to tell you about it really. It's only a sort of pipe dream that a girl friend and I have been amusing ourselves with for the past few months. We had the idea of running a mobile grocery store. With all these new housing estates on the edges of towns and a long way from the shops, I'm sure that if the stuff could be brought to the door one would do a roaring trade. One would have no rent to pay and could move from place to place with the seasons. We'd do Scotland in the summer, the East Coast in the autumn, then from Cornwall right along to Kent in the winter and the spring. With a little planning one could arrange things so as to spend the week-end in cathedral cities, or at seaside places; and so combine business with having lots of fun. Of course the snag is that we'd need two caravans, one for our mobile shop and one to sleep in, and two cars to draw them. So it's completely off the map, and one might just as well wish for a magic carpet right away.'

'But it's not off the map!' I exclaimed. 'Far from it. You shall have your caravans and cars. You can go out and buy them tomorrow if you like.'

Her eyes grew round as saucers. 'Daddy! You don't . . . you can't possibly mean it!'

'Of course I do. The fact that I've got to stay here for a while does not prevent me from signing cheques.'

'But it would cost goodness knows how much. Three thousand at least, and several hundred more to stock the shop.'

'You won't do it on that,' I told her. 'Not if you buy new

cars, and it is no good starting off with old crocks. But that doesn't matter. You can spend up to five thousand and send the bills to me.'

'Oh, Daddy darling!' she burst into tears and again threw her arms round my neck.

When she had gone I felt happier than I had for years. All that evening a warm glow ran through me at the thought that even if I had to die I had first given someone else a break.

But I have got to die. There is no escaping that. I have now come to the end of recording my strange and terrifying experiences during these past weeks. Eddie has been having a typescript made from the tape daily, and tomorrow I shall give him this last section. But it won't do Johnny or myself any good.

It is so utterly fantastic that no one will believe it. The fact that every single details fits will not weigh with them. They will regard it as a brilliant *tour de force* in imaginative fiction —or as the outpourings of a madman. But not of a madman mad enough to be sent to Broadmoor. While Sue eats her heart out Johnny has got to rot in prison. And I've got to swing. The case for the prosecution is unshakable, and nothing short of a miracle can save us now.

Postscript

The miracle has happened.

Directly Sue learned that Johnny had been charged with abetting me she realised that the only hope for him lay in solving the original crime. She therefore took up his investigation where he had left off.

Bill willingly gave her the run of Longshot; and while I have been dictating my long statement she conducted a systematic search there. As Ankaret and I were both inclined to be hoarders, it took Sue nearly a week to go through all our papers, the books in the library and every drawer and cupboard in the house. None of them yielded even a ghost of a clue so, depressed but still determined, she went up to the attics.

The mass of stuff she found there appalled her, and as most of it had not been disturbed for years it seemed most unlikely that she would find among it the sort of thing for which she was seeking. Nevertheless, she set to work and toiled away for three long days in the dust and dirt. On the third evening her labours were rewarded. She came upon an old tin uniform case that had belonged to Bill when he was a young officer in the Life Guards.

It was full of Ankaret's early drawings. Among them was her historical scrap-book, containing her almost faultless copies of the writing of Napoleon, Charles II, Marie Antoinette and a score of other famous people. It had her name inside the front cover, and loose in it were some amusing sketches of her father, mother and brother, with captions faked in their writings. But even that was not the most conclusive of Sue's finds.

There were two letters. The first had been written from Wellington Barracks and was simply signed: 'Dick'. It read:

Ankaret, my sweet,
  Apart from any question of dishonesty, how can you have

been so incredibly stupid as to bring the night-dress you obtained from Harrods in Grace's name with you when you came to stay with us last week-end? If you were so hard up for a tenner why on earth didn't you ask me for one? I would have given it to you willingly. A moment's thought should have told you that the description given of you and of the night-dress by the saleswoman could lead to your being found out. Unfortunately it seems that there was no love lost between you and Grace when you were at school together, and she is furious. I am doing my utmost to persuade her to keep this wretched business to herself; but her price is a signed confession. I am afraid your only way out is to send me one to show her, and if you will give me your solemn promise never to forge anyone's name again I'll do my damnedest to get it back for you.*

The second was Ankaret's confession, which had been returned to her. The dates on the two letters showed the episode to have taken place only a few months before I married her. That, being so hard put to it to make ends meet, she should have chosen to forge an ex-school friend's name on a shopping bill rather than have asked her lover for money, and then have been so careless about being caught out, was typical of her. The affair explained, too, why she had given copying people's writing for fun, and made no further additions to her historical scrap-book.

Two days later Johnny and I were taken before a judge in Chambers. The new evidence that Sue had found was produced. The two handwriting experts who had previously hesitated to risk their reputation by stating that the suicide letter was a forgery now declared it to be so. On that the case for the prosecution fell to the ground. The judge ruled that there was no case to answer. Johnny and I walked out free men.